William Prickett

Dearly Beloved

Dearly Beloved

by William Prickett

Wilmington, Delaware

Dearly Beloved

First Edition

Title: Dearly Beloved

Author: William Prickett

Published by:

Cedar Tree Books Ltd.
Nine Germay Drive
Wilmington, DE 19804

Editor: Nicholas L. Cerchio III

Cover Illustration: Adam Cruz

Layout and Page Design: Phil Maggitti

Copyright: William Prickett 2002

ISBN: 1-892-142-17-1

PRINTED IN THE UNITED STATES OF AMERICA

ACKNOWLEDGMENTS AND DEDICATION

I acknowledge with profound thanks the indispensable help of my secretary, Mrs. Phyllis Zehr, who not only declined to accept total and well-earned retirement due in part to my needs to have her type and retype *Dearly Beloved* but also encouraged me greatly by her continued interest in the evolution of *Dearly Beloved*.

I also, again gratefully, acknowledge the editorial advice of Mrs. Dorrie Ross of the English Department of the University of Delaware.

I would be remiss if I did not recognize and acknowledge the debt I owe to all my former partners at the law firm of Prickett, Jones & Elliott, who have graciously continued to make my office fully available to me as a place to work on this book as well as various pro bono projects. They and the whole staff have made it possible for me to try to spend my retirement years to date productively as well as pleasantly.

Once again I dedicate this book to my young wife, Caroline, who, besides her work as Chairman and C.E.O. of Summit Aviation Company, as the President of St. Anne's Episcopal School, a new school built for 300 children in grades K to 8, and until recently owner of a herd of 80 bison, has managed to support me fully in all my various other endeavors since I retired as a Delaware corporate trial lawyer.

Finally, I am again in debt to all those who read this book. A book such as *Dearly Beloved* is, after all, written for the pleasure of the reader. I hope each and every reader will enjoy reading *Dearly Beloved* as much as I enjoyed writing it.

William Prickett
July 2002

Table of Contents

Chapter 1
In the Face of God and This Company — 1

Chapter 2
For Better, For Worse — 19

Chapter 3
Wilt Thou Have This Man — 57

Chapter 4
Who Giveth This Woman in Marriage? — 99

Chapter 5
Or Forever Hold His Peace — 147

Chapter 6
If Any Man Can Show Just Cause — 169

Chapter 7
Will You Do All in Your Power? — 191

Chapter 8
Let No Man Put Asunder — 203

Chapter 9
We Are Come Together — 227

Social Note — 239

Out of Control — 240

Dearly Beloved

Chapter One
In the Face of God and This Company

At about 3:45 P.M. on Saturday September 18, 1973, Reverend William Piccard drove slowly and carefully around the sharp left curve at the bottom of the hill on Bluner Road. As always he checked to make sure there was not a car coming the other way down the long hill. At the very top of the hill stood his Episcopal Church, St. James, surrounded by old maple, beech and oak trees, surmounted by the bell tower and by the tall spire of the steeple. Reverend Piccard drove on up the hill. The parking lot was still virtually empty. He drove through the main parking lot around to the smaller back parking lot. He parked and let himself in the back door.

As the last stroke of four from the clock in the belfry died away, Reverend Piccard sat down at his desk in his study behind the sacristy. He heard the organist start playing the music for the Secant wedding scheduled for 4:30. Reverend Piccard knew that his small church would be completely full for this September society wedding. His starched white surplice had been carefully laid out on a chair together with his well-worn *Book of Common Prayer* with an old leather marker at page 300, "The Form for Solemnization of Matrimony." There was nothing for him to do for another 25 minutes. He therefore decided just to sit in his study and think about the wedding he was about to perform. Would it come off as other weddings had, or would it turn into a matrimonial fiasco?

Reverend Piccard looked just like what one would expect the Episcopalian priest of a church in a fashionable suburb of Philadelphia to look like: "pale, male & Yale," rather handsome and graying at the temples. Nothing in his manner or tone would even faintly betray that, of all his many duties, he detested most having to conduct society weddings. He had originally thought that this wedding would not be any different at all from dozens of other such weddings he had had to conduct. (How wrong he thought he had been!) Sarah Secant, the mother of the bride, who never darkened the doors of St. James except for other fashionable weddings or funerals or at Easter, had telephoned quite out of the blue early one Monday morning in April and, in effect, almost "made a reservation" for Saturday September 18. Mrs. Donald Perry, a social secretary, had driven out from Philadelphia without an appointment. As always, and in an almost patronizing manner, she in effect had told him just how the whole wedding would be "staged." Henry Dienst, the fussy florist from Philadelphia, had come, as usual, earlier that day to direct the placing of the large tubs of giant green ferns and the other floral decorations of the altar and first pews of his rather simple church. All of this attention to what he regarded as extraneous detail angered Reverend Piccard. These elaborate peripheral matters had really nothing to do with his church or, in fact, with the sacred ceremony of marriage. He frankly detested all of it.

However, he always had to admit in private that a good deal of his annoyance stemmed from purely personal pique that the marriage sacrament which he was about to have to perform had so little importance in the overall scheme of a full-fledged society wedding. The bachelors' dinner, the multitude of showers for the bride and the gala rehearsal dinner the night before, not to mention the elaborate reception at the Club that would follow, were all far more important to the bride and the groom, their families and the multitude of guests than the relatively short service that he was about to perform. Further, most of those now beginning to arrive at St. James were not there for a religious ceremony at all. The older women were there to look at the bride, relive their own weddings, carp at the dress of the mother of the bride and the mother of the groom and display their own wardrobes and hats. The men, on the other hand, for the most part never darkened the doors of this church or any other church

Chapter 1 -- In the Face of God and This Company

except perhaps at Easter, funerals, christenings or weddings such as this, preferring golf or simply sleeping late on Sundays after a hard Saturday night. These men were largely dragooned by their wives or came because they were relatives or friends or business friends of either the bride or the groom's family. Of course, there was a circle of men who came to the church regularly. This group consisted of members of the vestry. But even as to most of his vestrymen, Reverend Piccard had wry reservations. How many served on the vestry out of the love of the Lord, Jesus Christ, as contrasted with those who served on the vestry simply because it was just another secular step in their upward climb toward worldly success and the inevitable heart attack. Alfred Oakley Oliver, a cousin of the bride's mother, Sarah Secant, was certainly in the latter category of vestrymen.

Reverend Piccard had a soft spot for young people such as the couple in *Love Story*, who dispensed entirely with the church and took a do-it-yourself approach toward marriage. It was more Christian – that is, more early Christian than the great barbarian tribal gatherings such as the one that was just getting underway in his own church. Such feelings could not possibly be his official line or even his semiprivate view as long as old Bishop Kendrick continued to mete out a progressive 18th century policy for this diocese. Certainly, it could not be his line in this elegant conservative parish which collectively looked forward to such weddings as one of the recurrent features of social life, along with cocktail parties, dinner parties, funerals and coming out parties. He wished that he had had an opportunity to hint to the young groom, Phillip MacPherson, who was now waiting in the little chapel with his best man for 4:30, that a "do-it-yourself" marriage was acceptable in the eyes of at least some priests, himself among them, provided such a marriage was later consecrated by a blessing from a fully ordained Episcopal priest. He thought until the wedding rehearsal that this wedding would be no different from the seventy, eighty, or was it one hundred such weddings he had conducted since he had become the rector of this church some twelve years or so ago.

It was at moments like this that Reverend Piccard liked to imagine once again the consternation and surprise that would rock the parish, the vestry, Bishop Kendrick and his own wife Ruth (who enjoyed being the rector's wife in this parish) if he suddenly announced from the pulpit that he was resigning to become a missionary in Alaska as he had intended to do even before he had graduated from seminary and been ordained and had himself gone through a similar but less grandiose form of marriage than the one that was about to get underway. But he knew deep down that at this point in his church career he would never take such a drastic step. Through the years he had lost the strength and really even the zeal to do so. Furthermore, there was always the grim problem of money: His two youngest girls were still at that expensive country day school, Green Valley, with college and probably even graduate school that would have to be paid for after college.

Further, Bishop Kendrick would never allow him to resign gracefully as rector of this parish since the Bishop counted heavily on this parish for a substantial part of diocesan funds. Reverend Piccard knew that a significant part of the contributions stemmed from the fact that he was well liked by those in the parish who counted or, more accurately, contributed. But the Bishop, Reverend Piccard knew from years of useless attempts at gentle persuasion, had little truck with those in the church who felt that the church had better begin to concern itself with real problems. Bishop Kendrick had been furious when he had found out that Reverend Piccard had taken a drug orientation course given by the state police to familiarize church and civic leaders with the realities of the drug problem. The Bishop had thundered, "Pot is not the business of the Episcopal Church."

He knew that some of the six ushers and even some of the congregation would be looking at their watches to time how long it would take to "tie the knot." His momentary popularity on this particular afternoon would be inversely proportional to the length of the service. The length of the service would, of course, depend on the length of the prayers. But he had a different sort of game which he played with himself. It was far more challenging than merely counting the minutes and seconds until the wedding was over and the dash to the Club for the reception began.

As he interviewed each prospective bride and groom, he tried

Chapter 1 -- In the Face of God and This Company

to forecast in his mind just what lay in store for them. So many of these couples were so young, so inexperienced and so naïve. They were far too often getting married for reasons that were totally wrong. Thus, there was no logical reason to expect that such marriages would in fact endure "until death us do part." The variety of circumstances and reasons that led couples to the altar at St. James were often such it seemed that virtually all the marriages he performed were doomed from the very outset. Even though his parish had about the usual rate of divorce and scandal for a "Country Club" parish, Reverend Piccard was always slightly amazed that any of the marriages which he performed lasted.

Reverend Piccard had made it a practice of talking individually well before the wedding to the bride and the groom in his study. He knew that the grooms especially regarded this chat as simply another boring chore that had to be gotten through. They were pleasant enough but totally uninterested as he attempted to discuss the function of marriage and warn them that marriage would not be a sort of perpetual Disneyland with legitimate sex thrown in. Reverend Piccard admitted deep down to himself that these premarital chats were probably a total waste of time in most cases. The recipients of his advice were not capable or inclined to understand the implications of what they were about to undertake so lightly. It would take a dash of bitter adversity and even animosity to make them really consider the reasons why they had entered into marriage. The words of the marriage contract were so easily murmured by these couples, but most of them had little or no idea of just how long the contract they were entering into would turn out to be, or how rocky an institution marriage really is. He wondered how many people would marry if they had, like Scrooge, the benefit of a tour by the Ghost of Marriage Yet to Come. "Precious few," he thought wryly, "including myself in all probability.

"And what about the couple that was going to go through the marriage sacrament in twenty minutes? What will the future hold for them?" Reverend Piccard thought.

The bride, of course, was Susanne Oakley Secant, the only living child of Thomas Secant and his wife, Sarah. Their other child,

Thomas, Jr., had died, Reverend Piccard faintly remembered, in infancy of scarlet fever or some other childhood disease before Reverend Piccard had become the rector of St. James.

Sarah Secant, the mother of the bride, was a daughter of Robert Oakley, whose ancestors had come over with William Penn. Robert Oakley had been a vestryman of the church but had died long before Reverend Piccard had come to this parish. Mrs. Elizabeth Oakley, the grandmother of the bride, now well over seventy, had returned to the Quaker Church of her youth after her husband's death. However, Alfred Oakley Oliver, a nephew of Elizabeth Oakley and, hence, a first cousin of Sarah Secant, was on the vestry. Alfred's wife, Jane, was active in the Altar Guild. Together they made a handsome contribution each year to St. James.

The bride, Susanne Secant, was dark, having none of her father Tom Secant's fair Irish coloring. Susanne had her mother's aristocratic good looks though she was a bit shorter. But there was something hard and wild in her animated face, particularly her large bright black eyes. Even Reverend Piccard had heard of her reputation in the "junior set." In addition, he had been given to believe by his wife, Ruth, that everyone was surprised that Susanne was marrying this tall, serious-looking young man now waiting in the chapel rather than erratic, longhaired Stewart Bellak Jennings, whose mother, Dol Jennings, had been a Delp, another old family.

Susanne Secant's appointment with Reverend Piccard had been scheduled for her by her mother for 11:00 A.M. on a Thursday morning two weeks before the wedding. Reverend Piccard had looked forward to the interview: he was mildly curious to meet the bride and find out how she happened to be marrying a tall young man from Connecticut rather than young Jennings. However, just an hour before Susanne's appointment, her mother had telephoned, saying almost casually, "Reverend Piccard, this is Sarah Secant, Susanne's mother. I made an appointment for Susanne to see you later this morning. Unfortunately, she seems to have forgotten the appointment. She has already gone to the hairdresser, and I was not able to catch her. She will not be back until after she's been to a bridal shower."

Reverend Piccard had replied rather icily, "Well, just when

Chapter 1 -- In the Face of God and This Company

can she make it?"

Sarah Secant had paused and then replied coolly, "I just don't think that the child has a minute between now and the wedding. However, perhaps you and she can have a chat after the wedding. Maybe when she's back from her honeymoon. How would that do?"

Reverend Piccard jumped to his feet. "Now you listen to me, Mrs. Secant. That will not be at all satisfactory. Please tell Miss Secant that unless she calls and makes an appointment with me which she keeps between now and the wedding, I will not perform the marriage sacrament for her! That's final! Is that clear?" His voice had fairly crackled with anger.

There was a pause. Then Mrs. Secant had said smoothly, "Well, I see. I had not realized that the Episcopalian marriage ceremony required the bride to have a talk with the priest before the wedding. It was not required in my day but then I suppose there have been a lot of changes. I'll talk to Susie. We'll be in touch. I'm sorry for the mix-up. Good-bye, Dr. Piccard."

Reverend Piccard was shaking with so much rage that his hands trembled. He sat back down in his chair in the study and thought about what had just happened. He was quickly ashamed at having once again lost his temper, especially since he knew that his rage at the missed appointment was generated somewhat by his curiosity about the bride. In about half an hour, he had calmed down and was, in fact, about to call Mrs. Secant and tell her that it was unnecessary for Susanne to call him or to see him. However, before he could telephone Mrs. Secant, he got a phone call from Alfred Oliver's office in Philadelphia.

"Hello, Reverend Piccard, hold the line for a moment, if you would, for Alfred Oliver," said the brisk telephone girl at the brokerage firm of Oakley, Oliver and Tarrant. Once again anger swept over Reverend Piccard. However, just then, Alfred Oliver's suave voice came on the line. "Hello Father Bill, this is Al Oliver. Say, I just got a call from my cousin, Sarah Secant. She told me that there was some sort of a mix-up and Susie missed an appointment with you. This seems to have upset the apple cart for the wedding. Sarah called me because this sort of thing is so upsetting to the ladies, especially when

Dearly Beloved

they have sent out invitations and set up a wedding and all that sort of thing. What's it all about? Can I help square it away? I know that Susie is a sort of a scatterbrain, but I'd hate to see this marriage not come off at St. James simply because the child failed to keep a date with you."

At the start of the conversation, when he was in the heat of his rekindled anger, Reverend Piccard had been momentarily tempted to reaffirm to the smooth-talking Alfred Oliver just what he had told the bride's mother. However, after a brief pause and an inward sigh, he replied, "Oh, no real problem, Al. I flew off the handle and was a little bit more abrupt than I should have been with Mrs. Secant. I must be getting old and crotchety. I was at the point of calling her back and telling her that it was probably unnecessary for Susanne to come in and see me, though of course, she is free to do so if she cares to. I know she is busy, and I have comparatively nothing to do between now and the wedding," he added somewhat sarcastically.

He immediately regretted his sarcasm. However, Alfred Oliver was a practical and busy man. Finding that the problem had apparently been resolved before his telephone call, he simply said, "Thanks, Father Bill, see you Sunday at Church or at vestry a week from Wednesday. I'll call Sarah and tell her that there's no real problem or, if there was one, it has been resolved. Thanks again."

After the call from Alfred Oliver, Reverend Piccard thought the incident through once again. Then he got down on his knees at his prie dieu. "Oh God, forgive me for losing my temper at that silly woman, Mrs. Secant, and her even sillier daughter, Susanne – both, however, God's creatures – especially as the reason for my anger was in large part my own idle curiosity. Anger, like sloth, has always been one of my faults. I humbly pray again that you, oh God, will understand my weaknesses and strengthen me to overcome these failings and indeed all of my many other weaknesses.

"I sometimes dream of resigning my ministry in this parish and going to work in Alaska among the natives and Eskimos. Forgive such vain thoughts, oh Lord. I am here because it is Thy will. There is work aplenty to be done among the heathen that live here in this parish. Give me strength and energy to do Thy work here if that be

Chapter 1 -- In the Face of God and This Company

Thy will. Let me not be like Jonah who tried to avoid the tasks that You had set out for him.

"I pray, oh Lord, for those in my parish. Deliver them from their love of violence, their greed, their avarice, their pride and, above all, their sexual lust. I include myself, oh Lord, among them in my prayer for Your help and deliverance from these and other failings.

"Oh Lord, I pray once again that Thou will strengthen my flickering faith. Do not, oh Lord, allow it to go out as it has, as You well know, twice already. I pray not for secular or spiritual preeminence, but rather just faith.

"Finally, hear my prayer, oh Lord, for the young people, Susanne and Phillip, whom I am to join in holy wedlock. In spite of the barbaric rituals which have grown up around the first miracle at Cana, let Thy favor be shown to these two young people who are about to enter into the holy state of matrimony.

"All this I ask in the name of our Lord, Jesus Christ, who liveth and reignith forever. Amen."

He got up. As always, he felt somewhat better. The prayer softened the memory of the flaming anger that had twice just engulfed him.

As Reverend Piccard looked out the leaded windows of his study, he saw some of the ushers on the church lawn roughhousing, joking and smoking cigarettes before their nominal duties of ushering people into the pews commenced. For a moment, watching them, it seemed that the impending ceremony might turn out to be like an episode from "The Three Stooges." As Reverend Piccard was watching, an old white Corvette drew up to the curb. A very fat young man in a cutaway got out. Reverend Piccard recognized John Oliver, son of Alfred Oliver, and the best man. Oliver called all of the ushers together. After they were assembled, he took a white florist box from the back seat of the Corvette. Looking cautiously around, he set the box on the ground in the midst of the clustered groomsmen, cut the green string and opened the box: the group exploded and doubled up with laughter. Oliver, obviously well pleased with the effect of his disclosure, clapped the lid back on the box. He made motions cautioning the group to secrecy. He then carried the box out of view around toward the front doors of St. James. "Bridal flowers," thought Reverend Piccard, "but what caused all the merriment?"

Reverend Piccard's thoughts again turned to the groom. Phillip MacPherson's appointment was for 2:00 P.M. the same afternoon as the aborted appointment of the bride. Unlike most young grooms, he was right on time. He was wearing a blazer and a tie rather than Levis and a shirt without a tie. This pleased Reverend Piccard. Of course, he knew nothing of Phillip's family since they came from West Hartford, Connecticut. He knew very little about the groom except that he had just graduated from Princeton and would be going into the Navy for three years later in the fall. Tall and thin, he had an angular face, the length of which was emphasized somewhat by his horn-rimmed glasses and the sideburns which grew down below his ears. But his hair itself was reasonably short by present day standards, and certainly by the standards of some of the ushers who looked queerly out of place in cutaways with hair down to their shoulders.

MacPherson showed his Scotch ancestry by his tallness and the angularity of his face. He was thin and lanky now but in years to come, as he filled out and as his face took on more character, he would be better looking. The promise of better looks was marred somewhat by the fact that he often blinked involuntarily once, twice or three times in rapid succession.

Reverend Piccard had said in a genial tone as the interview got underway, "Well, Phillip, it's nice of you to take the time to come in. Actually, it is not absolutely required that either you or your bride come to see me. But I like to get to know those whom I am going to do something as important as marry before the actual ceremony or even the rehearsal gets underway. This is especially true of out-of-towners. But, then, I can't really claim to know your Susanne except very slightly through her cousins, the Olivers, and, frankly, by her reputation as a lively member of the younger generation. Actually, I know very little about you, except that you come from West Hartford, Connecticut, and have just graduated from Princeton – cum laude from what I hear – and that you are going to marry Susanne Secant. Tell me a little bit about yourself."

Chapter 1 -- In the Face of God and This Company

Phil replied, "There's not really much more to tell you, Dr. Piccard. I am from outside Hartford, Connecticut. Incidentally, I was confirmed at St. John's in West Hartford about ten years ago but I haven't really been very regular at church since going to Princeton, though I am a believer. I was an only child until my mother remarried after my father's death, so I now have two little half sisters. At Princeton I was in the Woodrow Wilson School of Public and International Affairs. I am going into the Navy in October to fulfill my military obligations and to avoid a low draft number and becoming cannon fodder with the infantry in Vietnam. I have a small trust fund, which, together with my pay from the Navy, will be enough for Susie and me to start out on. I had hoped to accept a rotating internship from the State Department and the Department of Defense and thus avoid this whole Vietnam business, but the Navy is insisting on its pound of flesh. Of course, the Navy has a perfect right to do so – it's just a three-year nuisance for Susie and me.

"We haven't known each other for all that long. In fact, I first met Susie last Christmas but I really want to marry her. I think or rather hope she still wants to marry me."

Reverend Piccard quietly noted that a troubled look came across MacPherson's face. He blinked several times as he said the last words.

Reverend Piccard said, "Now, we're getting quite close to 'Here Comes the Bride.' I hope that you and your Susie have made up your minds once and for all about the serious step that you both are about to take. If either of you have any serious doubts about the advisability of getting married, then the wedding should not take place. It should be postponed until both of you are firmly convinced that this is not only a good step but a permanent lifetime step. If either one of you has reservations about your marriage, then, as a matter of church law, you should not and cannot enter into the sacrament of marriage. On a more practical basis, I caution you that marriage is usually a long and often difficult evolution of the relationship between a man and a woman. If there are real uncertainties about entering into marriage even before the ceremony is performed, then it is elementary that the ceremony should be postponed until all such doubts are resolved."

Reverend Piccard looked sideways to see if any of these warnings were sinking in. The young man sitting in the chair next to his desk was obviously quite far away and not paying attention. There was a long pause. However, he suddenly turned and faced Reverend Piccard directly and said rather slowly and deliberately in his deep voice, "Thank you, Dr. Piccard, for this advice. I agree with you. All of what you are saying is perfectly true. Frankly, I am somewhat doubtful at this point that this wedding is actually going to come off for at least two compelling reasons."

Reverend Piccard recalled that he had sat bolt upright in his chair, surprised in spite of himself. "What do you mean, young man? Have you and Miss Secant had a tiff, or is this something more serious?"

MacPherson had replied evenly, "I really don't want to discuss the whole thing with you. Please do not attempt to get deeply into this situation to see if you can mediate or resolve it. Susie and I have not had a tiff. Rather, she and I have found that we have reached a fundamental parting of the ways. We just don't agree on the basics. Perhaps I'm too serious, but I want to do something meaningful with my life. On the other hand, Susie has got to grow up and decide here and now whether she too wants to realize her immense potential or whether she wants to go on being a 'madcap' and cutup all of her life. However, Susie doesn't agree with any of this. That's where the matter now stands. Second, as you may know, Susie carried on for a long time with Stewart Jennings, who is from around here. I think that he may well be planning some highjinks for the wedding ceremony itself. I really want to marry Susie. I'll always be sorry if this really wonderful girl gets away from me. Once we are married and out of the Philadelphia area, Susie'll see things my way. She will grow up and make a go of her life. However, things are touch and go at present. Again, I repeat, please do not try to intervene. I am reasonably sure that Susie didn't come for her interview with you principally because she does not want to discuss the situation with you, but I could be wrong. The best thing is simply to wait and see if things resolve themselves."

Chapter 1 -- In the Face of God and This Company

Reverend Piccard blew gently on his fingers and said, "I see. This is not usual, I must say, Phillip. Are you certain that it would not be a good idea for the three of us to meet and go over the matter?"

"No, no, Father Piccard, " MacPherson replied firmly. "This is really between Susie and me. Either we resolve it ourselves or we don't. But I am sure that neither one of us wants to go into the matter with you. I appreciate your offer and I hope you're not mad that I don't avail myself of it."

"No," Reverend Piccard said. "In the end, this marriage is a decision for the two of you to make. I can at times help, but if the two of you don't really want to talk together with me, you are probably right that it would only hurt things at this point. Let me say that you are a couple of years older than Susanne. While I don't know her personally, I've been told that she has a reputation for fun and antics. Remember that you need to supply leadership and maturity to a young person such as Susanne. At the same time, you can't be inflexible and unbending. Marriage is, as you will discover quickly, a never ending compromise between two people. Both you and Susanne are going to have to bend in order to make a go of the marriage that you are about to enter into. The delicate balance is how to compromise and get along without sacrificing principles. Your present problem may be beneficial in the long run in the sense that you and Susanne are already seeing what some people don't see and learn until after its too late – that is, that marriage is not all one continual bed of roses."

MacPherson replied, "I agree, but it remains to be seen whether Susie and I are going to go through with this marriage. Of course, as it stands now, the wedding is on. Susie's old nurse, Rebe, is coming up from Nevis just to see Susie get married. Rebe really raised Susie from the time Susie was little. Maybe she can help. But I will get in touch if things definitely come apart between now and the wedding or rather the rehearsal on Friday night. In the meanwhile, thanks for your help and understanding. Also, let's hope Stewart Jennings does not make good on his vague threats."

The interview had ended on that somber note. Reverend Piccard liked MacPherson: he had poise and gave off a feeling of strength and quiet determination in the face of major problems, which he was unwilling to share with a stranger..

At the rehearsal on the Friday evening, Susanne had stayed seated in the pew at the very back of the church while Joan Platen, her maid of honor, stood in. Reverend Piccard had wondered at the time whether Susanne's non-participation was actually due to the silly superstition that it was bad luck for the bride to participate in the rehearsal or whether it was due to the underlying problem that the groom had alluded to.

The rehearsal had started out routinely. However, in the middle of the rehearsal the sound of a motorcycle was heard coming up the long hill leading to St. James at a high rate of speed. Everyone froze. The motorcycle roared as it went around St. James and stopped at the main door. Everyone turned around as a young man pushed open the big door with a bang and strode into the back of the church, taking off his shiny black helmet and dark sunglasses. His long blond hair extended way down over the collar of his blue denim shirt. His faded Levis were tucked into scuffed black motorcycle boots. He stood there, obviously savoring the dramatic effect that his sudden appearance was having on the proceedings.

The father of the bride shouted, "Stewart, what do you think you are doing here? We are in the midst of the rehearsal for Susie's wedding!"

Jennings said, "No offense, Mr. Secant. I was just checking to see if Susie is still thinking she is going to marry Lurch, the big guy from Princeton. Maybe she will and maybe she won't. Let's just wait and see, shall we? Well, folks, see you all tomorrow! Same time, same station. Stay tuned for some real matrimonial entertainment!"

With that, he smirked at the bride, turned on his heel and walked out. The motorcycle circled the church again and left with a roar. The motorcycle went on back down the long hill at high speed. Then, as it rounded the sharp corner at the bottom of the hill, the noise gradually faded away.

Mrs. Secant was crying uncontrollably. She whispered hysterically to her husband, "Oh my God, Tom. This is all my fault. Why does what happened years ago now rise to ruin Susie's wedding?"

Chapter 1 -- In the Face of God and This Company

Tom Secant and a tall black lady tried to hush Sarah Secant up as they hustled her out of St. James and into the Secants' black Mercedes. As the Mercedes swiftly left the parking lot, the bride's mother could be seen through the side window of the big car, gesturing and talking hysterically. The rehearsal was then quickly completed, but everyone was in shock. After the rehearsal, the groom had come to see Reverend Piccard and asked for an appointment on Saturday morning at 9:00 A.M. There was no indication whatsoever what the appointment was all about.

Again, Reverend Piccard thought with astonishment at the surprising events earlier that Saturday morning. But just as he started to think what had happened, he glanced at the grandfather clock solemnly ticking across the room: it was now 4:25. Soon the sacristan would be knocking on his door. So he got up and put on his starched white surplice. With his *Book of Common Prayer* in hand, he was at the door when the discreet knock came. As the organist began the traditional "Here Comes the Bride," Reverend Piccard entered the chancel, came forward and stood waiting at the top of the two little steps, his hands folded in front of him holding his *Book of Common Prayer*.

The church was full, as he knew it would be. There were some late arrivals nervously scurrying about for seats at the back or standing along the side aisles. As Reverend Piccard reached the top of the two steps, the three bridesmaids came up the aisle, one by one, with downcast eyes and timid smiles. Then the six little boys and girls followed by the six groomsmen came somewhat awkwardly up the aisle, reached the steps and turned around and faced the congregation, following Mrs. Perry's directions. From his right, out of the corner of his eye, Reverend Piccard could see the little chapel door open. Tall, lanky Phillip MacPherson and fat John Oliver appeared and walked self-consciously to their appointed places. The atmosphere in the church was tense. The little windows along the side of the aisles had been tilted fully open. Four small electric fans below the windows made a purring noise as they went rhythmically back and forth.

Just ahead of the bride came the maid of honor, Joan Platen. Reverend Piccard noticed tears in her eyes in back of her horn-rimmed glasses as she looked up after she had reached the steps. "Why do some women always cry at weddings?" Reverend Piccard wondered what would happen.

Reverend Piccard thought that a young woman always looked her best in her wedding gown as she came up the aisle on her father's arm. Watching the approaching bride, Reverend Piccard thought that Susanne Secant was certainly no exception: her naturally dark complexion, emphasized by a summer tan, set off the whites of her large black eyes and her small very white teeth and her jet black hair. Her dark coloring was also emphasized by the snow white dress and small white cap she was wearing. In her arms she carried a large natural bouquet of greenery without any flowers in it at all. Unlike most brides who smiled and looked radiant, the bride's face was troubled – she looked downright frightened, though she was trying to smile bravely.

The bride's small stature contrasted with the bulk of her father. Tom Secant was big. In his younger days, as he was fond of saying, he had played in the front line of the Dartmouth football team "before the game became professionalized by scholarships." When Tom Secant was young and in his prime, he must have been quite handsome, but now in his late 40s, he was becoming stout. His florid but kindly face was somewhat pudgy and lined. Reverend Piccard had heard Tom Secant was now more apt to be in the bar at the Club than on the squash or tennis courts. It was no secret that Tom Secant's career as a stockbroker in Philadelphia in Oakley, Oliver and Tarrant had "plateaued," even though he had been made a partner early in his career. Still, today, the day of his only child's wedding, he looked quite his best, with his crisp graying brown hair neatly combed, his still handsome face and his large frame encased in a well-fitting cutaway.

In the first pew on the left, Reverend Piccard saw a rather tall, thin, severely dressed woman, obviously the mother of the groom. Reverend Piccard would have recognized the relationship if by nothing else than by her strong angular face. Like her son, she wore horn-rimmed glasses. Next to her were two rather plain little girls, Phillip's half sisters. The tall, portly man must be Phillip's stepfather..

Chapter 1 -- In the Face of God and This Company

Behind Susanne and to his right, Reverend Piccard could seeSarah Secant, standing alone in the first pew waiting for her husband to finish his role in the marriage ritual and then step back to her side. She stood erect. She had the same dark coloring that Susanne had, but her hair was white. She must have been a beautiful woman, Reverend Piccard thought, when she was Susanne's age. As it was, she was handsome and crisp. She had none of the decayed middle-age spread that was beginning to destroy her husband's looks. She wore a simple beige linen dress. Her feathered hat added an elegant flair. However, the forced smile on her face betrayed the heavy strain she was under. In the last pew, all the way to the side, standing by herself and very erect was a tall thin black woman. She was dressed in a long black dress and was wearing a simple straw hat. "That must be Rebe, Susanne's old nurse originally from somewhere in the Caribbean," Reverend Piccard thought.

In the third pew, Reverend Piccard could see Mrs. Elizabeth Oakley, the petite grandmother of the bride and the mother of Mrs. Secant. "Perhaps," Reverend Piccard thought, "Susanne comes by her fairly small size from her." In spite of the fact that she was over 70, she stood up, ramrod straight, though she carried a small white cane. Her hair underneath her small hat was as white as her daughter's. She had bright blue eyes. Mrs. Secant's and her daughter's coloring must have come from Robert Oakley since Mrs. Oakley was fair and had a ruddiness in her cheeks that is sometimes seen in older people.

Next to Mrs. Oakley were Alfred Oliver and his wife, Jane. The Olivers were in their late 40s. He was slightly shorter and smaller than his wife. His bald head and his thinness made him look smaller and older than he was. Though his somewhat crafty-looking face was free of wrinkles, he too had a real look of dread as the marriage service was about to begin.

The organ, which had been murmuring chords quietly, faded away. The very last arrivals were stealthily sliding down the side aisles to join more prompt members of the families. Reverend Piccard deliberately opened his well worn copy of the *Book of Common Prayer* to page 300, and was about to begin.

There was a moment of almost complete silence in the

church. Aside from a muffled cough or two, the only sounds in the church came from the four small, old-fashioned electric fans that continued to purr rhythmically.

As Reverend Piccard was about to begin with the familiar words, "Dearly Beloved," the bride said in a quiet but firm whisper, "Just a moment please, Father Piccard, before you begin."

Chapter Two

For Better, for Worse

As the clock in the steeple at St. James struck four, Phillip MacPherson, sitting alone in the chapel waiting for his best man, felt a wave of panic sweep over him. Though it was cool in the chapel, his palms were moist. He mopped his forehead with his handkerchief and then polished his horn-rimmed glasses, which had fogged up. He said to himself, "Christ, what in God's name am I doing here, sitting alone in this bloody chapel on the Main Line? In half an hour I'm going to marry Miss Susanne Oakley Secant. But Stewart Jennings is probably going to do something drastic. This wedding may be shot to hell."

It had all happened so quickly. There had not been any point almost from the very beginning when he would have wanted to turn back or, for that matter, could have turned back or even just stood still and considered things fully, unless it was the time in the early spring when Susie had seemed to have gone back to Stewart Jennings.

Where and when had it all started? Obviously, it started last winter on the weekend between Christmas and New Year. Phillip could remember every detail of that first weekend with utter clarity. He had spent Christmas Day with his mother, his half sisters, Doris and Alice, and his stepfather in West Hartford. He had planned to go back to Princeton to work on his thesis, "The Balfour Declaration and the Emergence of the State of Israel." John Oliver, however, had called and persuaded him to go skiing between Christmas and New Year's. He'd come down the day after Christmas and spent the night at the Olivers'. He and John had planned to leave the next day, taking John's beat-up old Corvette to ski at Mad River. However, Sandy, a friend who had gone up by train on Christmas night, had telephoned to say that there was no snow in spite of the snow reports. Sandy had said, "It would be a waste of your time and money to come up here." Therefore, the two of them had stayed at the Olivers', hoping that New England would soon be blanketed with snow. He said to himself, "If it had snowed, I would not be here waiting for the organ to begin playing 'Here Comes the Bride.' Rather, while waiting for orders to begin my three-year stint with the Navy, I might have been starting the basic CIA course in Quantico, Virginia (under the guise of a civilian training for the Department of Defense)."

On the Saturday after Christmas, he and John had been playing lackadaisically at squash at the Apple Orchard Club down the road from the Oliver house. In spite of the fact that he weighed more than 225 pounds, spoke with a slight lisp and was only about five-feet-five tall, John was amazingly agile and had played squash for years. He could lick Phil with one hand tied behind his back. Since they played together at Princeton occasionally, they were playing in a relaxed fashion, more for the exercise and to work off Christmas dinner than anything else.

In the next court they could hear the thump, thump of a squash ball. Occasionally the sound of girls' voices floated down into their court. Then the sound of the ball hitting the wall in the next court stopped. As Phil was picking up the ball the next time, he looked up into the gallery and saw two girls leaning on their elbows, looking down into their court. Susie's dark coloring and shoulder length black hair stood out against the white squash court and the man's white button-down shirt that she was wearing. Alongside her was her brown-haired roommate, Joan Platen, in a tennis dress. Oliver saw the girls the same time as Phil had and called out, "Hi, Cousin Susie. Come down and give us a lesson." Then he said to MacPherson, "Susie is a real pro at squash like her old man."

"Yeah," Susanne had called back derisively and in a somewhat coarse tone. "My old man was OK before he put on almost as

Chapter 2 -- For Better, for Worse

much blubber as you have, Olive the Pitt, old boy. It was also before he got to like to hear the sound of his own empty whiskey glass hitting the men's bar."

"Nevertheless," Oliver retorted, "he can still beat me when he's trying."

"Bullshit, who are you kidding, partner?" Susie replied. "Why even I can beat his fat old ass now!"

"Cousin Susanne, what a naughty girl thou art – what would Grandmother Oakley say to thee for using such coarse language? Rebe used to smack your little bun with her hairbrush whenever she caught you using such foul language. She'd still use her hairbrush on you today if she was around. We'll just have to get Rebe to come out of retirement and teach you your manners all over again!"

Susanne stuck out her tongue at Oliver and turned on her heel, saying, "Come on, Joanie, there are far better things to do than watch a fat cousin try to play squash with a string bean."

As the two girls walked away, Oliver called after then, "Hey, stick around, Cos, we'll buy you two a Coke in the grill when we have washed our honest sweat off after this terrific exhibition match. Besides, Cos, I've heard that Rebe had taught you never, never to stick your tongue out at anyone. Right?"

But the girls were gone. Phil was still looking after them. He turned to Oliver and asked, "Who are they, especially the well-stacked little number with all the lip? What say, let's quit and have a Coke with them?"

"OK with me," said Oliver. "As for Susie, she's my cousin and lives near us. Her name is Susanne Secant. I must have told you about her. Sue's quite a numero. She's mean as a snake at times. She got bounced from Bennett for smoking or selling pot last year. Do you know Stewart Jennings? No? Well, he's a cross-eyed freak who lives in the gatehouse on the Dulaire place down Bluner Road past the woods. He goes to Boston College, plays the piano and is interested in the avant-garde theatre, protest movements, you name it. But, it's all talk. Susie's been going around with Stewart for quite a while. They seem to be two of a kind. However, from what I hear, Stew suddenly gave Susie her walking papers. She's pretty unhappy right now.

The other girl is Joan Platen, Susie's old roommate from Bennett. Joan's from Winnetka – her grandfather put together Platen Mining & Refining. She's as rich as Croesus. I met her here at the Thanksgiving dance last year. She's just the opposite from Sue – cool, calm and collected, doesn't say very much but takes it all in. Underneath her quiet exterior, Joan is three times the girl Cousin Susie is or at least now is."

From Susie's parting remarks, Phil had not expected to see the girls again. To his surprise, once he and John had finished their showers, they found the two girls in the grill room. When Susie stood up from the sofa near the open fire where she and Joan had been sitting, Phil was surprised to see that she was quite small. Besides the frayed button-down shirt open so far down that he could see the top of her brassiere, she had on ragged cutoff jeans and scuffed sneakers. He also noticed her muscular, suntanned legs. Certainly the combination of jet black hair, large black eyes with blue eye shadow and small white teeth with spaces between them, coupled with her intense animation, gave her a striking look. On her brown forearm above the elbow she was wearing a gold slave bracelet, and she had large gold wire loops in her ears.

Susie said to Oliver, "John, you remember Joan Platen, my roommate before I got bounced the hell out of Bennett? Joan, you may remember my cousin, John Oliver, a/k/a Olive the Pitt. You probably met him at the Thanksgiving dance here last year." Then, turning to MacPherson, she looked up at him and held her hand to her eyes as if looking up into the mountains, saying, "But who the hell is this here tall man? No, no, let me guess. Is it Wilt the Stilt? Or is it the son of Paul Bunyan?"

Oliver said to the girls, "Hi, Joan, nice to see you again. No, Susie, wrong again. This is not the Neanderthal Man. It's my roommate, Phil MacPherson from West Hartford, better known as Blinky to those who know and love him, and there have been many and one in particular at Princeton. Right, Blinky?"

Turning to Phil, Oliver continued, "Blinky, lean down and shake Susie's hand. She won't bite, or she usually doesn't." Oliver

Chapter 2 -- For Better, for Worse

then turned to Joan, "It's nice to be a normal human being. The hell with those two freaks."

Susie snapped back, "If I'm a biting dog and your friend Blinky could get a job as the tall man, you certainly qualify as the fat man in any side show outfit without adding another pound." She added smiling, "Let's put a freak show on tonight, what say? Maybe Joan here could sell tickets and add to the Platen family fortune. What do you think, Joan?"

They all laughed and built on the idea. The ice had been broken. The four of them sat down and spent the shank of the afternoon on the oversized couches before the fireplace, drinking Cokes and playing "Who do you know?" and listening to John Oliver, who liked to talk, telling funny stories, mostly about himself. At one point when John was talking to Joan, Susanne leaned back on the couch, snuffed out her cigarette, put her hands back of her head, looked over at Phil, sizing him up, and then said, "Well, to hell with the Olivers, the Oakleys, the Secants and all that crowd." Laying her hand on his arm, she said, "But, what about you, Stretch, what's your claim to fame?"

Phil was electrified by her touch and disconcerted by her directness. He involuntarily blinked through his glasses and said, "Not much to report, sir. I was born and raised in West Hartford. My father was an insurance broker. Died when I was twelve. Fortunately, after a couple of years, Mother remarried. I now have two half sisters: Alice, age five, and little Doris, age three. I went to public school and then won a scholarship to Exeter. At Exeter I got the West Hartford Princeton Alumni Scholarship to Princeton. I'm now studying Russian, but my senior thesis is on the Balfour Declaration. I have successfully avoided the consequences of a low draft lottery number by agreeing to serve in the Navy for a couple of years after graduation, but I hope to be able to accept the joint internship in Washington that I was offered before I have to make good with the Navy." Realizing that he was sounding rather like a page from a yearbook, he added, "Seriously, I wear a size 17½ collar and occasionally have athlete's foot, worse on the right than on the left, ma'am, but I'm in a period of remission right now. Anything else you'd like to know?"

"Nope," Susie replied briskly. "You pass muster. I'd say that you're a long tall cube being shaped up in the Establishment block factories. They're busy polishing your edges so that you'll fit squarely in place and grow up into an even taller establishment brick some day."

"Thanks, pal, and you?" Phil replied. "Turnabout is fair play. Let me see if I have your dimensions correctly in mind at this point. Shoulder-length hair like nearly every other teenage girl in America, miniskirts and a mini-radical attitude against the Establishment, Vietnam, Nixon, Daddy and all that. Graciously in favor of all blacks and the civil rights movement, women's lib, a sneaky admiration for the Weathermen and a nodding acquaintance with the sayings of Mao Tse Tung. Smokes like a chimney. You are tone deaf but, of course, have the conventional love for outrageously loud music. Favorite group, The Doors. Unless I miss my guess, you probably didn't make the scene at Woodstock because you were in some fancy boarding school. For all of the foregoing, you are gracious enough to accept all the good things that are your natural due and that your trust and the Main Line have to offer. That's about it, I guess."

"Superficially on target, pal," Susie replied with a smile. "Touché. But truce, at least for the moment. Appearances are often deceiving, as you may find out, Buster., OK?"

"Fair enough, but is there anything else you care to know?" Phil asked.

"Well, now that you ask, how does a he-man like you end up with a rich fat fag like Cousin Zazu Pitts?" she said quietly with a malicious smile. Phil was swept with anger. He had accepted Oliver's situation long ago and never thought much about it. He quickly controlled his anger and replied easily, "Oh, Ollie, he's OK. I've known him since boarding school days. He's a nice guy and a good friend. It's just his manner. Any other questions, ma'am? And, incidentally, am I allowed to take the Fifth Amendment?"

Susie laughed and said brightly, "No, the questioning is finished for the moment. Hold out your hands." She pretended to snap on a pair of imaginary handcuffs. "The prisoner is to be returned to his cell subject to later recall for further examination." Phillip was

Chapter 2 -- For Better, for Worse

again electrified by the touch of her fingers.

John said as they were leaving the grill at the end of the afternoon, "What do you say, Blinky, shall we give these poor girls a break and take them out tonight? What about it, girls? Are you socially engaged or would you entrust yourselves to us?"

Susie said to Joan, "What say, Joan? Shall we go slumming with these two mismatched wolves, or would you rather sit home tonight and watch TV or listen to the old man bitch about his finances after he's gotten a couple of jolts of Jack Daniels in him?"

Without waiting for Joan's answer, Sue said, "Sure, I'll play Repunzel and let down my long black hair. So, what time are you and Don Quixote going to come around, Sancho Panza? How about 8:00 or 8:30? We should be through dinner by then. By the way, Ollie, could you drop Joanie home? We came on my Honda. Joanie is terrified at the very thought of having to ride again behind me for some reason."

"I don't blame Joan one little bit," said Oliver. "You damn near ran me off the road with that goddamned machine last summer at that sharp corner at the bottom of the hill on Bluner's Lane near Colonel Rider's place. You're going to get it sometime, Miss Smarty Pants. You may meet the nicest people on a Honda, but you are going to meet the nicest truck or telephone pole if you keep jazzing around the countryside at seventy miles an hour!"

Susie said, "Well, Fatso, all you gotta do is keep the hell out of my way!"

On their way to the door they passed the trophy cases. Oliver said, "Susie, seriously, why don't you take up a legitimate sport again instead of playing at Hell's Angels? Phil, this trophy case is full of silver that Susie won, either alone or with her old man. But you haven't hit a ball in anger in a good two years."

"Different strokes for different folks," Susie replied with defiance. "You win one, you've won 'em all. Besides, I've taken up a new sport: men. I eat 'em alive! By the way, Blinky, what do you do by way of games? Basketball, I suppose?"

Oliver replied for him, "Nope, wrong again, Susie. Blinky does cross-country."

Susie said, "See you wolves tonight." With that she was gone. They heard her motorcycle's roar as she sped out the circular drive of the Club.

Phil was totally astonished by Susie. He had been "Coke" dating Ann Livingstone, a sophomore at Princeton he'd met in the Russian section of the Firestone Library. She was studious, shy and nervous. Phil had thought he was quite intrigued with Ann. Though she didn't ski at all, Phil had asked her to come to Mad River for New Year's Eve, quite hopeful that he might finally overcome Ann's timidity and get her to sleep with him. But now Ann seemed pale and colorless compared with Susie, who, if nothing else, was intensely, almost aggressively, feminine. In spite of her manner, Phil felt that what Susie said was deliberately intended to shock and that she was often intentionally rude and cutting. He also disliked the smell of tobacco from all the cigarettes she smoked, one after another. Nevertheless, as they dropped Joan off, he found that he was looking forward to the evening with mounting excitement: the evening might well be enlivened with a little bit of sex with Miss Susie!

At dinner, John said to his parents, "Blinky met Cousin Susie and Joan today at the Club. I think Blinky here is quite smitten with our little cousin. In any case, we are going out with them tonight."

Mrs. Oliver sniffed and said in her deep voice, "And just what is Susie up to now. It seems to me that all she does is hang around the taverns with that worthless Stewart Jennings. Cousin Sarah is quite worried about her and with good reason. But, after all, what can you expect with the upbringing that Susie has had from Tom after Rebe retired? He has just about succeeded in raising Susie as a tomboy except that now Susie's turning out to be quite a tough girl. I can see why Sarah is worried. I dare say Sarah will be only too happy to see both of you instead of Stewart."

Mr. Oliver smiled and said, "It seems to me, Jane, that you are somewhat unfair to my goddaughter. You shouldn't prejudice Phillip against her. After all, she's basically an attractive and very intelligent girl even if she does talk in an exaggerated manner and puts on a few antics, especially when she is aided and abetted by that worthless Stewart Jennings. I was told the other day by the chairman of the

Chapter 2 -- For Better, for Worse

board of the Tilton Center for Disadvantaged Children that Susie's a real hard worker with a gift for helping kids who are speech impaired. She can't be all bad." Then, turning to Phillip, he said, "You can see, Phillip, I have a soft spot for Susie. I think she has a lot of spunk though right now she is busy going around shocking people." He chuckled, "Don't mind what Jane says. She just a little bit conservative and always afraid of what Susie is going to say or do. Susie makes her nervous."

Mrs. Oliver rose from the table and said dryly, "Well, Alfred, I guess we're all entitled to our own opinion. We'll just have to see what develops from that young gypsy. Don't let us keep you. Give our best to Cousin Sarah." She paused and then added, "And, of course, to Tom."

As they drove over to the Secants' in John's Corvette, he said, "Blinky, you'll like Tom, Sue's father. He's great. He's as friendly as his Labrador, Inky. He was a terrific athlete in his day at Dartmouth though it is true he's going to seed, as Susie so coarsely remarked this afternoon. She used to worship him but for the last three years or so, she's made no bones about the fact that she despises him. Why, I don't know, except that Tom can't stand Jennings and all he stands for. On the other hand, her mother, Cousin Sarah, is not quite my dish of tea. She's handsome, polite and ladylike. Of course, I get along OK with her, but it is just that she's as cold as ice. I don't need to tell you that Mother despises Susie – simply can't stand seeing her. I suppose the same is true of Susie. They are complete opposites. You should see them at a family gathering. Mother involuntarily flinches every time Susie starts to say anything."

The Secants' large Georgian house was only five places away from the Olivers'. The formal S-curved graveled drive led up from the road to the house. After parking at the door and patting Inky, the Labrador, who had come bounding around the corner of the house and frisking up to them, John pushed the front door open without knocking or ringing the bell. They paused in the front hall. From the living room there came the sound of an angry male voice punctured now and then by the sounds of a calm female voice. The actual words could not be made out, but clearly there was an argument going on.

From upstairs came the blasting beat of a stereo playing "Jesus Christ Superstar."

"Ah, the sounds of domestic bliss," said Oliver quietly to Phil. Then in a louder voice he shouted, "Anyone home?"

Out of the living room and into the brick hall came Mrs. Secant, a good-looking woman in her mid-forties. She resembled Susie in some ways but was a good deal taller and had white hair. Lines were just beginning to show in her handsome aristocratic features.

"Hi, Cousin Sarah," Oliver said. "We are two wolves looking for two Little Red Riding Hoods. This is Wolf MacPherson, my elongated roommate. Growl hello to Little Red Riding Hood's mother, Phil."

Mrs. Secant smiled and said easily, "My, I am frightened, but I'll call my resident 'Hood' and Joan." Then, going to the edge of the stairs, she called loudly, "Girls, please turn down that awful racket." The stereo was turned off abruptly. She then called, "There are two animals down here calling themselves wolves and saying that they are here for the two of you." She then turned and looked up at Phil and said in mock terror, "My, you certainly are a tall order of wolf. What long legs you have. Good evening, Sir Wolf." As Mrs. Secant shook hands with Phil, he got the distinct impression that she was looking him over carefully.

At this point Mr. Secant, the male voice, came out of the living room and joined them in the hallway. He gave the impression of filling the entire spacious hallway. After being introduced and hearing that Phillip was Oliver's roommate and that they had played squash that day, he said, "Phil, you certainly ought to be able to beat John here at squash with your reach. However, he's beginning to learn how to hit the ball. Why, he even gives me some trouble, though I can still beat him. If you want, sometime I'll show you a few tricks that can help a tall man on the squash court."

As he finished speaking, the girls appeared at the head of the steps. They were both dressed in pant suits. Susie's was gray flannel with a green collar and piping. She had a matching green butterfly bow in her black hair. Joan was in dark blue. Phil could still remember the attractive picture that the two contrasting girls made in the

Chapter 2 -- For Better, for Worse

moment they stood at the head of the stairs. Susie then came flying down the stairs two at a time, while Joan came down at a graceful leisurely pace. Mrs. Secant looked her daughter over and said, "It certainly is nice to see you in something other than cutoff blue jeans and a motorcycle helmet for a change. Here are the two waiting wolves, girls. Are you ready to be devoured?"

John said, "Phil, it certainly is mighty nice when the mother turns the Little Red Riding Hoods over to the wolves directly instead of making them go through all that bull of trotting through the woods, picking wildflowers and going to grandma's house."

"Nonsense, John" answered Mrs. Secant, "I certainly can tell the difference between wolves and woodchoppers."

"Well," said Susie. "Let's not stand here ringing changes on Little Red Riding Hood. Come on, Blinky, whether you're a wolf in sheep's clothing, a woodcutter in grandma's nightgown, or just a plain wolf, let's go. As Porky the Pig says, 'That, that, that's all folks.' Don't wait up cause we're gonna swing till sunup. Goodnight all."

Susie went right by her father, who was standing there waiting, obviously hoping for a goodnight hug from her. Rudely disregarding him, Susie went out into the hall, where she grabbed her blue maxi-coat as well as Joan's fur coat from the front hall coat closet. She put hers on and handed Joan hers and then marched out the front door, again pointedly disregarding her father. John, Joan and Phil trailed after Susie saying their goodnights to Mr. and Mrs. Secant.

John was driving and Joan sat beside him. Susie and Phil sat in the back. The drive out to the Yellow Lantern took only ten minutes or so. John was busy explaining to Joan his theory on the Lieutenant Calley case.

Susie leaned over toward Phil. He could still remember the thrilling sensation that swept over him as she came close in the darkness and he caught a whiff of her perfume tinged with the smell of tobacco. She put her arm on his and said quietly, "Well, did Old Lady give you the usual third degree? She's always prying into my business and finding out who I'm going out with."

"No," Phil replied. "We only talked about Little Red Riding

Hood. There was some question as to whether she would entrust her Little Red Riding Hoods to Ollie and me."

"No question about that. Ma and old Dads are glad enough to see me go out with anyone besides Stew Jennings. They both hate his guts. I suppose old blabbermouth Ollie the Pitt has told you that Jennings and I have busted up for good and all." She paused for a moment and then added grimly, "Well, maybe we have. I suppose what goes up must come down. It sure seems to have come down this time."

Phil mumbled, "Yeah, I heard something to that effect."

"Christ!" Susie muttered testily. "I sure will be glad to get the hell out of this dump. Nothing that anyone does or says doesn't become common property to be hashed over in the hair houses, bridge parties, the locker rooms and bars all around the Main Line. I am finished with Jennings. He's erratic, irresponsible and a neurotic like his mother, Dol."

At this point Phil thought that Susie was talking more loudly than was necessary to make sure John heard her. However, John was now explaining that President Nixon should share the blame with Calley so that Susie's remarks were lost on both John and Joan.

Susie lit a cigarette and said, "Let's change the subject. OK?"

"OK, whatever you say, boss," said Phil. "What's next?"

"Since you put it that way, up against the wall for more questioning. One wrong answer and I'll bust your noggin with my nightstick." She again took his hands in hers and pretended to unlock imaginary handcuffs.

"OK, officer. I'll come clean, but I reserve the right to interrupt the questioning and call my lawyer. By the way, I also reserve the right to take the Fifth Amendment. What's on your mind, officer?" Phil said, reaching his hands up to the top of the car.

Susie said, "Martha Mitchell gave me the right and the power to grant the witness immunity so that you don't have the right to take the Fifth, Fourth, Nineteenth, or any other amendment. What Martha Mitchell and I demand to know is, are you a virgin?"

Phil had been so surprised that he dropped his hands and blinked several times in the darkness. Susie laughed softly and con-

Chapter 2 -- For Better, for Worse

tinued, "Hey, you, back up against the wall. I've been wondering about this ever since this afternoon. You look so Saint Bernardy, so true blue, you know what I mean? In fact, I offered to bet Joan while we were getting dressed but she wouldn't take my bet even though I was willing to give her damned good odds."

Phil had looked over his upraised left arm at her and said to her, "Which way were you going to bet, officer, and what were the odds? I might take some of the bet myself. I am something of an expert on the subject. Of course, don't answer that question if I'm getting too personal."

Susie laughed, "I told Joan I would give her three-to-one that you weren't or at least that you wouldn't be within a month, didn't I, Joanie?"

MacPherson laughed this time and said, "Well, you would have won the bet even without the do-it-yourself option play. However, pray don't let me stand in your way of making dead sure of such an important fact. Of course, I could be wrong after all, and I sure would want a lady to be firmly satisfied."

"Whoa, hold on. I think I'm being run away with. But it's my own damned fault. As old Tom Ryan once warned me, 'Susie, learn to hold a horse at the trot before you put him into a gallop. Then he'll never run away with you.'" She added, "Let's change the subject. OK? Do you smoke, Blinky?"

"No," Phil replied. "But I know you're hooked from the number you sucked down this afternoon."

"No, silly, I mean grass, not just plain old cigs," Susie said. Phil had, in fact, smoked grass several times at Princeton, but it didn't do anything for him except make him sleepy and give him an awful sore throat. He said, "Yeah, I've tried pot but it didn't do anything for me. Do you? But, of course, you do. I'd forgotten," he chuckled.

"Yep, I do and so did all the girls on my hallway except, of course, for Joan. She doesn't smoke at all, never has and never will. Right, Joan of Arc?"

Joan said dryly from the front seat, "Right, Susie. And you shouldn't smoke at all if you know what's good for you."

Susie said, "Pish tush, Joan. They all say smoking pot is bad for you and even that it's habit forming. Stew says that's a lot of bullshit. If anyone should know, he should. Anyway, I've been smoking for more than a year and I've never gone beyond more than one or two joints a week. I've never taken anything more so far." She paused and then added, "Stewart takes some weird pill that he says has the same effect as hash but isn't habit forming. I may just try out those pills."

As they pulled into the parking lot of the Yellow Lantern, Susie said quietly to Phil, again putting her hand on his arm, "Maybe you and I can have a little smoke later tonight, OK? Probably what you smoked before hasn't been any good."

She flashed him a smile in the darkness and gave his arm a little squeeze. But then, as they started up the stairs into the Yellow Lantern, Susie stopped suddenly, turned to him and said, "Oh, God, how I dread going through the crowd at the bar in this place tonight! If Stewart is here, promise you'll take me home right away, Blinky. Deal?" She didn't wait for him to answer but went up the stairs and briskly entered the bar room from which came the sounds of Joan Baez on the jukebox.

Since it was the Saturday night after Christmas, the bar was full of college students besides the regular crowd. Joe Horgan, the manager, was next to the door. When Horgan saw Susie, he said quietly to her, "Nice to see you this evening, Miss Secant, but please don't smoke no joints tonight. It gives the place a bad name and a bad smell. Besides, Corporal Tim Roberts of the county police has been keeping an eye on this place and particularly for Stewart Jennings."

Susie said, "Joe, you know me. I am as good as gold now that Stewart is history."

John put his arms up against the wall and said, "Joe, we're clean, man, clean as a bloodhound's tooth. My name is Rapp Brown. I ain't never smoked nothin' but Virginia Slims. Blinky here has been specially sent by Big Dick Nixon to clean this town up. Blinky and Martha Mitchell have just returned from France by way of Turkey. Of course, Joan here is Agent 99."

Joe smiled then and said, "OK, I guess I won't have to frisk

Chapter 2 -- For Better, for Worse

any of you this time. But, tell your tall friend there to watch his head. The last guy who was as tall as he is knocked a chip out of his head and a piece out of my wagon wheel chandelier as he went through. There's an empty booth in the back. I'll send Claire over directly for your drink order."

Oliver and Susie exchanged remarks, insults, greetings and taunts with half a dozen people on their way past the bar to the booth in the back part of the bar room. After they had all been seated in the booth, John had ordered their first round of drinks from the waitress, Claire.

A girl who had been standing at the bar with a longhaired boy in a turtleneck sweater sidled over through the crowded room. Lydia was introduced by Oliver to Phil and Joan. She talked briefly about various inconsequential things and then, with an innocent air, said, "By the way, Jennings dropped in here last night. Sue, you should have been here. He was as funny as all hell. He played the old upright piano for a while and then did his Czech Chevaliers and 'Harry the Hamlet' routines. He was just great. Around midnight he began to get really high, started sailing glasses around and lighting and throwing kitchen matches about. You know how he gets, Sue. It was like that night you were with him here in November, only funnier.

"Finally Horgan came over and said, 'Jennings, you shut up and calm down or leave.' Of course, Jennings loved that.

"Stew told Horgan, 'Hey, Horgan, you can go and pack sand.' So Horgan really got red in the face and his neck swelled all up. He told Jennings, 'Jennings, you are not going to ever be allowed back in the Yellow Lantern if you break another single solitary glass! You hear?'

"Well, that did it. Jennings reached out and picked up a glass off the nearest table, held it out just in front of Horgan's big red nose, and then dropped it right smack on the tile floor. It broke in a jillion pieces.

"Horgan was hopping mad by this time but Jennings said very calmly, 'Horgan, if you don't shape up and quit annoying me, I am going to burn the Yellow Lantern down right around your ears as a protest.' Jennings started lighting blue matches on his jeans and throwing them around the joint Everybody in the place was watching by this time.

"Horgan hurried off to the telephone, saying, 'By Christ! I don't have to put up with this! I am calling Tim Roberts of the County Police.' Jennings put on his raunchy trench coat and stamped over to the front door, imitating Horgan's walk. Then he turned around, held up his hands for silence, pulled a beer glass out of his left pocket and said dramatically, 'One for the road' and let the glass smash. He pulled another glass out of his right coat pocket and said, 'I dedicate this one to Joseph Francis Horgan' and he let that one smash.

"Jennings got on his beat-up old motorcycle. We could hear him revving it up and doing 'wheelies' three or four times around the Yellow Lantern parking lot. Then, after several backfires, he roared off down Bluner lane toward Route 11.

"About five minutes later Corporal Roberts finally got there. Horgan said to him, 'Tim, you just missed Jennings. He just left riding his wheel.' Corporal Roberts said, 'Damn! But I'll get that cross-eyed creep one of these days, you see if I don't!'

"Horgan gets mad as hell at Stew when he gets drunk and busts the glasses and starts throwing matches around." She then added innocently, "Wonder where Stew is tonight. I doubt that he'll show up. He told everyone he was going to New York and back up to Boston. Well, nice to see you all. Have a ball. See you, Susie. Nice to meet you, Phil. Nice to see you again, Joan." Lydia then threaded her way back through the throng to her date.

"That lousy bitch!" Susie said angrily, grinding out her cigarette in the ashtray. "That little speech was all for my special delight and benefit. I hope she catches a nasty social disease from one of the many longhaired bums she's screwing!"

"Come on, Susie," Oliver said. "You can do better than that. Why not wish her a screw-up in her birth control pills so that she produces six stillborn Siamese gorillas."

"Too good for her and too tough on the gorilla world 'cause they are an endangered species, but I like your approach," said Susie grimly. She added menacingly, her eyes flashing, "Some day, just you wait. I'll fix that rotten bitch, Lydia, but good!"

Chapter 2 -- For Better, for Worse

They were sitting in a booth. The jukebox was not far away and was continually playing folk, jazz or rock. The sound was deafening. It virtually prevented any conversation between the couples sitting opposite each other in the booth. As a result, Phil and Susie talked almost entirely to each other. They only occasionally leaned across to shout to John and Joan. Phil mostly listened since Susie did most of the talking while smoking one cigarette after another.

At one point Phil said, "Tell me, Susie, why did you quit sports? Ollie says that you were a real competitor until about three years ago. Certainly the collection of silver at the Club shows that you were no slouch."

"My old man tried to raise me as a boy. I suppose this was because my older brother, Thomas, died and the old man and the old lady never had any other kids. He always wanted a son who would be a fullback at Dartmouth. He taught me all sorts of sports. I wanted to be better than any boy at sports, and for a damned long time I was. I suppose it was because I was small and a girl that, like Avis, I always tried harder and usually succeeded. I could beat the girls at all the dumb racket games, and I could beat a fair number of the boys. Rebe, my old nanny before I was sent away to Ethel Walker's when I was fourteen, was strict as hell with me – proper manners, prayers, clean clothes, good food and lots of sleep. It was Rebe who really raised me and made me toe the line. Mother forced her into retirement when I was packed off to boarding school. Rebe went back to live in Nevis. I had nobody to turn to.

"About three years ago I discovered that I had been pointed in the wrong direction. I was running for the wrong goal posts. I was all by myself, trying to be a boy when all of the other girls were trying to be girls."

She finished her vodka and tonic at a gulp and signaled the waitress for another. "You ready for another, Blinky?" She continued, "I was so goddamned dumb and innocent. I never realized that I was on the wrong track, even though Mother kept telling me that I should stop trying to be a boy. However, when I saw all these simpering silly girls around here, they kind of made me want to throw up. All that changed the day one of my gym teachers at Ethel Walker's

Dearly Beloved

invited me to her apartment for tea. I thought nothing about it until she tried to feel me up. Christ, I threw a shit fit and belted her. She thought I was queer as a three-dollar bill. Maybe if I had continued to think that a hockey stick was the most important stick in the whole world, I would have ended up as mixed up as she was, and probably still is."

Susie continued, "But she really did help me see the light even though she was trying to help herself to a little innocent goody. I made up my mind that no one would ever make that mistake about Susie Secant again. I chucked my tennis rackets, squash rackets, hockey sticks and all that junk into the back of my closet. I told everyone at Walker's in no uncertain terms that I wasn't gong to be the captain of any team or, in fact, play any more sports. I lost twelve pounds and bought myself a miniskirt and cut it even shorter. Then I spent the weekend with a roommate in Danbury. I wore my miniskirt and stopped all the traffic in Danbury. It was great finding out that I was a girl and that I could compete now that I was headed in the right direction. Of course, I still had old Dad's competitive spirit so, like Avis, I am still trying harder. I want to be the best girl-girl now that I've discovered what it's all about."

She continued, "As for the hardware at the Club, they can stuff all of that you-know-where. They don't give any trophies to the girl who has been a virgin the longest or, on the other hand, the best screwer in the Club, so I'm not interested in what they have to offer."

Phil said to her, "Susie, isn't all of that just for shock value? Who are you trying to snow?"

Susie glared at him and said, "Look, I may not be one of the hundred and fifty feminine brains that you've just admitted to the hallowed walls of Princeton, but I decided that I'm going to be honest and say what I think. How about you, Blinky my boy, are you honest?"

Phil said, "I guess so." His tone was a little uncertain.

Susie said, "OK, let's see about that. Let's take the black question for example. Are you unprejudiced so far as black people are concerned?"

Phil replied, "Sure."

Chapter 2 -- For Better, for Worse

Susie said, "We'll see about that. Tell me whether honestly way down deep inside you, you really dislike American radical blacks and distrust them. I am not talking about what you say or do, but way down inside of you, what you really think."

Phil replied, " I guess everyone down deep inside of them has some prejudice against radicals of other races. We try to stifle such feelings since we know that we've got to get along and work things out with others. But I wouldn't suppose that there are many people who can really say that they are totally without prejudice so far as radical blacks are concerned."

Susie said, "Horse shit, buddy! Why don't you say what you believe instead of saying what you believe you ought to say? You really are racially prejudiced against blacks. Why don't you say so? Why not be honest? See what I mean by honesty?" She then raised her voice and interrupted John and Joan and said loudly enough to be heard over the din of the jukebox, "Say, did you know that Blinky here hates niggers? He just admitted to me that he really hates them. Doesn't that surprise you, Ollie? Doesn't that surprise you, Joan, especially as you are such a bleeding heart on that subject?"

Phil said to her, "Goddamn it, Susie. That's not what I said."

Susie laughed and said, "Don't get your dander up, big boy, I was just putting you on."

Phil replied, "Then what's all this happy horse shit about being honest? I think most of what you say is designed to amuse and shock. You just end up making me mad at you."

Susie answered quietly, "The score is Wolf 2, Susie 0, first down and ten for the Susies at the end of the first half. I think the Susies had better have a good halftime pep talk by Joan or this ain't gonna be much of a game. Come on Joan, let's go to the can."

When the two girls had gone, John said to Phil, "Blinky, how are you making out with Mighty Mouse? She's talking a blue streak and sucking down vodka and tonic like it was going out of style. This isn't at all Susie's usual way. She usually doesn't drink very much but coming here is a big strain since she and Jennings used to keep this place on its ear. Everyone here knows that Stew gave Susie the axe."

Phil replied, "She'd be much better off if she'd relax instead of trying to be such a smarty pants all the time." Any further exchange was interrupted by the return of the two girls.

"Say, Blinky, how about another drink for me and you, pal?" Susie said.

"Okay, Lilly. By the way," Phil said, "you might try calling me Phil instead of Blinky."

"How's that, Buster? Are you smashed or something? My name is Susie, Susie Secant, remember? I don't know why you call me Lilly. Is this Lilly a childhood sweetheart of yours?" Without letting him answer, she said "Besides, I like the name Blinky for you. It fits you and you don't seem to mind Ollie calling you that. But," she added coming back to her first point, "what's this Lilly routine?"

"I'm going to call you Lilly each time you call me Blinky," Phil replied, "'cause it's short for Lilliputian."

"Score Phillip 3, Susie 0, fourth quarter, fourth down on the Lilliputians' one yard line. What are the Lilliputians going to do? Why, they're going to try for a 99 yard drop kick? But, to make it, I've got to steady my nerves. Order me another vodka and tonic while I unlimber my drop kick foot."

She went on, "After trying dear old Dad's recipe for success – that is, being a jock, I looked around for a different recipe. Of course, Rebe was long gone back to Nevis and her little house, her family and her prayers as a Deaconess of St. John's Episcopal Church. Rebe had raised me and taught me my manners and no nonsense about right and wrong, but she wasn't around. So I looked at Mother. But I couldn't go her route. Mother is like a zombie: controlled, and as cold as an iceberg. Maybe she is fond of me, but she has never once showed or even said it. She's afraid of all emotion and feeling. Perhaps it betrayed her or something, but I see no signs of it now. Her own world is bounded by the Philadelphia Orchestra, the bridge table, her charitable and artistic boards and the orderly running of her house. I don't want to go through life like that, forever moving in a prearranged ordered sequence. I want to let it all hang out and take it and give it as it comes. If I like someone. I want to show him in every possible way. On the other hand, if I don't like someone, I

Chapter 2 -- For Better, for Worse

want to show him that I hate him in the strongest way."

"But Susie," said Phil, "suppose everybody in the world was like you. The world wouldn't last more than a quarter of an hour. It would be terrible with everybody fighting."

"But," said Susie, "Blinky, excuse me, Phil I mean, not everyone is like me. I'm just selfish enough to want it that way."

"You certainly are going to end up in the other extreme from your mother, but you'll be just as far off course. Why not try the middle."

Susie said, "Bravo. Spoken like a true oracle of the Establishment. Did you say that you are going into the ministry?"

Phil changed the subject, "Ollie says you were suspended last year from Bennett for smoking grass, or was it selling grass. Were you permanently bounced, or are you going to get back in?"

Susie said, "My, how tongues do clack! You've forgotten to give the accused the required warning. Therefore, this confession will not be admissible against me in case you turn out to be a federal narc. The plain fact is that there were a couple of girls from some place, God knows where, in the Middle West who had never smoked in their whole lives and who wanted to try pot. So, naturally, they came to little Susie since I made no particular secret of the fact that I enjoyed a smoke once in a while. One of them coughed and gagged for a while, so she ran right down to the infirmary thinking she was going to croak and go to hell for having taken a few puffs on a joint. This led to a Committee of Inquiry or something like that. They decided to draw and quarter me for the good of my soul, as the Inquisition used to say, and as a shining example to others. I was nailed because the girls had insisted on paying for the two joints. I was willing to give them a smoke, but they firmly insisted on paying me. I didn't particularly care one way or the other, but they insisted so I didn't decline. This apparently raised my status to that of a drug pusher. Neither of my drug clients was willing to make it clear to the Gestapo that they had insisted on paying for the stuff.

"Well, my Uncle Alfred and the old man came up to Bennett once I'd explained the whole thing to them. Uncle Alfred threatened to sue the hell out of Bennett unless Bennett took me back unconditionally. It's become a kind of a mini Angela Davis affair. I want to be vindicated, but I really couldn't care less about going back. In fact, if I am reinstated, I'll probably just stay around long enough to write what I think of the whole place on the blackboards and then resign, mostly because I always wanted to go to a college with a serious program on handling disabled kids, particularly those with speech impairments. But I need to be reinstated unconditionally in order to start over again at a serous college instead of a finishing school. Do you understand, Blinky? No one takes my interest in disabled kids seriously."

"I think I understand, but while you're waiting to return and burn Bennett down, what do you do with yourself?" Phil asked.

"I work in an underground bomb factory," she replied. "We don't care about the politics of our customers as long as they use our products and are reasonably satisfied with the results. All you have to be is against the Establishment."

"Very funny," said Phil. "Seriously, what do you do? You must do something."

The jukebox had been momentarily silent. Joan and John heard the latter part of the conversation. Susie said, "I play hide and go seek in lower Philadelphia."

Looking at Phillip, Joan said, "Susie, I don't know why you don't tell Phil what you do. Phil, Susie got herself a non-paying job at Tilton's Day Care Center in Philadelphia in the black and Puerto Rican section. The center is supposed to take care of children of working mothers. But actually, from what Susie says, Tilton takes on battered and neglected kids, particularly kids with speech impediments. Right, Susie?"

Susie said, "Yep, that's right. I am roughhouse and games director four days a week with the toughest group of four-year-olds you ever saw. The regular staff, all social workers, have fancy degrees in this or that. They all secretly hate me because I get along with the kids so much better than they do. But Mrs. Lacey, the mother-type who runs the outfit, says you really have to love little kids in order to handle them effectively. No amount of courses at a teacher's college is going to help someone who really doesn't care. If nothing else, I

Chapter 2 -- For Better, for Worse

do care about the kids at Tilton. Do you understand, Blinky? There I go again. I mean Phil."

"Yes, but why only four days if you are all that interested?" Phil asked.

"I don't think they would want me any more than that," Susie said. "Besides, I have other things I need to do." She then added briskly, "Well, we've talked long enough about the number one suspect. Let's see what the number two suspect, Blinky MacPherson, does with himself. I'm pretty suspicious of him. Will you please account for your movements from December 13, 1937, until ten minutes ago, omitting nothing that might point one way or the other."

Phil replied, "Well, right now I should be finishing a term paper on tribalism rather than playing goo-goo eyes with an attractive longhaired dope peddler."

Susie said, 'So, what's your paper on tribalism about anyway?"

Phil replied, "I don't suppose it would interest you very much but there is a real question as to what the emerging nations of Africa are going to do about tribalism. There's a lot of fuzzy thinking in the United States about tribalism stemming partly from the backlash on our own thinking of what we did to our own American Indians. There are thousands of separate tribes in Africa. Peace was kept among them by the colonial powers. Now that the colonial powers have all been sent packing, with the possible exception of the Portuguese, who haven't heard about the Twentieth Century, and the South Africans, who have heard but don't care, the new African nations are either being torn apart by tribalism or are threatened with it. On the other hand, a detribalized African is very often apt to become a person without status. The situation is confused by the angling of the Russians and, now, the Chinese communists. Our own thinking on this issue is confused. We are apt to end up one hundred percent on the side of the Ebos. I am trying to write a paper on the whole problem with a focus on the Biafran situation. Does that clear it up for you? If not, I will give you an autographed copy of the paper provided it ever gets done."

Susie said, "For your information but not for publication,

I'm a member of a tribe that lives around here, but my problem is I want to be detribalized."

Phil answered, "But a detribalized native is apt to end up without status or a sense of belonging."

Susie said, "Well, I've already been detribalized since I have no status on the Main Line. I didn't know I'd been through detribalization. I guess Stew performed that ceremony for me."

John had an amazing capacity for beer. Phil had seen him, studying Russian literature, quietly consume half a case of beer in their dorm in an afternoon and be none the worse for wear. However, Phil and Susie were drinking vodka and tonics faster than John was drinking beer. Joan was drinking only Coke. By the end of the evening, Phil couldn't remember whether he had had seven, nine or a dozen vodka and tonics. As soon as Susie finished one, she asked Phil or Zazu Pitts (as she was calling him) to get Claire to bring another one. Finally, Oliver turned to her and said, "Hold the phone, Cousin Susie old girl, they are making vodka faster than you can drink it, no matter how hard you try." Phil only had ten dollars with him and was worried about the bill though he knew from experience that John would insist on paying the whole tab. Susie started talking to Phil about Jennings again over the strident sounds of the jukebox. It was a subject that she couldn't seem to stay off.

"What a selfish bastard Stew really is," said Susie. "All the time I went around with him, he treated me like some sort of a serving girl, just for his special pleasure. I guess I asked for it, but just who in the hell does Jennings think he is, Mr. J. C. Superstar himself? I always had to be there at his beck and call while he played the piano all night. Even worse, I had to sit and listen to him recite from Brecht or Kafka or preach about the revolution. I also had to act in any sort of hair-brained play or charade that he wanted to put on. If he had something more amusing to do, like meditate, or another girl uncrossed her legs, then I had to sit home and wait while my lord and master went out and jazzed around." Her voice rose. "If I said hello in a friendly way to any other guy, I got the riot act. He was jealous as an orangutan. It was pure slavery for several years."

She paused, "You know what Stew did last year?" Without

Chapter 2 -- For Better, for Worse

waiting for his response, she went on, "Last spring he asked me to come to a house party weekend at BU. Half way through the weekend, I found out that he had two other girls that were supposed to be his date for the weekend. He was juggling the three of us! I still don't know whether Jennings deliberately set it up to see if he could juggle all of us or whether his roommates asked some of us for him." She grinned and then said briskly, "Actually, it was pretty funny all the way around except for the one girl from New York. She couldn't see anything funny about it and packed her bag and stalked off to the station. The other girl and I decided to teach Stew a lesson. We ran up big bar bills with other guys and telephoned everybody all over the country at his expense. The other girl and I ended up pretty good friends. We had a ball."

Susie seemed to forget Phil and was reflectively talking to herself, "But I really can't understand what came over Stew. Sure, we fought like cats and dogs, sometimes over important things and sometimes over nothing. I put up with his guff and he's put up with mine. But we didn't have a real fight all fall. I thought Stew was beginning to emotionally grow up. He acted more seriously, don't you know, and wasn't such a cutup at parties. Then he started going to New York. I am goddamned certain he had another girlfriend – probably a NYU liberal or an actress or something like that.

"Then one afternoon, about a month ago, he came over to the house. Usually he wouldn't do that because Mother and the old man had made it brutally clear that they didn't like him one damn bit. I think Mother's dislike for Stew stemmed from the fact that she disliked Stew's father years ago. He died in a jet fighter crash when Stew was just a little boy. Or, maybe it was Stew's mother, Dol Jennings. She and Mother were fast friends even before they both went to Ethel Walker's but Mother now never even asks about Dol, though God knows Dol could sure use some friendship and understanding. She's in the local funny farm, the Philadelphia Institute, and has been for years.

"But, anyway, six weeks ago on Friday, or was it Saturday, Stew was home from Boston to see his mother in the institute. He came over to the house. We were watching TV when, quite suddenly, out of the blue, Stew said, 'Susie, let's face it. It's all over between you and me.'

"At first, I thought he was playing one of his nasty elaborate jokes and had something up his sleeve. Perhaps he does," she said bitterly, "but, if it's a joke, it's a damned poor one. I'll make him pay for it. By Christ, I'll show him a thing or two."

She went on sadly, "I didn't take it very seriously at first. I didn't realize what he was saying or at least what it meant, so I never asked him the reason. It was only later that it sank in. I called him to find out why. He never did give me any reason. Maybe we'd been going together too long and knew each other too well. Maybe he was just plain tired of little Susanne Secant who is more interested in helping little kids who have speech and auditory problems than in doing outlandish pranks. Of course, Mother and the old man were ecstatic when the local gossips relayed this tasty bit of info to them."

As Phil listened to Susie, he felt overwhelmingly sorry for her. In place of her earlier put-on gaiety and bravura, she looked very small, very helpless and very sad. Jennings must be an egotistical son of a bitch to have hurt Susie like that. He patted her on the shoulder and said as she sat there with tears slowly running down her cheeks, "Never mind, Sue. You're still very young. There will be a lot of other guys in your life. In six months you will have forgotten Stew Jennings. Besides, I don't think you are really in love with Jennings."

"Yeah, what have I had for the last three years, indigestion?" Susie said despondently.

"I think it's a case of 'Hell hath no fury like a woman scorned,'" Phil said.

Recovering herself, Susie took Phil's handkerchief from the breast pocket of his blazer, dried her tears and snuffed her nose. Then a determinedly cheerful Susie said, "Things aren't really that bad. Look what's just dropped off the Christmas tree and into Susie's waiting lap: you, Blinky Wolf."

"Lilly" said Phil, laughing, "I should be so lucky."

"In the meantime, how about buying your new lady love another vodka and tonic? They just flashed the lights for last call," Susie said.

Chapter 2 -- For Better, for Worse

Phil said, "Don't you think we've both had enough vodka?"

Susie said nothing but put her fingers to her mouth and let fly a piercing whistle. Claire, who had heard the whistle before, started over to the table. Phil was getting angry and said, "Susie, I'm not going to buy you another drink." By this time Claire was at their table.

Susie said, "Claire, this tightwad giant here refuses to shell out for another vodka for me, but my favorite cousin is going to buy me another tiny little vodka and tonic, aren't you, Zazu Pitts?"

Phil signaled John with his eyes. John said, "No dice, Cousin Sue. Rien ne va plus." To the waitress, he said, "Claire, thanks anyway, but we'll pass up the last call."

Just at that moment Joe Horgan leaned over and unplugged the jukebox. The Yellow Lantern was totally quiet for the first time. Susie said in a voice which could be heard all over the Yellow Lantern, "Fuck you, you goddamn queer!"

Phil's temper exploded. He slapped Susie across the face, first one way and then with the back of his hand the other way, saying, "Shut your filthy mouth, you goddamned little bitch!"

Joan put her hands to her mouth and said, "Oh no, Susie, how could you say such a thing." She turned to John and laid a hand gently on his arm and said, "Disregard it. Susie's just had too many vodkas."

John, looking hurt, said roughly, "Cousin Susie, I reminded you earlier today that your nanny, Rebe, taught you good manners. Where has all her training gone? Maybe your old man does drink a little bit too much but at least he can hold his liquor and his tongue. Come on, let's get the hell out of here."

Susie was crumpled up in a corner of the booth. Her eyes blazed with anger at Phil as she hissed at him, "You bastard! No one has ever dared do that, at least not since Rebe slapped me. No one! Why in the hell did you slap me?"

Phil was still angry, "'Cuz, Miss Secant, that's what I do when someone is playing at being a bitch and succeeding. I'm surprised you haven't been slapped before. You sure were in need of it tonight, and I expect pretty generally. Stop sniffling – you're not hurt. Next time you pull that kind of crap on me, I'll really knock your block off. Put your coat on, we're leaving."

Susie sat up, felt her jaw, snuffed her nose, then looked at him and said weakly, "I guess I was asking for it. No one has slapped me since Rebe did when I stuck my tongue out at her in the nursery. I have never, no never, stuck my tongue at anyone since then. I cried all night. It must be good for my character 'cause it's so damn unpleasant. Good God, if I get a roundhouse every time I'm a bitch, I'm not going to have any teeth in a week. Come on, Frazier, time to take Mrs. Mohammed Ali home."

John had, in the meanwhile, paid the bill.

Joe Horgan was standing at the front door with Corporal Tim Roberts. He said to Oliver as he looked at Susie, "I hope, Mr. Oliver, that Miss Secant isn't driving tonight."

John, recovering his usual good humor, said, "Of course not, Joe. If nothing more, John Oliver values his own neck and his Corvette, such as it is, too much to allow Cousin Susie to rack it up against a phone pole, making me and the Corvette just another highway statistic. Also, we don't want Corporal Tim Roberts to nab Susie for DUI, now do we? No, Joan here is our driver tonight. She only drank Coke. But it was very thoughtful of you to think of it, Joe. Goodnight."

"Goodnight, Mr. Oliver.. It's my pleasure to have you and your cousin here especially now that she is no longer with that no-good Jennings!"

"My fervent amen to that, Joe," John said as he went out the door.

As Phil and Susie came out of the hot barroom and hit the cold air, crossing the parking lot to the car, Phil realized that it wasn't only Susie who had had too much to drink: he too was "under the weather."

On the far side of the parking lot, Phil noticed a police car, its revolving light flashing. Corporal Roberts called over, "Say, Mr. Oliver, Stewart Jennings isn't around, is he?"

Oliver answered, "Nope. He's not with us, thank God. But we do have Susie in tow!"

Chapter 2 -- For Better, for Worse

Corporal Roberts replied, "Take good care of Susie: she is a favorite, especially ever since she helped Lt. Riley's youngest kid to get in that special speech therapy program. Safe home, Mr. Oliver."

When they got into the car, Susie leaned her head on Phillip's shoulder. He again smelled the fragrance of her perfume though it was mixed with the smell of vodka and tobacco. As Joan drove out of the Yellow Lantern parking lot, he put his right arm around Susie's waist. Feeling no resistance, he slid his hand between the buttons of her maxi coat. He cautiously fumbled with the buttons to her pants suit coat. Phillip thought that Susie was asleep until he heard her murmur sleepily and languorously, "That's nice, Blinky Wolf." Then she seemed to relax even more and be completely asleep. He slid his hand further in and found that Susie was wearing nothing underneath her suit coat. She just groaned slightly as his trembling fingers closed around her warm firm breast. He was surprised at how well built she was. He was delighted with his success though he admitted that it was probably due to the fact that Susie was either drunk or asleep.

No one said anything as they drove homeward. But all of a sudden Susie jerked awake and said, "Oh, Christ, stop the car, Joan. Stop the car for Christ's sweet sake! I'm going to puke!"

She sat bolt upright as Joan pulled the car off to the side of the road. Susie scrambled out of the car, leaned over and began to vomit. Phil also jumped out. He put his arms around Susie's small waist while she leaned over and retched again and again in the glare of the headlights of oncoming cars. He tried to shield her so that passing motorists would not see what she was doing or at least who she was. Finally, she said weakly, "Thanks. I guess I am OK now. Got a hanky?"

Supporting her with one hand, Phil reached under his duffel coat to find his handkerchief, quite forgetting that Susie had already taken it for her crying jag. Joan, who had also gotten out of the car after turning the flashers on, produced a package of Kleenex. For just a moment, Phil thought that he himself would be sick from the stench of vomit and tobacco and all the vodka he had drunk. But in the cold night air, his moment of nausea passed.

Phil said, "Hold on, Susie, the cold air will do you good."

Susie mumbled weakly as she leaned against him, "Thanks, pal. Say, you are nice! Jennings would have been there making fun of me or selling tickets."

When they got back in the car, John took over the driving. Joan got in the back seat with Susie who lay back and said lugubriously, "And for my final act, folks, I'm going to barf and then barf again. Red Riding Hood pukes on Wolf. Exit Wolf laughing. What a god-awful night for you, Blinky, and for me!" The rest of the short trip home was silent.

Phil could still remember the smell of vomit which had permeated the car for the rest of the trip home. He felt so sorry for Susie. When they drew up in front of the Secant house, she got right out of the car and went to the front door without saying anything to anyone and went inside.

Joan said, "I won't make it long, John. Thanks. I, at least, had a very pleasant evening. Phil, it's been nice to meet you. Never mind about Susie, it's a bad time for her and she's showing it."

John said to her, "Joan, it's OK. Poor kid, she has been through the ringer, but she shouldn't attempt to support the Russian economy by drinking up all the vodka that the Commies can make in one night. We may drop by tomorrow after lunch to see how the patient is. In the meanwhile, I prescribe a liberal dose of Alka Seltzer though Susie may be clearer than the rest of us now that she has painted the side of Bluner Lane with a few dollars worth of Smirnoff's best."

When they got back in the car, Oliver said, "Well, Blinky, old buddy, and what do you think of our local talent? Ain't Cousin Susie a bird?"

Phil replied, "She sure is one screwed up little girl." Then, to change the subject, he added, "I sure hope that while we have been reveling at the Yellow Lantern, it has been snowing like hell and that Sandy has telephoned to say that New England has nine inches of new powder."

As Phil tried to go to sleep that night, he told himself that he had probably seen the last of Susie Secant, but he continued to lie

Chapter 2 -- For Better, for Worse

awake for a long time thinking about Susie and her muscular body.

Sandy phoned the next morning from New England, "Hey, guys, there still is no snow, but the weather forecaster says it's on its way!"

Phil had a crashing hangover and felt rotten. He thought ruefully, "This is the price I pay for drinking neck and neck with Susie." He thought that he might not make it to the Sunday lunch, especially when the smell of roast lamb reached his nostrils. At lunch Mrs. Oliver looked over at him and said, "Phillip, are you all right? I think you're coming down with something. Probably the grippe. It's going around. Your eyes look red. Do you have a fever?"

Alfred laughed as he said, "Jane, dear, lay off. Don't you yet know the classic signs of a hangover when you see one? You should've let me give Phillip a milk punch before lunch. That always fixes things."

Mrs. Oliver said solicitously, "Phillip, don't say I didn't warn you about Miss Susie. That young pub crawler takes after her father."

Turning to his wife, Mr. Oliver said, "Now don't get broody, Jane, about Phil. No one that I know of ever died of a hangover, but many wish they could and would when in its grip. Not that I would know personally," he added smugly.

Phil somehow got through Sunday lunch. Then all he wanted to do was curl up and die. But John said, "Come on, Blinky, let's go over to the Secants' and see how your sparring partner is faring. Besides, I want to watch the game on their color TV – ours is on the fritz as usual."

Phil replied, "To hell with your little cousin, John. I sure don't want to see her again, and I'm sure she doesn't want to see."

John smiled, "Come on now, Blinky, it wasn't all that bad, especially on the way home, was it? You weren't exactly thinking of Ann Livingstone then, were you? That is, before Susie started tossing her cookies." Phil looked at him and blinked several times.

When they got to the Secants', John again pushed the front door open and walked in with Phil trailing. John called out in an exaggeratedly lugubrious voice, "Put out your dead! Put out your dead! We're here to pick up the bodies that were killed by the vodka and tonic plague that swept the Yellow Lantern last night. I've got one in tow."

Mrs. Secant called from the dining room dryly, "Ollie, why don't you and Phillip go into the library while the girls and I finish lunch. Tom has gone off to the awful Eagles football game, but you can fix yourselves a drink or a beer or whatever and turn on the TV. We won't be long."

Ollie replied, "Right you are, Cousin Sarah." He led Phil down to the end of the hallway and into the library. In sharp contrast to the rest of the house, which was furnished with elegant early American furniture, the library was obviously Mr. Secant's room and reflected his tastes. A giant color TV had been built into the bookcase and an oversize leather couch was placed in front of the fireplace to provide a perfect view of the TV. There was a small wet bar in one corner of the room. The desk was littered with papers. The walls were covered with framed photographs, mostly team pictures or pictures of Tom accepting trophies or shooting skeet.

Soon John had the TV on, had a beer in hand and was wrapped up in the Eagles game. Ordinarily Phil spent Sunday afternoons watching pro football and drinking beer, either at home or at college. In view of his hangover, he was dully looking forward to doing so on this afternoon. When Mrs. Secant and the girls came in, she looked at him and said with mock gravity, "My, my, girls, this looks like a rather battered wolf. How do you feel, Phillip? Do I detect the marks of a hangover? Can I get you anything, or did Cousin Alfred prescribe for you?"

Susie, who had followed her mother, cut in before Phil could reply, "Anyone who spends a lovely winter afternoon like this watching pro football on TV is a slob. That includes you, Ollie. Anyone for a walk? Come on, Blinky, let's get some air – it will do you good. Leave Ollie in solitary splendor in front of the boob tube."

Joan said, "If it's all the same to you, Sue, I think I'll join your mother on the winter porch and listen to the Philharmonic."

Susie said, "OK, if that's the way you want to spend the afternoon. Come on, Blinky," she said, grabbing his arm. Phil caught a whiff of the fragrance she was wearing. Susie looked lovely: fresh and clean, her long black hair glistening in the winter sunlight streaming

Chapter 2 -- For Better, for Worse

in through the window of the hallway.

Phil and Susie left the house. They walked down the road toward the woods. It was a clear, cold winter day without any wind. As they started out, the Labrador, Inky, came bounding around the corner of the house and joined them, obviously delighted with the prospect of a Sunday walk.

"Blinky, I want you to meet Daddy's dog, Miss Devlin," Susie said. "Her real name is Inky but I call her Miss Devlin because she had a litter but wouldn't reveal the father," she added as she stroked the head of the dog, who wiggled wildly with pleasure in the unexpected attention she was getting.

Susie had on her long blue maxi coat on with the fur hood up, haloing her face. For a while they walked through the woods. The only noise was the sound of their feet crunching in the dry brown leaves and the yipping barks of Inky, who was tearing around. Finally Susie said slowly, "Well, Blinky, or rather Phil, I guess I made an ass of myself last night, crying my eyes out and drinking up everything in sight. I should have a crashing hangover. I would too except for the 'piece de resistance,' that is, yorking my guts out on the side of Bluner Lane in plain view of the whole damn county."

Phil said, holding his aching head, "Plainly, Susie, I have the hangover that you think you should have. I would have been better off if I had joined you by the side of the road. If had, I might be clear-headed today." He added, "I'm sorry I had to slap you. Are you OK?"

Susie said, rubbing her jaw, "Yeah, I guess so. You really flatten a girl with that 'Me Tarzan – You Jane' technique. Do you use it often?"

Phil replied, "Sorry, I just lost my temper."

Susie said, "And I'm so sorry that you ended up with the hangover that should have been mine." Then she added, "I guess I slept all the way home on your shoulder before I barfed. Pretty messy performance all the way around. I don't usually drink that much. I don't really care for it and it doesn't do anything for me. Besides, I don't want to deaden my brain as dear old Dads seems intent on doing. Am I forgiven, Phil?"

"Nothing to forgive," replied Phil. "Shoulders are made to cry on and mine is available," he added gravely with a mock bow.

"Then I'll use it freely," Susie replied. "It's big enough to serve."

"Until Jennings returns to the roost," Phil added caustically.

"Not likely," she said. She took his hand in hers and examined it. "My, what big long cold fingers you have."

"The better to feel you with, my dear," Phil replied before thinking of the implications. He was covered with confusion and blinked several times involuntarily as he looked sideways down at Susie to see if she'd picked it up. She noticed his confusion and laughed uproariously, squeezing his hand and saying, "So I noticed, so I noticed, icy fingers, before I yorked." She then squeezed his hand again and put it in her pocket.

They walked on, hand in hand, and spent the rest of the glorious afternoon enjoying the wintry Pennsylvania countryside with Inky. She told him in detail just how she had become interested in teaching children who stuttered or had other speaking difficulties and all about the technique she had learned to help speech impaired children. Phil was surprised at what good company Susie was when she was not trying to shock him and make an impression. His head suddenly cleared. He felt completely well again as they returned to the Secant house just as the sun was setting back of the woods. It had been a fun walk.

Phil and Susie were laughing together at something in the hallway as they were taking off their coats when Mrs. Secant came in from the winter porch. She said, "Well, well, Little Miss Red Riding Hood, I'm glad to see that you brought the wolf home in better shape than when you went out. John said that he and Phil are not required at the Olivers' tonight, so they are going to join us for our pot luck Sunday night supper. Tom has gotten back from his awful game. But he and Ollie and even poor Joan are glued to the television. Mercifully, the game is coming to an end so we can all become civilized and talk without watching those great big gorillas racing around. Now, how would a drink sound to you, Phillip?"

Again Phil had the distinct impression that Mrs. Secant was

Chapter 2 -- For Better, for Worse

sizing him up. He made a mock bow and replied, "Your wish is my command, ma'am."

"Such courtesy is a thing rarely seen in wolves these days. You certainly are most mannerly, Sir Wolf," replied Mrs. Secant.

Susie commented sarcastically to her mother, "I suppose that you and Joan spent the afternoon on the winter porch listening to the Philharmonic, doing the Sunday crossword puzzle in *The Times* and looking at the after-Christmas sale ads as well as at the society column?"

Her mother smiled tolerantly. "As a matter of fact, you're right. Joan and I did spend the afternoon just that way. It was a most pleasant way to spend a wintry Sunday afternoon, though I envied the two of you for your winter afternoon walk."

Phil thought back on that Sunday night supper with real pleasure. Supper was hot soup, cold roast beef and salad set out on the dining room table. They had all taken their plates and eaten in the library before the fire watching an episode of "The First Churchills" on Masterpiece Theatre. After eating his supper, Tom Secant sat down in his favorite red leather wing chair and promptly went to sleep just after the episode started. At 10:00, Phil and John sad good night and drove back to the Olivers'.

John said on the way home, "Now, that wasn't all bad, now was it, Blinky, old buddy?"

When they got back to the Olivers', Mrs. Oliver said, "Good evening. Nice day? You look better, Phillip. By the way, Sandy called again: it's snowing. He's sure you'll now have good skiing."

"Great," said Phil with feigned enthusiasm. He found he had been unconsciously hoping it would not snow. He felt a wave of dread sweep across him as he remembered that he would have to spend New Year's Eve with Ann Livingstone pretending to be interested when he knew he would be thinking all the while about Susie.

"Maybe," he thought as he sat alone in the chapel of St. James, "it would all have turned out differently if it had not snowed."

Just then, John Oliver opened the door of the small chapel, "Blinky, you look as cheerful as Lieutenant Calley after the verdict. Cheer up, Blinky, in five minutes more or less, you are going to make an honest woman of Susie."

"Yeah, well maybe. That is if Jennings doesn't show up and upset the apple cart," Phil replied dourly.

John replied, "Stewart's threat at the wedding lunch was probably all bluff. No sign of Stewart yet. Also, he was pretty far gone at lunch and Joan and I were able to give him a vodka nightcap, so to speak, at his house. When we left him, he was crapped out in his bed. Stewart will have trouble starting his Czech racing motorcycle without a key. But I still wouldn't put anything past that guy. By the way, I just delivered the bridal bouquet. It was a real gasser."

Phil replied, "Well, I hope Susie gets the point." He thought to himself, "Reverend Piccard may be right: I may well have to make some compromises with Susie, but I hope that it works both ways."

"She'll get the point," John said. "Susie's not thick, you know. Also, Joan handed me this as I presented the bridal flowers: she told me to be sure to give it to you before the wedding." He handed Phil a small white package.

Phil unwrapped it and smiled and shook his head and said, "Well, I'll be damned."

John cocked his head as the sound of "Here Comes the Bride" filtered through the door. "Well, pal, that's the death march," John said, "ready, quick step, march."

Phil opened the chapel door quietly and walked with downcast eyes to the spot before Reverend Piccard as he had been directed to do by Mrs. Perry at the rehearsal. He was followed by John.

Phillip then turned around and faced the congregation. All of the six little children were peeping wide-eyed over the back of the second pew. The ushers and bridesmaids were all standing there except for Joan, who was just coming up the aisle. Joan looked at Phil and tried to give him an encouraging smile. Joan, when she got to the front of the church, turned around and faced the congregation with all the other bridesmaids and ushers as Susie and her father came up the aisle.

Then as Phil stood there waiting for Reverend Piccard to begin with the words "Dearly Beloved," Susie leaned forward and peeped around the huge figure of her father, saying in a whisper that

Chapter 2 -- For Better, for Worse

could only be heard by Phil himself, her father and Reverend Piccard, "Just a moment, Father Piccard, before you begin."

Chapter Three

Wilt Thou Have This Man?

A little past 4:00, Susie came out of the front door of the Secant house, gathering the heavy wide folds of her white silk wedding dress and train around her as she went down the front steps. Inky came bounding up. Susie said sternly, "No, down Inky. Down, girl. I haven't time to wrestle with you or race you on my Honda – besides, it's smashed and I even had to pay to get the wreckage towed to a junkyard!"

As she left the air conditioned coolness of the front hall of the house and the afternoon sunlight hit her, she said to the lady from Nan Duskin coming out behind her, "Oh, Lord, what a hot day for a wedding. I'm already dripping wet and I've just stepped out the front door."

Rebe came out the door. She was dressed in a simple long black dress and had a white straw hat with a blue and green ribbon decorating it. She had a small white cross hanging around her neck. She turned to Susie, smiled and said, "Now just you hush your mouth, child. Such words from Susiekins on her wedding day! Everything's going to be just fine. You just wait and see."

The uniformed driver standing at the door of the Cadillac limousine said, "Miss, the car is air conditioned and I've had it here for ten minutes with the air conditioning on, so you'll be nice and cool in there. Your father left with your mother a minute ago."

Susie said, "Yes. Thanks." She got into the limousine. The lady from the bridal salon arranged the dress, saying emotionally, "You look perfectly beautiful, dear. I wish you all happiness." She then got in the front seat of the car. Then Rebe got in Joan's car and the two of them drove off to the church.

Susie said in a depressed tone to the lady from Nan Duskin, "Thanks for all your help and your good wishes. I am going to need both if this wedding comes off rather than being broken up."

Susie sat back and relaxed in the air conditioned comfort of the big limousine. The driver got in and the Cadillac glided forward down the curved drive and on its way toward St. James.

Susie thought, "I'll be damned. So, here I am, on my way to the church to marry Phil MacPherson. After all the ups and downs, I wonder if it's going to come off or whether Stewart will really show up and shoot the whole wedding down. I would not put it past him."

Her thoughts turned to the Sunday morning after that first evening with Phil. She remembered lying awake in her bed, listening for some time to Joan's regular breathing in the other bed. Finally, about 9:00, she got up and shook Joan and said, "Come on, Joan, wake up. I need to talk to you."

Joan had rolled over, put her glasses on, looked at the clock and had said sleepily, "Gosh, kid, it's awfully early to wake a person up, especially after the shenanigans that you put all of us through last night." Joan yawned. "However, the nasty deed is done. What's on your mind?"

Susie said, "Well, what did you think of Goliath?"

Joan said, "Goliath? Oh, you mean Phil what's-his-name. Well, Little David, you certainly emptied your little bag of tricks last night."

Susie said, "That's probably right. Fair enough. But, just the same, what did you really think of him?"

Joan said with a smile, "Susie, you certainly do go from one extreme to the other. First, you take up with Stewart Bellak Jennings, a real do-nothing type who smokes pot and probably takes dope. All he does as far as I can see, besides drinking too much, is play the piano and his stereo and ride his motorcycle. He talks all the time about the injustice of the system, but as you yourself told me he lives off a handsome trust fund.

"Now Blinky is the other extreme – a dinosaur type, if you know what I mean, a relic from another age. A late-blooming Horatic

Chapter 3 -- Wilt Thou Have This Man?

Alger or large size reincarnation of Dick Wittington. He's probably as unhappy as Jennings with things but doesn't think that tearing things down is going to change them for the better. He looks like a real go-getter to me."

Susie had said, "You're too hard on Stew, Joan. You're still sore from this time last year when he pushed your trunk out the dorm window to illustrate the defenestration of the Czech Parliament or whatever the hell it was."

Joan said with a frown, "I didn't think that was funny then and still don't. If anyone had been underneath, they would've been killed. Sometime my poor innocent steamer trunk will have its revenge on Stewart. Mark my words! But, going back to Blinky, I think that you'll be seeing him again. Unless I miss my guess, I think he was intrigued with your efforts to shock him, at least in the early part of the evening. Also, I take it that Miss Susie is somewhat interested in the tall Princeton senior who gallantly held her around the waist while she barfed last night all over Bluner Lane. Right?"

Susie grinned, "Not really, but a man in the bush is worth two on the wing."

Joan said dryly, "Very funny, kid, but if you are really interested and smart, you won't let him jump in the bushes with you the first chance he gets or he'll leave you faster than you can say Simmons Beautyrest."

Susie replied, "Any more words of wisdom from Ben Franklin on this sunny winter morning? Hell, let's get up and see what there is in this Youth Hostel for breakfast. I am ravenous! How about you?"

Susie remembered her excitement when she heard Ollie's voice in the hall when they were at Sunday lunch and then had seen Phil MacPherson's tall form plodding with his head down on his way past the dining room toward the library. As they left the table, Susie had said quietly to Joan, "Say, Joanie, do me a favor? I want to take Blinky on a walk. Stay here with Fat Stuff, or, if you prefer, spend the afternoon with Mother listening to the Philharmonic. You'd probably like that better than watching pro football, wouldn't you?"

Susie thought back on that wonderful Sunday afternoon walk with Phil. He had loosened up and talked about his paper on tribalism and his thesis on the Balfour Declaration and how he hoped to go to Washington after graduation from Princeton and after serving in the Navy. Phil and John had stayed for Sunday night supper. Phil had seemed to get along well with two people as different as her mother and father. As she went to sleep that night, Susie had felt a tingling feeling of anticipation and pleasure at the thought that she would be seeing Phil again during the coming week.

On Monday morning, however, she had gotten a rude shock. She answered the telephone in her room, hoping it would be Phil or John. It was Mrs. Oliver, who said briskly in her deep voice, "Hello, Susanne, this is Cousin Jane. How are you? We haven't seen you in quite a while. Is your mother there? I want to talk to her about New Year's Day Dinner. She's not there? I see. Well, I'll call her back or, better yet, could you get her to call me? Actually, it's not necessary for her to call. I just want to say that John won't be there for New Year's Day Dinner. He and his friend, Phillip, left at the crack of dawn this morning to go skiing. Would you please tell your mother that? We'll, of course, be glad to come. We'll see you then."

Susie felt like she had been slapped once again. She mumbled, "Thanks for calling, Cousin Jane. I'll be sure to tell Mother. Goodbye." She sat there for a while at the phone and then said to herself, "Well, easy come, easy go, or to put it another way, you've seen one, you've seen em all."

However, later that week, her mother handed her a post card:

> Dear Little Red Riding Hood,
> Sorry we ducked out Monday, but the snow finally came. It's cold as hell here. Please give my regards to Miss Devlin. How about another walk? Perhaps I can explain chapter two of my thesis.
>
> Icy Fingers

Susie had written a long letter to him but tore it up and wrote him a post card in reply:

> Blinky Wolf,

Chapter 3 -- Wilt Thou Have This Man?

When? Miss Devlin is straining at her leash to hear chapter two. So am I!

L.R.R.H.

In response Phil had telephoned and made a date. On that day, however, Phil had called from the Olivers' when he had gotten down from Princeton. He said, "Susie, bad luck. I have a fever of 102. I may have the flu that's going around. I'm going to take the train back and turn myself into the Princeton Infirmary."

Susie had taken her father's Mercedes without his permission and insisted on driving Phil back herself. Picking him up at the Olivers', she said, "Poor Blinky. You look plain awful but it's the least that I can do for you after you held my head by the side of the road." Phil had smiled weakly, but it had been a miserable trip. He'd felt so rotten that they hadn't said much as she drove him through the driving rain back up to Princeton and deposited him at the front door of the infirmary. He walked in with his head down and the collar of his raincoat pulled up around his neck.

Once again Susie thought that Phil MacPherson was a closed chapter for her. About ten days later, she got a call from Phil, who said, "Susie, this is Phil. Yes, I'm in the land of the living again. How about coming up to Princeton this Saturday afternoon. There's nothing special going on except a cocktail party where I have to make an appearance because it's being given by my thesis advisor, but there's a dance at the club. Ollie is going to be away for the weekend, so I have the use of his Corvette. I can put you up at some married friends' who have room in their apartment. What do you say?"

Susie said, "You betcha, Blinky. Can't wait!"

Susie gave Phil a big friendly hug when she got off the little train from Princeton Junction to Princeton. Phil returned her embrace and kissed her lightly on the mouth. As they were walking to the cocktail party at the professor's house, Phil said, eyeing Susie's mini-mini-skirt, "Say, Susie, take it easy at this cocktail party, will you? It's going to be mostly professors and graduate students and their wives with practically no undergraduates. Just remember, there are no points to be scored by shocking these people."

Susie stopped and made him a small mock curtsy, saying, "Yes, Nanny Rebe, I do have my white gloves on and a clean handkerchief in my sleeve. Don't worry, Mr. MacPherson, I won't destroy your reputation with your intellectual colleagues."

Susie remembered, noting with quiet pleasure, that when she and Phil walked in, the older men had given her a real looking over and that the faculty wives had looked sour. Susie had remained fairly quiet and bored until one young intellectual girl started talking seriously about women's liberation. The men were putting her on. She was getting quite flustered. A bald headed man in horn-rimmed glasses said genially to Susie, looking at her legs, "Well and you, young lady, just what do you think of women's liberation?"

Susie, after checking and finding that Phil was all the way across the room talking to a tall gray haired lady, said innocently, "Well, you men seem to think women's lib is a great joke. Some women are simply talking about it, but others of us are really doing something."

The bald headed man said to the young woman, "Sally, it seems you have a pretty little ally. And, young lady, just what are you doing to promote women's lib?"

Susie replied, "I have a little project which I think is going to work. I am organizing a new professional football team made up of nothing but women. I'm going to sue for the right to play the Chicago Bears. I'm sure that the Supreme Court will grant us equal rights and equal time. I will then field a women's team with a topless line. The Bears team will be goggle-eyed. We'll walk right through 'em. We'll get excellent TV coverage. Of course, the only thing that could really beat my topless aggregation would be a team from the gay world."

Susie turned to the young woman who had been seriously talking about women's liberation and, eyeing her skeptically up and down, said, "I think I have one opening in the suicide squad. Would you like to try out? Perhaps you would be more interested in being a pass receiver, though I kind of have my heart set on that position."

The young woman looked daggers at Susie, but everyone

Chapter 3 -- Wilt Thou Have This Man?

else was highly amused. The bald professor said, "Young lady, I never thought that I would be interested in professional football, but let me know when you field your team. I will try out with the Bears, at least for that game."

Susie replied, "Why wait? Why don't we scrimmage tonight? However," she said, looking over at Phil, who, in fact, had heard the whole interchange and was glowering at her, "I think that any plans I might make are going to be replaced by a lecture on proper conduct for young ladies at faculty cocktail parties."

Phil got her out of there quickly though she would like to have stayed and talked more to the bald headed professor. After a good dinner at Lahiere's Restaurant, they parked and walked down Prospect Street in the rain to an informal dance in the dimly lit basement bar at Phil's club. The music was by The Five Aces and was loud and very good. Phil did not have Susie's endless love of dancing, so she danced continuously with him, some of Phil's friends and even some strangers, interrupting only occasionally to go over to the bar and have a drink with Phil. By 12:30 or so, Susie came over to the bar, where Phil was, and shouted over the loud music, "It's hot as the hinges of hell in here, isn't it?"

Phil replied, "Yeah. I guess so – why? Do you want to go?"

Susie shook her head and said, "No, I am having fun. I just love to dance, Blinky, and this band is just great." She turned away from Phil and started pulling the turtleneck sweater she was wearing over her head.

"Jesus, Susie," Phil gasped, afraid that Susie would be wearing nothing underneath.

"What's the matter," Susie said, smiling unconcernedly at him as she tossed the sweater on a table and went right on dancing with her current partner. She did, in fact, have on a purple bra. She saw Phil was frowning and she went over to him and said, "Hell, Phil, relax. This Pucci bra looks like a Mother Hubbard compared to my bikini. Besides, it's cooler and more comfortable."

She quickly became the center of attraction, much to Phil's annoyance, especially when someone turned on the glaring overhead lights. Susie loved it, particularly when everyone else stopped dancing and grouped around her and her partner. When the set was done, there was applause, even from the girls and not a few whistles. Susie said in a husky voice, "Now, if any of the gentlemen in the group would favor a little more light entertainment, please form a line and follow me upstairs, one at a time, giving this tall Jasper," pointing to Blinky, "four bits in specie as you pass him." The group standing around all laughed uproariously and made ribald comments.

Phil grabbed Susie's upper arm and squeezed it hard. He gave her the turtleneck sweater and said quietly but firmly, "Come on, Susie! For Christ's sake, put your sweater on, damn it! Don't make me bop you again!"

Susie replied, "OK, big boy, don't get excited." She then turned to her audience and said, "Well, boys, that's it. Give your four bits to your own dates."

She pulled the turtleneck sweater down over her head and spread her long black hair over her shoulders, saying to Phil, "Well, we've livened the joint up. This will give the other girls some incentive later. What's the matter, make you a little mad, Blinky Wolf? That's why I did it."

As they were about to leave the club, Phil said angrily to Susie, "Why don't you grow up, for Christ's sweet sake, instead of making an ass of yourself. First you tick a professor's wife off at the cocktail party, making her look like a fool, and then you come to a club party and act like a long-haired Italian streetwalker!"

Susie, chastened, said, "Sorry, Boss, I really was having fun. I don't mean to embarrass you or make you mad."

As they got to the door of the club, the rain was pelting down. They dashed for John's Corvette with their raincoats over their heads. The door was locked and they got drenched while Phil fumbled, found the key and finally got it in the lock and opened the door. Once inside, the car steamed up. Phil said, "Here, Sue, take your raincoat off, it's sopped." He moved over to help her wrestle out of the soggy coat. Once they had it off, he slid his arm around her. She threw both her arms around his neck and took his big head in her hands and pulled it over and kissed him fully on the mouth. He had his mouth closed for a moment but quickly opened it. Finally, she

Chapter 3 -- Wilt Thou Have This Man?

pulled away from him. Both of them gasped for breath. She laughed gently and said, "Christ, that was nice, but you're crushing me and I'm getting sopped from your own raincoat which, in your haste, you forgot to take off." Then, she said with mock dignity, "Besides, Blinky, I'm surprised at you. You've just lectured me about my improper behavior and here you are with as many hands as an octopus and slobbering like a cocker spaniel and breathing as hard as an express train. For all your fine talk, Blinky, you're as horny as a unicorn. I would hardly have thought that necking on Prospect Street would be your dish of tea in view of your lofty reputation and especially after the lectures you've given me all evening!"

Phil said, "Yeah, I guess you're right." He started the car and drove quickly around to the back of his dorm and parked the car. He led Susie into his room and took off her raincoat and his and threw them on a chair. He then locked the door and turned off all the lights. He led Susie in the darkness over to the dilapidated couch, roughly pulled her down next to him and took her in his arms. She had an awful feeling of panic as she felt Phil's strength and sensed his determination. He was breathing heavily. She resisted him as he tried, at first gently and then more forcibly, to pull her turtleneck sweater up over her head. Her resistance had seemed to egg him on. Finally, he managed in spite of her struggling to pull her sweater entirely off and was attempting to unfasten her brassiere. Susie was now thoroughly scared. She fought back as hard as she could, crying out, "No, no, Blinky, stop it!"

Phil had paused and had said, "Come on, Susie. What's the matter?"

Susie had said, "No, Phil. No. You're hurting me!"

But Phil had only redoubled his efforts. Susie had begun to cry. Suddenly, Phil stopped and said with real surprise, "Say, Susie, you are crying, aren't you? You're really scared, aren't you?"

She replied, "You're damned right I am. Christ, you're so goddamn rough. Say, why don't you practice a little bit of what you preach. You just finished giving me a lecture on my behavior and now you act like King Kong. You men are all just alike." She scrambled away from him. There was a pause. The two of them sat at opposite ends of the couch, saying nothing in the darkness. Phil then went over and turned on a light. Susie had, in the meanwhile, pulled her sweater back down and was crouched in the corner.

Phil said, "Say, you really were unhappy, weren't you? After all your talk and egging me and every man in range. It is just talk, isn't it, Susie? I thought from your line that you had worn out regiments of men. I would simply be one of a large number, but all your antics turn out to be nothing but a big bluff. Right?"

Susie responded timidly, "Well, Blinky, it's not all quite bluff, but I would be less than frank if I didn't own up that my experience with sex to date has been unsuccessful. I won't go into details. I'm fascinated, but I haven't had anything that has been halfway satisfactory."

She continued, "I just don't want another messy unsatisfactory sexual crumb taken on the Q.T., at least not now. If I'm going to have it, I want a whole slice."

Phil said bitterly, "Do me a favor, will you, Susie? Let me know when the loaf is really going to be sliced." He added with a doubtful tone, "And what about Stewart, your great Czech lover boy?"

Susie replied, "Oh, Stewart. He isn't really interested in sex. He says he is, but he really isn't. Maybe that's one of the reasons why I got along with him. He never was after me that way. I still don't know what, if anything, turns him on – it certainly was not me. He's more interested in just cutting up and having a good time."

Phil had laughed mockingly, "So, Susie Secant, the self-acclaimed answer to Bridget Bardot turns out to be a fumbling disappointed amateur." Then he added in an amused tone, "Somehow, Susie, I like you better for it. Incidentally, if it's any satisfaction, we had the same sexual career to date. I've been the usual route – the sailing councilor's wife, a couple of trips to New York and two or three casual lucky hits now and then, but none of it has worked out as well as it's cracked up to be. Well, come on, Susie, pull yourself together. I'll take you back to where you're staying." He had added, "Nobody will believe me if I try to tell your many admirers tonight that I didn't score with you."

Susie reached behind her and hooked her brassiere under

Chapter 3 -- Wilt Thou Have This Man?

her sweater. She gathered up her wet raincoat and her purse. As they were leaving, she laid her hand on Phil's arm and said, "Poor Blinky, are you awfully disappointed? Here you bring me all the way to Princeton with one thought in mind, and I disappoint you. I guess this is another leftover from an unpleasant incident involving my dear old Dad."

Phil said, "Just what do you mean by that?"

Susie replied testily, "Oh, nothing really, damn it. But, I suppose that this is the last time I'll be seeing Phil MacPherson, right? Of course, I can't complain. I put out a big sex line and when it comes time to produce, I don't want to. Exit the aroused erotic wolf, right?

Phil said,, "Susie, don't get me wrong. I had that very much in mind but you can't exactly blame me. You put on a very convincing act." He had added somewhat lamely, "Of course, Susie, I do like you and have fun with you and sex wasn't the only reason I asked you. You're fun to be with."

Susie said, "Keep saying that, Blinky. It's music to my ears." She had slipped her hand into his pocket as they left the dorm, "My what icy fingers you have." But Phil pointedly did not pick up on Susie's obvious opening. They walked back to the Corvette. They then drove back to Phil's married friends' apartment in almost total silence.

Sunday had been a disaster. Phil was painfully eager to get back to work on his thesis. As Phil put her on the little train to Princeton Junction, she tried to give him an affectionate hug just as she had done when she had arrived, but it was an empty gesture for both of them. As she rode the train home at noon, Susie thought again that she had seen Phil MacPherson for the last time. When Joan telephoned her two weeks later and invited her to spend a week at Hobe Sound, Susie was at first reluctant. Joan, hearing the hesitation in her voice, added, "By the way, Ollie is coming down for a long weekend. I told him to get Phil to come, too."

This put a new light on things. Susie had asked Mrs. Lacey, her superior at the Tilton Center, for a week off and had flown down Sunday.

Susie made an appointment with the hairdresser on Monday and had her long hair cut off. When she reappeared at the house that afternoon, Joan's eyes behind her horn-rimmed glasses opened wide and she said in astonished tones, "Susie! Good Lord! What have you done to yourself?"

"Yep, it's me," Susie replied. "Who did you expect? Charlie Brown or Snoopy?"

Joan answered, "Lord, Susie, why did you do that to yourself? Your long hair looked so well on you."

Susie said, "Well, Blinky really doesn't like it. He said my long hair rather made me look like an Italian streetwalker. Besides, I'm tired of looking like every other American teenage girl."

Joan looked at her and said, "Well, kid, after the initial shock, your feather cut does look nice. It softens your face." Joan continued after a moment, "You really do like Phil, don't you?"

Susie tried to feign indifference, saying, "Oh, I don't know, he's OK."

Joan said, "Come on, friend, who are you trying to kid?"

Susie said, "Well, there's no use kidding you or myself. I guess I do like Phil. He's so different from all the other guys. He's the complete opposite from Stew. But I don't think Mr. MacPherson has any real interest in little Susie Secant, the Main Line cut-up and pot smoker. Like most men, I think he's only interested in sex."

Joan said, "I think that Phil is probably interested in something more than sex but you've got to recognize that he's a serious sort of a guy and is intent on making his way in the world. It's refreshing to meet somebody like that these days."

Susie said, "Maybe you're right, Joan. But where, if anywhere, do I fit into that picture? As that old dragon, Cousin Jane, is fond of pointing out to everyone who's at all interested and some who aren't even interested, I'm a college dropout, a pot smoker, a pocket rebel and a pub crawler. Hardly the type who is likely to interest the Horatio Alger type."

Joan replied forcefully, "Kid, for Lord's sake, don't worry about your Cousin Jane or her generation. They think that you represent a threat to their sacred way of life, and you do. But, that's neither

Chapter 3 -- Wilt Thou Have This Man?

here nor there. Just don't sell yourself short. You're a very compassionate person underneath your façade. You have a good brain, which you might just use some day, and, boy, do you have determination! This in itself may help you with Phil MacPherson, who is himself pretty determined. I personally think you went off the track when Rebe retired. You should remember and practice all the good habits she taught you!"

Susie thought for a little while. "Joan, you just might be right. Rebe would be real disappointed in me after all the work, love and care she expended on me when I was a little girl. I wish I had never turned my back on all Rebe taught me. But it's too late now."

Joan had replied, "No, no it isn't too late. You've just got to make up your mind to do it."

Susie replied, "Well, maybe but, in the meanwhile, I am looking forward to the time when Blinky gets here!"

All that week Susie had thought about Phil MacPherson while she worked on a suntan so as to look her very best. On Friday, while she was sunbathing in her bikini at the pool out behind the Platen house, Ollie had casually come around the corner of the house. Seeing Susie, he mockingly said, "My, Cousin Susie, who are you baking that nice pie for? Could it be for my roommate, Blinky, by any chance?"

Susie looked up from under her sunglasses and said cheerfully, "Hi, Fat Stuff. You certainly are an unappetizing spectacle in a bathing suit. But you better be careful – this Florida sun will bake your lily white skin like a French fried onion ring if you're not careful. Say, by the way, where is Blinky?"

John replied, "Oh, Blinky. He is not coming down after all."

Susie felt like she had been punched in the stomach. Trying to mask her sharp disappointment, she said, "Oh, and why not? Joan said that he was coming down with you. Is he working hard on the Balfour Declaration or whatever his thesis is about?"

John replied with a teasing smile, "Nope, he's not working all that hard, at least not on his thesis. Matter of fact, I bet he's off skiing again with his girlfriend, Ann."

Susie sat bolt upright and took off her sunglasses and said angrily, "Just what in the hell do you mean by that, wise guy?"

John was taken aback by Susie's obvious anger and said defensively, "Now, Cousin Susie, don't get worked up. I was just putting you on. Can't you take a little joke? Actually, he's grinding away in the library as far as I know. Really, Blinky said he couldn't come because of his thesis and the plane fare was too much."

Susie said, "Just who in the goddamn hell is this girlfriend, Ann, anyway?"

John replied, "Oh hell, Susie, don't get your piss hot. She's no one. If you must know, her name is Ann Livingstone. She's just a little sophomore that Blinky occasionally has a Coke with or takes to the movies. Of course, he had asked her up to Mad River for New Year's Eve, but she doesn't even ski."

Susie said, "Cut out the crap, Ollie! Tell me about this Ann bimbo!"

John said, "No fooling, Susie, I've told you just about all I know. She is just some sophomore Blinky ran across mousing around the Russian section of the Firestone Library. She comes from San Diego or some such place like that in California. Blinky sometimes dates her, as I told you. She thinks Blinky is God." John added inconsequentially, "She's a Catholic and wears a gold medal of the Virgin Mary around her neck."

Susie said, "Medal or no medal, I'm dead sure she is sleeping with Blinky – goddamn her Catholic ass!"

John said, "Now, don't get excited, Susie. I didn't think that you really gave a damn. Besides Blinky really doesn't see that much of Ann, at least so far as I know.

Joan did her best to keep Susie's spirits up for the rest of the weekend but Susie could not hide her disappointment. She left early that Sunday morning, thanking Joan lamely for an excellent time. As she was driven by airline limousine to the airport, she mentally dismissed Phil MacPherson, thinking again she would probably never see him again. But she was dead wrong.

In fact, she saw Phil on three consecutive weekends after her return from Florida. These were quiet weekends spent either at the Secant house or at the Olivers' and at the Yellow Lantern. Susie enjoyed being with Phil and felt that she could be natural with him

Chapter 3 -- Wilt Thou Have This Man?

though she was apt to put on her act when other people were around. Phil commented at one point, "Why, Susie, do you put on that act when other people are around? You don't do it with me. You're more interesting and a better person when you're just being Susie rather than trying to shock and scare people."

Susie thought for a moment, "Well, maybe it's because I like you, Phil, and respect you. You don't need to be shocked to pay attention to me. On the other hand, which do you think is the real me, Phil? I sometimes have trouble in knowing myself."

Phil replied, "Have you ever thought of going to a head shrink and getting rid of some of these things that seem to be driving you up the wall all the time?"

Susie looked at him and said firmly, "No thanks, not on your Nelly. None of that stuff for me. Stew has told me what the shrinks are doing and have done to him and to his poor mother, Dol Jennings. I'd rather struggle with my own problems and nightmares rather than have those people muck up my problems and keep me sedated up for years on end in the Institute."

Phil said, "Hey, take it easy, Sue. I was just kidding you know. You don't need a belfry mechanic."

Susie replied, "Phil, you're the best shrink I know of." She remembered the somewhat astonished look that had come in Phil's eyes as she said this. She realized he was amused with her and liked her, but given any sort of encouragement he would again pounce on her as he had at Princeton. As it was, she simply stood on her tiptoes and gave him a kiss on the cheek at the end of the evening. Phil seemed content, or, at least, made no attempt to go any further.

However, at the end of the third weekend, Susie had driven Phil to the Thirtieth Street Station. They were waiting for the train to Trenton and on to Princeton. If the train had been on time, their conversation probably never would have taken place. As it was, Susie had slipped her hand inside his coat pocket and said as they walked along the dim cold platform, "You know, old Icy Fingers, I think I'm beginning to fall for you. I guess that you're really just interested in getting a chance to sleep with me. At least you never seem to indicate anything else."

Phil had kept on walking and then replied slowly, "You know, Susie, that I'm very fond of you, but …," he paused and blinked several times.

Susie had said snappily, "But, what?"

Phil replied uneasily, "Well, while this is fun for both of us, it's just as much a dead end for us as it was for you with Stew Jennings." Phil had blinked several times involuntarily as he said this, looking sideways at Susie.

Susie stopped short. She looked up into his face, her eyes wide with surprise. She had withdrawn her hand and said, "Blinky, you have the nasty habit of slapping girls. This time you've done it without even raising your hand. You're getting much better at it. What in the hell do you specifically mean by that last remark?"

Phil looked astonished at the bitterness in Susie's tone and said, blinking again, "Well, Susie, you know very well that I'm slated to do three years in the Navy after Princeton. Also, I'm going to Washington on an internship when the Navy dispenses with my services. Unlike Ollie and some of the other guys around here, I have only a few bonds to clip, so, other things apart, I'm not going to be in a position to do anything serious for some time to come. Of course, you and I have both known this all along but I just want to make sure there's no misunderstanding."

"Well," said Susie angrily, "there's no mistaking those words and what they mean. Christ, Phil, don't you trust me at all? So you're going in the Navy. Big Deal! So what! There are plenty of Navy men who have taken the plunge, so to speak, and gotten married. But it seems you'd rather have a girl in every port, rather than an anchor in one port. Don't give me that economic two-step bullshit, Phil. If you aren't serious, then you don't have to pretend that its economically impossible because both of us know that is a bunch of crap!"

She continued sadly, "So, where does that leave us? Let me see. Phil is interested in sleeping with Susie, who originally encouraged him along these lines. However, it turns out that Susie really doesn't want that but might like to have Phil as a lifetime roommate. However, Phil has absolutely no interest in this. It looks to me like the end of the trail. What do you think, partner?"

Chapter 3 -- Wilt Thou Have This Man?

Phil replied, "Not at all, partner. I don't see why things can't go along just as they have."

Susie said loudly, "Who are you kidding? All you've ever wanted to do is to get into me. Why don't you just come out and say that you're really not interested in anything else. You're nothing but a shit in wolf's clothing!" She began to cry, "Goddamn it, now look what you've done. You've made me cry again and I hate it."

Phillip had been surprised and touched and had said softly as he gave her his handkerchief, "Don't cry, Susie. Of course, I care very, very much for you, but I think that you should keep your eyes open so far as the future and the two of us are concerned."

Just then, the train came noisily into the station. Phil said with relief he was not able to disguise, "Here's my train, Susie. I've got to run. I'll see you in two weeks. Ollie and I are coming down that Friday. Then we'll all go into Philadelphia. See you then."

He kissed her quickly on the cheek and patted her on the shoulder. He then turned and dashed to the train and got on. He did not look back but hurried into the car. Susie was still crying as she turned to go to her car in the parking lot.

Susie was very depressed and irritable all that week at home and at the nursery. On Friday afternoon at the drugstore in the shopping center, she ran into Stewart Jennings. It was the first time she had seen him since long before Christmas.

Stewart said, "Hi, Susie, haven't seen you in a long time. How's tricks?"

Susie replied, "Not bad! What's new with you?"

Stewart said, "How are you and Lurch getting along?"

Susie knew, of course, that Stewart was referring to Phil but said, "Who?"

Stewart said, "Come off it, Susie. Don't play dumb with me."

Susie replied, "OK, I guess, why?"

Stewart said, "Well, I just hate to see a good girl like you fall for a dull craphead and social square like MacPherson. You can do better than that, Susie."

Susie said, "I don't seem to remember any such parting advice from you when you gave me my notice last winter. You let me go without even a friendly recommendation so that I could get another position."

Stew said, "I hardly expected you to commit social hari-kari." Then, changing his tone, he said, "Look, I'm home to see Mom in the Institute this afternoon, but how about it, why don't we go out to the Yellow Lantern tonight? Or, does the Jolly Green Giant have you under house arrest?"

Susie said, "He ain't so jolly and anyway, nobody runs me. Tell you what, Stew. Come to the house on your cycle at 8:00. When I hear it, I'll come out, and I'll race you cross-country to the Yellow Lantern, winner take all."

Stewart said, "You better have had a piston job done on that secondhand pile of junk or you're going to be eating my gravel all the way out to the Yellow Lantern." He continued, "I wish my new Tatra competition wheel would come from Prague. Then I'd really show you."

When Stewart arrived at the Secant house on his Harley, Susie was already sitting on her motorcycle in the garage with the light off and the engine purring quietly. Stewart turned his engine off and pulled out a cigarette. As he lit the match, Susie roared out around the side of the house and on down the "S" curves of the drive. She had not decreased her speed as she came down the lane and had not even stopped for the stop sign down at the end of the lane. She went down the long hill on Bluner Lane full speed and scarcely touched her brakes as she went around the sharp corner, skidding slightly. Even with that head start, she barely got to the Yellow Lantern ahead of Stewart. The race set the tone for the evening. She and Stewart went through some of their old tricks and ended up getting thrown out by Joe Horgan. But somehow it wasn't at all the same for Susie. Her heart just wasn't in it.

On Monday Mr. Secant telephoned Susie at the Tilton Nursery and said, "Sue, I've got great news. Bennett College just phoned me. They are willing to take you back without any conditions. Isn't that great! You have your Uncle Alfred to thank for that. When can you be ready? I'll, of course, drive you up."

Susie said, "Big deal! To hell with Bennett! I wouldn't go

Chapter 3 -- Wilt Thou Have This Man?

back if you paid me. Besides, it's right in the middle of the spring semester."

Mr. Secant said bitterly, "That's fine. Your Uncle Alfred and I have worked like hell for months to get you back into Bennett without conditions. Now, when we have finally succeeded, you say you don't want to go back. You might at least say thanks for the huge effort that we have made on your behalf."

Susie said, "Thanks. But after working at Tilton with speech impaired kids for six months, I don't want to go to a finishing school! I want to go to a serious college and then go on to get my master's in speech therapy."

Her father said, "All that's great but in order to get into a 'serious' college, to use your words, don't you realize it is vital to get Bennett to retract your dismissal?"

Susie thought for a moment and said in a softer tone, "I had not thought of it in that light. So I really mean it when I say, thank you. And I will write Uncle Alfred a note of thanks today."

That same day at dinner Mrs. Secant remarked with careful casualness, "We hear you were out with Stewart Saturday night. I thought that you were finished with him."

Susie's eyes flashed, "Yes, I was out with him. And, why not? The Twenty-Ninth Amendment to the Constitution provides nine new freedoms, one of which is that a girl can go out with any guy whatsoever she likes. By the way, how the hell did you and Guildersterne find this out, if I might be so bold as to ask? No, let me guess." Turning to her father, she said, "Could it have been your girlfriend, Sally, or is there a new one – maybe Mother's cute Italian hairdresser or the hostess at that cocktail bar in Cherry Hill, New Jersey?" Turning back to her mother, she said, "Oh, maybe it was one of your fat martini-drinking, bridge buddies?'"

Mr. Secant said angrily, throwing down his napkin, "No, goddamn it, Susie! As a matter of fact, Joe Horgan telephoned me at the office and told me that you and Jennings had broken the banisters and railings at the Yellow Lantern by riding your motorcycles off the porch when you left. The cost, you'll be glad to know, was about $200. Joe Horgan called me because he couldn't raise Jennings."

Susie said saucily, "So!"

Her father's face turned red and the muscles and veins in his great neck swelled up. He snapped at her, "So – that's a fine way to talk to your mother and I."

"Your mother and me," Susie cut in. "But I get your drift."

Tom continued, disregarding her remark, "I have a good mind to take that motorcycle away from you and sell it to pay for the damages, young lady. Who is going to pay the damage? You? The bank wrote me that you have been overdrawn consistently since October in spite of the allowance that we have continued though it was originally based on the idea that you were going back to Bennett College. Of course, Jennings is not going to pay for any of the damages from his trust funds. Oh no, not him! He's back in Boston, highly amused, I suppose, at having busted up Joe Horgan's property without any thought of who was going to pay for it. You and he, of course, think that money grows on trees. Well, we'll just see about that." He was breathing heavily.

Susie said sarcastically, "So, Daddeo's gonna take little Susie's wheel away from Susie and sell it, is he? Forget that little idea, Buster. That bike is titled in my name alone. Relax, I'll pay for those lousy banisters myself. What's your next charge, officer, or would you like to hear a certain countercharge I have against you?" She gave him a menacing look. She and her father were glaring at each other across the table.

Mrs. Secant had broken in at that point, saying smoothly, "All right, all right now. Everyone calm down, please. There is no need for anyone to raise their voice. After all, there is no reason for the help to hear you two bickering." Mrs. Secant then said, obviously trying to change the subject, "By the way, where is Phillip MacPherson these days? He seemed like such a nice boy."

Susie whirled around and said to her mother, "Goddamn it, keep your nose out of my business, both of you! What concern is it of yours what happened to Phillip MacPherson. How should I know? Maybe the Red Baron got him and Snoopy both at the same time with a butterfly net." As an afterthought she had added, "As a matter of fact, Stewart and I are soon going to get married. Now, put that in

Chapter 3 -- Wilt Thou Have This Man?

your pipe and smoke it."

Mrs. Secant looked aghast and said weakly, "Susie, I just don't believe you – you can't be serious!"

Susie said in the same menacing tone she had used to her father, "Can't I though? That's what you think. Maybe you'll both believe it when you read it in the Sunday Bulletin." She threw down her napkin and stamped out of the dining room. She heard her mother say, "Well, Tom, don't just sit there, do something."

Her father said in a defeated tone, "Sarah, I wish I could. Christ, I wish I could but I can't do anything. You know as well as I do that if I say anything to Susie, that's all the more likely to make her do it."

Unfortunately, that same evening about an hour later, Phil had called her from Princeton. Susie answered the phone in her room. Phillip started by saying, "Hello, Susie, is that you?"

Susie, still smarting from the conversation with her mother and father, said snappily, "Yes, there's only one Susanne Secant in this house and I'm she and I'm talking to you. Now, what's on your mind?"

Phillip had paused for a second, obviously put off by her frigid tone. Then he said, "Well, I was calling to make certain that everything is still OK for this coming Friday. Ollie and I are both cutting an afternoon class so we can be down there Friday and go into Philadelphia. We've managed to get tickets to the Mahalia Jackson Concert. I just want to make sure that everything is OK on your end."

Susie said, "Damn, Phillip, I had completely forgotten all about it. As a matter of fact, it turns out I can't make it. I was going to call you and let you know," she added.

"When?" Phillip snapped back testily.

"When, what?" Susie replied, pretending not to understand.

"When, what – what in the hell do you think I mean? When were you going to have the common courtesy to let me know that you had made other plans?"

Susie shot back, "Hey, big boy, I seem to remember in our last conversation that you didn't feel that you had any permanent claims on me and vice versa. What now makes you think that you run me or own me? As a matter of fact, why don't you goddamn well go and pack sand!"

Phil replied angrily, "Susie, why don't you have the common decency to tell me that Jennings has surfaced again instead of stringing me along that you had forgotten or that you were going to let me know about this weekend." Then he had added icily, "It seems to me that I remember that you once told me with a considerable amount of solemn pride that you gloried in your own honesty."

Susie by this time was shouting, "Goddamn you! You knew that I'd been out with Jennings, but instead of coming right out with it and telling me that you're pissed about it, you pussyfoot around. From now on, why don't you keep your goddamned big nose out of my business! I must have been crazy to think that it would be fun to play the heroine in 'Good-bye Mr. Chips' or Florence Nitingshirt to your Dr. Kildare. Go play stinky finger with that intellectual mackerel snapper in the Firestone Library but leave me goddamned well alone!"

Susie was referring to Ann Livingstone, but Phil had tried to play dumb and had said, "Who?"

Susie said, "Come on, stupid, Ann Livingstone. Who the hell did you think I was talking about, the Duchess of Kent?"

Phil paused, "If that's the way you want it, I guess that's the way it'll have to be." He paused again, obviously hoping that she would say something else. When she did not, he added, "Well, Susie, I guess this is good-bye. It's been an education knowing you. See you around."

She replied, "It will be too soon if and when I see you again. So long you blinking idiot." Susie clicked the receiver firmly down.

Susie thought that if she had been miserable in the week before, certainly the week that followed was the worst that she had ever been through. There was no one that she could really turn to. Finally, she telephoned Joan. After discussing the fact that she had been readmitted to Bennett but had decided not to go back, Susie said, "Yeah, things are dull as always around here except that about a week ago, I went out to the Yellow Lantern with Stew again. It was like old times. Stew set the place on its ear and, in the end, we were

Chapter 3 -- Wilt Thou Have This Man?

thrown out by Joe Horgan. We had parked our motorcycles on the porch and we must have busted the old place up pretty good with a racing start off the porch because Horgan called the old man and the old man read the riot act to me. Horgan claims we did about $200 worth of damage to that ratty old porch. Personally, I wouldn't give you a hundred dollars for the whole place. Of course, I'm in the doghouse with the family about that and about my general lifestyle which they don't fancy any more than I fancy their respective lifestyles. Joanie, what's the matter with me? I seem to be good for nothing."

Joan confronted her, "Nuts, kid. You can't fool me. It's not the trouble with your old man and old lady. You have been on the outs with them, especially your father, since Rebe retired. Come clean. The plain fact is that you and Blinky have had a parting of ways, right? That's really what's gotten you down, isn't it?"

Susie said, "It's so unfair. Why should I get hooked on Phillip MacPherson? He is a big, tall, serious intellectual guy who is intent on being a life scout or a Nobel prize winner or something along that line. I'm not at all interested in that sort of thing. I'm quite content to settle for a few laughs. The maddening thing about it is that I am hooked on him but he's really not interested in me. Sure, he's amused, but he's not really seriously interested in Susie Secant. I think it's all water over the dam. Phil called me just after I had gotten the Chinese water treatment from the old man and the old lady about my evening with Stew at the Yellow Lantern. I gave it to Phillip MacPherson with both barrels right between the eyes when he started kind of giving me the razzmataz about having gone out with Stew. If there was any chance of making a good thing out of Phillip MacPherson, I sank it with that verbal salvo."

Joan said, "Kid, it certainly sounds to me like Susie has been bitten, but good. But, you know, kid, you do yank people's chains pretty hard at times. You may well have yanked Blinky's too hard. Have you ever thought of apologizing or is that still not part of your lifestyle as yet?"

Susie said, "Oh no, Joan, I couldn't bring myself to do that. He was pretty mad himself. I think he'd just laugh if I called him now. I'm afraid that I've only my own sharp tongue to blame at this point.

All I will ever have to show from my serious love for Phil will be the loss of my long hair and the tattoo of a wolf on my fanny."

"What do you mean by that?" Joan asked.

Susie laughed as she replied, "In my salad days I thought it would be a cute idea to have a tattoo of a wolf on my derriere. I had it done while I was visiting you in Florida. It was the same day that I had my hair chopped off. The tattoo hurt like hell. It's only now that I can really appreciate the cute little design since the scab has come off. However, a fat lot of good it does me now. I guess I'll have to have it tattooed out. You don't happen to know any good tattoo parlors do you?"

Joan also laughed and said, "Kid, I wondered why you were so uncomfortable sitting down when we were in Florida. Don't eradicate the brand mark just yet. After all, Rome wasn't burned down in a day. Cheer up, Susie. Things are bound to get better. I just might be able to help. I'll call you Monday. So long, kid."

Joan did call her back on Wednesday. "Hello, Kid, this is Joan. I was in Old Nassau over the weekend. I saw your friend Blinky. I had a chat with him and pointed out to him that Stew wasn't really a serious contender for your favors and that you were very, very sorry that you had cranked off at him."

Susie said, "Oh, Joan, you shouldn't have done that." Then she quickly asked, "What did Phil say?"

Joan said, "I guess you did turn the tap off pretty hard because I wasn't very successful in my Dear Abby mission. Blinky said in effect that he wasn't sore, but I really think that he is. He then went on to say that he wasn't going to get back on the Susie Secant merry-go-round now that he's been pushed off. He ended up saying that he might give you a call just to let you know that there are no hard feelings. That's about the sum and substance of it, Sue. Why don't you give him a call?"

Susie said, "Thanks a lot, Joanie, for trying to act as a peacemaker. You know that there is a special reward in heaven for those who perform such missions. I don't think I'm going to call Phil. I am not quite up to that yet."

Joan said, "And just what do you mean by that?"

Chapter 3 -- Wilt Thou Have This Man?

Susie replied, "Oh, nothing much as it turns out. Monday afternoon I was going to the record store on my wheel. It was raining. I guess I thought I knew Bluner's Lane by heart and got a little careless. As I came bombing down the long hill past Colonel Rider's place on Bluner's Lane, I hit some loose gravel going around the curve. The gravel was slippery due to the rain. The damn bike skidded right out from under me. When I looked up, I saw the bike coming down right smack dab on top of me. I managed to roll away and the bike missed me. It skidded over and hit the post-and-rail fence on the side of the road. The gas tank must have cracked open. The motorcycle burst into flames and burned up and set the fence on fire. I got a cut on my arm. There was blood everywhere."

Joan broke in, "Good God, Susie! You might have been killed!"

Susie said, "Yeah, or even worse. I could have been fried to a crisp and lived through it. I was so frightened that I damn near passed out. The Partridge Farm bread man saw it all happen and stopped. He was about as shaken up as I was. I thought he was going to faint. I had to help him. My pal Joe Horgan from the Yellow Lantern was the first car to come along and Joe was great, as always. The whole damned volunteer fire company turned out. There were five fire engines with sirens screaming and lights flashing. Also, my buddy Corporal Tim Roberts came -- he could have given me a ticket but he didn't, thank God. I was taken to the hospital in an ambulance. It was quite a show, I can tell you."

Joan broke in again, "Were you hurt at all?"

Susie replied, "Not really. As it turned out, I didn't have any serious injuries at all except for some bruises, cuts and scrapes. However, they kept me overnight thinking that there must be some internal injuries or something. As it turned out, all I got was bruises and a cut on my arm and a general feeling of stiffness. I wanted to rent a motorcycle to ride back home from the hospital, but you can imagine the parental veto that I got on that idea."

Joan interrupted and said, "Kid, I have an idea. Stick around tonight. You may just get another phone call. OK?"

Susie had said, "What do you mean, Joanie?" But Joan had

hung up.

About half an hour later, the telephone rang. It was Phillip, "Susie, this is Blinky. I am calling to find out if you're really OK."

Susie said, "How nice of you to call, Phil! Yeah, I'm OK, I guess. I'm stiff and I have some stitches for the cut on my left arm but I wasn't really hurt, thank God. Fortunately, I was wearing my helmet or I might have had my brains, if I have any, knocked out by skidding on some wet gravel on the curve on Bluner's Lane. You know the place. Say, how did you hear about it? Bad news travels fast!"

Phil said, "Oh, Joan telephoned me a while back. She said that you'd been in an accident. She said she thought that you weren't hurt, but she wasn't sure. Incidentally, she said that you wanted to rent a motorcycle to ride home from the hospital. Is that right?"

Susie had laughed, "Right. That's what they do to give horseback riders and airplane pilots their nerve back when they've had a crack-up. You can imagine, Mother and old Dads made short shrift of that idea. I doubt that any further bike riding by me is going to be greeted with wild applause by either Mother or the old man."

Susie was pleased when Phil replied, "Well, you can count me in on that sentiment. Susie, you've just got to be a nut to ride a motorcycle, especially when you ride as fast as you do." He paused and then said, "I know that you told me to pack sand a couple of weeks ago. I've really tried hard, Susie. But it doesn't work. I am still hooked on you and I guess I always will be. How about it? Do you think you'll be well enough to go out Saturday if I were to come down? More important, do you want to go out with me?"

Susie said, "Hell, Phil, I'm OK except for a few bruises and some stitches that are coming out Friday. I could and would go out with you tonight. I'd just love to go out Saturday with you. Phil, I'm sorry I was so damn mean to you two weeks ago. As you know, I often say things that I don't mean. Deep down, I didn't really want to hurt you. I'm so glad you called. Am I forgiven again, Phillip Wolf?"

"Nothing to forgive," Phil said, echoing the conversation that had started their glorious walk in the woods months ago in December.

Chapter 3 -- Wilt Thou Have This Man?

Susie remembered the conversation and said, "My, what long icy fingers you have, Phillip Wolf – don't say it – see you Saturday night. But I still love you. Bye for now." Then she had hung up. She found she was in tears. Suddenly, she was so happy that she hugged herself. She spent the rest of the evening dancing to records in her room in spite of her stiffness.

She said nothing about the phone call from Phil, but the atmosphere in the whole Secant house reflected Susie's own serene good humor. Though the time had dragged for Susie, she had not minded but had savored the anticipation of seeing Phil again. On Saturday night while Susie and her mother and father were at dinner, she had heard the front door open and called from the dining room, "Is that you, Phil? Come on in. We're just finishing dinner." She saw out of the corner of her eye that her mother gave her father a small sidelong glance.

As Phil came into the candle lit dining room, her mother looked him over and said coolly, "Good evening, Phillip. It's nice to see you again." Her father rose and slapped Phil on the shoulder and said, "Hi, Phil. We're just having dessert. Do you want some? Just say the word and Mrs. Secant can ring for another plate. Meanwhile, pull up a chair and sit down with us."

Phil had replied, "No thanks, Mr. Secant. I've just eaten. I couldn't touch another thing." Susie discovered later that he had not had any dinner at all. By then, Susie had already jumped up, chucked her napkin on the table, and went out the dining room door saying, "Goodnight, folks. See you tomorrow. Come on, Phillip, let's go." She had deliberately worn the same gray pants suit piped in green that she had worn the first time that they had gone out.

Mrs. Secant called after her, "Susie, take a raincoat – it's going to rain again."

"OK, Ma," Susie called back. "OK if I borrow your fleece-lined raincoat?"

Mrs. Secant had called, "Certainly, my dear. Goodnight." Then came Tom Secant's deep voice, "Goodnight dear girl, goodnight Phil."

As they were putting on their coats, Phillip said, "I'm staying at the Olivers' and I've got John's car. When I got back to the room today, I found a note from Ollie. Here it is." He handed the note to Susie.

> Pyramus:
> I'm afraid that you'll have to go to Thisbe all by yourself. I am in the grip of the grippe and I'm going into the infirmary for the weekend. Don't think of changing your weekend plans. Take the Corvette and stay at the house. Mother expects you. Toujour l'amour.
>
> Snugg, the Joiner

As they got into the Corvette, they were both somewhat tongue-tied. Neither one of them knew quite where to begin and neither one wanted to upset things. Phil had started to make a right turn right at the end of the drive, taking the familiar road down Bluner's Lane and out to the Yellow Lantern. Susie said, laying her hand on his arm, "Oh Phil, let's not go to the Yellow Lantern again tonight."

Phil said, "I hoped you wouldn't want to go there."

Susie said, "I know. Let's go to the Fox's Den. It's a little bit of a drive, but I don't think you've been there. We're not likely to run into people we know."

They had driven out through the pelting April rain to the Fox's Den. On the trip out they circled around the questions that were in the very front of both of their minds, neither one wanting to break the pleasant mood of just being together by bringing up matters that were unresolved. Finally, however, they were settled on opposite sides of a secluded booth in the Fox's Den with a drink, a candle and an ashtray for Susie. Susie took a deep drag on her cigarette and then said, "You know, Phil, I'm so sorry for what happened. I knew it was totally wrong even as I did it, but I just could not seem to help myself. I've done just that sort of thing ever since Rebe, my nanny, left. I seem to want to hurt people, especially people who are close to me and love me most. Somehow, I seem to want to make them hate me yet, at the same time, I want them to love me. When I

Chapter 3 -- Wilt Thou Have This Man?

do that sort of thing, I hate myself the most. God, I hope you don't hate me as much as I hate myself."

Phil responded with a gentle smile, "I don't hate you, Susie. I never have, not since the first time I saw you and Joan looking down at Ollie and me in the squash court. I don't hate you now. I guess I never will, no matter what happens."

Susie smiled and put her hand over Phil's big hand. "I still don't hear the magic word 'love,' but never mind. I love you very much anyway. Maybe that's enough for both of us. Can you understand that I need you very much?"

"Isn't this kind of where I came in?" Phil said. "We seem to be back in square one, or I, at least, seem to be back in square one."

Susie replied quickly, "No, no, Phil. Don't say that. We're not back where we started from and we both know it, or at least I do. You're talking about Stew, aren't you? You're afraid that I will go back to him. I suppose you have every right to think so, but it won't happen, and I hope you know it won't. Stew and I have been friends. I think that our attraction lay in the fact that we have both been so terribly lonely. He's practically an orphan with his father dead and his mother, poor old Dol, in the institute for the last five years. I've, of course, been an orphan in many ways since Rebe retired."

Susie paused and then continued, "But I'm not in love with Stewart and, God knows, he's not in love with me. Even if we were, we couldn't make a go of anything for longer than three weeks." Then she added, "Maybe it means that I'm growing up. Isn't that what everybody wants Susie to do? But, God, it's lonely. Mother has her own perfect well ordered life into which I don't fit and which doesn't interest me, though Lord knows I've tried. Dad – the perpetual college athlete, growing fat and rotting away whatever little brain he had with alcohol in the men's bar and getting a little on the side whenever and wherever he can. The worst of it is that he was my complete idol for so many years until – well, never mind, but just where does that leave me? A college dropout or rather, kickout, with no brains and no convictions, playing at being a madcap and shocking mother's friends and playing at social work four days a week. I'm sick of myself, sick of what I'm doing and sick of the world in general. I have never seemed to be able to do anything right since Rebe left and went back to Nevis."

Phil said, "It sounds like you have growing pains. I'm sure that you will outgrow your shocking period. Don't worry, Susie, the best is yet to come."

Susie had then said, "Yeah. What's the best that's yet to come? Never mind – don't answer that. Phil, you're always so nice to me. Why? You're too damned kind to me. Keep it up, I love it." Then she added, "Do you love me, just a little? No, don't answer that. I don't want to know. Besides, I've got to go to the ladies' room."

When she returned, she sat next to him in the booth on his side rather than across from him. She put her head on his shoulder and said, "God, Phil, you're so good to me. Why? We both know I'm a bitch."

Phil said loyally, "You're no bitch, Susie, you just try to be one sometimes and you occasionally succeed but basically you're not, you know."

Susie said in a mocking tone, "Hurray for the Susies. It looks like they may score after all. Keep on saying it Phil, you sound like you're beginning to convince yourself. You may even convince me, but I've got to point out to you that there are a whole hell of a lot of others who wouldn't believe you on a stack of Bibles."

Phil replied, "Who gives a shit about them? Fuck all of them!"

Susie sat up with mock dignity, "Why Phillip, I never heard you use those expressions before. They're favorites of mine, but I'm quite shocked to hear you use them. It's so out of character. I'm obviously not only a bitch but a bad influence on you. Please don't ever use that coarse expression in my presence again. If it must be used, I'll use it, darling. If I hear you use it, I'll get Rebe to use her hairbrush on you as she did so often on me, or I'll wash out your mouth with brown soap."

They sat there for a couple of hours. Susie could not remember what they talked about. All she could remember was that it was a happy and relaxed time without really much need to say anything on either side. They even left well before closing time.

When they got to the Corvette, the rain had stopped. Susie

Chapter 3 -- Wilt Thou Have This Man?

grabbed Phil before he unlocked the car, stood on her tiptoes and gave him a passionate kiss on the mouth. They were still locked in one another's arms when another car came up and loudly blew its horn. Susie said, "Let's just go back to my house. The old man and the old lady will have hit the feathers by this time, and we can watch the late late show. OK? As a matter of fact, Blinky Wolf, we might just put on a late show that Mr. Johnny Carson himself might want to watch. But, be gentle when the time comes, Blinky."

When they got the house, it turned out that Susie was right. Her parents were upstairs. The lights were out except for a light on the front hall table. Phil closed the front door quietly. Susie turned to him and said, "Don't worry about waking Mummy or the old man. She takes a sleeping pill most nights and the old man sleeps like a pile of bricks. Come on, let's go in the library. Let me slide into the pantry and get some ice out of the icemaker."

When she came back, Phil had turned on several of the lights and the big color TV.

"Hey," said Susie, "what are you setting up here, a sol and lumiere? What we need is more heat and less light. Why don't you throw a few more sticks of wood on the fire while I blow out a few Philadelphia Electric candles." She proceeded to turn out all the lights except for the small one by the bar. "That's more like it," she said judiciously as the logs, which Phil had put on the fire, flamed up. She continued., "Scotch still your favorite poison? I'm still all for vodka."

Without waiting for his answer, she prepared two on the rocks and brought them over to the leather couch. She set the drinks down on the low plank table and sat down on the couch. Phil was still standing by the fireplace pretending to use the tongs to arrange the logs. Susie said, "Take off your coat, partner, and sit and rock for a spell."

Phil dropped his coat over a chair and pulled his tie down. He then sat down at the other end of the couch. There was a pause while both of them looked at the fire. Susie suddenly jumped up and ran over to the bookcase. She looked at the titles of the books by the firelight and then selected one saying, "Descartes. He and Montesquieu are my favorite philosophers, at least in this library. They can be counted on never to let me down and disclose my secrets. I am certain that no one in this household is going to pry into their works."

She brought the book over to the couch and opened it. From the binding, she pulled out a white cigar tube and opened it. Out of it came several small brown cigarettes. She took one, "Shall we light up a joint, Blinky? If we do, we'll have to open the windows because it stinks this room up terribly. I did it once. Mother was sore for a week though, of course, she knows I've been smoking pot for a year."

Phillip answered, "Let's not smoke tonight, Susie."

Susie thought for a moment, "I guess you're right, Phil. Here, let me put these away." She put the cigarettes carefully back in the cigar tube, slipped it back in the binding of the Descartes and carefully put the book back in its place. She came back to the sofa, "Where in the goddamned hell did I put my drink."

Phillip answered, "Forget about the drink, Susie. Come here." She sat down next to him on the couch and relaxed while Phil attempted to undress her.

Susie struggled away from him, laughed and said, "I never understood exactly why the women wore skirts until now. Phil, my dear, you just can't fight your way subtlety into a pants suit. Pants suits are an invention of the women's lib group. If we're going to get anywhere, I've got to give you some help. In the meanwhile, turn that goddamned TV down."

Phil turned the TV down and for good measure, went over and turned off the light on the bar table. As he came back toward the sofa he could see in the flickering light of the fire that Susie had taken the pants suit off. She now had only her white bra and brightly colored abbreviated underpants on. He walked swiftly over to her and took her in his arms and kissed her. He reached around behind her and tried to unhook her bra with one hand.

She said, "Blinky, you couldn't unhook that thing with one hand in a million years. Let me do it. In the meanwhile, your belt buckle is going to make a permanent brand on my tummy."

Phil let go of her and quickly stepped out of his moccasins, slipped out of his khaki pants and pulled his shirt over his head and threw these and his underwear haphazardly around the room. While

Chapter 3 -- Wilt Thou Have This Man?

he was doing this, Susie took a pair of cushions from the window seat and threw them in front of the fire. She then sat down on one of them, waiting in front of the fire, having removed the rest of her clothing. She said quietly, looking into the fire, "Well, I guess this is what you've been after since the beginning. Don't answer that, Blinky. I don't want to hear the answer, no matter what is it. Anyway, it's also what I want – now. It's kind of classic, isn't it?"

It had not been a classic at all. Phil was far too excited and had barely stretched outside beside her and touched her when he had exploded, covering both of them with warm, sticky, sickly smelling fluid. Phil lay there with his head in the cushion, "Oh Christ! Goddamn it! Goddamn it to hell!"

Susie had gotten a bar tower and cleaned up while Phil lay there. Then she giggled and lit a cigarette. "Relax, Phil, my love, it can happen to anyone. Besides, I think it's kind of funny. It reminds me of parts of 'Portnoy's Complaint.' Besides, we have all night unless you have a late date. So what difference does it make?"

They lay there on their stomachs looking into the fire while Susie smoked a cigarette and they drank their drinks and he stroked her back. Finally, he said dreamily, "Aren't you worried about getting pregnant, Susie?"

Susie said, "Jesus Christ, Phil, it's 1973 not 1873. You have heard of the pill, haven't you?"

Phil replied dryly, "Of course I have, Susie, only I just didn't think that you would be on them just now."

"Have been since I was fifteen-and-a-half," Susie replied. "It makes mother sleep better. Turn that damned TV off and throw another log on the fire. I'm getting cold." She went quietly out of the room and brought back a pair of comforters from her room.

In the course of their lovemaking, Phil's left leg had knocked over the end table. The lamp had fallen over with a terrific crash. Afterwards, Susie said, "How was that for you? It was great for me in spite of the pyrotechnics. I may not be good at much else but, by God, this is something that I want to be good at. I intend it always to be good with you and for you, Blinky Wolf."

Phil grinned, "Well, feel free to practice with me anytime

you want."

That was the last thing that Susie remembered before drifting off into a light doze before the fire with Phil's arm around her. When she woke up, the overhead light in the room had been turned on. As she looked over her shoulder and over the top of the leather couch, she could see the face of her mother in her bathrobe framed by the doorway and the darkness beyond. Her mother stood there for just a second and then turned the light out and closed the door without saying anything.

"Oh my God," Phil groaned. "Susie, what in the world are we going to do? That was your mother!"

Susie said somewhat dreamily, "For a moment, I thought it was Lady MacBeth sleepwalking and seeing Banquo's ghost. As a practical matter, I guess I'd better get mother's sleeping pills strengthened."

Phil said: "How can you kid around at a time like this? What will you say to your mother tomorrow or, probably far more to the point, what will I say to her or, even worse, what will she say to me?"

Susie leaned on one arm, "Let me see, you've given me several interesting questions. First, what will I say to mother tomorrow morning? I usually say 'Good morning, Mother, how did you sleep?' However, that would seem to be inappropriate under the circumstances since she obviously isn't sleeping too well probably due to the ungodly commotion that we have been making down here. Next, you ask me what she will say to me. She usually says, 'Susanne, how did you sleep?' I could reply very truthfully, 'Very well' without gilding the lily – you being the lily, of course.

"As to what you will say to Mother, I won't put words in your mouth. After all, you are a Christian, almost a Princeton graduate and quite a gentleman, if I do say so. If I am at breakfast, I would hope that you would give me a good reference, something like 'Mrs. Secant, your little Susie is a really one first-class screw.' You might polish that a little bit between now and daybreak, especially as I intend to make a further effort to deserve a kind word at breakfast from you to my sainted mother."

Chapter 3 -- Wilt Thou Have This Man?

Phil had pulled her toward him and said, "Christ, Susie, how can you laugh at a time like this?"

"Well, Phil, I can't cry when I'm happy, now can I? Besides, what are you worried about? I haven't got seven strapping brothers who are going to come in and castrate you for dishonoring their little sister and besmirching the family honor. Dad's role calls for him to pound you into a pulp, but he's asleep and anyway I know for a fact that he's hardly in a position to do that. Besides, even if he wanted to do it, what good would it do him or me or you or mother or anybody? Christ, Phil, don't let your New England conscience ruin everything."

Phil said dryly, "My conscience took the evening off sometime ago. It wasn't my conscience that just walked in and turned on the light: it was your mother."

"Well" Susie had said, "I noticed that she turned the light off again. That was very courteous of her and also saves on the electric bill."

Phil said, "What else could she do, for goodness sake?"

"She could have offered us the guest room. We might both catch our death of colds here. On the other hand, she might have offered us the garden though I doubt that she would consider that since we would undoubtedly trample her spring daffodils with this bacchanalia," Susie said.

Phil said, "Seriously, don't you think I'd better be going?"

She said, "Not by the hair of my chinny-chin-chin. You've made your bed, Sir Wolf, now lie in it."

Susie continued, "Don't leave, Phil. After all, this is what you've wanted from the beginning, and we're both enjoying it. Incidentally, don't worry, I'm not thinking any further than tonight."

They spent the night in the library dozing and talking and again making love, this time being careful not to knock over the furniture. By this time the fire had almost completely burned out and through the leaded pane of the window dawn was starting to break.

Phil sneezed loudly and sat up. He seemed terribly depressed. He dressed slowly and then turned on the lights and emptied the full ashtray and put the glasses in the sink and straightened the place up.

Susie followed his movements while peeping out from under the quilt. She put on his blue blazer and went out into the hall. There she took off his blazer and slid into her mother's fleece-lined coat and came out in her bare feet to the damp graveled driveway. The sun was about to come up. Susie said, "I love being up at this time after a rain, don't you? It's so clean and fresh."

Phil stood with his blazer over his arm and yawning, "Lady, I don't know about you, but I'm tired and I'd like to be in bed."

Susie replied, "Come on, I just happen to know of an empty available bed."

Phil ruffled her hair, "You're a nut, Susie. You better get inside before you catch cold. Also, the first church goers will soon be up and they'll quite an eyeful of you standing here in your bare feet at 6:00 A.M. in your mother's coat, dancing on the lawn." By then, Susie was doing ballet movements on the lawn.

Susie danced over to him, stood on her tip toes, kissed him and said, "Well, I guess you're right as always. Goodnight, Sweet Wolf, and angels hie thee to thy rest. I don't know what hieing is, but it had better be something non-sexual or the angels will hear from me. Parting is such sweet sorrow that I will die until it be morrow. Isn't that the line?"

Phil kissed her and said, "Goodnight or, rather, good morning, Susie, I'll see you tomorrow or, rather, later today. Tell your sainted mother that our motto is 'Honi Soit Qui Mal Y Pense.'"

Susie slept until about two o'clock. When she looked out and saw the white Corvette in the drive, she came downstairs. As she came down the stairs, she heard her mother and Phil on the winter porch. He was saying, "Mrs. Secant, I won't play games with you anymore than I'm playing games with Susanne. I want to marry Susanne just as soon as she agrees to have me. I think that she is going to agree to marry me now that she's convinced that she's over Stewart Jennings and that she loves me."

Susie was about to come in and when she heard her mother say angrily, "To hell with your honorable intentions, Mr. MacPherson! You are older than my daughter, Susanne. You knew that she had been through an emotional crisis with Stewart Jennings when you

Chapter 3 -- Wilt Thou Have This Man?

first came down here. I would suggest that you get Susanne's agreement to marriage before you talk about your intentions since I think your actions speak louder than your intentions."

Mrs. Secant continued in a calmer tone, "I know that among the younger generation marriage is not a fashionable institution. However, my mother is a Quaker and I still have some of the traces of my Quaker upbringing. I must say that I am shocked by your behavior. Incidentally, I must tell you, though Susanne isn't getting along very well with her father now, he is still completely devoted to his daughter. I would not put it past him to give in to his Irish temper and thrash you good and proper if he so much as suspected the scene which I saw last night in his own television den."

She then continued in a kindlier tone, "Phillip, please understand me. I do like you. I have since you and John first came to the house after Christmas. I would like to see you marry Susanne since I think you love her and I know that she loves you. However, until you and she decide this fairly simple question, you can hardly expect me to be overjoyed by what went on last night. I might add, Phillip, that I'm sure that Susanne's father would be genuinely pleased if you and she were to get married. Of course, there's no real reason why you and Susanne shouldn't get married if you want to. You are finishing college this spring and from what you've told me, you are going into the Navy this fall with a position in Washington thereafter. I suppose that we could have a wedding in September right after Labor Day if this is what the two of you want. Of course, I would like to announce Susanne's engagement to you formally at Easter time at a small cocktail party and then really have a proper wedding. How would this sound to you?"

Susie heard Phil say uncertainly, "Well, that sounds just great to me, Mrs. Secant. I'll let you know when I've talked to Susie."

At this point, Susie walked in, "You two look like Bruschnev and Koseygen. Have you decided to throttle poor little Israel?"

Mrs. Secant smiled and said to Susie, "No, dear, but Phil tells me that you and he have decided to get married. Of course, I can't tell you how happy that makes me for both of you. I might add that it will also make your father very happy to hear this. He's gone to a

76ers game."

Susie said, "Do tell. 'If thy intentions be honorable, secure to send by one that I shall send to thee.' Christ, there are some things even your best friends won't tell you. But, I'm certainly glad that I'm old enough to be let in on this delightful little family secret. Do you think I'm old enough to keep it? By the way, do I have the option to refuse to play on MacPherson's team or is there a reserve clause in my contract? Has it ever occurred to you, MacPherson, that I might say to hell with that?" Susie had stamped out of the room and into the library. Phil followed her, "What's gotten into you Susie? I thought that's what you wanted."

"Of course it is, Phil," she said, "but it's a hell of a way to hear a proposal of marriage. I didn't really expect a Victorian valentine scene with you on your knees passionately grasping my hand and my turning shyly away from you and saying, 'But, this is so sudden Mr. MacPherson.' On the other hand, I certainly hadn't expected to receive a proposal of marriage through Mummy." Susie had continued, "Now that it has finally come, I'm surprised and I want to think it over."

Phil said, "Take it easy Susie, don't lose your cool. There is nothing binding. There is no hurry."

Susie answered: "OK, pal, but that goes both ways. It seems to me that at this time yesterday, it was Blinky MacPherson, the Navy's secret threat who had skillfully steered his racing dinghy neatly through the reefs and shoals of marriage, right Mr. Admiral? What happened between you and the Mother Superior? Did she wield the shotgun in Dad's absence?"

Phil replied in an unconvincing tone, "Don't be silly Susie, of course not. I had made up my mind that I wanted to marry you long before I talked to your mother."

Susie replied, "Oh yeah, and just when did you come to this summit decision? It was a far better kept secret than the Pentagon Papers, pal. I know that I am something of a security risk but you might consider confiding in me."

They spent the rest of the afternoon miserably watching television in the library. Neither of them alluded in any way to the

Chapter 3 -- Wilt Thou Have This Man?

night before and warily avoided any subject that touched on the future. Mrs. Secant left them entirely alone, having retreated to the winter porch from whence they could hear the sounds of the Sunday Philharmonic Concert. At 5:00 o'clock, she came to the door of the library. Susie looked up and said, "You again – look Mother, Phil and I are not even talking, much less holding hands. You can relax for the moment. Mr. MacPherson, like the Indians, only mounts his attacks after midnight, not at sundown, especially when Wide World of Sports is on the TV. If this be married bliss, I'm beginning to see something in women's lib."

Phil said, "Never mind, Mrs. Secant, I'm told that lionesses always roar just before feeding time."

Susie smiled and relaxed somewhat, "Serve up two fricasseed Christians if you please."

Mrs. Secant smiled, "OK you two. But, Susie, would you please go up and change into something besides those awful cut off blue jeans and put some shoes on. Cousin Alfred and Jane are coming over for a drink in about half an hour and I don't want you looking like that. You might try a comb and brush on your hair at the same time."

"Love him, hate her, but anything to cheer up the House of Usher," Susie said moodily as she left.

Mrs. Secant said, "Never mind her, Phil. Susie is sometimes like that, as you know or certainly will get to know. By the way, could you set up the cocktail tray and bring it into the living room while I get some crackers and cheese? You know where the ice is. Old fashion glasses will do all the way around – even the martini drinkers drink them on the rocks these days."

Tom Secant got home about ten minutes after the Olivers arrived and he said with real warmth, "Well, this is a nice surprise. Alfred, how are you? You missed a good game today. That's right, you don't like basketball. Hi, Phil – Susie." He bussed Jane on the cheek and said, "How's my favorite cousin?" He than said to his wife, "How was the Philharmonic my dear?"

She replied, "I'm glad you finally got here, Tom. I think that here in the privacy of the family, it can now be told. Phil and Susanne are engaged. Of course, it is unofficial and completely private so that nobody is to say anything about it as yet, but I do think that this group is entitled to know the good news right away."

Phil had blinked hard several times and shot a look at Susie from the bar where he had been mixing and serving the drinks. Susie was totally surprised. She collected herself and then said, looking at her mother, "Oh, Mummy, Phil and I wanted this to be a secret for the present. It was only decided at exactly 2:30 this morning, wasn't it, Blinky? Actually, Blinky tried once before but he was premature, so to speak, and I just wasn't ready. It takes a woman longer for some reason. However, this second time, Blinky took his time and slowly worked up his most persuasive argument. When I found how forceful he could be, I was fully satisfied that he would make me a good and loving husband. However, in the course of persuading me, Blinky got so enthusiastic that he woke Mother up so that she came down and shared our little celebration."

Susie had looked over at her father who had looked surprised. She then had said, "Dad, we tried to wake you, but you sleep so soundly, you know. Besides, it was to be completely private for the present. However, I'll tell you what we'll do. I'll get Phil to persuade me all over again tonight, and then we will wake you and you can be equal with Mother. What do you think of that idea, Mummy dear?" Her mother looked pained.

Everyone was talking all at once. Tom Secant had pounded Phil on the back, "That's great – just great! Susie, I'm so happy for you. I will break out some champagne. Boy, this is really an occasion."

Alfred added, "Congratulations, MacPherson my boy. It will be nice to have you as a member of the family. Susie, you know that you have our best wishes. Jane and I congratulate you, Sarah, and Tom. I think that you have a grand son-in-law in prospect. When is the wedding?"

Mrs. Secant said, "Well, it's only April so that I would suppose a wedding in the early part of September would be appropriate if St. James is available, especially since Phil has got to do some Navy service in the latter part of September, don't you, Phil?"

Chapter 3 -- Wilt Thou Have This Man?

Alfred said, "Grand. Let me know if I can be of any help with Father Piccard at St. James. Jane and I would like to give the wedding lunch, wouldn't we, Jane?"

Susie remembered that Cousin Jane had said nothing at all up until that time. Then she murmured in her deep tones, "Of course. The summer garden will be in full bloom and it should be lovely. How many will there be, Sarah?"

Susie's mother smiled and said, "Well, Jane, it's just happened, so we really haven't had a chance to think it over, but Susie is our only daughter so that we will want to have a really proper wedding, especially since she refused categorically to come out. Right, Tom?"

Tom smiled, "Of course. Let's do the thing in style. We are, of course, assuming that it's OK with you kids."

Susie laughed and said, "Don't mind Phil and me. We don't really count in this. Do it any way you want."

Susie's thoughts were interrupted as the limousine drew gently up to the front door of St. James and stopped.

In the narthex Susie's dress was straightened out by her mother, the lady from Nan Duskin and Rebe. Ollie came up with a large white florist box, which he set down on the ground and opened. He stood up ad handed Susie a large bunch of greenery, smiling and saying, "Here, Susie, is your bridal bouquet from Blinky."

Susie giggled, as did the whole bridal party. Rebe straightened Susie's wedding dress and kissed her lightly saying quietly, "Susiekins, don't you worry! I am sure the Lord will not allow Stewart to interfere with your wedding."

With that, her father smiled and proffered his left arm to her. As she walked up the aisle, she thought to herself, "Dad looks his very best today. Boy, is he in for one big surprise!"

As she reached the chancel, she stopped and then took a half step forward and whispered to Reverend Piccard who had opened his *Book of Common Prayer* and was about to start the service, "Just a moment, Father Piccard, before you begin."

Chapter Four

Who Giveth This Woman in Marriage?

As the grandfather clock at the far end of the hall struck four, Tom Secant came slowly downstairs and stood in front of the large Duncan Phyfe mirror in the polished brick hallway, waiting for Sarah. He looked at himself in his new cutaway in the antique mirror and also glanced at his gold Rolex wristwatch. Before coming down, he had seen from his dressing room window the hired Cadillac limousine waiting for Susie. Sarah had given him strict instructions that they were to leave the house in the Mercedes no later than quarter after four with Susie to follow them at twenty minutes after four. There was no sign of Susie who was upstairs being helped into her bridal gown by the lady from Nan Duskin and, of course, Rebe. He thought of getting a drink from the decanter on the sideboard in the dining room. However, earlier he had solemnly promised himself that come hell or high water he would have nothing to drink except champagne at least until the reception was all over. He resisted his strong urge for a drink.

Finally, after walking somewhat stiffly around the hall, Tom sat down on one of the Chippendale chairs. The chair was uncomfortable but the air conditioning felt good. He wanted to be there and ready when Sarah came down. He pulled out a cigarette and lit it with his gold Ronson lighter.

"Christ," he thought, "how time flies. Only yesterday, Sarah and I moved into this damned expensive house. It wasn't long after little Tommy died. We wanted to try to rub out the bad memories of our first house and Tommy's death and make a new start. Of course, buying another house never really makes any difference. We never should have bought it. It's far too big, not only in the number of rooms but in the size of that mortgage which has, over the years, gotten larger.

"However," he thought, "when we bought it, the stock market was still going well and selling securities was no strain. Now, the damned market is down and the problems that the back office can't seem to solve are nothing short of horrible."

He had never really even tried to understand the workings of the back office. It irritated him that Alfred and the other senior partners had not simply told those "goddamn clerks" to straighten the back office situation out once and for all so that he and the others could buy and sell securities without continual foul-ups. "Now," he thought bitterly, "because of those problems, the SEC had not only been critical of the number of 'fails' of the firm, but had reviewed the capital accounts of the partners and limited partners." Neither Sarah nor Susie knew that they were in fact limited partners in the firm since all their capital that was not held firmly in trust was irrevocably tied up in the firm and could not be withdrawn, at least until the firm was through its present shaky condition. " God," he thought, "Nixon and the crowd from New York have sure screwed things up with their program to 'dampen the fire' or whatever the hell they call it."

Tom mentally ran over his own personal financial condition. The next mortgage payment would not be due until November 15, but his third quarterly federal tax return was not yet paid – that was $8,000. Mr. Finnegan of the IRS would undoubtedly be calling him the coming week or certainly by the first of October. Mr. Finnegan would remind him pleasantly that the payment was overdue. They would then go through the little charade that they had been through so often before. Tom would pretend to be surprised and suggest that because of the pressure of business, he must have overlooked taking care of that detail. Perhaps he could suggest that his tax picture was being reviewed by his CPA and a revised estimate was going to be filed. Maybe the wedding could be the excuse this time. However,

Chapter 4 -- Who Giveth This Woman in Marriage?

both he and Mr. Finnegan would know that the phone call was just a first discreet reminder to Tom not to allow his federal income tax to slide again.

Then there was his personal bank note of $239,000. He would be getting a phone call from Mr. Adams, the loan officer at the Girard Bank. Perhaps Mr. Adams would write him this time. Tom knew that he could get the note extended for another six months though there would be the usual grumbling by the bank about the inadequacy of the collateral.

Next there was that stack of bills: some were in the third drawer of his desk at the office and some were in the top drawer of the desk in the library. Some were unopened. A few were beginning to get some age on them but others, fortunately, were fairly current. These bills, he judged, would amount to better than $5,000, no, probably closer to $6,000 or even $7,500, including three back payments on his Mercedes. The total for the wedding would be in the neighborhood of $26,000 to $30,000 but it would be two months or more before he would have to think seriously about these bills since the reception was being held at the Club. The photographer had required a $500 payment in advance. The agent for the three-piece orchestra said stiffly that they were strictly on a cash basis so that Tom had had to come up with $500 in advance.

When he had finished his calculations, he found the situation no better but no worse than he anticipated. He was not overdrawn as yet this month, nor was Sarah so far he knew and she would be getting a trust fund check October 1st. "Thank God for Sarah's trust! Without it, I would have gone bankrupt years ago." Tom had lived so long in the shadow of debt that, to a certain extent, he had become almost immune to it. He said to himself somewhat grimly, "Well, I've been through worse financial straits before and I'm certainly not going to let a detail like that ruin Susie's wedding for me."

Tom looked around the formal brick hallway. Four old maps of parts of Chester and Delaware County, four Birch prints and the Duncan Phyfe mirror hung on the wall above the chair rail. The only furniture besides the simple drop-leaf table and the grandfather clock were the four Chippendale chairs. Sarah had always been adamant that nothing of any kind be left in the hallway. Hats, coats, boots and sports equipment all had to be put away. Today was exceptional: there were some late arriving wedding gifts stacked unopened in the hallway on the other side of the table. There was nothing on the table except the large pewter bowl. Tom, catching sight of it, leaned over and flicked the ash of his cigarette in it since there was nothing else handy. He knew this would make Sarah angry since the pewter bowl was ornamental and was never to be used for anything, especially an ashtray.

As a matter of fact, Tom thought, the whole house was pretty much like the hall. Everything was in perfect taste and in the appropriate place. The furniture and décor reflected Sarah's background and personality. The only exception aside from his little dressing room and bedroom was the "library" where Sarah had allowed him free rein. Actually, the library was really a TV room with a small bar, a leather couch, a couple of comfortable chairs and his desk. He thought with a certain amount of satisfaction that the library was the only warm room in the house. The other rooms were perfect maybe, but formal and cold – a kind of furniture reflection of Sarah herself. For all of the perfection of the other rooms, people by choice always congregated in his library.

As he continued to wait, his thoughts turned to Sarah. He thought of the time when he had first seen her. It had been at a crowded cocktail party somewhere on the Main Line following the Penn-Dartmouth lacrosse game in the spring of 1949. Though she was obviously quite young, Sarah looked strikingly handsome and rather above it all in the jostling crowd. He had played lacrosse for Dartmouth against Penn that day and was rather bored by the cocktail party since he neither smoked nor drank while in training for football or lacrosse.

Tom did not have a date and Sarah was obviously quite alone and not talking to anybody. He went over and struck up a conversation with her. He found right away that she was totally different from the girls that he had been used to. She, for her part, seemed to find something different in him from the young men she had known around Philadelphia. As a matter of fact, on their second date, while

Chapter 4 -- Who Giveth This Woman in Marriage?

he was driving her back to Sarah Lawrence in her car after the Yale-Dartmouth lacrosse game, Tom had remarked idly, "You know, Sarah, when I'm with you, I really feel like an Irish hick. I wish I were more sophisticated."

Sarah replied with some bitterness, "Well, I'm sick and tired of sophisticated Philadelphia types. Tom, I'm glad you aren't like that. I like you for your friendliness and gentleness, and for your uncomplicated and unbyzantine approach to people and life. You make friends with everyone you meet. I envy you for being able to do that so easily and genuinely. It instills trust in me for you. Don't ever lose your genuineness just to become more sophisticated."

Tom was puzzled by the amount of feeling that Sarah had put into her reply but he was intrigued by Sarah at that point and not too concerned about why she was interested in him. He wondered at the time if it was not a reaction to some recent situation, but he knew no one from Philadelphia who could fill him in on Sarah, so he let it go.

Tom replied lightly, "Don't trust me too far, Sarah, for I'm really after your lily white body, as you know."

The long and short of it was that she had either come to all of the Dartmouth lacrosse games that spring or he had come down to Philadelphia over the weekends to take her out. He could sense that she was getting her nerve up to sleep with him. He decided to take whatever time was necessary with her. Several times Sarah gave him reason to believe that she was ready, but just as he was sure that he was going to succeed, she would back off, no matter how firmly but gently he tried to persuade her.

Just as Tom was about to give up the chase, he suddenly succeeded when he least expected it. It happened one Saturday night in June when they were driving back from Far Hills, New Jersey. He had taken her to her cousin's wedding up in Far Hills. Alfred had married a rather plain, deep-voiced girl, Jane Liscomb. After the reception, as he was driving Sarah back, she suddenly said, "Tom, why don't we stop at that motel up ahead. I am dead tired and it's still a long way back to Philadelphia and even farther out to the Main Line?" Tom was surprised but delighted. They stopped at a motel outside

Dearly Beloved

New Hope. Sarah was very naïve and scared when they actually were in the motel room. Tom was very relaxed and took all the time necessary to calm her down. She said to him in a whisper as he very slowly undressed her with all the lights turned off, "Promise me that you'll be very gentle and promise me that you won't do anything unnatural to me. You know, Tom, I am still technically a virgin."

As Tom sat there in the hall, he wondered again for the twentieth time what Sarah had meant by that remark on that first evening so long ago.

Sarah had seemed happy that night and was deeply grateful to him the next day. Tom was touched. Though the night had been generally unsatisfactory for him, he found that he was fascinated with Sarah. He had never met anyone as delicate and as handsome as Sarah. He already had had plenty of encounters with all sorts of girls who were as experienced or more experienced than he was. As Tom thought back on it, he recognized that Sarah's decision to have an affair with him in June 1950 had stemmed only in part from her infatuation for him. It had in part been a belated act of rebellion and experiment by an otherwise obedient child against her domineering mother. He thought it was probably a reaction to something that had happened to her before he, Tom, had come along.

"Unfortunately," Tom thought, "the damned Korean War broke out just at that point. If it had not broken out, then undoubtedly Sarah and I would have drifted apart since neither one of us was the least bit interested in what the other one was doing or interested in. After twenty years she still does not care or understand about football, and she was always plainly bored with lacrosse. She never liked any of my friends at all except Charlie Jennings. "On the other hand," he said to himself, "I'm not much better. I still have no interest at all in art or music. It bores me stiff when Sarah drags me to an opening or to look at a bunch of junky sculpture."

Just then the swinging door at the end of the hall from the pantry opened and Inky wiggled through and bounded up to Tom. Though her tail was thrashing wildly, she was somewhat apprehensive, knowing that she was in territory that was strictly forbidden to her often muddy paws and exuberant personality. Tom stroked her

Chapter 4 -- Who Giveth This Woman in Marriage?

black head affectionately, "Well, Inky old girl, how did you get in here? Feel kind of left out of all the excitement, do you? If Sarah catches you in here, she'll raise hell with both you and me. Lie down, girl! No you can't put your head in my lap. I can't go to Susie's wedding with dog hairs all over my new wedding pants, can I? No, lie down. That's a good girl." The Lab lay at Tom's feet looking up fervently at him and wagging her tail with pleasure when he occasionally looked down at her or when he nudged her gently from time to time with his shoe.

Tom's thoughts reverted to his marriage to Sarah so many years ago. Since he was in the ROTC program, Tom had received orders about two weeks after the Korean War broke out. That night, he and Sarah had gone out for dinner alone. Sarah, for the first time since he'd known her, drank a martini and they had wine with dinner. After dinner, they were both feeling somewhat sentimental as they drove home and Tom had proposed to Sarah, never dreaming she would accept. To his intense surprise, she not only accepted with tearful joy but insisted that they drive up to Hanover the next Saturday and get married in the Dartmouth chapel. It all happened so quickly that Tom never really had time to think the matter through. He knew that Sarah was a handsome aristocratic girl with certain prospects of inherited wealth and came from one of the oldest Main Line families. These were all things that Tom aspired to. Suddenly, they were all his. But, on the other hand, his intuitive knowledge of people warned him that he was making a fatal mistake in rushing into a Protestant marriage with this proud, reserved girl.

Tom also sensed that Sarah knew it was wrong. Nevertheless, they had quickly gone through a wedding ceremony in the college chapel without telling either one of their families. Tom's father had died of cancer while Tom was still a child. His widowed mother had never forgiven her only son for marrying outside of the Catholic faith. She would not even talk to him or see him for six months. Thereafter, until her death, his mother had made it quite clear on their rare visits to Worcester that she had no use at all for Sarah. On the other hand, Mrs. Oakley had outwardly given her blessing to the marriage but Tom instinctively could sense from the outset that she was crushed by Sarah's marriage. Like his own father, Sarah's father had died some three or four years before their marriage.

"No," thought Tom, "it was a bloody mistake for either one of us to have gotten married. I should have married Catherine Duffy. I could have, too, at any time I wanted to, up until the time she married what's-his-name, the accountant. I wonder what my life would have been like if I had married her and returned to Worcester as I should have. I would probably be coach of one of the good Catholic high school teams there. I would have had some fine children with Catherine. All of her four are in college except, of course, for Mary Dee, the retarded one. I'd be in as good physical shape as I used to be. I wouldn't be drinking or smoking." He thought about this for a little while and then his thoughts turned again to Sarah. "Sarah, on the other hand," he thought, "should have married some Philadelphia type like Alfred Oliver or maybe even Alfred himself except that he is her cousin."

Alfred and his friends had been put out when Tom had married Sarah. Tom thought, "Sarah would have had an easier time if she had married some Philadelphia type who had come from the same surroundings that she had. No, it had been a mistake from the start for me to marry her just as it had been a mistake for her to marry me." While she was afraid of people and was, therefore, cold, he, Tom, did get along well with people. People were as necessary to him as food and drink. Tom knew that Sarah had always been envious of Tom's ability to make friends easily. Sarah resented the fact that he got along with her old friends quickly and easily. Tom even got along well with Sarah's mother.

Tom had supposed that he would be sent directly to Korea as a new second lieutenant, but it turned out that he had been retained at Ft. Bragg as the line coach for the football team. Sarah had stayed in Philadelphia after trying Ft. Bragg for about six weeks. When he was released from the Army, Tom and Sarah had come back together again. The first flush of their marriage had worn off and both of them recognized tacitly that they were in a marriage that was unsuitable. However, Sarah was unwilling to admit to herself, much less to her mother, that she had made an awful mistake. Tom, an opti-

Chapter 4 -- Who Giveth This Woman in Marriage?

mist, hoped that they could make a go of it. Almost as two strangers, therefore, they set about trying to make their marriage work. Tom had an offer as an assistant coach at Schuyler State College in Western New York, but Sarah immediately vetoed that idea. As a first concession, therefore, Tom decided temporarily to accept the position that was offered him as a stockbroker in the Oakley firm. For twenty years or so he had been trying to be a Philadelphia stockbroker. He knew that underneath it all he was still Thomas O'Malley Secant from Worcester (though he had long since dropped his middle name, O'Malley, at Sarah's suggestion or rather insistence).

As Tom continued to wait, he thought more about Sarah. Sarah had always been afraid of emotion, either in herself or in other people. She was afraid to give anything of herself. This made her brittle and afraid of other people and, in turn, people disliked her. But, Tom remembered that after the first glow of their marriage had worn off, even he had become somewhat afraid of Sarah for a while. He was surprised after he came back from his stint at Fort Bragg to find that her shell seemed to have gotten thicker and more impenetrable, at least to him. In addition, he found that Sarah really disliked sex. She had been naïve and excited before their marriage and even during their brief honeymoon, but, basically, she hated the whole business and made it clear to Tom on his return from the Army that she thought he was infantile and common to want to have sex as anything but a great exception. When she had conceived little Tommy, she immediately used that as a reason for terminating any sex at all. She took to sleeping in the guestroom. After Tommy was born, Tom looked forward eagerly to sleeping with Sarah again. However, Sarah firmly insisted that it was wrong to sleep together for at least three months after the birth of little Tommy. Then, she only allowed Tom to sleep with her at rare intervals. She was terribly cold and disagreeable before, during and afterwards. Once, she said to him afterwards, "God, how I hated that. It's so animal-like. You are usually so gentle and so kind. It brings out the worst in you, especially when you've been drinking."

Tom replied roughly, "Sarah, there's nothing wrong with sex. You used to enjoy it, or at least pretended you did anyway. Now, you're rejecting it, hating it and not participating. Worse, you're trying to make me feel bad because I like it. What's the matter with you, Sarah, anyway?" She had not replied but had turned over and said nothing more.

Tom thought of the last time that he had slept with Sarah. It had been almost two years after the birth of Tommy. They had been to a dinner party where Tom had had too much to drink. When they got home, Sarah had gone into the guestroom and gone to bed. Tom, after lying awake thinking for some time, talked himself into believing that Sarah might really enjoy it if he were to get rough. He had known some girls who loved being slapped around. He kept repeating to himself as he got up, "Treat a lady like a whore and a whore like a lady." He then went into the guestroom and had crawled quietly into the single bed next to Sarah, who was already asleep, determined to try a gentle approach first. He called to her gently, saying, "Come on, Sary." This was a pet name that he had called her during their courting days. She woke up. A look of loathing, disdain and horror crossed her face. "What are you doing? Get out of here!"

"Come on, Sary, relax and enjoy it. You used to, you know," he cajoled gently, reaching out to caress her.

"Keep your drunken hands off me," she snapped, recoiling from him as though he were a rattlesnake. Suddenly Tom was swept with anger: the liquor, his desire and the months of frustration produced a flash flood of liquid red rage that swept over the banks of his emotional self-control. He grabbed her by the wrists and jerked her upright, "Here you, by the living Christ, I'll soon teach you to have a little respect for your husband, you cold-ass bitch."

He had been pleased to see that she was really terrified. She had never seen him really angry before. Though he knew as he did it that it was a fatal mistake, he ripped her nightgown from top to bottom with one movement and then threw her back down on the bed and said roughly to her, "One peep out of you and I'll slap that smug puss of yours so hard your teeth will rattle for a week." He had then forced Sarah to give in to him but had hated himself for it. As he sat on the edge of the bed smoking and pulling his pajamas back on, she lay on her stomach crying. She hadn't said anything but had then

Chapter 4 -- Who Giveth This Woman in Marriage?

gotten up, put on her bathrobe and gone into the bathroom. Tom could hear her run a bath though it as 3:00 in the morning. He went slowly back into their bedroom. That had been the last time he had ever slept with Sarah.

As Tom continued to wait for Sarah to come downstairs, his thoughts turned to Charlie Jennings. Charlie had been his assigned roommate during his first year at Dartmouth. Charlie had arrived at Dartmouth freshman year on a scholarship, not knowing a soul and had been assigned to room with Tom. Tom was receiving financial aid because of his ability at sports. Though they were totally different, they hit it off immediately. They had remained fast friends throughout their four years at Dartmouth.

At Dartmouth Tom had lived, eaten and drunk the athletic program, especially football and lacrosse. Charlie Jennings' widowed father was a career foreign service officer who had served all over the world. Charlie could speak a touch of several foreign languages. His mother had been a noted Czech concert pianist. Though she had died when Charlie and his sister were young, Charlie had inherited her musical talent. He dabbled in all sorts of things at Dartmouth, including music, drama and skiing, but principally he was interested in just having a good time. He and Tom had one thing in common: they both loved chasing girls and each was successful in his own fashion. They spent considerable time together at various girls' colleges. As a matter of fact, both of them had caught gonorrhea the same weekend from the same sweet little Colby girl, Doris Davis. Charlie and Tom, after they had been cured, each jokingly accused the other of having given Doris the disease. After college, Charlie had been sent when he completed flight training to Korea as a Marine Corps jet pilot.

About two years after he was released from the Army and trying to settle into the routine of being a Philadelphia stockbroker, Tom had gotten a call out of the blue one Wednesday from Charlie in New York. Charlie had recently been separated from the Marine Corps. He was in New York and wanted to come down for the weekend to see Tom and to meet Sarah. Sarah had long since made it clear that she was not charmed with Tom's athletic friends. Indeed, Tom had not had many of them to the house simply because Sarah was so pointedly cold to them (and their wives) when they did come to relive with Tom the great days of college football or lacrosse victories or defeats. It was a world which bored Sarah and she took no pains to disguise it. However, Tom was insistent about having Charlie for the weekend though Sarah had said icily, "I want it perfectly clear that my house is not the Dartmouth locker room or reunions headquarters!"

 As Charlie got off the train, he slapped Tom on the back and said, "Glad to see you, Thomas old boy. My Lord, you're bigger and somewhat stouter than our days at Dartmouth. Let me get a good look at you. My, you always could wear the clothes, but you used to dress on the flashy side. Take a look at you now – a camel's hair polo coat, a J. Press sport coat, regimental tie, Brooks Brothers pumpkin-colored hat and Frank Brothers shoes with tassels! Say, somebody has taken you in hand and given you some real class, Thomas. I heard from some of the crew laboring on Wall Street that you had married a handsome Philadelphia heiress. I guess she's the one who's sharpened you up in the haberdashery department. As I remember, Thomas, waitresses used to be plenty good enough for you and also for me for that matter. Remember the time in Winsocki with those two girls that we picked up thinking they were certainly French Canadians. We tried out my French on them only to find out that yours was Polish. Mine was a Dago who couldn't understand a word of my fine Milanese Italian. Still, it didn't make any difference that night, did it old buddy? Those were the days and also the nights, eh?"

 Sarah's dinner party that night, Tom remembered, had been a big success. Besides Alfred and his new wife, Jane, they had asked Dol Delps, Sarah's best friend, as a date for Charlie. Tom could still see Dol as she looked that night when she drove herself over to the house: fresh, radiant, shy, nervous and sort of dumb. Dol, having come out in Philadelphia, could handle the local Philadelphia boys without any real difficulty but she had never run into anybody quite like Charlie. Charlie could really charm the ladies and loved doing so. That night was no exception. Besides telling war stories about Korea, he regaled them with stories about his schooling in Milan and places that he had been with his father during his father's tours of duty in

Chapter 4 -- Who Giveth This Woman in Marriage?

Singapore, the Philippines and elsewhere. In the course of the evening, it came out that Charlie's mother had been a concert pianist, that he knew good music and played the cello. This endeared him to the three ladies, all of whom knew and loved classical music. Dol was clearly mesmerized but so were Sarah and Jane. The only person who was not fascinated was Alfred: his nose was out of joint because of the girls' obvious fascination with Charlie.

How good things had seemed that year: too good to last. Charlie and Dol hit it off. Weekend after weekend Charlie was a guest at the Secant house. On weekends the six of them – that is, the Secants, Alfred and Jane Oliver, and Dol and Charlie – went out together. Things were not any better between Tom and Sarah but with the group around the problems between them seemed less acute. Tom liked Charlie and was endlessly amused by him. Charlie, in turn, was amused by Tom and used Tom as the butt for his wit and humor. Of course, Sarah and Dol were old friends. Jane Oliver, though she was very plain, was pleasant enough to the two other girls and intelligent enough so that she was good company to Charlie. Alfred remained a little grumpy.

Tom was not surprised when Dol eloped with Charlie. Dol's father, S. Stewart Delp, seemed to be angry, but that only lasted a week or so. Stewart was born seven months or so after they were married. Charlie told Tom after the elopement, "Thomas, I certainly am glad I took the trouble to call you that Wednesday afternoon from New York when I was bored with the prospect of spending that weekend alone in the city chasing another airline stewardess or a dumb model. I've wandered, following my father all of my life. Now that college and Korea are over and done, I want to settle down, get a regular job and become a part of the community and have scads of children. Dol and I are going to be happy because she and I want exactly the same things."

Dol and Charlie moved into the old gray three story gatehouse on the Dulaire place. Charlie set out to learn the insurance business. The securities business was good to Tom. Also, he was Club champion both in squash and tennis for the second straight year. He was getting along with Sarah just about as well as could be expected, but, of course, the real thing for him was his son. It seemed that nothing could mar the overall happy situation.

But Tom had had a nagging premonition that things were just too good to last. His premonition had been correct. After Dol and Charlie had been married two years, Dol had suffered a nervous breakdown or, rather, suffered another nervous breakdown. Sarah admitted to Tom that, in fact, Dol had had "spells" of depression even before she went away to Ethel Walker.

At the same time Tom started having money problems. His debts had quickly escalated to catastrophic proportions. Sarah could not seem to understand that all her money was in trust and there was no way she could make the Girard dole out more than the income. She lived on the same scale that her mother did and turned a deaf ear to Tom's weak protests that they were having money problems. As a matter of fact, Tom himself never really put his mind on attempting to limit their expenses even though their mounting debts hung over him like a dark cloud.

Tom shuddered as he recalled his only attempt to see if he could extricate himself from the financial quagmire by pulling off a smart financial move all on his own, just as he thought Alfred Oliver and some of his contemporaries in the Oakley firm were doing. It all looked so easy. The results had been horrendous: the SEC brought informal charges against Tom and two members of the New York house in connection with issuance of the stock of Venezuelan Ventures, Inc. The SEC pointed out that the stock should have been registered. The firm's attorneys, the Oakley name and influence and an informal understanding with the SEC that Tom would never do more than buy and sell stock extricated Tom from potential criminal charges. It had been smoothed over at the firm with the explanation that Tom had perhaps been naïve but innocent of actual wrongdoing. Alfred, however, had told Tom privately, "Look, we think that you knew or damn well should have known that that stock should have been registered. Furthermore, if the Venezuelan Venture was going to work, it was a firm opportunity rather than an opportunity for Tom Secant to make a private killing. One more caper like that and even your status as Sarah's husband won't save you from getting

Chapter 4 -- Who Giveth This Woman in Marriage?

canned from this firm. Is that clear?" Alfred had added maliciously as he was leaving, "Incidentally, you might be a little more discreet in your extramarital affairs. Please do not date the firm's secretaries from now on."

Tom's thoughts turned to a fateful night in June. Dol had again been admitted to the Philadelphia Institute about three weeks before. Tom and Sarah had taken Charlie with them to a dance at the Club, leaving Della, the cleaning woman, to sit with Tommy. It was not the first time that they had taken Charlie with them, nor was it the first time that Tom had gotten tight. Charlie drove them all back to the Secants'. Sarah had paid the babysitter who had walked home. Tom had clumsily checked on little Tommy asleep in the nursery. Then they had all gone out in the garden for a nightcap. Tom felt sleepy and decided to go off to bed. He remembered starting on his way up the lawn toward the house but he had either passed out or fallen down near the yew hedge back of the sandbox. Just how long he had been lying there he did not know but, when he woke up, it was still dark and he could hear a man and a woman arguing nearby. It turned out to be Sarah and Charlie. The first words that he heard distinctly when he realized who it was came from Charlie, "OK, Sarah, have it your way. Let's be honest. Frankly, I think that this is going to be a new experience for you but, if that's the way you want it, let's do it that way."

There was a pause and Sarah said something in a low voice which Tom didn't catch. Then Charlie said, "No, Sarah, for the last time, I'm not going to marry you. I never said I would and I never intended to and in fact I'm not going to. Sure we've slept together a couple of times over the last three months. However, the fact that we've gone to bed together doesn't necessarily mean that we've got to get married. Christ, I would be like Solomon if I had married every girl that I ever went to bed with. Don't interrupt. You said that we're going to be honest, so I'm laying it on the line for you, just as honestly as I can.

"Actually, you and I could never make a go of it, even if we did decide to chuck everything and get married. You're Philadelphia, pure and unadulterated, and I'm not and never will be. It was a mistake for me to try to settle here. I know the reasons. I had been wandering all my life with Dad. After Korea I just wanted a place to settle down. I envied those who came from somewhere, who had roots and whose children knew where home was and where Thanksgiving dinner would be held year after year and generation after generation. That's something that I never had. I'm not complaining about it in part because I had other things that those who have Thanksgiving dinner in the same place year after year will never have. There are thistles in every pasture and this one is no exception.

"I never should have married Dol. She is more than a very pretty girl. She's a really nice person and really nice people are hard to find. I guess Dol was part of the dream that I had. Why was it a very careful secret that Dol had longstanding psychological problems that antedate even Dol herself? Nobody ever told me about Dol's Aunt Caroline or where she's been off and on for thirty years or about Dol's previous depressions. I'm not complaining about this, but it does complicate the situation.

"In addition, even if I were prepared to dump Dol, who needs all the help that I can give her, and my little son, Stewart, who has crossed eyes, there is Tom. Tom, quite apart from the fact that he's your husband, is a hell of a good friend of mine. Tom is a thoroughly nice guy though you don't seem to realize it and probably never will. I'm sure that Tom has no inkling that you and I have had an affair though, God knows, he and I have chased and caught skirts together for years.

"OK, let's set all the other people to one side, including Dol, your mother, little Tommy and little Stewart, and say that, like the Duke of Windsor, we're going to chuck all for love. What a holocaust that would be! Where would we live and what would we do, just for openers?"

At this point, Sarah interrupted and said, "Charlie, all of this may well be true but I know this area and everything is accepted given time."

Charlie retorted, "Well, maybe this area can accept anything, but I can't and, furthermore, I won't."

Charlie continued, "I'll also be frank with you and give you a

Chapter 4 -- Who Giveth This Woman in Marriage?

good reason why the alluring prospect of divorce and marriage to you wouldn't work. I like sex – every part of it. I spend a good part of my waking and sleeping hours thinking about it and enjoying it. You hate sex. It's physical, it's sweaty, it's smelly, it's work – it's all of the things that you hate. Oh yes, you and I have had our little affair but, for you, the physical part has been disgusting and degrading. I might add for my money you aren't really much good at sex because you don't like it. I'm not blaming you for this. It's a matter of your training and strict Quaker upbringing."

Charlie went on, "Sarah, let's face it. You and I are sons of bitches, each in our own particular way. I'm a phony but that's because I like people too much and want to please and charm them, especially the ladies. You, on the other hand, have no heart and, I might add, no ass. Maybe your Quaker mother and Philadelphia father boiled it all out of you. What is left is nothing but a cold handsome statue, incapable of either giving or receiving human emotions, including sex. You say that you love me but you don't really know what love of any kind is and probably never will."

Sarah interrupted again and said, "Charlie, I agree with one thing – that you are a son of a bitch. Do you always destroy women after you've slept with them? Does this add to your sense of pleasure to completely disembowel a person as you've just done me? You're wrong, dead wrong, Charlie Jennings, about me. I do have feelings and I am sensitive to other people, no matter what you think. I'm fond of people: Dol, Alfred, Mother and Cousin Jane."

Charlie laughed. "Don't make me laugh! So far as Dol is concerned, you don't really like her. You tolerate her because she worships you. You felt no compunction about jumping into bed with me though you knew that this would likely put Dol in the Institute for good and all if she ever found out. So far as Oliver is concerned, don't make me laugh. He's a little Philadelphia stuffed shirt if there ever was one. You're not even fond of him. Furthermore, no one could arouse him for anything except business, especially as Jane keeps a pretty close eye on him."

Sarah said bitterly, "I guess none of us measures up in terms of sexual behavior to some of the European and Oriental numbers that you have run into in your career to date, but I'm sure that I don't care to compete with them. All I can say is that I'm sorry for Dol because of what you've done to her. I wish to hell that Tom had never brought you here. I curse you for having made so many people around here miserable!"

Tom could hear her walking angrily away on the graveled path. Charlie called after her, "There's no need to curse me, Sarah. I am miserable enough right now. May my curse follow you!"

Charlie left, and Tom heard his car start, then drive away. Tom lay back there in the damp grass. His first reaction was more surprise than anger with Sarah. She who hated sex had jumped down from her pedestal and had had an affair with Charlie even though Charlie seemed to have made it clear from the outset that he really didn't much like her. His second reaction was that this was a perfect opportunity to get back to real life after several years of trying to pretend that he was a Philadelphia gentleman. He could get back to coaching and to real people. Even as he lay there on his back looking up at the stars, he knew he wouldn't do that. There was little Tommy. He knew that if he divorced Sarah he would only see Tommy on alternate weekends and during the summer. He could not face such a grim prospect. In addition, inevitably, he thought about his financial problems. He knew that besides his regular debts, he had at that point temporarily "borrowed" against certain funds belonging to Sarah. These transactions would come to light immediately in any divorce or separation.

Tom had always imagined he would want to kill any man who dared to sleep with his wife. Now, however, that it had actually happened he felt no desire to kill Charlie. To his surprise, he found his attitude and feeling toward Charlie had not changed one way or the other. In addition, as he lay there, Tom found curiously enough that he felt terribly sorry for Sarah. Charlie had been brutally frank. Sarah would be devastated by what Charlie had told her. After mulling over what he had heard and analyzing his own reactions for about an hour, Tom got unsteadily to his feet, went into the house and went quietly to bed in his own room. He said nothing the following day or indeed at any time to indicate what he had overheard in the

Chapter 4 -- Who Giveth This Woman in Marriage?

garden. Instead, he watched Sarah to see what effect Charlie's talk had had on her. He knew that she was going through hell. She looked like a person who was sleepwalking. To the world Sarah was hyperactive and insisted on their going out to dinner parties and cocktail parties constantly. He didn't see how she could keep it up, knowing the strain she must be under.

One morning she told him that she was going to do some shopping in New York and that she would stay overnight at the Junior League rooms in the Waldorf Towers. Tom was sure that she was going to spend the night with Charlie. Though he told himself that he really didn't care, he called the Waldorf once during the day and then again at dinnertime and found that Sarah had not checked in and didn't even have a reservation. He was surprised and, in fact, relieved when Charlie himself came over that same night after dinner. Charlie was clearly depressed by Dol's continued mental illness. She was due to come home again in a week, but clearly she wasn't well. Tom spent the evening try to cheer Charlie up by recounting the "good old days" at Dartmouth and their escapades. He happened to mention Doris Davis and the time they both caught gonorrhea. Tom concluded by saying, "Hell, Charlie, like they say, it's no worse than a bad cold but we sure were two scared turkeys for a while, weren't we, eh Charlie?"

He had expected Charlie to laugh, thinking about how frightened they had been when they had caught gonorrhea. Charlie's face clouded over and he said quietly, "You know, Tom, clap may be a joke, but other venereal diseases are serious. I thought I had gotten clap again while on rest-and-recreation leave in Japan from Korea but it turned out to be something else – some Oriental crud that gummed up my plumbing. It took me a hell of a while to get over it. The Navy doctors said it could eventually make me sterile. It hasn't yet, but it scared the hell out of me for a while, I can tell you. Dol and I want lots more children when she's better." That was all Charlie had said, but it cast a pall over things. They had called it a night not long after.

Quite suddenly one Sunday afternoon about ten days later the telephone rang. Tom had been watching the Phillies on TV At first Tom could not make out who was on the telephone. All he could hear was incoherent weeping from an hysterical woman. Finally he figured out that it was Dol and he had said, "Dol, Dol, this is Tom. What in the world is the matter? You've got to listen to me, Dol. Tell me what's the matter, honey."

Dol had blurted out, "Tom, Charlie's been killed! He's dead!"

Tom had said, "Dead? What do you mean, Dol? That's impossible!"

Dol replied, "That's what I think but Willow Grove Naval Air Station called up and said that Charlie's jet trainer had collided with another plane and exploded. They said they were calling me because it was going to be on the radio and they wanted to get to me first. I didn't even know that he was flying. He had promised me he wouldn't." She dissolved into hysterics again.

Tom could still remember the look of horror and disbelief that crossed Sarah's face as he went into the little living room where she was doing her nails while listening to the Philharmonic. He told her what he had just heard. Sarah said, "Oh God, are you certain? There must be some mistake about it. Charlie had promised me, or rather Dol, that he wouldn't fly again."

Tom replied, "There's no mistake about it. Dol just called. The duty officer at Willow Grove called her. They would be absolutely certain before they called with news like that. Can you hang on? I've got to get over to Dol's. She was hysterical and God knows what she might do at this point."

Tom jumped into his car and raced over to the Jennings' gatehouse, half afraid of what he would find when he got there. Dol was weeping uncontrollably. Tom was able to get her into the car and drove her right to the Philadelphia Institute while Della agreed to stay and look after Stewart, who was taking a nap.

By the time he had gotten Dol readmitted to the Institute and had been to the Delps', it was past 9:00. Then he called his house but no one answered so he drove at breakneck speed back to his house. The downstairs phone was off the hook. Fearing the worst, he raced upstairs and into their bedroom. To his horror, he saw that there was an open box of sleeping pills on the bedside table beside

Chapter 4 -- Who Giveth This Woman in Marriage?

Sarah. He panicked and shook Sarah roughly awake. He was greatly relieved when she woke right up and wearily said, "Lord, Tom, why are you shaking me so? I'm so exhausted. That phone has been ringing ever since you left. I took it off the hook and went to bed about an hour ago."

Tom was relieved but said somewhat gruffly, "Well, I simply wanted you to know what you probably know already – that is, that Dol is OK physically but she's back in the Institute."

Sarah murmured, her eyes filling with tears, "Poor Dol, wouldn't you know that she would be the one who would take the brunt of all of this."

Tom had replied, "Poor Dol? Yeah, and what about poor Charlie?"

Sarah said, "Yes, what about poor Charlie? Well, he's out of it."

Charlie's funeral, Tom had remembered, was the worst that he had ever attended up until that time. Charlie's sister had come from St. Louis, but she was the only member of the Jennings family who could get to the funeral. Charlie's father was an invalid in his retirement apartment in Montreaux, Switzerland. Dol's family, the Delps, had turned out in numbers, but Dol herself was far too emotionally upset to attend. He, Tom, Alfred, Jane and Sarah, who was as white as a sheet, plus Charlie's sister were the only ones at the graveside on that rainy July morning as the Marine bugler sounded taps and the flag from the coffin was handed by the young Marine Captain to his sister as Charlie's coffin was lowered into the new grave in the Delps' plot at St. James.

About a week later, Tom was going over the stack of bills Sarah had left on his desk for payment. Among the bills was a note from Charlie. Tom would have recognized the handwriting anywhere:

> Sarah,
> You are very foolish to write. I am writing back in the hope that you will see the light on this whole situation. I did not mean to be unkind to you, but you have got to be reasonable. In the first place, we both know that

Dearly Beloved

we are not in love and never have been. We have had an affair, each for our own different reasons. The fact that you think you are pregnant should not be used as a reason to go through a divorce and marriage which both of us know even now couldn't possibly work. Furthermore, I doubt that you are pregnant. If you are pregnant, why do you believe the child is mine rather than Tom's? It has been quite some time since Easter weekend. In any case, as I told you, my allegiance, such as it is, has now got to be to Dol and Stewart."

C.

About two weeks later Sarah said dully to Tom at dinner, "The doctor tells me I'm pregnant."

Tom was about to blurt out bitterly, "By whom, my dear?" but he was able to hold his tongue. Instead, he got up and went to the end of the table and kissed Sarah on the forehead. Great tears rolled down her cheeks. She said between her tears, "Don't leave me, Tom. God, I need you especially at this time. Lord knows I don't want this child, not at a time like this. I am going to ask Dr. Pierson whether he can certify me for an abortion. I just don't think I can take it."

Tom replied, "Sarah, you just have the blues at this point. You know how much we want other children, brothers and sisters for Tommy. Don't even think of getting an abortion."

Sarah had been miserable and unhappy throughout the pregnancy even though Tom, feeling genuinely sorry for her, had done everything possible to alleviate her misery. In a curious sense, they were closer than they ever were before or afterwards. Sarah said frequently that she hoped that she would miscarry. She did not miscarry though she had delivered Susie prematurely by about a month.

When Tom saw little Susie for the first time, he could hardly believe what he saw: she was so small and so undeveloped as she lay in the incubator. Sarah, who rejected the little girl almost completely, did not even go to see the tiny infant being cared for in the incubator

Chapter 4 -- Who Giveth This Woman in Marriage?

as she (Sarah) was leaving the hospital two days later. Tom, in the weeks that followed, was half afraid Sarah would simply abandon the tiny child in the hospital. However, when Susie was about five weeks old, he and Sarah had driven to the hospital and taken her home in the child's basket that they had used for Tommy. Sarah barely looked at the child except to point out that her eyes were crossed. Fortunately Tom had arranged to have Mrs. Grogan, who had taken care of little Tommy when he was first born, on hand. Mrs. Grogan was enchanted with the tiny little girl. Dr. Pierson assured Tom that Susie's eyes would uncross spontaneously, and indeed they did.

Tom thought back on those days when he and Mrs. Grogan had cared for Susie. He thought it was strange that he had so quickly become attached to this little baby, especially as it was not his child but Charlie's. But, of course, Susie did not replace little Tommy.

At that point Tom again toyed with the idea of leaving Sarah since the curious closeness they had had together during Sarah's miserable pregnancy had vanished. She was as cold and as distant as before. It was as if she had hated Tom all the more for his kindness and gentleness to her during her pregnancy. However, Tommy, their continuing debts, and Tom's inability to take decisive action, all combined to keep him from leaving Sarah. Tom doted on little Tommy and could hardly wait to get home from the office to play until suppertime with his little boy.

Then it happened – the death of little Tommy. As always, sadness overwhelmed Tom as he thought back on that time. Little Tommy had come down with measles, or was it German measles, one morning. The little boy had been feverish when Tom got home from the office that Friday afternoon with a Donald Duck toy to amuse him. However, even the Donald Duck did not rouse the little figure lying in the spindle bed in the nursery. He was covered with spots and had a temperature that made him as red as a tomato. Tom had stayed there in the nursery until Sarah had come in and said rather sharply, "Tom, it's time for little Tommy's supper. You'd better think about getting dressed. We're due at the Club in twenty minutes for cocktails. It's black tie, you know."

Tommy had said, "Don't go, Daddy, don't leave me, Daddy.

Stay with Tommy."

Tom had gone to Sarah and suggested, "Look, Sarah, why don't we forget about the Club tonight? I'd rather stay here with Tommy."

Sarah replied, "Nonsense, we accepted this invitation three weeks ago and we've got to go. Tommy feels miserable with the measles, but they are not serious. His temperature is only 101½ and will probably break tonight, according to Dr. Lowell. Tommy will be getting some St. Josephs aspirin after supper and that will make him feel more comfortable. Jenny will be babysitting since it's Mrs. Grogan's day off. Certainly a fifteen-year-old is capable of telephoning the Club if anything develops. Now, come along. Let's not be late, shall we? We can simply come home from the Club early right after dinner if that's what you want. OK?"

They had gone to the Club. After dinner he had gone into the men's bar for a drink with several friends and had stayed there. Though Sarah had sent him two messages from the bridge table suggesting they leave, Tom had not responded, but had simply stayed in the men's bar until it closed.

As Sarah was driving them home, she said sarcastically, "Well, you're a fine one. You're the one who didn't want to come because Tommy is sick, and yet I haven't been able to get you to come home until now."

When they got home at 1:15 A.M., they found Jenny fast asleep on the couch in front of the television, which was still on. She had gone to sleep at about 10:00 and had not checked on Tommy. Tom had galloped upstairs to the nursery: Tommy was clearly worse. They took his temperature: it had gone up to 104.

As they were calling Dr. Lowell, little Tommy went into convulsions. The rest had been pure hell. Dr. Lowell was out for the evening. His answering service said that there was no one taking his calls. They called an ambulance. While they were waiting for the ambulance, they and Jenny stood helplessly around the crib as the little figure went through convulsion after convulsion. As Tom bathed Tommy's little body, he could feel the strength ebbing out of the child. Tom, as he thought back, was still not sure whether the child

Chapter 4 -- Who Giveth This Woman in Marriage?

was actually dead as he carried him down the front stairs to the ambulance which had finally arrived, its red light flashing.

He and Sarah had followed the ambulance, its siren wailing, in their own car, leaving Jenny at the front door of the house weeping uncontrollably. During the ride to the hospital, neither he nor Sarah had dared say anything. On the one hand, Tom thought, "If I had only just insisted on not going to that stupid party at the Club, but Sarah insisted on this sort of thing." On the other hand, he knew that she was thinking that if only he had not gone to the men's bar with the guys, they would have come home and could have gotten Tommy to a doctor.

Once they got to the hospital, the little figure was carried into the emergency ward by a fat nurse of the emergency ward staff. The Friday night crowd in the waiting room of the emergency ward gawked at Tom and Sarah in their evening clothes. The duty doctor was summoned. He was a small young man with a strong Spanish accent. He bent over the little figure lying in his red pajamas with blue chickens on them under the strong light. The doctor immediately ordered oxygen and hypodermics. However, after what seemed an eternity, the Spanish-speaking doctor had dropped his stethoscope, stood up and said partly to the fat nurse and partly to Sarah and Tom, who were standing there, "No use anymore, the baby is dead."

Tom went completely to pieces and wept uncontrollably. The same doctor had given him a shot. Sarah had driven him home. In spite of the shot, Tom had wept all the way home, but neither of them had said anything. Tom secretly had a Mass said in Worcester a week later for his little son buried in the Oakley plot in the St. James graveyard.

Even before Tommy's funeral was over, Tom had come to what he thought was a firm decision that the time had come to leave Sarah. After all, he thought, what was left for him other than their joint debts. However, Tom, as always, temporized and put off telling Sarah of his decision. He hoped almost daily that miraculously the grim state of their finances would somehow change for the better and then he would tell Sarah of his decision. Of course, there was no basis for such hopes.

Days, weeks and finally months passed. In the meanwhile there was only little Susie upstairs in the nursery. She remained an ugly, scrawny little child with black hair that stood straight out from her head. But her eyes, which had been completely crossed when she had come home from the hospital had, as promised, come uncrossed.

Tom, as he sat in the downstairs hall waiting for Susie, this girl-woman, to come down the stairs in her wedding dress, wondered how it was possible that that little bundle of ugly flesh could turn out to be something so beautiful and that he loved beyond all reason, especially as he had known from the very start that she was not truly his own daughter, but Charlie's child. Still, as he thought back on it, he knew what had happened. All of the love which he had had for Tommy was searching for a place to come to rest. Susie was the vacuum which had attracted and soaked up his love.

From the first he and Mrs. Grogan had taken entire care of the little girl. Sarah had little to do with Susie, having retreated into her own well-ordered life in which there was little time for or interest in Susie. Then Mrs. Grogan left as Susie was about to be four. Tom had in effect tried to become both the nurse and babysitter for the child. He drove her to nursery school in the mornings on his way to the office and came home as soon as he decently could leave the office so as to be there when the little girl awoke from her nap. But he simply could not make it work.

Then a miracle happened. At a squash tournament one weekend on Long Island, he heard of a Mrs. Rebecca Haight, a native of Nevis. She was a forty-year-old nanny looking for a position. Tom interviewed her on Sunday morning after she had attended church. He hired her right then and there. In fact, to Sarah's great surprise and dismay, Tom had driven Rebe straight back to the house that very Sunday night. Tom overruled all Sarah's protests, agreeing that he himself would pay Rebe's wages, though Sarah paid the wages of the cook, the maid, the gardener and the handyman through her mother's office. This arrangement had worked out.

Indeed, as he sat there, his mind was flooded with a hundred happy memories of Susie's childhood – buying her clothes, haircuts together on Saturday mornings by Succhi, the little Lebanese barber,

Chapter 4 -- Who Giveth This Woman in Marriage?

who was blind in one eye, recording her growth on her birthdays on his clothes closet door, right back of the hooks on which his ties and belts were hung, expeditions to the Philadelphia Zoo, the Planetarium and, later, to the Flyers, the Phillies, the 76'ers and the Eagles.

However, the best part of the day for Tom in those golden years had been the early morning. Susie's room was right across the hall from his. Every morning when his alarm clock would go off, the little girl would be waiting and would come flying across the hall, throw open the door and leap into his big bed and snuggle with him for a minute or so. Then the two of them would lie there on their backs looking at the ceiling and talk things over. In the spring, summer and early fall, they would pull off their pajamas, put on their bathrobes and bathing suits and run down and take an early morning plunge in the pool. In the fall, when it got too cold to swim, Tom would put on his old Dartmouth sweat suit while Susie would proudly put on the smallest size sweat suit available. Together they would jog, huge father and tiny daughter, through the fall foliage. In the middle of the winter or when it was raining or snowing, they would do calisthenics in place of jogging.

Since Sarah slept late and the cook didn't arrive until 8:00, Rebe would cook Tom and Susie a huge breakfast. After Rebe dressed Susie, Tom regretfully would leave her off at school. When Tom had been hung over or was even still slightly under the weather from the night before, he paid doubly for his sins because Susie would draw away from him if his breath smelled even faintly of stale alcohol when she gave him a good morning kiss.

Rebe from the very first day was strict with Susie. She enforced good manners, cleanliness, honesty and respect from Susie. Rebe firmly insisted that Tom also enforce her high standards for Susie. But though Susie adhered to Rebe's exacting standards, there was always lurking beneath the surface a wild and rebellious streak that surfaced at times in forbidden or bad conduct for which Susie was immediately punished by Rebe. What was far worse for Susie was Rebe's disapproval. Even Sarah respected Rebe for what she exacted from Susie in the way of behavior, manners and cleanliness. Sarah also tolerated the fact that in time Rebe set the tone for the other help and, to some extent, ran the house.

Tom had been amazed and delighted when he found that Susie was precocious as a child athlete. In spite of her small size, she could do things easily and quickly which children years older were either incapable of doing or afraid of doing. Tom had become very proud of his little girl even at that early age.

His life had quickly come to center around Susie. Though she was bright in school if somewhat erratic, Tom really had never cared much about her academic performance. As Susie went into grade school, Tom could not wait to teach her the sports that he now loved so well but which he had never had an opportunity to play when he was a poor boy growing up in Worcester. Though she received squash and tennis lessons from the pro at the Club, still it was Tom himself who really taught her by practicing endlessly with her. The result was that she was the local champion from the very start. In addition Tom had always been seriously competitive as an athlete. He had instilled in Susie his own burning desire to win at games.

Tom and Sarah now led almost completely separate lives. They saw each other at dinner and at parties. Sarah grudgingly accepted Tom's close and almost exclusive relationship with Susie, his sports, his friends and even tacitly tolerated his girlfriends. All she required was that he not offend the proprieties and that her bills be paid fairly promptly. She, for her part, led a well-ordered existence, ostensibly running the house and garden, playing bridge, women's tennis, attending concerts, sitting on boards and seeing her mother regularly for lunch on Thursdays.

So far as Tom was concerned, his real life centered around Susie just as it had around Tommy. Sarah pretended to be mildly amused but, as years went by, Tom could sense that Sarah was secretly jealous that Susie was as devoted to Tom as Tom was to the child and that Rebe's strict standards had made Susie into a well-mannered tidy little girl.

Then one Thursday evening when Susie was fourteen, Sarah said almost casually at the dinner table to Tom after Susie had left with Rebe after saying good night and going upstairs to finish her homework, "Tom, it is time to consider boarding school for Susie.

Chapter 4 -- Who Giveth This Woman in Marriage?

Don't you agree?"

Tom was crushed and angrily replied, "Sarah, you can forget that idea, here and now!"

Sarah said, "Look here, Tom, you've had fourteen good years with Susie, but you're fooling yourself if you think she's anything other than a girl and that she can find real happiness in beating girls and, in fact, boys at sports. It's time Susie learned something other than how to collect silverware at clubs in the Philadelphia area."

Tom had replied with increased anger, "Well, Sarah, if you think Susie should embrace your outlook on life, then forget that also. Susie is alive and enjoying herself. She's competitive and good at sports. That's one hell of a lot better than going around and not feeling anything as some people in this house do. Also, Susie is a real nice polite girl with good manners and habits. No thanks to you! Susie owes her proper upbringing mostly to Rebe, but partly to me, if I do say so myself. I know you've never liked Rebe and are jealous of her, but you owe her a world of thanks for what she has done for our daughter."

Sarah replied, "I will not get into an argument with you, Tom. Now it's time to think of Susie. I would like to send her to Walker's. I went there. It's a good school and will take some of the edges off Susie. Besides, my mother will pay Susie's tuition at Walker's so it won't cost you a cent."

Tom replied sullenly, "I don't want any of the edges taken off Susie. Of course, this is all your mother's idea. Yeah, as a matter of fact, today is Thursday. Of course, you had lunch with your mother as usual. I'll bet a cookie she is really back of all this fancy boarding school idea. I am sure she would like to turn Susie into one of those delicate wax figures she sees at concerts and picture galleries."

Sarah replied, "Perhaps you don't want any of the edges taken off Susie but again you might think of Susie. People are beginning to laugh at her, saying that she's nothing but a tomboy. Think about it. Do you want Susie to grow up into some sort of an athletic freak or do you want to see her be successful at what she really is – that is, an attractive girl. You might also keep in mind that they do have sports at Walker's. Susie will have a chance to meet new people and do other sports. Think of Susie, Tom, rather than your selfish pleasure in keeping her at home."

Tom replied, "That's a lot of bullshit, and you know it! Nobody's laughing at Susie Secant. Besides, she's happy and doing well. Why do you want to shut her up in some fancy girls' school with a lot of other girls? It's unnatural. Susie will hate losing her freedom and being away from home."

Sarah had said nothing more, but she had sown a seed of doubt in Tom's mind. It made him uneasy to think that anyone was laughing at his Susie, especially if it was any of their friends whom Tom still secretly despised though he had gotten along reasonably well with all of them for so many years.

Not long afterwards, one morning as Tom was sitting at his desk at Oakley, Oliver & Tarrant idly glancing over the *Wall Street Journal* after finishing the sports pages of the *Philadelphia Inquirer* and the crossword and wondering what to do until lunch, Alfred casually came in, closed the door and sat down. Tom knew instinctively something was in the wind. Alfred was far too busy to drop by Tom's desk just to "shoot the breeze." Tom waited as they went through the amenities and pleasantries. Then it came.

Alfred said suavely, "By the way, Tom old boy, I know you've had a tough time with Sarah over the years. You and she have had real guts to stick things out so long. At one time you hinted that you might like to be free of Sarah. Personally, and this is only a guess on my part, but I think maybe Sarah would consider giving you an amicable divorce at this point if you wanted one. You might think it over for a while or try it on for size, as they say. You're right in your prime as it were, you know, and could remarry if you want. Just an idea, Tommy, but think about it."

Tom was surprised and scared. Though he still toyed from time to time with the idea of leaving Sarah when he was angry, he had long since abandoned any serious thought of leaving her and starting over. He suddenly realized that he had become quite content with things as they were. Most important was the fact that such a change would upset his relationship with Susie. Panic swept over him. Sarah was trying to take Susie away from him. He also realized with a

Chapter 4 -- Who Giveth This Woman in Marriage?

jolt that his comfortable well-paid position with Oakley, Oliver & Tarrant would end the very day a divorce from Sarah became final. Also, his financial disarray would all come out.

He looked squarely at Alfred and said, "Tell Sarah to forget any such idea. I might welcome it personally, God knows, but Susie is entitled to grow up without her life being wrecked by divorce just when she's getting to be a teenager. It's just too bad about Sarah and me, but we don't count and Susie does!" He paused and added, "Alfred, I would fight a divorce to the bitter end. And there are some bitter, bitter matters which neither you nor anybody else knows about but which would damn well come out if Sarah ever tries to divorce me! I'll bet you ten dollars to a cookie that Sarah does not want her freedom enough at this point to have it all come out, especially as it would kill her mother who still thinks Sarah can do and has done no wrong. Unless I miss my guess, I am sure Sarah just does not have the guts to go through a contested divorce, including a custody battle over Susie." Tom had become red in the face and he was breathing heavily.

Alfred said easily, looking to make sure the door was closed, "Relax, Tom old boy. Don't get excited. No need to shout. I just seemed to remember that at one time you wanted to be shed of Sarah, but now I take it that's all changed."

"You are one hundred and ten percent correct, Alfred," Tom replied and then added, though it sounded as fake as it really was even as he said it, "Now, if you don't mind, Al, the market is about to open and I have telephoning to get done."

As Alfred left, Tom realized with a start that the little talk he had just had was directly related to Sarah's suggestion that Susie be sent to a boarding school. "Goddamn it, why does she always send Alfred around? I suppose the whole goddamned family is upset because Susie is not quite in the Oakley tradition. To hell with all of them!" But the seed of doubt which Sarah had planted about Susie grew. Was he thinking more of himself than of Susie's well-being?

Just how sensitive he really was about slights to Susie soon came to light quite unexpectedly ten days later at the semifinals of the Junior Single Tennis Championship at Cold Creek Country Club.

Tom had come to look on Cold Creek as a relatively second-rate club, but it ran a good "warm-up" junior tennis tournament, so Susie had been entered.

Tom had slipped away from the office. He was standing with some other people behind the back line screens watching Susie. She, as usual, was efficiently and savagely "creaming" some local girl who was both older and larger than Susie. At some point two Cold Creek members had come up behind him. Tom had not noticed them at the time. Then he heard one of the men say to the other with a slightly affected accent and manner that still annoyed Tom, even after all these years, "Who is that plump little black-haired girl on the far court? I haven't seen her around. She strokes the ball more like a boy than a girl."

Tom was ready to hear something flattering about Susie. Instead, the other man replied in the same Philadelphia accent, "Oh, I forget her name but it's something like Murphy or O'Toole. I'm told she's some little mick who does nothing but go from one club to another cleaning up on the amateurs …."

The rest of what he would have said was lost because Tom, blind with rage, knocked him to the ground with one blow of his huge left arm. For an instant Tom had been about to grab the man by the throat and throttle him but, fortunately, Tom came to his senses. He was afraid that he had killed the man, who was still unconscious and deathly pale.

To make a long story short, the matter had been hushed up by Alfred and smoothed over with apologies all the way around. The ultimate result, so far as Tom was concerned, was that he had had to subscribe to Sarah's wishes that Susie be sent to Ethel Walker's. He had gone to Susie and said, "Susie, your mother and I have talked it over and we are in agreement that you should go to Ethel Walker's. Rebe has been saying that her job with you is done and she wants to retire and go back to her home in Nevis. Rebe agrees with us that you should now go to a boarding school."

He was still ashamed because the part about Rebe was totally untrue. What Rebe had actually said was, "Mr. Secant, Susie is just becoming a teenager. She needs me and you to see her safely

Chapter 4 -- Who Giveth This Woman in Marriage?

through this period of her life. It's Mrs. Secant who is behind all this. It isn't right for Susie."

Tom had held up his hand in order to stop Susie from breaking in with a torrent of objections, which he saw coming. He continued, "Look at it this way, Honey. Here's a new ball game. You've done all there is to do around here. Walker's is a good girls' school. There will be a lot of new girls whom you can take on and beat in various sports."

But, it was, of course, Rebe who made Susie accept. Rebe had said, "Susiekins, Rebe is old and tired. I can't stand the cold and dampness up here any more. I need to go home to my house in Nevis. I have been asked to become a deacon in our church. Also, my daughters need me to help with my own grandchildren. Besides, there is nothing more that Rebe can do for her Susiekins. I'll promise to come back for Susiekins' wedding whenever that is. That will be a happy day for Rebe. Now don't you forget all I taught you and you'll be just fine."

That settled the matter. Actually, Rebe had said to Tom Secant, "You know I really don't want to leave Susie. She still needs my help, especially since Mrs. Secant has never done anything for her own daughter. Well, what must be, must be. Now, it's going to be all up to you. Don't let me down. Don't let Susie down! You hear?"

Tom had replied, "I won't, Rebe. I promise." But he had let Susie and Rebe down.

Susie had remained unconvinced and had gone sullenly off to Walker's that fall, her baggage consisting mostly of rackets and hockey sticks. The first four weeks Susie was terribly homesick. She called Tom almost nightly and pleaded with him to come and get her. Tom, fighting his own craving to have Susie near him, had to encourage her to stick it out. In the end she had come to accept Walker's. She had never openly admitted while she was there that she liked the school, but Tom knew that in the end she had been fond of the school, the girls, the teachers and, above all, the sports program.

However, when Susie was sixteen-and-a-half and a junior at Walker's, a change suddenly came over her. Tom had known that she would change from being a little girl into a woman but the change when it came was so dramatic and so sudden that it surprised him. At Christmastime she had been a child, excitedly recounting to Tom at the first dinner after she got home the final hockey match that fall and her part in the Walker victory. At Easter, when she got off the train for vacation, she was no longer at all the same. She had turned into a beautiful young woman.

Tom, as always, was in a high state of excitement as he went to meet her at 30th Street Station. To his surprise he saw that Susie was unconcernedly wearing the shortest miniskirt he had ever seen. She had let her black hair, which she had always kept short, grow long and she was wearing lipstick. She outwardly disregarded the glances that she was attracting, but Tom knew Susie well enough to know how much she was enjoying the attention she was generating. She told him on the way home that she had chucked lacrosse though she had been elected captain. Instead of the child whose cheeks had been flushed with excitement as she talked about sports, Tom found that Susie had become fascinated by boys and parties. Susie had shown no interest in working on her tennis with him during that vacation. Sarah was amused at Tom's obvious disappointment at the change that had dome over Susie.

Then about a year later, it happened. Tom, as he sat there, felt a rising current of anxiety and shame as he thought back on that awful five minutes in which he had heedlessly destroyed the mainspring of his own existence – that is, his relationship with Susie. Tom had never really been able to forget that Susie was not really his own flesh and blood but the daughter of Sarah and Charlie. He had never even hinted as much to anyone and had, of course, never mentioned what they both knew to Sarah, but it was always in the back of his mind. Even after Susie left for boarding school, she would still come across the hall during vacations and get into his bed when his alarm clock would go off. It was still Tom's favorite part of the day.

However, when Susie had come home for Easter vacation the following year, she had not come into his room in the mornings. Of course, she was going to parties and staying out late but, even so, Tom missed his special time with Susie. On that dreadful morning his alarm had gone off as usual and wakened him. He had been out

Chapter 4 -- Who Giveth This Woman in Marriage?

far too late the night before and had had too much to drink. He lay there and smoked a cigarette and thought about Susie across the hall. For some reason, he had gotten up and had gone across the hall to her room. He pushed open her door. She was asleep with her long black hair spread out on the pillow. He sat down on the edge of her bed and simply looked at her at first. He then bent over and kissed her on the forehead. She opened her eyes wide and said with surprise, "Why Daddy, what are you doing here?"

Tom had replied, "Well, Susie, I miss the mornings when you used to come over and snuggle and we used to talk about things. That's why I came into your room."

Susie laughed and said, "Daddy, I'm getting to be too big a girl to come over and snuggle in your bed." She looked at him and then said, "You know that, don't you?"

Tom hated to think back about what happened next and wished with all his heart that it had not happened or that he could somehow eradicate it. He had bent over and kissed Susie again, but this time he kissed her full on the mouth. He had smelled her hair and had put his hands under the covers. She had nothing on. He slid his hands along her firm body. Susie had said nothing and done nothing. She simply lay there motionless. Then, after a few moments, she grabbed his hands, pushed them roughly away, turned over and jumped out of the far side of the bed covering herself with the sheet. He was appalled at what he had done. She was very, very angry. He mumbled, "Sorry, Susie, I guess I kinda forgot myself for a moment there."

Susie stood there on the far side of the bed, glaring at him and then snarled, "You dirty son of a bitch. You're just some goddamned animal. What do you take me for? One of your cheap girlfriends, like Sally?" She snatched up her dressing gown from the foot of the bed and threw it around her as she ran into her bathroom, banging the door behind her as she went and locking it.

The episode had happened so quickly that Tom was dumbfounded. He also was surprised that Susie knew about Sally. He was deathly afraid that Susie would tell her mother. Most of all, he was sickened by what he knew he had done to the relationship between himself and his beloved Susie. His hands were shaking as he walked slowly back across the hall and into his own bedroom.

Susie did not tell her mother. However, from that moment on Susie had no use at all for him. She made no bones about showing her distaste for him not only to her mother but also to everybody else. Yet so far as Tom could tell, Susie never disclosed to anyone the reason for the sudden change in her relationship with him.

Tom had said to Susie as she was about to go out and get in her mother's car to go to 30th Street Station to go back to school after Easter vacation, "Susie, I need to talk to you. Please come with me to the library."

When Susie came into the library, Tom closed the door, turned around and said, "Now, Susie …." But Susie had interrupted, "I know just what you're going to say. Let me say it for you because I can say it faster and cleaner and get my reply out and over with. First, you're sorry. I'll bet you are. But that doesn't wipe out what you had in mind for me the other morning. Second, it won't ever happen again. You bet it won't because I won't ever get in a position to let it happen. Third, can't we just forget the whole thing. The answer to that one is no, no, no. Neither one of us will ever be able to forget it. Finally, I'll never forgive you. If you ever so much as touch me in any way, I swear to God I'll have you jailed, you dirty old son of a bitch! So far as I'm concerned, I'll never kiss you or touch you again as long as I live!" With that, she marched out of the library, banging the door behind her. She went right out to her mother's car.

After she had left, Tom sat alone in the library and cried. He reviewed the sorry course of his life since he had married Sarah, culminating now in a complete and apparently unhealable breach with Susie, the person around whom his life had centered. He had come to depend not only on his love for Susie but her love and admiration for him. All of this was forever gone. He admitted to himself for the first time that he was simply tolerated at Oakley, Oliver & Tarrant because he was Sarah's husband. He thought about his insoluble debt problems. In the past he had always taken comfort and refuge in athletics, but he was no longer champion of anything at the Club. Younger men beat him easily even when he got into shape, which was becoming more and more difficult.

Chapter 4 -- Who Giveth This Woman in Marriage?

Then, two months later, there was his prostate. Tom had never really known what it was except as an unpleasant detail of his yearly physical. One day out of the blue he was overcome by a severe attack of such excruciating pain that he was nauseated. Dr. Carton, the urologist to whom he was referred by Dr. Cates, his regular doctor, ran a series of tests. Dr. Cates then assured Tom it was not serious. "Just an early warning of old age," Dr. Carton had said to Tom, "You'll soon be right as rain again."

Tom insisted, "You're not kidding me, Doc, are you? It isn't cancer, is it? My father died of cancer of the colon, you know. An article in *Readers Digest* says cancer is hereditary."

Dr. Carton had replied, "No, sir, if it was cancerous, Mr. Secant, I probably would schedule you for major surgery tomorrow morning. It's not cancerous. It's just a slightly inflamed prostate that we are going to treat conservatively, at least for the present. Get this prescription filled promptly, take two pills as directed, and see me in a week."

In spite of Dr. Carton's assurance, Tom had been convinced about half the time that he was dying of inoperable cancer. He would wake up in the middle of the night or very early in the morning in a sweat. He would lie there for hours, awaiting apprehensively for the stabbing pain that he was certain signaled that he was being secretly devoured by forces within himself. About that time, Sally, his girlfriend of four years, moved to Oregon without even saying goodbye. Tom knew that Sally had been going out behind his back with a Merchant Marine officer from Oregon. But Tom never dreamed that she would up and leave without even so much as a thank you after all the fun they had had together and all of Tom's many kindnesses to her. He had even put up Sally's share of the money for the beauty parlor she and her girlfriend, Anita, had started. Of course, Tom's life with Sarah was a disaster and there was no prospect that it would get any better.

About a week later, Tom decided to end it all. As he sat there thinking about it, it seemed like such an easy solution, a complete answer to all of the problems that were crowding in on him. A feeling of peace and detachment such as he had not felt in years settled over him. "They'll be sorry, all of them, especially Susie. They'll realize when it's too late what a good guy Tom Secant really was."

Tears again came to his eyes in thinking about how sorry his family, his partners, his friends and acquaintances would be when he was gone. Though Tom had no reason for postponing his suicide now that he had decided on it, he decided to do it exactly one week later. Why he had decided to postpone it for a week he could not say, except that it seemed somehow inappropriate to do something as important, as tragic and as final on the spur of the moment.

He would always remember that "final" week. He found that he had heightened powers of observation: he saw all sorts of things and people with new clarity, in great detail and with new perspective. Though it had been a pleasant week, that had not deterred him, he remembered, from his basic decision, especially as a letter had come from Susie addressed, for the first time, only to Sarah. She never even mentioned or inquired about him. Also, on Thursday he had had such an intense pain while driving to the Club that it had made him gasp. It had been fully ten minutes before it had passed and he had been able to drive on.

On Sunday afternoon Sarah had gone out to make a fourth at bridge and had stayed on for Sunday night supper. Tom had been asked to join the bridge players for super but declined, saying he had work to do. He sat at his desk in the library for awhile, thinking that he should try to put the bills and other financial papers in some order. He started and then said to himself, "To hell with it! Let Alfred or the lawyers or CPA's figure it out!" He had then sat there and drew up and revised a note to Sarah:

> Sunday
> Dear Sarah,
> Susie was my last real interest in a life that has
> been one series of mistakes after another. Now
> Susie has indicated to me that she rejects me both
> as a father and as a friend. I also believe I have cancer.
>
> I know that you have had to put up with a great deal

Chapter 4 -- Who Giveth This Woman in Marriage?

in the way of my failings over the years. I hope that this release for both of us will work out for you.

Tom

P.S. Our financial affairs are in poor shape, as always, but I think that my insurance will cover most of our debts.

When Sarah returned home from bridge, she came into the library where he was sitting watching "Bonanza" while stroking Inky's silky head. Sarah had said, "Let me turn that awful western down. I can't hear myself think with all that gunfire and noise. I got a letter from Susie and she certainly is one changed girl. What do you think?" She smiled somewhat maliciously and said, "After all, you've been somewhat closer to Susie over the years than I have or at least you were until a couple of months ago."

Tom had looked up from the TV, which was still turned on though the sound was turned down. With a start, he realized that he had not been paying attention to what Sarah said. Though in a couple of hours he would be dead, he was far more interested in seeing what was happening on "Bonanza." He smiled at the incongruity of it and said to Sarah, still looking at TV, "Oh, I don't know. Kids all go through a stage."

Sarah said with annoyance, "Oh well, all you really ever cared about is how Susie does at sports. Goodnight. By the way, don't forget to put that dog of yours out before you come up. I don't want Inky sleeping in the upstairs hall again."

She turned on her heel and closed the door. Tom heard her go upstairs and then he could hear a bath running. He watched the end of "Bonanza." As he was about to turn off the TV, he sat there for a moment more. He became interested in the episode of "Mission Impossible." He watched it until the end, again wondering from time to time how he could possibly be interested in "Mission Impossible" when he had determined to end his life that very night.

When "Mission Impossible" was over, he quickly turned the TV off and remembered what Sarah had said about putting Inky out. After putting Inky out, he came back into the kitchen and turned to the question as to how he was going to commit suicide. He realized with a jolt that he had never thought about what means he would use. Actually, he had never gone beyond the fact that he was going to commit suicide.

He first thought about starting the engine of either the Mercedes or the station wagon in the garage. However, he realized that the sound of the engine running in the garage might well attract Sarah's attention. He then thought of taking a hose to hook up to the exhaust and driving to a secluded spot. He went out and bent down to look at the Mercedes' exhaust: the garden hose would never fit over the exhaust. He then turned to Sarah's station wagon but the exhaust on it was about the same size. He went from the garage back into the kitchen. Inky followed him in. He sat there and thought about the problem. He did not have a pistol. Besides, the thought of the horrible results of either using a pistol, if he had one, or one of his shotguns in his bathroom revolted him.

He remembered Sarah's sleeping pills and went quietly upstairs with Inky behind him. He got himself ready for bed, including taking a shower, putting on clean pajamas and brushing his teeth. He got into bed and lay there with Inky lying beside him reading *Sports Illustrated*, waiting for the light from under Sarah's door to go out. When it did, he waited another ten or fifteen minutes and then got up quietly and went out into the hall. He laid the note outside Sarah's door on his way to her bathroom. Then he went back and pushed the note under Sarah's door. Then he went on down the hall to her bathroom.

He opened the medicine cabinet. She kept her supply of sleeping pills in a pink prescription box. He found the pink box and took it back with him into his room, leaving Inky outside in the hall. He slowly counted the pills in the box: there were twenty-one. He first decided to take all of them, but then said, "Ten should do the trick." He got up and got a glass of water from his own bathroom and swallowed seven pills, one at a time, leaving three, for some rea-

Chapter 4 -- Who Giveth This Woman in Marriage?

son, next to the box that contained those that he wasn't going to take. He remembered thinking that it all seemed so simple and undramatic. He did not feel, after he swallowed the pills, that he had taken a deadly dose of anything. He looked at *Sports Illustrated* again. After a while, he finally began to get sleepy. The last thing that he remembered was wondering whether he should take up golf which he had always derided as an old man's game.

The next thing that he remembered had the awful quality of a bad dream. He was stumbling up and down the asphalt drive in his bare feet in the cold night air in front of the house. Sarah was on one side of him and Alfred was on the other. He could not remember just what he had said at first except that he had pleaded with them to let him sit down because he felt so tired. Alfred had said to him, "No, Tom, goddamn it! You can't sit down! You've got to keep on walking!"

Alfred leaned across him and said to Sarah, "Good, he's now awake. Quick, Sarah, go into the house and dissolve ten tablespoons of salt in a milk bottle of warm water. We've got to get him to vomit. I'll keep him walking in the meanwhile."

Sarah said, "But Alfred, we haven't got any milk bottles. Our milk comes in cardboard containers."

Alfred replied, "For Christ's sake, Sarah! Don't be so dumb! About a quart of water with a lot of salt in it will do. Precise measurement isn't necessary."

It had taken two quarts of salt water to make Tom vomit. In the meanwhile Alfred, like a martinet, kept marching Tom up and down. At one point after he had vomited for the third time, Tom said weakly to Sarah, "Please, Sarah, go call a priest. I'm going to die."

Alfred had broken in and said, "Nonsense, Tom! You're not going to die tonight! You'll die some time but not here tonight and not this way. Not at least if we can help it! Now, get up and keep walking!"

After what seemed an eternity of walking in the night, Alfred had turned to Sarah and said, 'Well, Sarah, I think we're over the hump. The Poison Information Center said that if we could wake him up and keep him moving and flush out whatever part of the

Phenobarbital has not gotten into his system, he would be OK with no after effects. We'll have to keep him on his feet or at least awake for the rest of the night but I think we're now OK. Why don't you put on some coffee?"

Alfred continued to march Tom up and down the driveway, having gotten Sarah to get him a raincoat. At one point Tom remembered Alfred saying to Sarah, "Thank God you discovered what Tom had done. How did you happen to discover what he had done?"

Sarah replied, "It was really an accident. I heard Tom go into my bathroom just as I was going to sleep. I couldn't imagine what he was doing there, but I didn't think anything about it. However, I couldn't sleep, so I turned on the light and went into the bathroom to get another sleeping pill. I could not find them, but I didn't put two and two together. I was about to turn out my light after getting back into bed when I saw the note. Again, I almost didn't pay any attention to it, but I heard Inky's tail thumping in the hall. I got up again to put her out. When I got back upstairs I read the note, which led me to believe that Tom had committed suicide."

Alfred broke in and said grimly, "Attempted suicide!"

Sarah said, "Thank God you weren't too far away. I panicked and couldn't think of anything to do. I never would have thought of the Poison Information Center until it was too late."

Finally, as the sun was about to come up, Sarah went upstairs. Tom and Alfred sat at the breakfast alcove drinking hot coffee. Tom no longer felt sleepy, just tired. Alfred pulled the note that Tom had written out of the pocket of his coat and handed it to Tom, saying, "Here, Tom, is your note. I suggest that you destroy it. Fortunately, only the three of us will ever know about what happened tonight. There wasn't time to call a doctor or an ambulance, but it turned out OK. This better be the last time you'll ever even think of something foolish like this. Hell, man, we all have debts! So far as Susie is concerned, don't let it get you down. You have been a wonderful father to Susie, if I do say so myself. If you really do love Susie, then don't humiliate her for life, as well as Sarah, by leaving them with the legacy of your suicide. Things have been tough for you, Tom, but I never thought I would see the day when you would

Chapter 4 -- Who Giveth This Woman in Marriage?

be a quitter. You're supposed to be the big competitive type. You mentioned earlier this morning that you wanted a priest because you thought you were going to die. If you still have some yearnings toward the Roman Catholic Church, keep in mind the doctrine of your church on suicide. You also mentioned cancer. What makes you think you've got cancer?"

Tom told Alfred about his two attacks, and concluded, "Hell, I don't believe Dr. Carton. They never tell you when you've got it. Besides, when I was a small kid, my father died a lingering death of colon cancer at Mass General. Everyone knows that cancer is hereditary."

Alfred laughed and slapped Tom on the back, "Relax, Tom. Your trouble is probably more your conscience than anything else. You've got trouble with your prostate, but who doesn't? Seriously, I've been to Carton for years for chronic prostatis. I can tell you he's not only a square shooter, but he is damned good at male plumbing repairs."

Tom said humbly, "You may be right. Thanks for everything. As always, you've bailed me out. I'm grateful. I wish I could find some way to repay you."

Alfred looked at him for a moment and then, after a pause, said, "Let's not end up on a sentimental note, shall we? Why don't you get a shower and put in an appearance at the shop later in the morning? I've got to be at One Wall Street in New York by 10:30 A.M." He looked at his watch, "I can just make it, if I catch the 8:42 Metroliner out of 30th Street. Say goodbye to Sarah for me. See you Friday night at dinner at Mrs. Oakley's. So long, Tom."

Tom thought back on the conversation with Alfred in the breakfast alcove that gloomy morning as dawn was about to break. It was, he thought, the only time that he ever really liked Alfred. Tom knew that he would never try suicide again. Alfred had been right about the prostate trouble: it had passed. Tom had hoped that the attempt at suicide would purge him of the awful load that he felt as a result of his fateful five minutes with Susie, but it hung over him like a dark cloud. In the past Tom had frequently gotten tight at parties at the Club or at Dartmouth reunions. However, he had always prided himself on the fact that, unlike many of his contemporaries, he was not a steady daily drinker. But from then on Tom found to his horror that he had begun to drink steadily. At times, he would stop completely and go two or three weeks without a single drink. He would exercise religiously and shake off two or three pounds. But in the end he would again have two martinis before lunch and the same at the men's bar at the Club in the late afternoon with another one at home before dinner. After dinner he would drink highballs as he watched TV until he went to bed. It was only when things were slightly blurred with alcohol that life was at all bearable.

One of the things that pained him most was that he blamed his break with Susie for what he saw happening to her. In place of the fiercely competitive athlete that he knew so well, to Tom's horror, he found that she not only smoked regular cigarettes one after another but made no secret of the fact that she smoked pot as well. Tom was terrified to say anything for fear that she would go on to something stronger than marijuana.

Tom thought of Stewart Jennings. He could feel his temper rising as he thought of Stewart. Tom had tried so hard after Charlie had died to become a kind of uncle or step-godfather to the boy. For some reason Tom had never succeeded in reaching Stewart. It was one of his few failures with people. Stewart always rejected Tom's efforts to make friends and had grown up into all the things that Tom hated: he was not athletic, he wore his hair shoulder length, he was at war with the established order of things run by the seniors of which Tom was now very much a part, he used drugs, he rode motorcycles and he was entirely unimpressed with Tom Secant and his generation.

In addition Tom, who never really cared for music except perhaps the songs on the Hit Parade, hated the music which young Jennings played. In the end Rebe had forbidden Stewart from ever coming to the Secant house or having anything to do with Susie, in fact overruling Sarah herself in the matter. Tom remembered that Rebe had repeatedly punished Stewart when he would lead Susie into trouble when they were children. Tom, as he thought about Stewart, wondered if Susie had not taken up with him two years ago as just

Chapter 4 -- Who Giveth This Woman in Marriage?

another way to show her defiance of Tom.

Tom wondered if the dreadful incident with Susie had not occurred whether he would have been able to open Susie's eyes to the fact that Stewart was a "nothing" character who surely was headed for serious trouble. Oddly enough Tom realized that he had been shocked when Susie said she was going to marry Stewart, not so much because he knew that she was Stewart's half-sister but simply because of his intense hatred of Stewart and all he stood for.

Tom once again thought how good a drink would taste. He felt the middle finger on his left hand twitching ever so slightly as he sat there. He tried to stop it but, as always, was unable to do so. But he was glad to see that the faint trembling was not visible. Finally, he thought, "Hell, just one won't hurt. In fact, it will help steady my nerves as I walk Susie up the aisle."

He got up and quickly went into the dining room with Inky at his heels. He took the square captain's decanter with the silver marker engraved with "Blended Whiskey" from the sideboard and looked for something to drink out of. Finding nothing, he glanced quickly over his shoulder to make sure Sarah had not come down and then swiftly took one of Sarah's precious Chinese export tea cups out of the lighted glass cupboard and filled it right to the top. He swallowed it in one gulp and carefully replaced the cup among its fellows and put the decanter back on the sideboard. He paused and almost took another.

He walked casually out of the dining room with Inky behind him. He went back to his chair, feeling better in one way for the burning liquor but worse for having given in again. He said to himself, "Hell, if Susie would only forgive me, I might be able to quit drinking and get back in shape."

When Tom was seated again, he pulled out another cigarette and lit it. His thoughts turned back to Stewart. Tom thought to himself, "Isn't it just like him to show up at the rehearsal and at Alfred and Jane's luncheon to which he wasn't asked." He thought about Stewart's riddle on incest and wondered if Susie had told Jennings about that awful morning three years ago. Then he thought, "That drunken toast of his really didn't make much sense. All it did was to upset people. By God, if he shows up at the wedding as he said he would and attempts any funny business, I'll kill that longhaired hippie bastard with my bare hands!"

Just then, he heard a blast of music as Susie's door opened and then he heard Sarah's sharp footsteps coming down the hall from Susie's room. Sarah came on down the stairs, briskly pulling on her elbow length white gloves and saying nervously, "Oh, there you are, Tom. All ready?"

Tom could see that Sarah was upset as she looked at herself briefly in the mirror. She turned and looked at him critically for a second. She ordered him to stand up. She pulled his vest down smartly and straightened his pocket handkerchief. She sniffed as she smelled alcohol and said sharply, "Tom, this is one day you might lay off whiskey for Susie's sake!" Sarah went on in a softer tone of voice, "You know you would still look quite handsome in this new cutaway, Tom, if you lost about fifty pounds. Here, you've got some cigarette ash on you." She took off one glove and brushed him off and was about to go out the door when she happened to see the two stumped out cigarette butts in the pewter bowl on the drop leaf table. She said to him with renewed anger, "Really, Tom, must you use that bowl for an ashtray especially today of all days when I'm trying to keep this house in some sort of shape. Damn it, Tom, even after all these years, you still treat my house as if it was a barroom!"

Tom replied, "Sorry, Sarah, I just couldn't find an ashtray while I was sitting here waiting for you. Where's Susie? I want to see her in her wedding dress coming down the stairs."

Sarah replied sternly, "Never mind, Tom. She's just finishing up and will be down in a minute. But you'll see her at the church. Come on, now, we really must leave so that we can get the car parked and be ready when Susie gets there."

Just then Sarah caught sight of Inky, who was lying back of the chair on which Tom had been sitting. Sarah said, "Inky!" The dog wagged her tail guiltily and cringed. Sarah exclaimed angrily, "That damned dog of yours! How did you get in here anyway, Inky? Tom, you know she's never, never allowed in this part of the house! She puts her muddy footprints everywhere and dog hairs all over and

Chapter 4 -- Who Giveth This Woman in Marriage?

she's always breaking things with her tail. Get her out of here, won't you?"

Tom let Inky out the front door saying, "Come on, Inky. Today's no different from any other day for you, old girl, is it?"

Sarah took one last look at herself and adjusted her feather hat. She looked at Tom in the mirror and said bitterly, "Well, let's go face the music, shall we? Stewart has already given us a prelude at lunch. I just know that Stewart will be there to mess things up this afternoon."

Tom said as they went out and got into the car, "How about Susie? What does she think? Joan and John Oliver took that drunken bum home after lunch for some reason."

Sarah replied nervously, "Susie, poor child, is scared and upset but who isn't on their wedding day, even without Stewart. She was sick at her stomach this morning. Goddamn it, why does Stewart have to try to ruin things at this point? Can't you do something for a change?"

Tom replied, "Just what can I do at this point? If Stewart does try anything, I'll smash him."

"That's great," Sarah said bitterly. "I can just see it now. The whole church service turned into an Irish free-for-all! Whatever happens, promise me you won't repeat the Cold Creek Club fiasco, will you?"

"OK, OK, you know best, as always," Tom replied testily as he started the Mercedes, "but just what do you want me to do?"

Tom and Sarah arrived at St. James at twenty minutes after four as Mrs. Donald Poiry, the social secretary, was trying to organize the six little children as well as the ushers and bridesmaids. John Oliver offered Mrs. Secant his arm and escorted her up the aisle while Tom stood waiting for the time when he would escort Susie. Tom was half proud and half fearful both of Susie herself and of Stewart Jennings. However, when the organist began Here Comes the Bride he gave his left arm to Susie and proudly escorted her up the aisle. He stopped before Father Piccard, waiting for him to begin the service with the words "Dearly Beloved."

Chapter Five

Or Forever Hold His Peace

Stewart Jennings suddenly opened his one good eye and glanced over his shoulder at the electric clock on the table in his room on the third floor of the Jennings' gatehouse on the Dulaire estate. "That's cookcoo," he thought dreamily. "That freaking clock is facing the wall." Then, he remembered. "Oh yes, that's right. Joan and John Oliver followed me here after that lunch at the Olivers'. That was a real gasser. I guess I was a little bit out of it after giving my toast. But I did manage to get home on my new Tatra bike. Let's see now. Joan helped get me upstairs, and I remember stretching out on the bed. Joanie said she was going to set the alarm. What the hell time is it now?"

He got up, went over and turned the clock around and said to himself, "Three-thirty. That's great! I can still relax for another fifteen minutes before the alarm goes off and I have to get shaved and dressed and prance off to Sister Susie's wedding to the Jolly Green Giant, only Susie ain't my sister after all." He turned the clock around and saw that, while the alarm was set for ten after four, the alarm wasn't pulled out. "Jesus Christ! That dumb Joanie doesn't even know how to set the alarm!" He snapped the alarm button out and set the clock back down again and lay back on the bed, relaxing.

He lay there and looked around the room. There were dirty clothes tossed all over and another pile of dirty clothes lay where he had tossed them in the fireplace. In one corner there was a two-foot stack of long-playing records with their covers all over the room. In another corner there was a pair of hiking boots and a backpack. His father's cello with several broken strings stood in another corner with a shirt hanging from one of the pegs. The top of the bureau was littered with change, pens, pencils and miscellaneous cards. Besides a tattered Czech flag there were posters all over the walls.

Stewart said to himself, "Thank God, Della is coming on Monday. Maybe she can clean this room up." He closed his eyes again and reached into the bedside table drawer and pulled out a small brown cigarette, stuck it between his lips and pulled out a blue kitchen match from a box on the bedside table. He lit the match on the plaster wall behind his head and flipped the match away after lighting his cigarette. He sucked hard on the little cigarette, inhaling deeply.

He said to himself, "Ah, nothing like a joint! But just what the hell is the real time?" He reached for the phone on the bedside table and could not find it. "Now, where the hell has the goddamn phone gone?" He lay there puffing on the marijuana cigarette, thinking, "Christ, I feel shitty. No matter how crappy I feel, I've got to go to Mighty Mouse's wedding. It wouldn't do to miss Susie's wedding, especially as I can dash in like the Seventh Cavalry to the rescue and break it all up. Boy, what a rip-off that would be. Think of it. Busting up a full-fledged society wedding at St. James Church!"

He smiled, rolling the attractive picture around in his head as he lay there. He thought, "As a matter of fact, the whole lot of them -- fat old Tom Secant, high and mighty Sarah Secant, Alfred Oakley Oliver, his nasty wife, Jane, and old Mrs. Oakley -- already had the pee scared out of them earlier in the day by my little toast at the wedding lunch."

He laughed out loud remembering their scared faces as he had stood with his glass in his hand on the sunlit lawn at the Olivers' house at lunch. "Take old Mrs. Oakley," he thought, "sitting in the shade of the big copper beach tree at the side of the lawn with two or three other Victorian relics. She was stiff as a ramrod in her white gloves and with her little white cane. She didn't move a muscle, but I'll bet her ass was twitching!" He thought back on his interview with Mrs. Oakley in April. "Christ, she is such a phony. And to think that I came away from her little tea convinced that I couldn't marry Susie. But God Almighty! Rather than being married to Susie I'd go back in

Chapter 5 -- Or Forever Hold His Peace

the Philadelphia Funny Farm for good and all."

Stewart thought again of Mrs. Oakley and said to himself, "That dried up old busybody probably thought that I'd been frightened off by her little tea time talk with me. It was so dramatic, especially when it was followed up by Dick Tracy of the Quaker City Detective Agency. Man, there was a guy with a sense of the dramatic! After long-distancing me, he comes here swaggering wearing a cloak and dagger raincoat and makes me sign in detail for the copies of the papers. True enough, the papers did show what Mrs. Oakley claimed – that is, that Tom Secant's blood type ruled him out as Susie's father and that my dear old dad could have been the father. However, Mrs. Oakley, with all of her detective work, jumped to a quick conclusion. It turns out she jumped to the wrong conclusion. She just didn't go to the end of the trail."

He took one last drag on the little brown cigarette, again inhaling deeply. He flipped the cigarette toward the fireplace. He missed. It hit a brick above the fireplace and bounced out and rolled over and came to rest on the floor. He got up and picked the cigarette butt up and put it out in an ashtray. He lay down again. He thought back on the events of the day. When he woke up that morning around 9:00, he felt lousy and had almost rolled over and gone back to sleep. However, he had wanted to make sure that his new Tatra motorcycle was still parked where he had left it the night before. As he got out of bed he had thought, "Jesus, I should have put it in the garage instead of just parking it outside! It'd be a bloody disaster if somebody pinched it, especially when its the only Czech competition bike in the area."

Stewart got up and went over to the window and looked out. There, three floors below, parked next to the garage was the big black-and-silver competition Tatra motorcycle, just where he had left it the night before. Just the sight of it glistening there made him want to ride it again in the daylight. Then he remembered that he had not gotten the Tatra registered or licensed. Instead, he had just taken the plates off his Honda and put them on the Tatra. "Well to hell with that. On that bike I could lose any old cop, including Corporal Tim Roberts."

Dearly Beloved

He was unsure where to go but decided to have a ride in the early morning before it got hot. He looked in the mirror and saw he needed a shave but said to himself, "To hell with doing it now!"

He dressed quickly. He gulped a cup of instant coffee in the kitchen and dashed out through the garage door. He put on his black helmet and pulled down his dark blue visor. The key was in the ignition where he had left it. The motorcycle started instantly with a satisfying roar. He came out around the gatehouse, through the woods and out onto the road. It was a beautiful day though it was already getting hot. However, as Stewart roared along at 60 and 70 miles an hour, the air felt cool. He got on the Schuylkill Expressway and went all the way into Philadelphia itself, weaving dexterously in and out of traffic. The Czech Tatra motorcycle was bigger and far more powerful than his Honda. Once or twice he came close to losing control momentarily.

When he got off the Schuylkill, he decided to stop in to see his mother. He made a slalom course in and out of the columns of the elevated until he got to the corner of 49th Street. He then made the familiar turn at the corner around the large gray masonry walls surrounding the grim buildings of the Philadelphia Institute. He parked his motorcycle in front of a parking meter and said "Hello" to his old friend Robert, one of the guards. Robert said, "Morning, Mr. Jennings. Say, that's a real nice looking bike. It's new, ain't it?"

Jennings replied, "Yep, Robert. Brand new. It's a Czech wheel. The only one in Philadelphia. The Czechs have been cleaning up at motorcrosses all over Europe with these Tatras. I intend to put her into competition. It's really not much good for riding on the road but it's one hell of a machine."

Robert said, "No need to put money in the meter on Saturday mornings if you were thinkin' about it. The place just ain't that crowded."

Stewart replied, "Screw putting money in the meter anytime, Robert, especially for a bike. Besides, Mother's trust fund supports this cruddy prison as it is. There's just no need for me to spend my money to support this dump by putting money in their lousy parking meters. See ya."

Chapter 5 -- Or Forever Hold His Peace

He walked in the front door of the institute, turned left and took the self-service elevator to the sixth floor, got off and went to the nursing station. The floor had the same familiar look and even the particular institution smell which he would never be able to forget. He was not certain whether he knew the nurse on duty, so he smiled and said, "Good morning, nurse. I'm Stewart Jennings and I'm here to see my mother, Mrs. Charles Jennings. I guess she's had breakfast and is back in her room. I'd like to see her."

The nurse flipped through the cards in the file on her desk and said, "Mrs. Jennings, let's see. 'No visitors without Dr. Rogian's permission.' I guess that wouldn't apply to her son. You're right, Mr. Jennings. The patents have finished breakfast and your mother's back in her room. She's had her morning medication. Of course, normally visiting hours are in the afternoon but I don't see any reason why you can't go in and see your mother now. You know where her room is? It's 649, third on the left."

Stewart recalled that he had been inwardly relieved: he had been half expecting a "hassle" about seeing his mother. He had just smiled and replied, "Yes, thank you, nurse. I know just where it is." He was tempted to tell the nurse that his mother had been in the same room for the last five-and-a-half years, so he was thoroughly familiar with the room and its location.

However, he said nothing more and walked down the hall and tapped on the door. His mother's gentle voice replied, "Come in." Then, seeing Stewart, she said with obvious surprise and pleasure, "Why, it's Stewart! How nice to have a visit from you early on this September morning. What a pleasant surprise. Come here in the light and let me get a good look at you. You do look a little tired, Son. Did you get enough sleep last night? Are you eating well? A proper diet is important, especially for someone your age, you know." She took another look and said gently, "You know, Son, you should get your hair trimmed a little bit. I don't mind your wearing it long, though I prefer the short hair that your father always had, but your hair does look a little bit unkempt. Also, it looks like you forgot to shave this morning."

Stewart replied somewhat testily, "Come on, Mother, lay off.

My hair's OK."

He looked around the room. It was just the same as it had always been. There was a mixture of institution furniture and some of his mother's own personal antique furniture. As always there was a smiling photograph of his father in flying clothes and a Marine overseas cap in a silver frame on her antique bureau. On the windowsill, there was a picture of Stewart himself, age ten, in shorts when he had been to a camp in Maine. Standing next to it was a picture of himself and his mother at a dude ranch in Montana. On the bureau there was a fading brown formal photograph of his mother at her coming out party.

Stewart went over to his mother and kissed her on the forehead and looked at her. Her face was pale behind her glasses, which she wore continually now. Her eyes were flat and watery. Her gray hair looked slightly unkempt and oily. She was wearing a nondescript gray dress and her favorite long sleeve brown sweater, which buttoned up the front. On her feet she had slightly soiled fluffy pink slippers. Stewart noticed that there was a book in her lap, but it was not open. So far as Stewart could see, there had been no change whatsoever in her since the last time he had seen her in the early summer. He said to her, "Well, how are you, Mother?"

She looked up at him and said with a slight sigh, "Oh, not too good but not much worse either. Dr. Rogian has given me some new medicine, and he seems to think that I'm making progress, but I doubt it."

Stewart said with exasperation, "Mother, you've got to tell Dr. Rogian to stop putting you on that junk. You've got to make a real effort; otherwise you'll never get out of here."

His mother shook her head indecisively, "Never mind about that, dear. Dr. Rogian knows what is best for me, and I do what he says. What brings you home from Boston? I would think you'd be back up there again. Let's see, it's the end of summer and college should be about ready to start again, unless they've changed that too."

"No," Stewart said. "College ended this year just as it always does in the middle of June. So I was out for the summer. I was

Chapter 5 -- Or Forever Hold His Peace

thinking of getting some sort of job in conservation or pollution control. But in the end I took my old bike out to get a look at what's left of America now that they've just about wrecked it. I went with a guy I know at BU who wanted to do a real live version of *Easy Rider*."

His mother looked up at him and said, "Why didn't you take up the piano seriously this summer? I'm sure that Mr. Esmre would have taken you on as a student again. He said you had real talent. Or maybe you could have spent the summer studying the cello again. Your father always hoped that you would be a really fine cello player. He never had the time."

Stewart replied wearily, "Mother, we've been over this subject a hundred times. I don't have the ability to play the classics and, besides, they don't interest me. So far as the cello is concerned, I haven't touched it in a year or so. Let's talk about something else, shall we? Please don't nag me again about piano or cello lessons."

Mrs. Jennings said, "All right, dear. If that's what you want. How is Della? Is she keeping the house clean and tidy?"

Stewart replied, "Ma, you know perfectly well that Della keeps the whole house spic and span. I don't like her in my room because she insists on putting things away. Then I can't find anything. So far as the rest of the house is concerned, I never use the lower two floors except for the kitchen and the breakfast room. I really don't know what Della does with herself three days a week."

Mrs. Jennings said, "Thank goodness for Della. I am glad that everything is still being kept up. I would hate to think the house is getting run down or dirty." She paused and said, "Let me see, isn't this the weekend of Susie Secant's wedding. I got an invitation but, of course, I'm not going. Still it was nice of Sarah and Tom to send me an invitation. Would you please be sure to thank them for me personally? I've answered the invitation, indicating that I won't be able to attend. Here, son, pull up that chair and sit down."

Stewart pulled up a chair and sat down. There was a long pause. He wondered what they could possibly talk about. This happened every time. After a while he said, "How are you, Mother? It's been a long time since I've been able to get in here to see you. Do you mind if I smoke, Mother?" Without waiting for her reply he pulled a

Camel from the pocket of his shirt and lit it with a blue kitchen match with his fingernail and dropped the match into the wastebasket.

Mrs. Jennings said to him, "Don't do that, Son! You'll start a fire. Put it in an ashtray if you must smoke."

Stewart leaned over and looked in the wastebasket and saw that the match had gone out. He said wearily, "OK, Mother, OK. The place isn't burning up."

Mrs. Jennings said, more to herself than to him, "My, I certainly am glad, my son, that you're not marrying Susie today. I haven't seen her for a while, so I really don't know what she's like now but, still, I'm glad you're not marrying her."

Stewart said, even though he knew that Dr. Rogian had repeatedly cautioned him not to talk to his mother about things that might upset her, "Well, there are quite a few people who are glad that I'm not marrying Susie but I bet I know the real reason that you wouldn't want me to marry Susie, Mother."

Mrs. Jennings looked slowly around at Stewart. After another pause she said gently, "Why, Son, do you think that I would not want you to marry Susie?"

Stewart paused and almost dropped the matter but finally said, "I suppose because of the rumors about Susie's parentage."

Mrs. Jennings said, "Well, my son, and just what are the rumors of Susie's parentage?"

Stewart said, somewhat irritably, "Oh, come off it, Mother! You know that it is said that Susie is my half-sister and that's the reason that I shouldn't marry her even if I wanted to."

Mrs. Jennings shook her head slowly, "Susie is not your half-sister. Although that might be a good reason for you not to marry Susie it's not the real reason. The last time I saw Susie she had become a complete tomboy. Though Rebe taught her her manners when she was a little girl, she now has absolutely no manners or taste. Unless she's suddenly changed quite a lot for the better, I wouldn't want to have my son marrying her."

Stewart said, "Quite apart from what Susie's like, I have it on pretty good authority that she is my half sister, Mother. Why is it that

Chapter 5 -- Or Forever Hold His Peace

you say with so much assurance that she's not my baby sister?" Stewart paused, knowing that it was wrong to go further into the matter. However, he decided to go on. "I take it that you do know Dad is supposed to have had an affair with Mrs. Secant, and Mr. and Mrs. Secant were pretty close to a divorce just about that time."

Mrs. Jennings looked at him steadily for a moment and then said with another sigh, "Of course, I found out that Sarah and your father had had an affair. Even at the time it was going on I suspected it. Though I didn't really want to know about it, I finally got up my courage and asked your father directly, though it nearly killed me. In the end he admitted that he had had an affair with Sarah. He swore to me by all that was holy that it was the only time he had violated our marriage vows. He also said that it was completely over and that it had been a purely physical thing – he never loved Sarah. In spite of what he said, it nearly killed me. I was desperately in love with your father and Sarah had been, in so many ways, like an older sister to me for years. I had looked up to her, admired her, copied her in every way and wanted to be like her and this happened. I didn't want to believe it, even when your father admitted it. The shock of learning about this brought me back to the institute."

His mother looked out the window, "Of course, Tom Secant never knew about it, poor dear, though he and Sarah weren't getting along very well. He was thinking of divorcing Sarah and starting life afresh. He told me so several times when he was in his cups."

Stewart said, "Well then, Mother, since you know that Mrs. Secant had an affair with Dad and that Tom Secant was thinking of divorcing Mrs. Secant, what makes you so flatly certain that Susie is not in fact my half sister?"

Mrs. Jennings turned around and smiled faintly. "What Sarah Secant did not know at the time when she came to me and told me that she was pregnant was that your father was completely sterile. After you were born, your father and I tried to have other children but we never succeeded, so your father and I were both medically examined. Your father explained to me that he had become sterile due to malaria, or something like that, that he had gotten while serving with the Marines during the Korean War. Apparently there was nothing that could be done about this. For some reason this embarrassed your father tremendously and he never wanted it discussed. I don't know exactly why. He felt, I think, that it sort of robbed him of his manhood. He explained that he had allowed Sarah to talk him into their short affair in part because he wondered whether he'd also lost some of his manhood. The long and short of it was that your father never could have been the father of Susie. That's why I know that she's not your half sister."

Stewart sat there for a moment thinking. Then he said, "OK, Mother, fair enough. But if Dad was sterile and couldn't have been Susie's father, neither was Tom Secant. The blood types are simply wrong." Stewart had said this, forgetting that his mother had not seen and knew nothing of the copies of the papers that he had received through Mrs. Oakley. He went on, "Who is Susie's father? Someone must have been."

Mrs. Jennings looked at him and said, "What real difference does it make now? It all happened more than twenty years ago. But, if you really want to know, about a month before your father's death, Sarah came to me and told me that she was pregnant by your father. She wanted me to give him up so that she could marry him. Of course, I knew that he didn't love Sarah and had no intention of divorcing me and marrying her. I also knew that he couldn't be the father of Sarah's child. I just laughed at her. Oh, how I laughed at her. I just couldn't stop laughing. Sarah got very angry and said, 'What are you laughing about, you fool?' For the first time in my life I stood up to Sarah. I told her in no uncertain terms that she was the fool for thinking that she was carrying my husband's child – that he was sterile and therefore he was not the father of her child."

Mrs. Jennings sat there for a moment, "I had never seen Sarah cry before, but she just broke down and cried and cried and cried. I felt terribly sorry for her and said, 'Sarah, why are you crying? You are far luckier than I am. You're going to have a child by your husband, a thing that will never happen for Charlie and me again.'

"That seemed to make things worse and Sarah cried even more bitterly and said, 'But it's not Tom's child. I hate him for what he is. He is nothing but an animal. He spends his time chasing and

Chapter 5 -- Or Forever Hold His Peace

catching hat check girls and waitresses, thinking that I don't know about it. I wouldn't sleep with him again if it was the last thing I did. But I'm at the end of my rope.'

"I felt so sorry for Sarah that I put my arm around her shoulder and said to her, 'So, it's Alfred's, isn't it?'

"Sarah said bitterly, 'Yes, it's Alfred's. You look surprised, Dol. You're no more surprised than I am. Tom once treated me like one of his tarts and Charlie killed me by telling me that I had no feelings at all and was incapable of either loving or being loved. Charlie left me with absolutely nothing, so I turned to Alfred again. I probably would have married Alfred except for one terrible evening the year I came out when he made me do horrible things to him that I'm still ashamed to remember. Actually, I guess I married Tom partly in revulsion for that awful night. In spite of what Alfred made me do, he and I became friends again and he always wanted to be forgiven. After what Charlie had said, I was so despondent and so desperate that I turned to Alfred. One night earlier this spring we tried to make believe that we were having fun. We went to the Hilltop Motel outside of West Chester. Lord, it was so grubby. We were both really so unhappy, trying desperately to pretend to each other that we were having fun as other people do. Neither one of us liked it. Alfred's marriage to Jane hadn't done anything to change his very peculiar ideas of sex. Oh God, Dol, it was just so awful. Sex is supposed to be so beautiful and so much fun but it's just ghastly and now, in spite of everything, this pregnancy. Christ, what am I going to do? I wish I could die.'"

Stewart sat there listening to his mother and then said quietly, "Alfred." His mother paid no attention but continued in a dreamy sort of way. "In a sense Sarah and I were reconciled briefly on that gray afternoon in the small living room at the gatehouse. We were both so miserably unhappy we cried all afternoon together. Not a month later your father's jet crashed and he was killed. I didn't even know that he had taken up flying again. He had promised me that he would never fly again. Everything in my world except for you, my son, had come unglued. I went completely to pieces. Thank God for this kindly place. If it hadn't been for the nurses and the doctors, I think I would have died at the time."

Stewart said dryly, "Well, why didn't everyone get to know the details of this cute situation?"

Mrs. Jennings shook her head slowly and said, "No, Son. As a matter of fact, I believe nobody knows except, of course, Sarah and Alfred and me and my doctor. Tom still thinks that he is Susie's father. Poor old Tom. Of course, Jane was always somewhat suspicious of Sarah since Sarah had been an old flame of Alfred's long before Jane married him, but I doubt that Jane has any idea about that night at the Hilltop."

Mrs. Jennings paused and then continued, "What difference does all this make? It's all such ancient history and a closed chapter, especially now. That's what Dr. Rogian tells me. The only person who is still trying to sort the pieces out is me. I don't understand yet why it all happened and why it all happened to me. Why to me? What had I done to deserve what happened? Why? Dr. Rogian keeps telling me that I should put all of it out of my mind and not think about it. Indeed, for a long time, I didn't think about what happened. I don't think about anything. I live from day to day in my quiet world here in the institute. But from time to time, it all comes back like a bad dream and makes me unhappy all over again. Why am I being punished? What did I do or what didn't I do? Susie's wedding seems to have reopened the whole thing."

Stewart and his mother sat there, neither one saying anything. He then looked at his mother and could see that her eyes were full of tears and that she was holding back sobs. She got up and went over to the bed and lay down with her face to the wall, murmuring over and over again between her sobs, "It's so unfair, it's all so unfair."

Stewart went over and sat on the edge of the bed and said, "Now, Mother, don't cry. It doesn't do any good. Besides, it happened so long ago. I think that Dr. Rogian is right when he says that you shouldn't think about these things. Come on, Mother, sit up and let's talk about other things. Who cares about Susie Secant or any of the Secants or Oakleys or Olivers for that matter? They don't matter to us now, do they, Mother? Come on now.

Chapter 5 -- Or Forever Hold His Peace

"Let's talk about the time that you and I went out to the Double B Ranch in Montana. Do you remember that, Mother? Do you remember the good time we had that summer riding together up in the mountains and fishing for trout?" He sat there for a quarter of an hour with his hand on her shoulder, patting her and talking about the West and the two weeks they had spent together out there so many summers ago. He made up details of long trail rides that had never taken place and described sunsets and mountain scenes from his imagination. He could tell that she was listening to what he said though she wasn't saying anything. The sobbing continued as he talked on about the West. Suddenly there came a firm knock at the door. Stewart said, 'Come in." The nurse from the nursing station stuck her head in the door and said, "Mr. Jennings, could I see you for a moment?"

Stewart replied, "Sure, nurse. Just a sec. Let me say goodbye to Mother." Then, turning to his mother, he said as he kissed the back of her head since she was still facing the wall, "Well, Mother, I think I've gotta be going. You take care of yourself and don't get excited. I'll be back again in a couple of weeks and maybe even sooner. You do what Dr. Rogian says and don't get worked up: maybe you can get him to begin to let you come out and be with me. How would you like that, Mother?"

She kept her face to the wall though she did shake her head vaguely. Stewart was sure that she would never venture forth from the institute again, even if she were given permission to do so by her doctors. He left the room quietly.

Outside in the hall the nurse said curtly to him, "Dr. Rogian is in the consulting room; he wants to see you. You should have told me that you were not supposed to see your mother without Dr. Rogian's permission. You got me in a lot of trouble."

Stewart said to her, "Sorry about that, nursie. Just where is Dr. Freud?"

The nurse pointed sullenly to a room at the end of the hall. Stewart walked down to the end of the hall and pushed the door open and walked in without knocking. Dr. Rogian was sitting there writing at the desk. He looked up over his glasses from his work.

Dearly Beloved

Stewart sat defiantly down in the chair facing the desk, pulled a Camel from his pocket and lit a blue match with his thumbnail. Dr. Rogian said quietly, "Stewart, it's nice to see you though I am disturbed that you have again come to see your mother without permission or advance warning and without having a staff member there. We've been through this before. You know that I feel that your visits to your mother can be upsetting to her and also can be upsetting to you. After one of your unscheduled visits she is upset for days and the old fantasies come back more strongly. If you would just talk about non-sensitive matters with her. I just happened to drop in this morning and the nurse told me…"

Stewart interrupted him and said, "Now, listen to me, Dr. Rogian. Don't push me too far. You and I both know that Mother is not committed here but is simply a voluntary patient. You think you've got a great thing going with Mother. You don't want to get her well and release her anymore than she, in her drugged state, wants to leave the security of this comfy little prison. But don't get too high and mighty with me about my visits to my mother or, by the living Christ, I will sic a certain young radical lawyer on you. He is just itching to bring an action against private mental institutions like yours to test the right of you doctors to keep a patient such as Mother over-medicated and charge them fancy fees. How would you and Mother's trustee, Alfred Oliver, like to have a big habeas corpus action splashed all over the *Bulletin*? Get off my back, Doctor, if you know what's good for you!"

Dr. Rogian simply sat there and listened to this while toying with a paperclip. He didn't seem to be upset by Stewart's threat. Stewart added, "You look skeptical, you self-satisfied old bastard. Be careful, one more snide remark out of you and we'll see who's bluffing about the lawsuit!"

Dr. Rogian sat there for a moment, looking at Stewart, and then he said gently, "You know, Stewart, the greatest mistake that you ever made was to interrupt your own course of treatment last year. You were doing well. All of us here had great hopes that you would in time be able to solve your own problems. Is there any possibility that I can persuade you to pick up where you left off? You know that

Chapter 5 -- Or Forever Hold His Peace

your mother's family is interested in having you do this and would be glad to defray the costs, without in any way cutting into your trust funds."

Stewart replied bitterly, "Motherfuck all the Delps. They've always been embarrassed by me, their Czech cousin. Sure, they would love to have you or one of your buddies get me in their grip again! There is no way, Doc, no way in hell that you or anyone like you is ever gonna get your tentacles on me again. You belfry mechanics are all alike – once you get a person in your grasp, they never get out of your grip again. What are you really after? Another fee? Maybe the fact of the matter is that Alfred Oliver is stalking me as he has Mother – oh, yes, I now know the incestuous little story of Sarah and her perverted cousin, Alfred, in the Hilltop Motel. I just heard it from Mother. I'm sure they would do anything to see that Mother rots in here forever. But as for my taking so-called therapy again, forget it. Remember also, Dr. Freud, if you rock the boat too hard about my seeing Mother when I want to, I'll tear this place apart. In the meanwhile, don't yank my chain again or you'll regret it. Is that clear?"

Dr. Rogian said patiently, "If that's your attitude, Stewart, I don't suppose there's anything that I can really do about it even if its for your own good. Let me repeat what Dr. Roberts told you. You must avoid drugs or pills of any kind. Drugs are dangerous for anybody but far more dangerous for anyone with a history like yours. Please promise me that you will avoid them?"

Stewart shot back, "Why don't you go to hell! Keep your nose out of my business will you? A fat lot you know about drugs! I'll bet you've never even tried smoking or taking a pill!"

Dr. Rogian replied evenly, "You're right. I haven't tried either one or anything else, but all you have to do is take a look on the eighth floor if you want to see the results of drugs even without a predisposition toward emotional problems. This isn't getting us anywhere. When and if you're ready to face up to things, call me or Dr. Roberts.

"In the meanwhile, I think that you would at least consider your mother's own best interests and lay off disturbing visits with her. Your mother has very vivid fantasies about what happened around the time of your father's death. I take it she has been talking to you about what she thinks happened at that time. Your mother is going to be fairly agitated for some time to come. This is not good for her. Why reopen matters which disturb her so much?"

Stewart replied, "Who are you kidding, Doc? Mother wasn't fantasizing about the Hilltop Motel. It really happened that way."

Dr. Rogian said, "So far as your mother is concerned, it's real for her whether it happened or not. The point is not whether it did happen, but the fact that your mother is terribly disturbed by the old events."

Stewart replied, "This is where I came in. I'll be seeing you, Doc. In the meanwhile, I think I'll check later today at Susie's wedding with some of the principals to see whether what you consider to be Mother's delusions and fantasies did in fact happen. It should be very interesting to see Mr. Oliver and Mrs. Secant's reactions to the mention of the Hilltop Motel. I'll be seeing you, Doc."

Stewart was pleased with his visit. He could see that Dr. Rogian was perturbed. As Stewart walked out the front door, he looked back at the huge gray building. As always he was depressed by the building itself. He thought back on his own uncompleted and seemingly never-ending course of psychotherapy and of the two weeks that he had spent as an in patient in the institute eighteen months ago. The sight of his mother whimpering with her face to the wall, afraid and unwilling to come out, frightened him. As he got to his Tatra, he saw Robert and said to him, "Just how in the hell do you stand working at this place? It gives me the creeps. I feel better every time I come out the front door."

Robert shrugged his shoulders and said, "It's a job like any other, Mr. Jennings. I'll see you."

As Stewart unlocked his motorcycle, just before stepping down on the crank, he looked at his watch: it was 12:45. He had not been asked to any of the pre-wedding festivities or even the wedding. However, he knew that the Olivers were giving a buffet wedding luncheon on the lawn of their house. He said to himself, "By God, I'll crash that lunch. I'm sure I'll be as welcome as Malcolm X at the Union League but I'm the best friend of the bride though perhaps

Chapter 5 -- Or Forever Hold His Peace

she doesn't realize it yet. I also now know a considerable amount about her ancestry. I know why that crafty little bastard, Alfred Oliver, Mother's trustee, has been so content to allow her to languish in the institute for all these many years. Let's see how a Bohemian toast livens up a rather sedate Philadelphia wedding luncheon!"

It was 1:30 by the time he drove into the Olivers' drive. He parked his Tatra motorcycle among the cars and went into the house. The bar had been set up in the dining room, so he went directly in there and got a vodka on the rocks from the bartender. He drank the first one down almost straight and then had the bartender give him another, which he took with him as he went through the house and into the living room. Then he came out through the French doors and out to the flagstone terrace and looked about him. He stood there for a moment, dazzled by the bright sunlight, looking at the peaceful wedding luncheon. The caterer had laid out eight tables, each seating eight people on the lawn with a large buffet table at one end. At one corner table in the shade of one of the huge copper beech trees, Mrs. Oakley was sitting with Mrs. Dulaire and two other ladies in their seventies. On the left, at a table that was larger than the others, Phil and Susie were at opposite ends with the ushers and bridesmaids. Stewart waved a greeting to Susie. Close to where he was standing there was a table at which only Mr. and Mrs. Secant and Mr. and Mrs. Oliver were sitting as well as a man and a woman Stewart did not recognize – they must be Phillip's parents.

As Stewart stood there by the door of the living room, he could see that a number of people had looked up, seen him and were surprised. Just then Joan Platen came up from the buffet table with a lunch plate in her hand. She looked at him for a second and then said casually, "Hi, Stewart. What's new in Bohemia? Have you defenestrated any trunks recently? It's nice to see you again. Are you interested in some lunch? If so, we've got a seat at our table over there."

Stewart had been surprised at her cordiality. Before, she had always made it pointedly clear that she didn't like him since he had visited Susie at Bennett. He said to her, "Say, that's nice of you, Joanie. Maybe I will join you. But come over with me and watch the fun as I say my how-do-you-dos to the Olivers and the Secants. After all, I wasn't exactly invited to this bash, but good manners call for me at least to say hello before eating and drinking."

Joan followed as Stewart went over to the Secants' and Olivers' table. Once he got there he took off his sunglasses and said, "Hi, Mr. and Mrs. Secant and Mr. and Mrs. Oliver. It was fun to check in at the rehearsal yesterday at St. James."

The four of them looked at him with stony faces as he went on. "I wanted in particular to say hello to all of you here since I probably won't get much of a chance later on in the day with everything that's going to go on. By the way, I stopped in at the institute this morning to see Mother. She asked me especially to say that she's alive and doing fairly well and how much she appreciates being asked to this particular wedding. Of course, she can't come."

Mrs. Secant said evenly, "Stewart, it's a happy day for all of us. It's too bad that Dol can't be here too. How is she?"

Stewart looked at Mrs. Secant and said directly to her, "You know how she is, Mrs. Secant, and why she never really recovered from the blows that were given to her about the time of Dad's death. I don't think that she's too well. Today she talked at considerable length about the things that happened about that time and it always makes her a little bit unhappy."

He saw with satisfaction that Mrs. Secant's eyes had widened ever so slightly and that Tom Secant's great neck was swelling. He continued. "Today, we went into things a little more deeply than ever before. Now I understand some of the things I never had before. Of course, all of this is old hat to all of you but a lot of people here would be fascinated to learn what all went on in those good old days."

Stewart savored the recollection of Mrs. Secant's mounting anguish. He continued. "I would be less than frank if I didn't say that I can't help but be jealous of Blinky. He's a lucky dog, and getting one hell of a good daughter. Don't you agree, Mr. Oliver? Of course, there's no reason in the world why I couldn't be marrying Susie in place of Blinky except that she preferred him to me."

All four of the people at the table said nothing. Joan plucked at Stewart's sleeve and said, "Come on, Stewart, my lunch is getting cold." Stewart said, "Just a sec, Joan, I won't keep you, but I did want

Chapter 5 -- Or Forever Hold His Peace

to tell all of these good people what a great day I think it's going to be all the way around. By the way, do any of you like riddles? Perhaps you haven't heard the latest one which I heard this morning at the hospital. What is the game that can only be played by members of a family, but any member of the family can participate but only two can play at a time? Give up?" He paused for three seconds and then said quietly, "Incest!"

As Stewart lay there in his bed, he smiled as he recalled his words' effect. Tom Secant turned purple and had half gotten to his feet. There was a look of pure horror on Mrs. Secant's face and she was deathly pale.

Mrs. Oliver said, "Stewart, that's not even funny."

Mr. Oliver said, "Steady there, Jane. Stewart, how about coming with me for a second." Mr. Oliver quietly but firmly said to Tom Secant, "No, Tom, sit down and let me see if I can't handle this, will you?"

Mr. Oliver laid his hand on Stewart's sleeve as they walked across the lawn and he said to him, "Stewart, my boy, I think you've had a little bit too much to drink."

Stewart stopped, looked Mr. Oliver in the eye, and said, "Listen, Mr. Alfred Oakley Oliver, one more stupid insult out of you, Buster, and I'll describe to your assembled guests in vivid minute detail just exactly what took place at the Hilltop Motel one night nineteen years ago."

Mr. Oliver looked at Stewart and said smoothly, "You think that you are going to upset us by recounting some of the fantasies that disturb your mother. You must feel free to say just exactly what you please and recount if you like what it is that is so disturbing to your mother."

Stewart was thrown off. He expected Mr. Oliver to be astounded and to ask him not to reveal what his mother had told him. Stewart replied uncertainly, "Fantasies my fanny! We both know that it's true. However, luckily for you and your cousin, I remain fond of Susie. She's the only one in this crowd who's ever been halfway decent to me, so I may not blow the situation wide open provided you keep a civil tongue in your head."

Mr. Oliver said quietly, "Stewart, you must do as you think best for Susie and for your mother." They turned around and walked back to the table. Stewart could see Mr. Oliver shaking his head to the others at the table indicating that they were to do nothing.

Stewart said to Joan, "Would you tap on a glass? I feel a toast coming upon me." Stewart saw the anguish in Mrs. Secant's eyes, but Mr. Oliver again made a small negative movement with his head.

Joan replied, "Stewart, we've had a lot of toasts. Do you really think another is necessary?"

Stewart said, "Nuts, Joanie. Here, if you won't do it, give me that knife." He clinked loudly on a glass. When the ringing had died away and most of the people had stopped talking and turned around, Stewart stepped out on the lawn.

"I know many in this crowd aren't regular churchgoers. I'm not, but I'm going to be at St. James today at 4:30 when Blinky thinks he's going to tame the shrew, Susie. The text for today in the Holy Calendar is found in Chapter 7, Verse 21 of St. Luke. As all of you know, this concerns the raising of Lazarus. The verse says, 'Lord, he stinketh.' This is, of course, not appropriate today for certainly, Blinky stinketh not. Far more appropriate is the fact that the wedding service will refer to the first miracle at Cana. You all know that the first miracle at Cana occurred when Christ happened to drop in at a wedding. There wasn't enough wine so that He used his magic power to turn the water into wine.

"I've always thought that the miracle at Cana was particularly appealing – here is a nice sort of a wedding going on when the wine runs short and a hippie-looking guy says something to the effect, 'Hey, man, I can do something about that,' and proceeds to do so. Today, of course, there is no need for any bearded hippie to drop in, at least at this nice party given by Mr. and Mrs. Oliver. There is more than enough to eat and especially to drink, as my remarks probably show."

There was a general laugh and Stewart continued, "I would therefore propose another toast, but not to the bride. She has already probably been toasted enough but, rather, a toast to Mr. Oliver. Why Mr. Oliver? Beneath his somewhat stuffy exterior he has always had

Chapter 5 -- Or Forever Hold His Peace

a soft spot in his heart for his Secant cousins, first Mrs. Secant and now Susie, his goddaughter. In fact, he's like a second father to her. I am going to betray a family confidence just so that you can share the pleasure that I have in learning of the true generosity of Mr. Alfred Oliver. I am sure that he in particular will be furious at me for betraying this confidence but I am going to take my chances. Mr. Oliver is settling a trust fund on Susie and the man she marries to alleviate any economic problems which they might otherwise undergo as a young married couple.

"Look at Mr. Alfred Oliver as he sits there at the table. He is so embarrassed and so modest that he can't say a thing. Come on, Mr. Oliver, don't be shy and make me tell all of the background details that led you to make this magnificent gesture.

"Please also forgive me for having disclosed this, but there is never any harm in the truth, is there? When I recently learned the true facts about all of this, I thought I should speak out. After all, this is 'just cause' and the reverend will tell us this afternoon to speak out now in a just cause or forever hold our peace. Here, then, is a toast to Mr. Oliver and his generous gift." Though most of the people had finished their champagne, they raised their glasses and drank the toast.

Mr. Oliver got to his feet and said smoothly, "Well, Stewart Jennings has always been one for surprises. I am a little surprised at this toast. I had rather hoped that this gesture of mine would remain private, but it is true that on Monday, assuming that Reverend Piccard does his job this afternoon, I will set up a small trust fund for Susie."

Stewart saw Mrs. Oliver looked very surprised and angry. Mrs. Secant looked relieved. Tom Secant was smiling broadly.

Susie came over to Mr. Oliver looking puzzled and kissed him, saying, "Cousin Alfred, what a nice surprise for Blinky and me. How lucky can a girl be on her wedding day!"

Joan came over and said quietly to Stewart, "Now, come on, Stew, finish that drink and get some lunch."

Stewart replied, "To hell with lunch, Joanie baby, I'm having too much fun."

Joan said, "Well, how about sitting down at this table and

telling me what this is all about? The toast didn't make complete sense to me." Joan led him over to a stone bench. They sat down and she said, "Now, just what is this all about, Stewart?"

Stewart lay there with his eyes closed, thinking back on what had happened next, when the alarm went off. He opened his one good eye: the clock said 4:15.

Stewart said to himself, "Jesus, up and at 'em! I better get moving cuz I sure want to hear the magic words 'Dearly Beloved'. I know that all the folks sitting in the pews at St. James are going to love to hear the tasty story I have to tell them when the Reverend Piccard asks the question as to whether any man has just cause and all that stuff."

Chapter Six

If Any Man Can Show Just Cause

Just before the clock at St. James struck four, Mrs. Robert Oakley's limousine drew up to St. James. The chauffeur opened the door for Mrs. Oakley. She got out of the limousine and walked in the big main door followed by her maid, Annie. Leaving Annie in the back pew, she walked slowly but firmly on her little white cane down the aisle to the third pew on the bride's side and sat down. After she was seated, she bent her head for about a minute and then she raised her head again. She sat with her back very straight, not allowing it to touch the back of the pew. Mrs. Oakley had arranged to be at the church at 4:00 P.M. sharp. She knew very well that according to Episcopal wedding protocol she was supposed to come up the aisle on the arm of an usher just before her daughter, the mother of the bride. However, in her view Episcopalian wedding services got underway with something very like a parade. She had decided quite deliberately not to be a part of it and had arrived at 4:00 o'clock. The organist started playing Bach's Prelude in F Sharp Minor. The ushers were not yet escorting people up the aisle but were still frolicking on the lawn at the side of the church.

Mrs. Oakley looked around the church. It had not changed at all since the days when she and her husband had come to St. James every Sunday morning. Now, as always for a fashionable wedding, the altar and chancel were adorned with pots of huge lacy green ferns. Mrs. Oakley thought, as she had many times before, that these jungle plants looked oddly out of place. She also thought again that for all their delicate tracery, these ferns must be as hardy as the weeds that grow along the tracks of the Penn Central since these tubs would appear this same week, not only at other weddings but also at funerals as well as all sorts of parties and civic functions, being shuttled in and out of churches, houses and halls in all sorts of weather. Mrs. Oakley far preferred the simplicity of her little Quaker church, which remained unadorned, even for a wedding. She thought, "I like the old-fashioned Quaker ceremony. In fact, it is very much like the new type of wedding, which some of the younger generation seems to think they invented, when they stand up and recite their own vows."

As she sat there listening to the music, she said to herself, "The organ here never was of first quality. It will do for hymn singing but it simply is not up to Bach." For that matter, she noted to herself as she sat listening, "Neither is the organist, so that it really does not make any difference about the quality of the organ." As Mrs. Oakley continued to listen, she was certain that her daughter, Sarah, must have selected the music. "Of course," she thought, "Bach for this wedding is certainly casting musical pearls before swine so far as these long-haired ushers are concerned. As for Phillip MacPherson, he might know Bach through a music appreciation course at Princeton. Of course, Stewart would know all of these familiar Bach pieces quite well."

Mrs. Oakley's thoughts turned to Susanne, "Here it is her wedding day. I liked Susie while she was under the thumb of her nurse, Rebecca or Rebe as Susie called her. Rebe taught Susie good manners and respect. But then when Susie went off to boarding school, Rebe had been let go by Tom and Sarah and had returned to Nevis." Mrs. Oakley thought to herself, "Susanne had gone into a downward spiral and, at least until very recently, still seemed to be spinning out of control. Susanne had no values. She seemed to have no regard for either the attractive things of this world or for any of the many people who do so many things for her. She is an almost totally selfish young woman whose only law is the gratification of her own pleasures. She is quite critical of everyone and everything but she has nothing really to suggest by way of improvement be-

Chapter 6 -- If Any Man Can Show Just Cause

cause she knows so little. Even if she did have something of value to suggest, she has neither the industry nor the readiness to work for anything. But I may be wrong. I have heard good things of Susanne's serious work with disabled children in downtown Philadelphia."

Mrs. Oakley thought for a moment and then said to herself, "The real truth of the matter is that I'm afraid of Susanne. Since Rebe left, I have never really been able to control or impose my values on Susanne as I was able to do with her mother. But I quite like Phillip MacPherson. He seems like a sensible and determined young man. I am amazed Susanne has the good fortune to come up with such a fine young man. Has Susanne reverted on the eve of her marriage?" To Mrs. Oakley's surprise and pleasure, Susanne and Phillip had in fact come to see Mrs. Oakley the day before their wedding, saying they probably would not get much of a chance to see her at the wedding.

Mrs. Oakley thought of how different Susanne was from her mother at the same age. A pleasant feeling suffused Mrs. Oakley as she thought back on the time when Sarah had been a young girl. From the time she had been a small child, she had been the embodiment of all that Mrs. Oakley had most wanted in a daughter – a pretty child growing into a beautiful young woman who was poised, polite and restrained. Sarah had been far more biddable than her older brother, Richard, who had always fought both his parents, beginning when he was a small boy. Sarah had seemed completely content as she grew up and went happily off to Ethel Walker's and then on to Sarah Lawrence.

Mrs. Oakley had supposed that Sarah would at the appropriate time marry someone very like her cousin Alfred, that is, until she had met Tom Secant. Mrs. Oakley was not sure when she had first become aware of Tom Secant as distinguished from a number of other out-of-town young men who were always around the house when Sarah was at home on weekends or vacations. Tom was big, handsome and athletic and, above all, kind and pleasant. She remembered that he had been popular with all of the girls and the other young men around the house. At that time, she had catalogued him as an attractive muscular Irish "pudding" with little to recommend him but his athletic body and his charm and freshness. Indeed, she could remember that, at some point during the spring of 1950, Tom Secant had on one occasion driven her into Philadelphia. She had tried hard to lead him into conversation on half a dozen subjects which she thought might be of interest to him. But while Tom was pleasant enough, he simply had no brains and no cultural background, so there had been nothing – literally nothing – that they could find to talk about. Thus, they had spent the drive discussing trivialities punctuated by long silences.

Mrs. Oakley thought about June 10, 1950, the date of the outbreak of the Korean War. She thought somewhat grimly for the thousandth time that the decision of the North Korean Communists to invade South Korea had been a tragedy for many people, including Sarah, since it was this event, she was sure, that had precipitated Sarah's hasty marriage to Tom Secant. Tom had received his orders shortly after the decision by the United States to send troops into Korea. It was not more than three weeks later that Tom appeared in a second lieutenant's uniform. But for the Korean War Mrs. Oakley was certain Sarah's infatuation with Tom would have quickly run its course. "Things also might have turned out quite differently," she thought, "if Robert had been alive or even if Sarah's older brother, Richard, had not died five years before."

Mrs. Oakley's thoughts turned back to Sarah. She had been surprised when Sarah came to her on that Sunday in August 1950, after driving Tom Secant to the train. Sarah had said with downcast eyes, "Mother, Tom Secant and I got married in Hanover, New Hampshire, last Saturday. We wanted to wait and have a regular wedding at St. James, but Tom had received his orders. We wanted to get married before he left."

Mrs. Oakley had had to summon all her strength so as not to lose her self control as she sat there and looked at Sarah, so guiltily happy about what she had done all on her own for the very first time in her life. Mrs. Oakley could still remember her instinctive feeling, "Oh, my poor silly goose, what have you gone and done!" However, she had actually managed to say, "Well, my dear, I hope that thee and Tom will be very happy."

Chapter 6 -- If Any Man Can Show Just Cause

It had taken her years to get over the inward bitterness and sense of waste she felt but could not say or show at seeing her treasured only child married to a handsome, weak, stupid athlete. She still did not know whether Sarah had panicked, thinking that she was pregnant and that this had triggered the hasty marriage. However, if she had married Tom Secant thinking she was pregnant, Sarah had been mistaken. When little Tommy Secant was born, it was fifteen months later.

While Tom was serving for two years in South Carolina during the Korean War, Sarah had continued to live at home with her mother even after little Tommy was born. It had been a pleasant time for both of them. Mrs. Oakley had felt that Sarah almost came to dread the time when Tom would come back and she would have to sleep in the bed that she had made, so to speak. But Sarah was too proud, Mrs. Oakley knew, to admit even to herself much less to her mother that she had made a ghastly mistake.

Tom Secant, Mrs. Oakley felt, soon knew as well as Sarah herself did that they had both made a terrible error. But Mrs. Oakley could see that he, like Sarah, was trying gamely to make a go of it. Little Tommy was the result. Tom was as proud of his son as any man on earth. Still, in spite of their genuine efforts, Mrs. Oakley knew that, without either of them having to say anything, the marriage was not working. Sarah, she could see, was impatient with Tom's continued lack of interest in music, literature, art or any of the things that Sarah had learned to cherish under Mrs. Oakley's careful guidance. On the other hand, Tom was clearly annoyed that Sarah made it clear that she had no interest whatsoever in the sports that were the center of Tom's life. As she watched the two of them struggling after Tom's return from the Army, all she could do was hope and pray that the trouble that was bound to result from the hasty and ill-conceived marriage would not hurt Sarah. However, all in all, she had become fond of Tom because of his unfailing kindness and thoughtfulness of others, including herself. She also appreciated the fact that he and Rebe had actually raised Susanne almost without Sarah.

Mrs. Oakley remembered clearly the first time she had seen Charles Jennings, Tom's best friend. Though it was twenty years ago and he was with Dol, his fiancée, Mrs. Oakley still remembered that she had inwardly trembled. Sarah was clearly captivated by his easy charm, his good looks and the patter of his sophisticated conversation. Mrs. Oakley remembered that she herself was delighted to find that Charlie Jennings was knowledgeable about music and was a gifted, if not very serous, cellist. The contrast between Charlie and Tom was devastating for Tom, an athletic vegetable, good looking and friendly but without any brains or culture.

She knew that, though Charles Jennings had died in a plane collision nineteen years ago, still he was very much a part of the proceedings that were going on today. With Charlie's death the situation should have been closed once and for all. The trouble was that it was not.

When Mrs. Oakley looked at Susanne, she saw not only something of the strong Oakley personality stemming from her husband, Robert Oakley and his forebears, but she thought she could also see some reflection of Charles' breezy personality as well as something of his looks. She often wondered that other people did not notice what seemed so obvious to her, especially as it was often remarked that Stewart and Susanne were "two of a kind" when one would lead the other one into some trouble, scrape or escapade. Of course, the fact that Susie and Stewart seemed to have an attraction one for the other was a source of vague uneasiness for Mrs. Oakley. However, she had thought, as long as the situation didn't ripen into anything more serious, there was little that she could or should do about it. She had, however, been inwardly relieved when, at one of their regular Thursday luncheons in January, Sarah had mentioned in passing the arrival on the scene of Phillip MacPherson. Her daughter continued to report on the growing interest not only of Susanne for Phillip but also his growing interest in Susanne. While neither one of them discussed their reasons, both were content to watch MacPherson replace Jennings in Susie's affections. This contented state of affairs had been shattered when Sarah came to lunch on the first Thursday in April.

Mrs. Oakley thought back on that day. As usual they were being served a light lunch by Annie in the little dining room. As Sa-

Chapter 6 -- If Any Man Can Show Just Cause

rah came in and kissed her mother, Mrs. Oakley could sense that she had something on her mind. After the usual conversation about the house, the weather, the flower show, Mrs. Oakley asked her daughter, "Well, is Ms. Susanne going back to college? Last week, thee told me that the authorities had lifted her suspension so that I suppose she's ether back there now or will go back at the beginning of the next school term.

Sarah gave a great sigh and replied, "No, Mother, on the contrary. Susie announced that she is not going to go back though heaven and earth was moved on her behalf by her father and Alfred."

Sarah added with a helpless shrug, "You know Susie."

Mrs. Oakley said, "But am I to take it from all this that Mr. MacPherson has displaced a college education for Susie? That doesn't seem a totally bad alternative to me."

Sarah had replied, "Well, not now it seems. The first time we got wind of the new situation was at dinner last week. Tom brought up the subject of some damage that Susie and Stewart Jennings had apparently done at the Yellow Lantern with their motorcycles the previous Friday night. Mr. Horgan, the manager, called Tom and said that the two of them had broken some banisters or a porch or something with their motorcycles as they were leaving. That was the first that we knew that Susie was seeing Stewart again. He had been completely out of the picture so far as we had known since before Christmas."

Mrs. Oakley asked, "Well, and what about Phillip MacPherson?"

Sarah continued, "Mother, that's the bad part. Tom, in the course of the row about the damage, alluded to Phil, or perhaps I did. In any case, it was like throwing gasoline on a fire. Susie flew into a rage and stalked out of the dining room blurting out that she was engaged to Stewart or that she would marry Stewart Jennings if it was the last thing she did, or something to that effect."

Mrs. Oakley was stunned, "Sarah! Thee don't suppose for a minute that Susanne's serious?"

Sarah said, "Mother, again, you know Susie. She likes to say things to shock and upset people. But she is now a very determined character, especially when she is opposed. As you know, Tom hates Jennings beyond all reason. He hates all young men who are not interested in athletics, who wear their hair long and go around in ratty dungarees. The worst thing is the music. Susie plays her hi-fi full blast all the time. That drives Tom wild. You know he walked out of *Hair*. Everyone thought it was because of the nudity. Actually, it was the music. It physically upset him. It doesn't help that Stewart is a musician. The modern generation scares Tom, who is nothing if not conservative. I have no use for Stewart either, and I've made that pretty clear to Susie. The problem is that Susie is just contrary enough to up and marry Stewart simply to shock us and to show us her determination. Worse, Stewart is just unstable enough to go along as a sort of lark or a way of protesting. It could happen. There just isn't a blessed thing Tom or I can do," she added with a resigned look.

Mrs. Oakley, as she thought back on it, was surprised at one thing; that is, that Sarah herself was not more upset at the dizzy prospect that Susie might really marry young Jennings. At that moment Mrs. Oakley decided that she herself would have to take an active part.

Mrs. Oakley still recalled Stewart's guarded tone when he telephoned from Boston in response to her note to him. Mrs. Oakley had said, "Thank you very much for telephoning me, Stewart. It is good of you to do so since I'm sure I could never have reached you myself by phone. I would like to talk to you if I might. I understand that you come down on some weekends to see your mother, is that right? I wonder if you could come and have tea with me on the next weekend you're down here."

Jennings was clearly surprised and he had said with hesitation, "Tea? Well, yes, Mrs. Oakley. I suppose I could do it this weekend, either on Friday or Saturday."

"Well," she had said, "on Friday afternoons Mrs. Dulaire and I are driven into Philadelphia for the Philadelphia Orchestra concert. Why don't you come on Saturday, say at 4:30? I would prefer that you not discuss our rendezvous with Susanne at least for the moment."

At 4:30 on Saturday, Stewart Jennings had been shown in by

Chapter 6 -- If Any Man Can Show Just Cause

Annie to the little paneled study overlooking the garden. Mrs. Oakley had been struck once again by the physical resemblance between Stewart and his father. Stewart had the same basic facial characteristics. The most striking physical difference between him and his dead father, besides Stewart's slightly crossed eyes, was that Stewart had shoulder length hair, whereas Charlie Jennings had always had a close cropped crew-cut, the mark of the generation that grew up after World War II. Above the mantelpiece in the little study was a portrait of Sarah's brother, Richard, in uniform. He had the same crew-cut. The other difference Mrs. Oakley found was that Stewart's face was weaker than his father's. There was also, she noticed, a difference in that Stewart did not have his father's engaging quality of looking the person he was talking to directly in the eye. Stewart did have some of his mother's shyness. His blue jeans and blue denim shirt, however, were clean. His worn sport coat still had a cleaning tag. It had obviously just come from the cleaners. As Stewart took off his sunglasses, Mrs. Oakley once again noticed his crossed eyes.

As Annie wheeled in the tea cart and began laying out the tea, Mrs. Oakley said, "How is your mother? Of course, I know she's still in the Pennsylvania Institute, but I keep hoping that she's getting stronger and soon will be out once and for all. You know that your mother and Sarah were inseparable as girls, though Sarah is older than your mother by about two years. Sarah was as much raised by your grandmother as she was by me and vice versa for Dol. The girls could walk through what used to be the Dulaires' woods to see each other. Your grandmother and I agreed that it would be better if the two of them saw more of other girls, so we were going to send them to different boarding schools, but they both chose to go to Walker's.

"I will never forget your mother as a debutante. She was so lovely with sandy hair and a fair complexion. She had a gentleness and shyness that was captivating. I knew that she had had some emotional problems, but there was nothing to indicate the long dark years for her after your father's tragic death. You must give your mother my very best when you see her. Please tell her that I would like to have her come to tea with me when she is allowed to leave the institute. I would like to go there myself to see her, but I'm told that visitors other than the members of the immediate family are not permitted.

"By the way, is Della still the housekeeper? Say hello to her for me. She certainly has been faithful to you and your mother over the years.

"I have heard, Stewart, that you have inherited your father's and your Czechoslovakian grandmother's musical gifts. I never met your grandmother. Of course, her reputation as a pianist was international. I did hear your father play once. He played the cello part in a Brahms quintet here at this house with some other young musicians, including two members, I believe, of a Curtis String Quartet and a visiting English pianist. Your father did remarkably well. Do you also play the cello?"

"Well," Jennings replied, "I still have the old man's fiddle someplace around the house. I took lessons for five or six years, mostly to please Mother. I still hack away at it now and then but not seriously. I certainly couldn't hold up the cello part in a Brahm's quintet. The piano is my instrument, if I have one. I thought at one time of being a composer, but my real musical talent, if I have any, seems to be to amuse people by doing musical imitations or singing folk songs."

"What a waste, Stewart, what a waste," Mrs. Oakley replied. "Well now," she said briskly after Annie had silently withdrawn, closing the door behind her. "I suppose you're wondering why an old lady living alone in this big house has asked you to come and have tea with her. You may think that it's simply because I want company at tea time. Indeed, that is true and I would welcome you at tea time any time you care to come. Also, I suppose that you might think it was because I wanted somebody to talk to about music, obviously a common interest. I could have asked Susanne to join us but if she did come, she would pretend to be bored to tears. Unfortunately, she has apparently lost her appreciation of real music, though it may come back in time."

She raised her hand slightly since she saw that Stewart was going to say something, "No, my boy, don't interrupt at this point. I

Chapter 6 -- If Any Man Can Show Just Cause

know Susanne's strong points as well as her weak ones. She needs no defense from you. After all, she is my only grandchild."

Mrs. Oakley paused. There was a moment of silence as she considered how to best approach the subject. "My daughter, Sarah, does come to see me regularly, unlike Susanne. I therefore am somewhat abreast of Susanne's activities apart from gossip, of which there is no lack I can tell you. I know that you and Susanne kept company, as we used to say years ago, mostly at the Yellow Lantern. All well and good. No harm in that except for something that does not concern you really. No, that's not right – it does concern you very much. There's no use saying it does not. What I am about to tell you happened many years ago but you must know about it since it poses a great threat to you and Susanne and, indeed, for all of us.

"Young man," Mrs. Oakley said, looking sideways at Jennings, "are you fond of Susanne?"

Jennings looked troubled and paused before he replied somewhat defensively, "Yes, Mrs. Oakley, I like Susie and she likes me. We have a ball together. But frankly, I dislike your fat son-in-law as much as he dislikes me. Mrs. Secant and I have cordially disliked one another for years and still do."

Mrs. Oakley said, "Well, I understand from her mother that Susanne has recently sworn that she will marry you if it's the last thing she does or something along those lines. Neither you nor I need to be reminded that when that young lady puts her mind on something, she is apt to succeed. Determination is one of Susanne's admirable traits, I might add. However, I take it that this statement may be a reaction at least in part to Mr. MacPherson who, until recently, as I understand it, seemed to have replaced you in Susanne's affections."

Again she paused, then continued quietly, "Your father was a most attractive person. He had a weakness for the ladies, to use a Victorian expression. I am, of course, not telling you anything that you probably do not already know. I am certainly not saying this out of disrespect for your father as you will soon see. On the contrary, it is most painful to me to have to go through this. The long and the short of it is that your father was in fact the father of Susanne."

She stopped. There was complete silence broken only by the ticking of the empire clock on the mantelpiece.

Jennings broke the silence, "Oh, Christ!" He reached in his shirt pocket and pulled out a Camel cigarette, saying, "I need a smoke. This is quite a jolt!"

"Why of course,'" Mrs. Oakley said. "You'll find an ashtray over on the windowsill."

Jennings lit the cigarette almost automatically with a blue tipped kitchen match. He inhaled deeply as he sat down again, after getting the ashtray. His hand trembled slightly as he raised the cigarette to his lips.

"Let's see. That would make Susie my stepsister, wouldn't it?"

"Wrong," Mrs. Oakley said briskly. "Susanne is your halfsister by blood, but not by marriage."

"That would make any relationship between me and Susanne incestuous. Good God!" Jennings said with a sigh. "I've done many things but I never expected that I might be in for incest. Fortunately, I never slept with Susie!"

"Oh, come, come," said Mrs. Oakley. "Don't go into an Orestes-Electra funk about what is past. There is no use crying over spilled milk, especially when you had nothing to do with the spilling of it. The point is not to compound the situation at this point. That's why I am talking to you."

Jennings slumped back in his chair blowing smoke toward the ceiling. Finally he said reflectively, "Well, this sure goes a hell of a way toward explaining several things. For example, it explains why Susie and I are so alike."

He chuckled slightly and then continued, "It also explains why the Secants have always had the needle out for me and have put it in so hard and so often."

Mrs. Oakley said, "You may be right that you and Susanne have so many qualities that are alike. But you're dead wrong about why Mr. Secant doesn't like you. The reason he doesn't like you is probably because you're part of the younger generation of which he is afraid. This is because he doesn't understand the younger genera-

Chapter 6 -- If Any Man Can Show Just Cause

tion and thinks that it represents a threat to him. I don't believe that his dislike of you has anything to do with what I have told you. I am certain that he does not even suspect that he is not Susanne's father. So far as my daughter is concerned, she knows that your father was Susanne's father. However, she has never said so to me and probably doesn't admit it even to herself. Susanne herself has no inkling at all. I might add that I don't think your mother knows anything about this. At the time, she was in the Pennsylvania Institute. I don't need to tell you that any disclosure of this might well have an adverse effect on your mother." She paused and then added, "Also, it would drive Tom even more to drink if he knew that his pride and joy, his only daughter, his Susanne, was not his child. I don't need to tell you that Tom dotes on his daughter even though for some reason she has behaved abominably toward her father for the past several years."

Jennings said to her after another pause, "Do you mind if I ask you a question, Mrs. Oakley?"

"I would be most surprised if you didn't have several questions. You have a perfect right to an answer now that I have opened this Pandora's box to you." Mrs. Oakley continued, "What is your first question?"

Stewart replied, "How in the hell, if you'll pardon the expression, do you know about this tasty bit of history? Why are you so sure about it when you say that even Susie's mother has never admitted it to you, and her father doesn't even know?" He was clearly angry.

"This isn't a fantasy of a crackpot old Quaker living alone too long who wants to break up a possible marriage between you and her granddaughter. You and I both know that this isn't so. You are entitled to know why I am so certain.

After Susanne was born, I saw a good deal of her and came to be very fond of her. Her mother almost rejected Susanne completely for a while. Susanne's care was at first left pretty much to old Mrs. Grogan and Mr. Secant and then to Susanne's wonderful nanny, Rebe. I saw a good deal of her. Susanne was totally unlike Tommy, Jr., who died about that time. Sarah did intimate to me after Tommy's death that she had had an affair with your father before he died.

What she actually said was that she had been on the verge of leaving Tom Secant with the thought that she would marry your father after he divorced your mother. However, your father told my daughter that he wasn't going to become involved in a nasty divorce situation simply over an infatuation. Not long after, the jet trainer that your father was flying collided with another plane and he was killed."

"Well," said Stewart somewhat aggressively, "that's a long way from backing up your accusation, Mrs. Oakley."

"I haven't finished but you have every right to be skeptical," Mrs. Oakley said. "I decided to check on my own to see whether Susanne was truly Tom Secant's child or your father's. I'm not sure why I wanted to know this. Certainly at the time, with your father dead and Tom Secant's obvious growing fondness for Susanne, there did not seem to be any real reason for prying into the past. Anyway, I hired a detective agency in Philadelphia."

"How could a detective agency find out without going to Mr. or Mrs. Secant? After all, my father was dead, so there was no way of asking him," Jennings said doubtingly.

"It really was not all that difficult. You yourself would and could solve the problem, given a little time. The agency determined your father's blood group from his Navy medical records. They then obtained the blood grouping for my daughter, Sarah, Tom Secant and little Susanne. The first two were simple – I simply offered each of them an insurance policy which required a physical examination and, of course, a blood sample.

"So far as Susanne was concerned, there was no difficulty. The agency got the pediatrician's nurse to give us her blood grouping for a small fee. Once they had the basic blood samples, the rest was all science. Perhaps you haven't taken biology, but I am sure that you know from reports of paternity suits in the tabloids that this sort of thing is child's play. The long and short of it was that it established conclusively that Tom Secant could not have been the father of Susanne and that your father could be."

Again she paused and then continued, "Once I had the information, I paid the fee to the detective and sealed the whole business in an envelope and put it in my strong box in the Girard Trust

Chapter 6 -- If Any Man Can Show Just Cause

Company. I marked it clearly that it was to be destroyed in the event of my death. If I had died, as I probably should have ten years ago, no one would have known what you and I now know."

"I suppose you would have no objection to my looking at the contents of the envelope?" Jennings asked.

"No, of course not," she replied, "but I destroyed the envelope. Two winters ago, I was ill with grippe – it really wasn't very serious. Alfred Oliver was the executor of my will and had a power of attorney from me. When I recovered, I went to my strong box at the Girard about something else. The envelope had been opened and then resealed. When I asked Alfred about it, he first denied that he'd opened it, though he did say that he'd gone into the safe deposit box. Of course, he had the legal right to do so. But it made me angry that he had gone to my safe deposit box even before my death. He said he only wanted to see that any cash or securities in the box were converted into deep discount bonds or something like that to save on estate taxes. Of course, he was fond of Susanne and Sarah so no real harm could come of his knowing the contents of the envelope. But I was angry since it was clearly marked in my writing – 'To be destroyed at the time of my death.' Alfred said he had simply determined that there was no cash or securities in the envelope. It seemed obvious to me that there would not be either cash or securities in the envelope. Why would I want any cash or securities destroyed?

"Anyway, I decided it was dangerous to have such information about. Quite apart from Alfred, some bank officer or tax official might be required to look at the contents before destroying the envelope. Besides, at the time, it seemed like a closed matter. The long and short of it was that I tore up the envelope and its contents."

"OK," said Jennings. "If I was really interested I could get a copy from the detective agency or you could get one for me?"

"Yes," Mrs. Oakley replied. "Or, if necessary, we could go through the same process all over again. You need to be entirely satisfied that this is fact, not just invention on my part. Just say the word."

Jennings replied, "I would rather like to have a look. Could you get a copy and send it to me at home? I'll look at it next time I'm home, then destroy it. I don't want it at college. Really, however, I'm satisfied, Mrs. Oakley. More to the point, what is it you want me to do or not to do now? Obviously, you don't want me to marry Susie. Quite obviously, I'm not going to. However, that is only part of the story."

At this point, Annie, after knocking discreetly, came into the room and asked, 'Would you like some more tea, ma'am?"

"No, thank you, Annie, you may clear," Mrs. Oakley had replied after looking inquiringly at Jennings, who had shaken his head. "But, the sun is now over the yardarm and Mr. Jennings would probably like a drink What would you like?" she asked, turning to Jennings.

"Vodka on the rocks," Jennings replied.

Mrs. Oakley said, "Sounds dreadful but get it all the same, Annie. Though it's a trifle early, I'll have my usual bourbon old-fashioned."

"Very well," Annie said as she left with the tea cart, quietly closing the door once again behind her.

"Where were we?" asked Mrs. Oakley. "Oh yes, where do we go from here? Well, I suggest that we keep this a secret between the two of us. Soon I will be dead and gone."

Again she raised her hand slightly as Jennings indicated that he might break in.

"Nonsense," the old lady continued. "I have lived too long already but, thank goodness, I have lived long enough to prevent what might otherwise have been another catastrophe. Soon you will be the only person with the secret, other than Sarah. That is why I wanted your assurance that you were truly fond of Susanne. Susanne is not very secure right now. The revelation of her actual father would be a great shock to her. I don't need to elaborate on that. I don't think that it would be a good thing if Mr. MacPherson got wind of his little bit of family history. In the first place, it does not concern him and never will. In the second place, it conceivably might frighten him off. I detect a certain straight-laced quality about that young man that might not quite stomach this detail. I am told that he is bright and has admirable qualities. He may well be the best possible husband for Susanne. Therefore, I am encouraging to my limited ability

Chapter 6 -- If Any Man Can Show Just Cause

Susanne's marriage to this young man. However, Susanne and her Phillip are bound to have a rocky road in store for them. Phillip should not be armed with this fatal piece of unnecessary information.

"Of course, you could destroy Tom Secant by disclosing to him that he had been cuckolded by his best friend and that his only remaining child was not his. That would be pure cruelty to a nice but very weak man.

"You might be tempted to settle your long-standing score with my daughter. She has been unfair to you over the years and, more particularly, recently. You now have the means to pay her back ten times over. Overkill seems to fit the situation, but I hope that you would not deliberately do so. No doubt, whatever immediate satisfaction you might get would be at Susanne's expense as well as everyone else's, including possibly your own. Also, it would be downright despicable for you to do so now that you understand the true facts.

"I'm not really worried, Stewart, about your deliberately revealing what I have told you in confidence. Rather, I am concerned that this situation might spontaneously come out at 3:00 A.M. some morning in some after hours bar or might be told by you in strictest confidence to some trusted friend or even some girlfriend. This would be fatal. If I have learned anything in the course of my years, it is that a secret shared by two people is a secret. But if a secret is shared by more than two people it is only a question of time before it is general knowledge."

Jennings was about to reply when there was another quiet knock on the door. Mrs. Oakley said, "Come in, Annie."

Annie appeared with a silver tray with the two drinks on it. She silently passed the old-fashioned to Mrs. Oakley and the vodka to Stewart and then left, again closing the door quietly behind her. In the fading light Mrs. Oakley sipped her drink. Jennings took a large swallow of his. Neither one said anything. Jennings got up and looked out at the garden.

Jennings finally broke the silence after lighting another cigarette and sitting down again. "Well, I don't mind telling you, Mrs. Oakley, that what you have told me this afternoon is a real shocker. I need some time to absorb what you've said and figure it out. To use a common expression, 'It's a new ball game.' I think I'm going to have to reverse my field and start running in a completely different direction. To carry the analogy a little bit further, I think that I will probably end up running interference for my former rival so that he can now become my brother-in-law, so to speak."

Mrs. Oakley cut in sharply. "That's what worries me. It's just that sort of smart remark that is likely to make what I have told you common knowledge. If you do it now, what are you likely to do when you get a few more vodkas on the rocks under your belt or you get angry with Phillip or Susanne or her parents."

"Don't worry," Jennings said evenly. "I think I'll take the rest of this weekend off and go see my aunt and uncle in Lancaster. I owe them a visit, and I like to play with their kids. When I get back, I will have digested the situation. I won't spill the beans either by smart remarks, drunken confidences or too sudden a reversal of form. Can I come back to have tea with you later in the spring? I may need to talk to somebody. You are the only one I can talk to, isn't that right?"

"Of course," Mrs. Oakley said. "Come any time. Quite apart from this situation, I would enjoy talking to you. Would you like another vodka? I can ring for Annie," she said, indicating the tapestry bell pull.

"No, thanks very much," Jennings said wearily. "I think I've had enough stimulants for one day. Thanks for everything."

"Nonsense, on the contrary, my thanks to you. If the Secant family knew it, they would also be thanking you. You are showing real control in a most difficult situation. I am counting on you, Stewart, to continue to be steadfast," said Mrs. Oakley.

"Don't worry, Mrs. Oakley. Mum's the word. Goodbye. Thank you for the information, the tea and the much-needed drink. I'll call you in a week or ten days when I have recovered my cool somewhat. Perhaps I can join you again for tea. I may have some more questions at that point. I do hope you don't have any more family problems that you want to disclose. I've had quite enough."

Mrs. Oakley replied "Never fear, my boy. You know all the unpleasant details. Goodbye again. Thank you for coming and thank

Chapter 6 -- If Any Man Can Show Just Cause

you for understanding and taking it all in stride. Do call me and come to tea again if you have further questions."

With that Stewart left. Mrs. Oakley sat there alone in the little study, looking out the window until it was quite dark, wondering whether she had done the right thing. Stewart, though he had taken her revelations calmly, was a weak reed to lean on in view of his radical ideas, his erratic emotional background, his drinking and the use of drugs and his strong hatred of Tom and Sarah.

Though she was not at ease, Mrs. Oakley consoled herself that there was no other alternative. Even Stewart must realize that if he disclosed what she had told him, it would not help him and would bring a good deal of unhappiness to others, including Susie and his own mother.

In spite of his suggestion that he come and see her later in the spring, Mrs. Oakley had not seen him again or even heard from him. She felt a mounting uneasiness all spring, especially when she recalled the weak lines of his face and knew that this weakness was in some measure a reflection of the unstable emotional heritage from his mother and his Delp forebears. As a matter of fact, the next time she saw him was when he got somewhat unsteadily to his feet in the center of the wedding luncheon hosted on the lawn by the Olivers at their house. For an awful moment, when Stewart had looked around at the guests and had paused when he saw her sitting with Mrs. Dulaire in the shade of the copper beech, she thought that he was going to disclose what she had told him, but it turned out to be one of those spontaneous rambling humorous toasts to Alfred. She could not hear all of what he said but it seemed to amuse the younger guests. She herself preferred the toasts of her childhood which were the subject of a good deal of advanced effort and were short, humorous and to the point.

Her thoughts turned back to her son-in-law. She felt really sorry for him especially since Susie had for some unexplained reason turned relentlessly against him. Mrs. Oakley knew he had with Rebe raised Susanne almost without help from her daughter, Sarah. More important, her nephew, Alfred, had horrified her last week by disclosing Tom's attempted suicide, his mounting addiction to alcohol, his disastrous financial affairs and the huge amount of debt that Tom had incurred over the years. Mrs. Oakley knew in her heart that Sarah's extravagant lifestyle was at least in part the cause of Tom's financial ruin and recurrent tax problems. Mrs. Oakley had really come to like Tom over the years. She decided right then that she would take decisive steps to clear up Tom's financial problems on the Monday after Susie's marriage to Phil McPherson. "After all," Mrs. Oakley mused, "Tom has basically been a good soldier – a good loyal husband to my Sarah and a caring father to Susanne. I don't want to have my son-in-law's life come to an end with the disgrace of suicide. Tom's suicide would forever humiliate my Sarah and leave a lifelong blight on Susie. No," she said to herself, "I will use some of my money now to set Tom's financial and tax house in order. That may be what is needed to help Tom straighten his whole life out, particularly if Susie would end her savage treatment of him."

Her thoughts were interrupted. An usher appeared beside her pew escorting Jane with Alfred following. As Jane slid into the pew, Mrs. Oakley thought to herself that she had never seen Jane looking quite so sour. "Of course," Mrs. Oakley thought, "Jane has never liked Susanne. She probably dislikes having to come to this wedding."

The Olivers had just been seated and were at their prayers when Sarah swept up the aisle on the arm of an usher and stood alone in the first pew. Mrs. Oakley looked at her Sarah. Her maternal pride in Sarah in spite of all that had happened was reaffirmed. Sarah, in Mrs. Oakley's eyes, looked exactly what the mother of the bride should look like.

Mrs. Oakley shuddered as the organist suddenly chopped off the organ transcription of Bach's cantata "The Heavens Laugh, The Earth Exults" and began the traditional "Here Comes the Bride." Mrs. Oakley allowed herself to turn her head around and watch Tom escorting Susie up the aisle. Mrs. Oakley thought that Tom looked very serious as did Susanne. Mrs. Oakley looked at Tom and thought, "Poor Tom. But with this marriage, what he doesn't know at this point will never hurt him. Furthermore, this wedding will make it all a closed chapter."

Chapter 6 -- If Any Man Can Show Just Cause

She turned back and waited for Reverend Piccard to begin the service with the familiar words "Dearly Beloved."

Chapter Seven

Will You Do All in Your Power?

Rebe was driven to St. James Church by Joan. As Rebe got out of Joan's car, the big bell in the belfry struck 4:00. A flood of recollections swept over Rebe as she recalled the countless Sunday mornings years ago when she and Susie had come to this very church. Susie went to Sunday school while Rebe attended the 10:00 o'clock service, always sitting by herself in the last pew. Rebe stood in the sunlight and savored her memories for a few moments. Then she went into the church and sat down in the last pew on the bride's side. She went down on her knees and prayed, "Oh Lord, please hear this my special prayer for my dear little Susie, who is getting married today at this very church in half an hour. Please do not allow Stewart Jennings to interfere with your Holy Sacrament of Marriage. I pray that You will extend Your special favor, grace and blessing to Susie and Phillip and their marriage. All of this I ask in the name of Christ our Lord and our Savior. Amen." She got up from her knees, then sat back and thought of the recent course of events that had brought her back to St. James Church for Susie's wedding.

One day about a month ago, Tom Secant had telephoned her right out of the blue at her house in Nevis. She could tell right away that Mr. Secant was quite upset. But he started off quietly enough.

"Rebe, it's so nice to hear your voice again. I hope that you and your daughters and all your family are keeping well. I call you to give you a wonderful surprise. Since the time of my Christmas card to you, your little Susie has fallen in love and has become engaged to be married. In fact, Susie is going to get married at St. James Church on September 18 — that is, if all goes well and Stewart Jennings does not interfere." Mr. Secant continued, "But, Rebe, Susie really needs you badly now. I beg you. Please try to come up before Susie's wedding."

She had replied, "I will certainly come to my Susiekin's wedding. Mr. Secant, you know, of course, that you can count on me. If there is anything on which I can be of help to Susie, let me know. I will certainly do my best for my Susie, you know that!"

Mr. Secant continued, "Good, Rebe. I always could count on you. I have arranged for you to come up here before the wedding. In fact, I am mailing you an airline ticket to come from Nevis to Philadelphia. I can't wait, Rebe, to talk to you and get your advice and help on all the problems that Susie is having as she moves so quickly toward her wedding on September 18."

So Rebe had flown into the Philadelphia airport four days ago. Mr. Secant had met her at the Philadelphia airport. She could tell right away from Mr. Secant's agitated state that all was not well. Also, she could smell alcohol on his breath as he welcomed her with a big affectionate bear hug. When they got into his car, Tom had started to unburden himself right away saying, "Rebe, Susie is not at all the same nice little girl that you left as she went away to boarding school simply because of her mother's and her grandmother's wishes. As we both know, I did not want Susie to go to boarding school, and neither did you for that matter. All of a sudden, Susie grew up in lots of ways. Susie changed from being a really nice youngster into a wild young teenager. Susie seemed to deliberately turn her back on all the good things that you had taught her – manners, good behavior, cleanliness, going to church and all of that. Susie began to use bad language. Susie suddenly stopped playing all sports. Rebe, you remember how much Susie loved to play sports of all kinds. She was a good little athlete. But, as I say, all of a sudden, she stopped playing all sports. Then Susie began to smoke. In fact, I also know that she even smokes pot now from time to time and right in our very own house! I just don't understand it. Also, though she really doesn't drink that much, Susie began to use alcohol when she started going out with Stewart Jennings and the awful crowd he hangs out with. Beyond

Chapter 7 -- Will You Do All In Your Power?

that, Susie has broken my heart. She no longer is close to me at all like she was from the time she was a little girl. Remember, Rebe?" Tom looked sideways at Rebe as he said this.

Rebe recalled that she had turned to him and said, "Mr. Secant, tell me just what happened to cause all this trouble. Most important, tell me why Susie is no longer close to you. When I was made to leave by her mother, Mrs. Secant, Susie was devoted to you. You were a very good father to Susie. You had every reason to be proud of your daughter."

Tom looked aside uneasily and finally said, "Rebe, I don't really know why. But Susie has made it all too clear that she doesn't like me anymore. In fact, Susie won't have anything to do with me. She doesn't kiss or embrace me or allow me to hug her. She won't take directions or correction from me. She likes to make fun of me. Susie runs me down to my face and to all sorts of other people behind my back. Can you believe that? Rebe, without Susie my life lost all its meaning. I came damn close to ending it all one night two years ago."

Rebe could tell right then that there must have been something terrible that had caused this split between the devoted father and the loving daughter. She mused to herself, "I am going to have to find out just what seems to have led Mr. Secant to think about ending his own life." But she replied out loud to reassure Tom, "Mr. Secant, young girls like our Susie sometimes go through strange periods. Let's get this situation between you and Susie straightened out, shall we? But first let's turn to happier things. Just who is my Susiekins marrying? I hope he is worthy of her."

Tom replied, "Well, Rebe, you probably remember Stewart Jennings. He was the spoiled child of Dol Jennings. He was impossible as a small boy. He was the one who taught Susie to stick her tongue out. He got worse and worse as a teenager: smoking pot, riding motorcycles, playing the piano in bars and cutting up generally. He was always getting Susie in trouble even when they were little kids. You probably remember the time when Susie was about seven years old and she and Stewart smashed a hundred panes of glass in Colonel Rider's greenhouse. You first gave Susie a good spanking with your hairbrush. Stewart lied and tried to blame it all on Susie. But you did not believe him one bit and took him over your knee and also gave him a good spanking with your hairbrush. Remember, Rebe?

"Well, when Susie was about eighteen, she took up with Stewart as a boyfriend, partly as another way of spiting me. The two of them were a holy terror. Susie defied me and bought herself a secondhand Honda motorcycle. Susie damn near got herself killed on Bluner's Lane when she tried to go around that sharp corner at Colonel Rider's place at an ungodly high rate of speed. Mercifully, Susie was not killed or hurt. Rebe, I still have constant nightmares about Susie's accident.

"Well, just after Christmas she left off going out with Stewart Jennings, thank God, and took up with a young man named Phil MacPherson from Hartford, Connecticut. Phil is really a wonderful young man. He has just graduated from a fine college and has a career all planned out in governmental service. He is steady and serious. Phil is just perfect for Susie. He's everything that Stewart isn't. But damn it all to hell, Rebe, just now, almost on the very eve of their wedding, some sort of a disagreement has sprung up between Susie and Phil. Maybe, just maybe, they will make up and the wedding will go forward. I certainly hope so. But to complicate matters, Stewart has turned jealous and is threatening to make trouble at the wedding itself."

Rebe said, "But just what does Susie do with herself since she left college or was dismissed? Surely she must do something!"

Tom said, "Rebe, that's about the only good part. Susie found that she has a real knack with kids, especially those who have trouble talking. Susie seems to be a natural speech therapist. She has worked four days a week at the Tilton Center for Disabled Children in South Philly without pay. They worship her there! She has even talked of finishing college and getting a master's degree in speech."

Rebe had said, "Well, that's good, real good. Underneath all this foolishness, Susie is doing something useful for other people."

At that point they had gotten to the house. How familiar it was, Rebe thought as she came in the house. Rebe thought back on the many years that she had spent there almost solely in charge of

Chapter 7 -- Will You Do All In Your Power?

Susie except for athletics, which Mr. Secant handled. Rebe also remembered that Mrs. Secant had made no bones about the fact that she disliked, resented and was envious of Rebe. In fact, it had always been Mr. Secant who had paid Rebe's wages each week in cash.

Rebe took her old black cardboard suitcase through the kitchen door and up the steep little back stairs and into the nursery. It was just the same as it always had been when Susie was a little girl growing up, always under Rebe's strict and watchful eye. She found that her old bedroom behind the nursery had been made up for her. She set her suitcase down and came on back into the nursery. As Rebe came in one door, Susie had come running in the other door. Susie was dressed in cutoff blue jeans, a slightly soiled T-shirt and scuffed sneakers. Rebe and Susie stood for just a moment and then had fallen into each other's arms. Rebe at first thought how good it was to have her arms around her beloved Susie once again. However, Susie was no longer the sweet smelling little girl that Rebe had left with so much pain six years ago. Instead, Rebe instinctively recoiled as she smelled tobacco on Susie. Rebe had gently pushed Susie away and said, "Susiekins, what's this I smell? Don't tell me you smoke!"

Susie had said, "Yep, Rebe. You betcha. I smoke cigarettes and even a bit of pot now and then." Susie added a little defiantly, "What do you think of that, Rebe old girl?"

Rebe had held Susie at arm's length and said sternly, "Child, I don't believe you. How can you soil the beautiful body the Lord gave you with tobacco and drugs and I suppose drink? You should know better! I taught you better than that!"

Susie herself stepped back, pulled herself out of Rebe's grasp and said more defiantly, "God Almighty, Rebe, I'm now too old for you to scold and lecture me anymore. I'm not a little girl now. In fact, I am almost a full-grown woman. Shit, Rebe, I'm about to get married!"

Rebe remembered she was overcome by a flash of anger. She said sharply to Susie, "Young miss, I told you when we first met that you were never, never to sass Rebe. Now you have gone and done just that!" With that, Rebe had slapped Susie right across her face, first with the front of her hand and then with the back of her hand. "I think it best if I return right away to Nevis now that I see what Susie has turned out to be in spite of all I tried to do for her and teach her; a smoker of cigarettes and, yes, pot, a user of foul language and dressed in dirty ragged clothes on the eve of her wedding! What a pity? What a waste!"

Susie looked staggered and took two more steps backwards, her face contorted with anger. Then suddenly Susie began to cry. Rebe recalled that she had gently enfolded Susie once again in her arms. Susie had stood there, leaning against Rebe and cried and cried for a good five minutes. Susie then ended up sobbing just as she had done when she was a little girl and been bad. Susie, through her sobs, finally said, "Rebe, Rebe, I did not mean to sass you. Honest I didn't! How could I ever do that to you? You're the person who means the most to me in the whole wide world and has done the most for me. Please, Rebe, please don't leave me now, especially as I've gotten myself a whole mess of problems. Rebe, I am worried sick that my marriage to the man I love is going to fail at the last moment mostly because of my own stupidity!"

Rebe had continued to hold Susie, who was still sobbing in her arms, and said, "There, there, Susiekens. Just tell Rebe what is the matter. Then you and I will see what we can do about it."

Susie had said between sobs as they sat down on the old couch, "Well, Rebe, I got engaged to a wonderful guy but he and I are now mad as hell at one another. Neither one of us seems to be able to back off. I really cannot remember quite what started it, but I am not at all sure that Phil is really going to go through with our marriage. I have to admit he has lots of reasons not to do so. Also, there is Stewart Jennings. You remember him? He was always getting me in trouble when we were little kids. Then he sort of became my boyfriend a couple of years ago. He taught me to smoke, use pot and how to zip about on a motorcycle. For some reason Stewart dumped me all of a sudden about Christmastime. But when I ended up with Phil, Jennings became jealous. Now he keeps saying that he is going to break up our wedding at St. James. I know that I am partly responsible for that because I know I sort of egged Stewart on. I am terrified that, because I have been playing games, this whole wedding is

Chapter 7 -- Will You Do All In Your Power?

going to come crashing down around my ears on Saturday. Rebe, I'm really in love with Phil MacPherson. I know he is in love with me. Also, Phil is my only real chance of getting out of this house, away from my family, especially my father, and Philadelphia and the Main Line. I wish I could be a little girl again growing up under your care and love, Rebe. I really want to do something worthwhile with my life rather than just being a continual screw-up. I want to learn speech therapy so I can really help little kids professionally who can't seem to talk. I also want kids of my own with Phil. Help me, Rebe, for God's sake, help me. Help me if you can, as you always have before. Please, oh please do what you can to help me! Say you will. Rebe. I beg of you!"

Rebe then said to Susie, "Well, my child, calm down. The first thing that you've got to do is to go right upstairs and take a good hot bath. Wash your body, wash your hair and brush your teeth. Let's get rid of the awful smell of tobacco." Rebe remembered she laughed as she said, "Susie, why whoever heard of a bride who smelled of cigarettes! Then throw those trashy dirty clothes and filthy sneakers you are wearing right into the garbage can! Even the poorest girls in Nevis would be ashamed to be seen in what you are wearing. Susie, I taught you to know better. When you've done that, come on back down. Please don't swear or use dirty words any more. It hurts me so to hear you use such foul language. By then I will have unpacked. You and I will have a good cup of hot tea like old times. We will sit down and talk things over. I am sure that you and I can sort things out. We always could: no reason why we can't now. It's going to all come right, just you wait and see, Susiekins."

Rebe smiled as she thought back on the rest of that first afternoon. Susie had come back an hour later. She was spanking clean from head to toe. Susie was wearing a simple skirt and a clean white man's shirt and had polished loafers on her feet. Susie's black hair glistened as Rebe brushed it out just as she had done so often when Susie was a little girl. Rebe and Susie then sat down in the breakfast room and had a good long talk over a pot of tea.

Susie had begun, "Rebe, I don't know just where to begin. However, everything seems to be screwed up or messed up when everything should be going perfectly. I am engaged to a wonderful guy who will, I know, give me the support I need and give me a wonderful and interesting life. However, since you left me, I have developed the habit of deliberately doing exactly the wrong thing and ticking people off at me. Somehow, I get pleasure out of it. Why? Why, I sometimes ask myself. I don't know the answer. I may well have crossed Phil so severely that he may well and probably should throw our marriage over and go on his own way."

Rebe said, "Well, Susiekens, how did this start anyway?"

Susie said, "I don't really remember. Also, Stewart has decided it would be neat to shock the whole parish by coming into St. James and busting my wedding up. Jennings is mean enough to do something like that just for kicks. I can't stop him. It's driving my mother crazy. She is just beside herself. As for the old man, he and I had a bust-up some two years ago. Since then I have gotten my jollies in being just as mean as a snake to Dad. As I think back on it, my meanness has surely helped drive him to drink. Also, when I stopped playing sports, again just to be ornery, the old man then laid off any effort to be serious in sports. Now he is physically going to pieces before my very eyes. He has become an alcoholic. On the one hand I love teasing him and making him miserable but on the other hand inside I bleed for him. I am really sorry for all the pain I have deliberately caused him."

Rebe interrupted and said, "But tell me, child, what was it that led to this split between you and your father? When I left, you two were devoted to each other. He lived and breathed your success. Just what happened? Tell me, Susie."

Susie looked away and said, "Rebe, I really don't want to talk to you about it. Can't we just leave it at that?"

Rebe took Susie's chin in her hand and said firmly, "Young lady, now you look at me straight in the eye. I have come all the way from Nevis in spite of my age and my arthritis. You have asked for my help. Yes, I am willing to help you all I can but you have to come clean with me. Now tell me just what happened between you and your father. Then maybe we can figure out how to straighten it out. OK?"

Chapter 7 -- Will You Do All In Your Power?

Susie took Rebe's hand away from her chin and said, "Well, Rebe, if you must know, you remember that I used to run across the hall and snuggle with my father before we came down to breakfast with you. One spring vacation when I was home from boarding school, my father, probably still in his cups from the night before, came into my room. When I awoke, he was there with his hands all over me. I am sure he wanted to sleep with me, his own daughter! Now, Rebe, you know it all! Does it surprise you that I am no longer close to my father?"

Rebe recalled that she had controlled a look of surprise and anger and had said as matter of factly as she could to Susie, "Well, and so nothing further happened, did it, Susanne?"

Susie said, "Well, no, I guess it didn't, but that was because I rolled out of the other side of the bed."

Rebe said, "Well, Miss Susanne, the fact is that you have been making your father's life miserable for the past several years over something that never really happened? Right? Furthermore, tell me honestly, and yourself as well, young lady, did you yourself scramble out on the other side of the bed as quickly as you could have and should have? Ask yourself that before continuing to try to destroy your father, who raised and loved you, over something that never really happened."

Susie thought for a while without saying anything. Finally, she said slowly, "Well, Rebe, as I think back on it, I guess you, as always, are right. I should have jumped right out of bed on the far side just as soon as I woke up. However, I had begun to like playing with fire. I guess I waited for a while just to see what would happen. You're right. Nothing really did happen. But I was frightened and scared! I used that incident as a weapon to torture my father at the time and I have done so ever since. But when I punish him, I am punishing myself because I really know deep down that I didn't act as quickly as I should have. I have blamed him entirely for something in which, however briefly, I participated. Also, down deep, I really love my silly old dad."

There was silence for a while and then Susie said, "Rebe, you now know what happened and didn't happen and what stands between my father and myself. But how in the world do I get over the wall that I have deliberately built up between my father and me? My father, whom I love deep down and whom I really don't want to hurt, is now a total stranger to me and on his way to becoming a confirmed alcoholic. How, Rebe, just how?"

Rebe remembered that she had said, "Well, child. That is quite simple. All you've got to do is to pick the right time and simply tell your father straight out that you are sorry for having put him through the wringer for all these years for something that didn't happen. You don't have to go into detail. He will know right away. Simply make it clear that you don't really have anything against him and that you love him as you always did. After all, that doesn't seem too hard, does it?"

Susie had sat there sipping her tea and finally said, "No, Rebe, it all seems so simple and straightforward when you explain it. No, there's nothing hard at all about doing what you say. I just must pick out the right time and then just do it. It might make a big difference to Dad. Maybe he will even stop drinking, lose weight and take up sports again. Wouldn't that be great! But just when would be the right time I wonder."

Rebe said, "Think it over carefully. Then do it before it is too late. But, changing the subject, Susiekins, who at St. James is going to marry you and Phillip?"

Susie had replied, "Rebe, honestly, I don't really know him at all. He is Reverend Piccard. He came to St. James after you left, but I have never been near St. James since you left except, of course, for Christmas, Easter, weddings and funerals and that sort of thing."

Rebe had deliberately looked shocked and said, "What, Susie? You've left off going to church! You don't know the priest who is going to do the most important thing for you maybe in your whole life?"

Susie had said, "No, Rebe, I am ashamed to say that's right. But it's worse than that. Reverend Piccard invited me to come and have a little chat with him a week or so ago. But just at that point, Phil and I were starting our disagreement. I didn't want Reverend Piccard poking into my love life especially as I was seducing Phil regularly. So

Chapter 7 -- Will You Do All In Your Power?

I deliberately missed my appointment with him. I understand from Mother that he was pissed or, excuse me, Rebe, rather I meant to say, upset that I had missed the appointment."

Rebe said, "Susie, how could you think of doing such a thing as that! You must take steps to come clean with Reverend Piccard and indeed the Lord before you can go through the sacred ceremony of marriage."

Susie said, "But, Rebe, how can I do that at this point?"

Rebe said, "Well, if I were you, I would ask him after the rehearsal if you and Phil can come to St. James on Saturday morning and meet with him."

Susie's bright eyes opened wide as she said, "Yes, but what would we do there with him?"

Rebe said, "Why, make your peace with God, to be sure. Ask Reverend Piccard to administer the Holy Sacrament of Confession to both of you. Then follow that by taking Holy Communion."

Susie said, "Rebe, I never would have thought of that. But I can already feel that a full confession by me of all that I have so deliberately done wrong almost since the time you left and receiving absolution from Reverend Piccard as well as the Sacrament of Communion would be a wonderful way to start my marriage to Phil. I can also assure you, Rebe, that Phil will be totally surprised and delighted when I make this suggestion to him. He will just love the whole idea."

Rebe then continued thoughtfully, "But now let's turn to Master Stewart Jennings. I remember Stewart from the days I took care of you. He always was a little brat, a liar and a coward to boot. He was the one who taught you to stick out your tongue at people. Remember? He was forever in one kind of trouble or another. Indeed, I remember the last time I saw him before I left and you went off to boarding school. He came over to our house and called me nasty names from the other side of the fence. I told him to apologize to me but he ran away when I tried to grab him to give him another good spanking. I told him, though he was age 13, that what he needed was a good spanking and his mouth washed out with brown soap again as I had done on several occasions before. It didn't do any good. But Stewart, even though he was 13, was scared to death of me then and he probably still is. Susiekins, what reason is there to believe that Stewart will really come to your wedding on Saturday and commit the sacrilege of interfering with the marriage just for fun and games. I doubt that even Stewart would be up to that. But, mind you, if by chance he does, I will do what I can to prevent him from doing anything. Just how, I don't quite know, but put your faith in the Lord as I do."

Susie said as she finished the last of her tea, "Rebe, how wonderful to have you here for my wedding. Already you have shown me how to solve most of the problems that were standing in my way. How can I ever thank you?"

Rebe remembered that she had said, "Well, Susie, if you want to thank me, then don't ever forget again all that I taught you when you were a little girl. Listen to your conscience and do things right."

"Rebe, I will. I promise you I will," Susie said. "Will you read one of the lessons at our wedding service?"

Rebe replied, "Susie, nothing would please me more!"

Just then Mr. and Mrs. Secant arrived at St. James. Rebe went over to Mrs. Secant who was looking distraught. Rebe said, "Mrs. Secant, are you OK?"

Mrs. Secant said, "Rebe, Joan has just told me Stewart Jennings is on his way here to speak up when Reverend Piccard asks if any man knows of any just cause why Susie and Phillip cannot be married. What possibly can be done to stop Stewart's wickedness?"

Rebe said quietly, "Now just calm yourself, Mrs. Secant. Nothing at all is going to happen. Just you wait and see. Now here is John Oliver, your nephew, come to take you down the aisle."

After Mrs. Secant had gone up the aisle, Rebe watched the bridesmaids, the groomsmen and the little children all go up the aisle. Finally, Susie and her father went slowly up the aisle and stopped in front of Father Piccard who opened his prayer book and was about to start the marriage service with the words "Dearly Beloved."

Chapter Eight

Let No Man Put Asunder

Joan Platen heard the steeple clock striking four as she drove back up Bluner Lane and into the St. James Church parking lot. She drew up in the shade of one of the large maple trees and sat there for a few moments, trying to collect herself.

Mrs. Oakley's Cadillac drove sedately up to the main door of the church. The chauffeur and Annie, who had been sitting in the front seat, got out and stood by the rear door of the long black car as the old lady got brittlely out of the back seat. Then, with Annie behind her, Mrs. Oakley walked briskly on her little white cane into the church. Joan said to herself, "Though she doesn't realize it, her stiff-necked upbringing of her daughter is in large measure responsible for what may be a tragedy that is about to happen!"

Just then John Oliver drove up in his battered white Corvette and took a white florist box out of the back. Joan smiled when she saw John open the box and the effect that its contents had on the ushers gathered closely around him.

Joan thought back to the time when Susie had telephoned her on the first Monday in April and said blithely, "Joan, this is Susie. How's your love life? Are you sitting down? I'm still in bed. You'll never guess what's happened. Blinky and I are engaged! He proposed in a roundabout way this weekend. I suppose I have accepted. I'll give you all of the somewhat sloppy and humorous details about how we became engaged. When can you come down for the night? Our engagement is not binding or formal, but the cat is somewhat out of the bag since Mother saw to it that Alfred and Jane knew about it very promptly and she also couldn't wait to tell Grandmother Oakley. So now it's all over the place. They are all very pleased, principally, I suppose, because Blinky represents to their way of thinking an end to the Stewart Jennings phase of Susie Secant's life. Yes, I'm happy. But now that it's actually come about, I feel kind of funny. I am not really at all certain about it. Mother is planning to throw a cocktail party at the end of this month or early in May for the formal announcement."

Susie continued, "The date of the wedding hasn't been set as yet, but I guess it will be on a day in September after Labor Day. You've got to be my maid of honor. Naturally, Mother wants to do the whole thing up in style at St. James with a reception at the Club afterwards. I'm sure she is set on this is because she and the old man didn't have a formal wedding. Or it may be because I told them all to pack sand when Mother suggested a coming out party two years ago. Personally, I'd rather forget about all the formal 'shoot 'em up' and simply start living with Blinky or maybe go through some sort of a recitation of vows. Mother won't hear of any such thing. She says it would kill Grandmother Oakley. I suppose it would. On the other hand you might know Blinky wouldn't hear of any such simple sinful approach. So Mother has the social bit in her teeth and things are proceeding at a swift pace."

Joan's thoughts then turned to the time earlier in the week when she had flown in for the pre-wedding festivities. It was the first time she had seen Susie since the engagement party. The night that Joan arrived she and Susie sat up in the twin beds in Susie's room to hash things over. Joan said, "Well, kid, you must be on top of the world at this point. That's a gorgeous engagement ring you are sporting."

"Yeah, I guess it is. Blinky tells me it was his grandmother's ring. Joanie, if you must know the truth, I'm not at all certain. I am in love with Blinky, that's for sure and certain. But at this point I'm not sure this wedding is going to work out. I thought when you were in love with someone that somehow everything would be perfect from then on. But it isn't so, or at least not with me or us. Blinky is such a straight article in so many ways. I guess that's one reason I fell for

Chapter 8 -- Let No Man Put Asunder

him, but I'm already a little bit sick of his preaching at me. We had fun together before we got engaged but since then I feel like a new girl at a camp assigned to some sort of a senior counselor. I'm not sure I can go through life following in the sainted footsteps of a major in the Salvation Army or Parsifal.

"Of course, when he's not running a revival meeting, we have fun. Blinky loves to make love. Mother, as I told you, raised the roof that night in April when she was troubled with insomnia and came in at an inappropriate moment. I told her a little white lie to calm her fears – that is, that I was still on the pill. She's tried to forbid us from touching one another until we are actually married, but it just doesn't seem to work out that way. I think Phil promised her that he wouldn't sleep with me until we were married. Maybe he really meant it. But what the hell. I could seduce Phil in Center City Philadelphia, during the Mummers Parade in about thirty seconds. We have great fun. I think that we might have a great future on television or perhaps as a nightclub act. Maybe if things don't work out financially, we could give a correspondence course or franchise ourselves. Of course, we would have to practice all the time like figure skaters. But that wouldn't be so damn bad. We could call it 'The MacPherson Do-It-Yourself Intercourse.' Maybe we could get bank financing for poor but meritorious couples and even throw in a wedding."

Joan said, "Susie, you're a nut!"

Susie went on in a somber note. "Joanie, I would chuck the big wedding if I could. My heart isn't in it. Among other things it's going to put the old man further in debt. He sure as hell doesn't need that. He's got enough other troubles."

Joan replied, "Well, kid, you're only a couple of days away from the big day, so there really isn't much you can do about it at this point."

"Yeah, I guess so," Susie had replied moodily. "But who would have ever thought that Susie Secant would tamely submit to being the traditional little bride in white at a church wedding. It's all so bloody square, if you know what I mean."

Joan remembered that she had been disturbed by Susie's mood and felt that a violent reaction was going to follow shortly. She was correct. After a black tie dinner given by the Dulaires on Wednesday at the Club in honor of Phil and Susie, Phil had driven Susie and Joan back to the Secants'. Susie had been irritable at little things all the way home. Once home they all had gone into the library. Susie had gone directly to the bookcase and pulled out a volume and had taken a white cigar tube from the binding in the back of the volume and said, "Lord, I haven't had a smoke in such a long time. I think I'll light up. How about you, Phil? Do you feel like trying one? Of course, Joan has never smoked and never will."

Phil said, "Susie, for me, please don't smoke one of those goddamn joints. Why don't you give them to me and I'll throw them all down the john."

Susie said defiantly, "Are you crazy or something! I like to smoke, and I'm going to do it until the day I die. What's wrong with a quiet smoke once in a while for God's sake!"

Phil looked at Susie and blinked several times and then said, "You're what? You're going to smoke pot after we're married? Oh no you're not! Once we get married you're not going to smoke pot! As a matter of fact, I'm rather hoping that you're going to quit smoking ordinary cigarettes, let alone grass. How about it, what do you think, Joan?"

Joan looked at Susie and had seen the dangerous thunderheads of anger rising in her flashing black eyes as Susie replied, "Hey, keep Joanie out of this! This is not her business. Besides we both know how Joanie feels about smoking. Her approach is purely Victorian. But, Blinky my boy, you've got to get off your Excelsior kick. I'm not Sadie Thompson. I don't relish the thought of going through life climbing one puritanical peak after another. If that's your idea of life, forget it or at least forget it so far as I'm concerned. I'm quite content to remain in the valley below and let you do the climbing."

Joan tried to mediate and said, "Hey, come on now. Come off it, both of you. You're both wound up and tired from all that you've been going through. For God's sake, don't get in a wrangle at this point."

Phil said, "Joanie, I quite agree that Susie is overwrought and tired from getting ready for the wedding. But, she shouldn't com-

Chapter 8 -- Let No Man Put Asunder

plicate things by smoking grass just before our wedding. Smoking grass is against the law if nothing else, and Susie should damn well not do it."

Susie was now clearly angry, "Principle my ass! Come off it, big boy! You don't enjoy it, so you don't want me to do it. What about screwing me before the wedding? That's also wrong, but that doesn't seem to count. Is that because you've enjoyed it? Now how do you square your fine principles with that, Buster?"

Phil looked surprised, but Susie gave him no chance to reply as she went on, "If you want to know, you can take this fancy wedding and stuff it you know where. It wasn't my idea to go through this goddamn farce. I would have been satisfied to go through whatever was necessary in front of a justice of the peace or simply recite our own wedding vows or whatever you have to do with a few friends. You agreed with me at one time. Why did you change your mind and back up the old lady as she mapped out this elaborate social do? Was it because you like this big social stuff, or was it because you can't stand up to the old lady anymore than my old man can?"

Phil broke in, "Well, what's so wrong with your old man? Susie, you treat him like a dog. He's very fond of you, and all you do is turn him off. Why are you so goddamn mean to him, Susie?"

Susie snapped back, "To hell with him and his so-called affection for me. He's a stupid animal. He drinks too much, and he plays around. So far as I'm concerned, I couldn't care less if he dropped dead tomorrow!"

Phil stood up, "Susie, why don't you grow up? Some day you may wake up to find that your father has dropped dead of a heart attack just as mine did. You'll know then, just as I do, that you only have one father."

Susie replied, "Get off my back, Oliver Twist! You're bringing tears as big as golf balls to my eyes with that Life with Father routine. You ought to be on television on Father's Day." Susie paused for a moment and then turned to Phil and said, "Sweetheart, what would you say if I told you that dear old dads, whom you seem to revere, made a serious attempt to sleep with me early one April morning three years ago when I had just turned sweet 16. How would that sort of display of affection strike you?"

Joan looked at Phil. For once he did not blink as he quietly replied to Susie, "So what, Sue. You've trotted out this little piece of information just to shock Joan and me. First, you make it clear that it never happened. So I say, so what? Could it be, Susie, that you love to dish out shocks but you really can't take them? Second, what am I now supposed to do about your little shocker? Cancel our wedding? Or maybe you think I should go up and punch your father or burn the house down or something in protest for what did not happen three years ago? This finally explains why you're always so bitchy to your old man and why you're always giving him the needle. You've been holding this against him and rubbing his nose in it, right? Did you ever think that the constant needling you give him is probably one of the things that's driving him to drink? Damn it, Susie, why don't you grow up a little bit?"

Susie looked surprised and then said bitterly, "Well, so that's all you think of me? To hell with you, Buster! I'll show you a thing or two." She then stamped out of the room.

Joan and Phil sat there in the library, neither one saying anything or looking at one another. Finally, Phil said angrily, "This is a pretty state of affairs a few days before the wedding." Then he continued, "Joan, I'd rather expected from what Susie has indirectly hinted from time to time that something like this had happened. I knew that there must have been something that generated Susie's meanness to her old man. She simply has to face the fact that it didn't happen and get over it. I didn't want to show any surprise because that's what she so clearly wanted. It must have come as a terrific shock to her when her father made a pass at her since he was her idol. Something of the kind did happen though Susie probably exaggerates it. Underneath I bet she really loves her father, but she is just mean enough to be making him pay and pay and pay for what did not happen. The old boy was probably in his cups. I don't want Susie going around with this chip on her shoulder for all time to come. It's just something she's got to get over."

Joan said, "You're right, Phil. That was just the way to handle it. Susie has made Mr. Secant pay many times over for whatever went

Chapter 8 -- Let No Man Put Asunder

on. Poor guy. He just dotes on Susie."

Phil disregarded what she said and continued more to himself than to her, "You know, I certainly never dreamed that first night at the Yellow Lantern that I would end up marrying Susie. At first I thought she was just a screwed up little girl with hot pants. Now I really love Susie. I also have seen through the act she is always putting on. She is an intelligent and very determined young woman. God, I see a lot of problems though. I can just see Susie doing to me what she is doing to her old man, can't you? On the one hand I want to marry Susie, but I know that it may be a hell of a mistake. She's bound to make me miserable a good deal of the time. But I know it would be a worse mistake for me not to marry her. I'd be miserable always if I didn't marry her, and she gets away from me. I'm damned if I do and damned if I don't. I'd never be happy with someone like Ann Livingstone." He looked over at Joan. "That's right. You don't know Ann, do you? She's a sweet kid. Nothing like Mt. Vesuvius upstairs. Damn it, the plain fact of the matter is that I need Susie much more than she needs me." He turned to Joan and continued, "Do you understand what I mean? Do you agree?"

Joan replied, "Sure, I understand. You've taken on quite an assignment with Susie, but as you've just said, she's a terrific girl. She has great potential, which you can bring out if anyone can. She needs to get her priorities straightened out and do that soon. The time for hijinks is past. You've got to realize that Susie is going to take a lot of careful handling. She thinks you're too serious. For example, coming down so hard on her about smoking just as a matter of principle was perhaps a little tough."

She continued, "Phil, remember when you and Susie reached an impasse like this before? I told you that if you wanted to restore things with Susie it would be up to you to make the first move. You weren't willing to do so until Susie's motorcycle accident. The situation is somewhat similar now. You need to convince Susie that she's wrong in feeling that you're a stuffed shirt. I'm sure that if you do something along these lines, Susie would be happy to show you that she really loves you. After all isn't that the way it happened after the motorcycle accident?"

Phil said gloomily, "I don't know what more I can do to show Susie that I really love her. What started all this off was her childish desire to smoke grass though she knows my feelings. I don't think pot will hurt her, but it's the principle of the thing and the awful risk that it can lead her to try really dangerous and addictive drugs as so many other people have done. I also am damn sure that Susie doesn't really get much satisfaction out of it. She originally smoked pot as a childish rebellion. She's doing it now to bug me because she knows I don't like it. Hell, I don't want Susie to smoke pot, but it's her whole attitude that really distresses me as I look down the road."

Joan sad, "I certainly don't like the way things stand now. I hope that you find some way to tell Susie what you just said to me."

Phil looked perplexed. "Maybe you're right. But I don't know exactly what I should have done. Say I think its great to smoke grass on the eve of our wedding when I think it's terrible? More to the point, what am I supposed to do now? Am I supposed to take a speed pill to show that I'm a regular guy and that I don't think there's anything wrong with drugs? Perhaps I should shoot a little something into my arm before the wedding. Any other ideas?"

Joan smiled, "Well, Phil, I don't see you doing either one of those, and I don't know exactly what you can do. But you might try to think of something to show Susie that you're more than willing to meet her halfway on things."

Phil replied somberly, "I'll think about it, but it beats me how to do it. Also, it defeats me that every time Susie is crossed in any way, she immediately trots out that bum Jennings. Is this going to go on all of our lives together? Is he really the standard against which Susie is going to measure my many failings? Jesus Christ, I must be crazy to marry this girl. Maybe I am crazy, but that's the way it is. We'd best turn in. I'll see you tomorrow."

After Phil drove away, Joan turned out the lights downstairs and went up to the bedroom. Susie was lying on her bed and turned somewhat defiantly toward Joan, "Well, don't just stand there looking at me like that. I'm so sick of hearing old Reverend MacPherson moralizing at me I could scream. Since our engagement he's been like

Chapter 8 -- Let No Man Put Asunder

a probation officer. Joan, I can't go through life with a guy who is leading the children's crusade, if you know what I mean."

Joan said, "Listen here, Susie. You have a suicidal streak that surfaces every once in a while. But so does everyone. You're no different. Everyone once in a while can't seem to help doing the very thing that is contrary to their best interest. What you've just done tonight is a perfect example. You and I both know that more than anything in the world you want to stop being Susie Secant, the county cutup, and instead do something serious and worthwhile with your life. You're on the verge of being able to do that with a guy who really thinks you're great. Yet on the eve of your wedding you can't help making it appear that you are going to kick it apart just for the hell of it. Why in God's name do you give in to this?"

Susie said dully, "I couldn't care less at this point."

Joan continued, "You really do care, but look out. You seem to think that you're something unique and special in having an urge for self-destruction. Forget it, kid. We all have this urge but you've got to control it, especially now."

Susie replied cuttingly, "You wouldn't by any chance have just finished a child psychology course at dear old Bennett, would you? Besides, you yourself told me that Blinky at times is as serious as a bull moose. Be fair, Joan, don't you agree that Blinky does like to hear the sound of himself lecturing me? If he's like this now, what's he going to be like later on? He makes married life sound like double drill and no canteen."

Joan said, "Blinky does come on strong at times. It's up to you to loosen him up. You certainly don't seem to be going about it in the right way, not from the little scene you just put on tonight."

Susie answered, "Well, what do you suggest for openers – sackcloth and ashes or a little self-flagellation? Is that the path of penance that I should now follow? What do you counsel, Pallas Athena?"

Joan said, "Be serious. This may be the last of the ninth inning. I'm not going to tell you how to run your life or your marriage, but you'd better straighten up, and do it right now!"

Susie replied, "Thanks, Dear Abby. I will certainly consider your words of wisdom carefully. Now, Dr. Spock, if tonight's feature program is over, I'd like to turn in and get a couple of hours of shut-eye before the next round of this circus gets underway."

They said nothing more to one another, but as they were getting ready for bed, Joan noticed that Susie put the cigar tube carefully in her top bureau drawer. They turned out the lights and lay there awake in the darkness, neither one saying anything. Joan could hear Susie sobbing quietly in the other bed. After lying awake and worrying for what seemed a long time, Joan finally dozed off.

Later that week as they were getting dressed to go out to cocktails, Joan said to Susie, "Well, kid, I hear from your mother that you missed an appointment with Reverend Piccard."

Susie said, "I sure did. What a drag to have to talk to that old bird. He would probably pry into all sorts of things that I don't particularly want to discuss with him right now or at any time. According to Mother, he threw a real shit fit but calmed down when Cousin Alfred yanked his chain some."

Joan said, "I don't mean to pry, but where do you stand with Phil? Are you going to patch things up, or are you simply going to let things slide and take the very real risk that Stewart will show up and make a hash of your wedding just for the hell of it? If so, please understand, Susie, that you can count me out here and now!"

Susie looked frightened but said defiantly, "Just what do you mean by that grim statement? What do you think is going to happen?"

Joan lost her temper and said angrily, "OK, smarty pants, I think Jennings is going to try to break up your wedding and your only chance to marry Blinky will end once and for all." She added, "I think Jennings is going to hurt you terribly as well as all your family. That's what I think is going to happen. I think it may well happen whether you like it or not. That's what I think, now that you asked. I also think that Phil would be well advised to look up Ann Livingstone – he's far too good for you."

Joan saw fear and uncertainty in Susie's eyes. Susie said nothing for a long while and then said quietly to Joan, "Oh my God. What the hell have I gone and done? Joan, help me if you can. I am going

Chapter 8 -- Let No Man Put Asunder

to try to make this wedding work and also make my life with Phil a success. Rebe is flying in this very afternoon. Maybe she can help me. She always has."

Joan said, "Good girl, Susie. Now you're talking. You can count on me. You know Rebe will stand behind you but what can she really do? And just how are we going to stop Stewart at this point?" Joan's worst fears were confirmed at the wedding rehearsal when Stewart had driven up to the main doors of St. James on his motorcycle and came right on in and intimated that he would return the next day at the wedding service itself.

On the morning of the wedding Joan was wakened by the sound of Susie vomiting in the bathroom. Susie emerged looking pale, saying, "Joan, what a wretched night I've had, cursing my stupidity in bitching up my own wedding to a guy I really love and care about. How could I have done such a dumb thing!" She continued as she threw on a pair of slacks and a white shirt, "I'll see you later. There's something I have to do now. I'll be back in time to dress for the wedding luncheon at Alfred and Jane's. See you!"

Saturday at noon, as Joan and Susie were getting dressed to go to the wedding luncheon, the telephone between the beds rang. Susie said, "Joanie, would you mind answering that?"

Joan answered and the voice on he other end said, "Hello. Is Mrs. Secant there?"

Joan replied, "No, I'm sorry. Mrs. Secant has left for the wedding luncheon. Can I give her a message?"

The voice had replied, "This is Dr. Rogian. I have an important message for her. Will you be seeing her? It is vital that she get this message. Who am I talking to?"

Joan replied, "This is Joan Platen, Susie's roommate and her maid of honor. We are leaving for the wedding luncheon in a few minutes. I will see Mrs. Secant there."

Dr. Rogian said, "Fine. Would you tell Mrs. Secant that Dr. Rogian called. Tell her Stewart Jennings came to the hospital this morning and saw his mother. He then came to see me and said he was going to make trouble at the wedding. Tell Ms. Secant that Stewart is going to make trouble about the Hilltop matter. I want to make sure that Mrs. Secant is forewarned. Have you got that? The Hilltop matter – it's important."

Joan looked over at Susie, who was looking at her, and said into the phone, "I understand, and I also understand the importance of the message. I will give Mrs. Secant the message just as soon as we get to the wedding luncheon."

Susie said inquiringly, "Who was it, Joanie? What did they want? What's so important?"

Joan replied, "Oh, nothing really. A Mr. Robertson's wife has been admitted to the hospital so they can't come to the wedding. Big deal! I'll tell your mother at the Olivers'. Let's get going. We're late as it is now. Don't worry about Stewart. Certainly all of us can deal with that screwball now that you have finally come to your senses, kid."

When they got to the Olivers', Joan went directly to Mrs. Secant and said, "Mrs. Secant, can I talk to you privately for a moment?"

She replied, 'Why of course, Joan dear. How about in the library? What's on your mind?"

Joan replied, "I don't know whether it's significant or not, but a Dr. Rogian, I believe that was his name, telephoned the house just before we came over here and said that Stewart Jennings had been to the institute to see his mother and then came in and talked to Dr. Rogian. The doctor went on to say that Stewart was threatening to upset the wedding. He said it had something to do with Hilltop or the Hilltop matter. He asked that I pass this message along to you."

Joan could see Mrs. Secant's hand tighten around her sherry glass. However, she said lightly to Joan, "Well, thanks for the message. I certainly hope that Stewart really doesn't try to upset the apple cart. Let me see, I think it would be best if you didn't mention this to Mr. Secant since the mention of Stewart drives him into a frenzy. It's probably also best that Susie doesn't know of this, at least for the present. Don't you agree? On the other hand I think I will mention it to Mr. Oliver. Of course, Stewart wasn't asked to this luncheon, so maybe something can be done to see that Stewart doesn't really carry out his threat."

Chapter 8 -- Let No Man Put Asunder

Joan said, "I think I know a way to stop Stewart if he does try to break up the wedding."

Mrs. Secant said, "Thanks, Joan dear. That's very nice of you, but I don't see how you could stop Stewart if he does make good on his threat, just as he did at the rehearsal last night. However, I do appreciate your offer. Now, go get yourself some lunch, child."

As Joan came out of the French doors leading from the living room to the sunlit terrace, she looked over the lawn and garden. Beyond the flagstone terrace the lawn was alternately in sunlight and in shadow from the huge old trees that stood around the edge of the lawn itself. At the edge of the lawn the carefully tended flower gardens were in full bloom. On the lawn the caterer had set out tables with white linen tablecloths. There were pink and blue ribbons decorating the table and the carnations were also pink and blue. At the long buffet table at the far end of the lawn there were large silver candelabra with white candles. The guests were at the tables, and there was the quiet hum of conversation and laughter. It looked so calm and beautiful. It seemed impossible that anything might happen to prevent the wedding from taking place.

Indeed, as Joan looked around, there was no sign that marred the outward serenity of the wedding lunch except for Mrs. Secant's pale face as she talked animatedly to Mr. Oliver at one side of the terrace. The hurried conference ended as Mr. Oliver patted Mrs. Secant on the shoulder and led her over to the corner table where Mr. Secant, Mrs. Oliver as well as Mr. and Mrs. Charles Simmons, Phillip's mother and stepfather, were already seated and were waiting to begin their lunch.

Joan went to the buffet table and got herself a plate. As the guests were finishing the blue and pink sherbet and were drinking demitasses and smoking, there was the sound of a large motorcycle coming up the Olivers' driveway. The noise stopped. Shortly afterward Stewart stepped dramatically out of the glass doors and the darkness of the living room and into the bright sunlight. He stood on the flagstone terrace with an old-fashion glass in one hand and his other hand in his pocket. He had taken off his black motorcycle jacket and was wearing a blue denim shirt, Levi's and sneakers. He was wearing aviator sunglasses. His long blond hair, released from his black helmet, stood out halo-like from his head. Many of the guests looked around at Stewart, surprised to see him and wondering what he was going to do. Stewart, obviously savoring the effect his appearance was having, stood there looking around. He deliberately took a cigarette from the pocket of his denim shirt and pulled a blue kitchen match from his pants pocket and lit it with his thumbnail. He flipped the match away on the lawn in a contemptuous gesture. Joan could see Stewart smile maliciously as he spotted the corner table where the Secants, the Olivers and the Simmons were sitting and started over to them. She intercepted him and tried unsuccessfully to head him off.

    Joan stood behind Stewart while he talked to the Olivers, the Secants and the Simmons. Joan could see the effect and the anguish that he caused with his toast. The toast had some special significance for the people sitting at the table. After his toast she laid a hand on Stewart's sleeve and led him over to an empty stone bench.

    Stewart said, "Say, that was quite a little toast, wasn't it, baby? Not bad for having been made up on the spur of the moment. My inspiration just got a nice little trust fund for Susie which I'm sure she can use. But I'm just warming up these people for the real show that's going to take place this afternoon. I've really got the goods on the whole crowd. By God, just you wait and see." He called to a passing waitress. "Say, please bring me a vodka on the rocks."

    Joan could see that Stewart was already showing the effect of the previous vodkas. She said, "Just a sec, Stewart, don't you think you've had enough, at least for the moment?"

    He replied, "Joan, just whose side are you on anyway? You sound like old Alfred Oliver himself."

    She said, "I'm on Susie's side, naturally. What is this all about anyway, Stewart?"

    He replied, "Do you really want to know? I have a plan to rescue her from the Hartford giant. Would you like to hear how?"

    Joan nodded her head affirmatively and passed Stewart the vodka on the rocks which the waitress had brought. Stewart took a long drink and wiped his mouth on his sleeve. "For a while I was led

Chapter 8 -- Let No Man Put Asunder

to believe for family reasons that I couldn't really legally marry Susie even if I wanted to, which is a joke because I never wanted to anyway. There's no use going into all of that now, but the long and short of it is there wasn't any reason why I couldn't marry Susie this very afternoon if I wanted to. This afternoon, when old Piccard asks if there's anyone in the house who knows any just cause why these two shouldn't be joined together, well, I'll pop up out of my pew and tell them once and for all that Susie is too good for MacPherson, a blinking conservative shithead if there ever was one. For my money he's nothing but a tall social climber. I'll also disclose that that great hunk of flesh, Tom Secant, is not really Susie's father and doesn't have the right to give her away. What a rip-off that will be, don't you agree?"

Stewart was looking at Joan. She looked shocked. She said to him, "Christ, Stewart, what a hell of an idea. I knew Susie and Phil were a little on the outs, but your little plan solves all Susie's problems. But what's all this about Susie's father?"

Stewart said, "I won't spill the beans now, but Susie doesn't need to take any more crap from Tom Secant – he's a complete stranger to her. The trouble is, her true father isn't any better – maybe worse."

Stunned, Joan signaled to the waitress. "I know the bar is closed, but we are two of the bride's best friends. We need to have just two more drinks, one double vodka on the rocks and one champagne on the rocks."

The waitress said doubtfully, "Well, I don't know, Miss. I'll try." In just a moment, the waitress returned with the drinks. Joan took her glass and handed Stewart his, saying, "Come on, drink up, Stewart. Then I'll drive you home. Leave your motorcycle here, and I'll pick you up on the way to the church this afternoon."

Stewart said, "Nuts! I can drive the box that Czech wheel came in."

Joan said, "Sure you can. OK, then John and I will follow you to your place. I want you to tell me just what you plan to do so that Susie will be prepared."

Stewart looked at her and said, "OK, Joan. Let's get out of here!"

By this time most of the guests were leaving. Joan saw Susie and John Oliver standing talking on the other side of the lawn and beckoned to them. When Susie and John came over, Joan said, "Say, guys, I've got my car here. I told Stewart that I'd follow him to the gatehouse. I'll go with him so that Stewart can explain to me what lay back of his toast and his plan for the wedding this afternoon. OK? John, please come with me. Stewart, why don't you go out through the garden to your motorcycle. I'll say goodbye to the Olivers and join you there."

Susie threw a troubled look at Joan and was about to say something but Stewart broke in and said, "Right on, Joan. Let's get the hell out of here. Susie, I can hardly wait for the ceremony and my part in it. I think I'll grab another drink on our way out."

Joan could see that Phil was very angry as he saw Susie talking to Stewart, who was somewhat unsteady. Joan went over. "You look mad, Phil. I don't blame you. Try to understand that John and I are trying to manage things so that Stewart won't interfere this afternoon."

Phil replied, "Joan, I have confidence in you and John, but it makes me furious to see Susie talking at our bridal luncheon to Stewart Jennings, who is drunk as a lord, in case you hadn't noticed."

Joan said, "I had noticed. Phil, there are more ways than one to skin a Czech cat. Don't lose your cool. John and I think we may know how to handle Mr. Stewart Bellak Jennings. Please say my goodbyes and thanks to the Olivers."

Joan and John went to her car. John got in. Stewart was sitting on his black-and-gold motorcycle. As she was about to get in her car, Joan said pleasantly to Stewart, "That sure is a beautiful machine. Susie says it's Czech."

He replied, "It sure is; it will go to 100 kilometers in 20 seconds and outrun any cop car!"

Joan said, "Stew boy, before you leave, why don't you tell John and me just what your plan is?"

Stewart still had a drink. He took a swallow and announced in a loud voice, "By God, Joanie, old girl, I intend to fix all of them but good, including her mother, that hard-hearted Philadelphia bitch, Tom Secant, ex-athlete and drunk, and, yes, old Mrs. Oakley, the dean

Chapter 8 -- Let No Man Put Asunder

of the community, as well as Alfred Oakley Oliver, in outward appearance a pillar of society and the church but really a sneaking little pervert, running a crooked brokerage house. By God, I hate them one and all. I'll fix them today for what they have done to my mother. But most especially, I intend to tumble Blinky MacPherson, boy scholar from Hartford, who can't wait to become a part of the crumbling establishment with Susie, his society wife. Let the chips fall where they may and God help whoever is under them because there are going to be some pretty heavy chips falling this afternoon about 4:30." He handed Joan his empty glass.

Joan said, "OK, Stew boy, take it easy. You've told us who you don't like and who is going to be revenged upon, but you don't tell us how you're going to do it."

Stewart smiled maliciously, "Well, when old Piccard asks if any man knows just cause why these two should not be joined together, I'll pop up in my seat and tell them one and all. Won't that be a gas, Joanie? "

Joan said, 'Yeah, Stew, sounds like just what the doctor ordered."

Stewart gunned his motorcycle and roared out of the Olivers' driveway. Susie came over and said, "Joan, I know Stewart is mean enough to break up my wedding just for the fun of it. Joanie, Stewart's just drunk enough to do what he says. I think I'm going to upchuck again."

Joan said with exasperation, "For Pete's sake, kid, pull yourself together. Don't sit there sniveling and wringing your hands. Puking is not going to help. No, go get dressed in your lovely wedding dress. John and I will outfox Mr. Jennings and arrange things so that he will never get to St. James' this afternoon. Come on now, kid. Don't falter now that you have finally come to your senses and want to stop this cross-eyed jerk from permanently messing up your whole life."

Susie threw her arms around Joan and gave her a big hug, saying, "What can I say but thanks? If I do end up as Mrs. Phillip MacPherson, it will be due to your help!"

Joan and John Oliver got into her car and she drove quickly

over to the Dulaires' gatehouse. Both of them got out of the car and walked to where Stewart was fumbling with the front door key, trying to get it in the front door lock of the gatehouse.

Joan said pleasantly, "Why not ring the bell, Stew?"

Stewart said, "'Cause there ain't no one home, that's why. Della has the whole damn weekend off, that's why!"

Joan said, "OK, Stew boy, give me the key; I'll open the door for you." She inserted the key in the lock and opened the heavy old front door. She handed Stewart the key and he dropped the key on the hall table, walked over and turned on the light switch in the hallway. As he did so, the sound of his stereo hi-fi player came on from speakers all over the house. Stewart turned around, smiled and said to Joan and John, both of whom were surprised by the deafening noise, "You look surprised. I have my stereo tape player hooked up to the lights in the house. It plays all over the house."

Joan shouted to Stewart as he was about to go upstairs, "Hey, Stew, where do you keep the liquor in this joint? You, Ollie and I should drink a little toast to this afternoon's events."

He replied, "Joanie, I didn't know you were one for liquor. That's an excellent idea. You really are a very bright girl. A very excellent idea. Vodka, gin, whiskey and all that sort of crap are in the pantry between the kitchen and the dining room. There may be some tomato or V8 juice in the fridge if you want a Bloody Mary. Why not bring the drinks up to my room on the third floor? I'm going to go up and crap out for a little while before the wedding." Stewart slowly climbed up the stairs using the banisters for support.

Joan shouted, "OK, Stewart, hang on. We'll be up in a second." Then she turned and said quietly in Oliver's ear, "Come on, Ollie, shake a leg. Don't just stand there looking helpless!"

Oliver said forcefully, "Jesus, Joan, don't give Stewart another drink of vodka. It'll just make things worse."

"Nonsense," Joan replied briskly. "Unless I miss my guess, with about one more solid double vodka, Stewart will have had it for this day. He'll be in the land of la-la at 4:30. Come on, let's make it happen."

Oliver said, "By golly, Joan, you may well be right. It's worth

Chapter 8 -- Let No Man Put Asunder

a shot, or maybe two shots. Let's go!"

In the pantry they found a half-empty bottle of vodka as well as gin and whiskey. Joan got three oversize old-fashion glasses out of the cupboard, filled them with ice, filled one with vodka and the other two with cold water . She handed the one with vodka to Oliver, saying "Here, Ollie, you take the one with vodka I'll take the two with water. But for God's sake, let's not get them mixed up. If I drank the one with vodka, I'd be on my ear for days. So will you if you get Stewart's potion; that's a fatal potion!"

When they got upstairs, Stewart was stretched out in his clothes and shoes on his unmade bed with his eyes closed. Joan tasted the old-fashion glass just to make sure that she had one without vodka. Then she tapped Stewart on the arm and handed him the glass which Oliver had handed her. Then she raised her own glass and said, "Well, Stewart, here's to the bride, Susie, and all that takes place this afternoon."

Stewart sat up unsteadily in his bed and said sort of dreamily, "Right. Right on. That's a bottoms up toast, guys." The three of them finished their respective drinks in a series of gulps. Then Stewart lay back down on the disheveled bed and lit a cigarette with a blue match that he had pulled out of his blue-jean pocket. Joan said, "Stewart, old boy, the two of us have got to trot on home and get into our wedding finery. I'll set your alarm for 4:00. That should give you plenty of time to get to St. James. Right? See you there!"

Stewart said dreamily, "OK, OK. Right on." Then he sang dreamily, "Get me to the church on time, get me to the church ..."

As Joan and Ollie were going toward the door, Stewart lay there with his eyes closed and muttered, "They'll all be getting their just deserts this afternoon about 4:35 P.M., just you wait and see. Wait and see." His voice trailed off and he was silent with his eyes closed.

Joan said quietly to Ollie, "You go ahead on down. I'll be down in just a second." As he went quietly out of the room, Joan pulled the shades down, turned on the air conditioner and said, "Stewart, boy, are you OK?"

Stewart did not reply. She could hear him breathing heavily.

Dearly Beloved

His mouth was open. Joan said to herself, "Well, let's see. The time has come for my poor trunk's revenge. One good defenistration deserves another." She took the phone cord and gave it a smart pull. The cord snapped loose from the connection in the wall. She went over to the window, raised the shade, opened the window and dropped the phone out. She watched as it spiraled downward three stories and smashed to pieces on the cobbled drive in front of the garage narrowly missing the big black Czech motorcycle parked there. Joan then quietly closed the window, pulled the shade back down again and went quickly down the steps. She picked up the front door key and went out the front door, locking the heavy door behind her and then throwing the front door key in the bushes. She said to Ollie, "Stewart is out like a light. I very much doubt that he will be able to make the wedding this afternoon. But I locked the front door just in case!"

Ollie said, "Well done. But let's take a couple of additional steps just to make sure that old Stew can't get over to St. James."

Joan said, "Ollie, what more can we possibly do?"

Ollie said, "Follow me." He went back over to where the big black motorcycle was parked. The key was in the ignition. He pulled the key out and tossed it into the thick bushes. He then picked up a stone and went back to the motorcycle. He gave the ignition hole a couple of smart taps with the rock, saying, "Now even if Stewart does manage to get up and somehow finds his way down and out the door and over to his motorcycle, he will find no key to start it. Even if he does have a second key in the house somewhere, he won't be able to get the key into the ignition. Between us we have three reasons why Stewart is not going to be able to get to St. James to disrupt the wedding ceremony this afternoon."

Joan said, "Ollie, those were brilliant ideas. But if I know Stewart, he might somehow still manage to show up. Let's get back to St. James and make sure our final backup is in place."

John said to her, "Joan, please drop me off at home so I can get my Corvette. I'll make sure our backup plan is all ready. By the way, I had my research assistant recheck with Harrisburg: they confirm that the only motorcycle Stewart has registered with them is his old 1965 Honda. Also, tell Susie that Stewart will probably not be

Chapter 8 -- Let No Man Put Asunder

able to show up. She is worried sick. Also, please be sure to tell Aunt Sarah about Stewart's sadness about being unable to attend the wedding. In spite of her outward appearance and aristocratic coolness, my aunt is just about at the end of her tether."

When Joan got back at the Secants, she went up to Susie's room and said, "Well, kid, Ollie and I have done all that's possible to prevent Stewart from getting to the wedding. First, he is dead to the world – that is, passed out on his bed from a little overdose of vodka. Next, if he were to arise from his vodka potion, he is going to find that he is unable to start his big Bohemian motorcycle."

Susie replied doubtfully, "Joanie, if I know Stewart, he'll somehow show up. But if this wedding does actually come off, it will be thanks to you and Ollie's effort. I don't have to tell you again how grateful I am. Let's tell Daddy and the old lady. They're both frantic." Susie hesitated and then said, "By the way, what with everything else, Joanie, can you remember to give this to Ollie with instructions that he must absolutely give this to Phil before the service gets underway? I want to be sure that Phil gets it and knows just what it is." With that, Susie opened her purse and pulled out the battered white cigar tube which came from the back of the volume in the library. A small white ribbon had been wrapped around it with a sprightly bow. Joan took it and smiled at Susie and said, "Sure, kid. I am certain that Phil will get the message from this little gift."

After dressing, Joan went down and saw Mr. Secant, who was already dressed and waiting in the front hall. "Mr. Secant, Stewart is passed out on his bed at the top of the gatehouse. It is unlikely that he'll be able to repeat his performance at the rehearsal dinner and do what he warned us about at the wedding luncheon today."

He replied warily, "Joan, thank goodness! Good, good! I just hope to God that Stewart stays that way until Susie is safely married and away on her honeymoon." He added, "I'll tell Mrs. Secant. You don't know the strain that she has been under at the prospect of Stewart Jennings coming to St. James to bust up the wedding. She will be immensely relieved to receive this good news. Thank you, child."

At 3:45, Joan was dressed and ready to go. Susie was still

being helped into her white wedding dress by the lady from Nan Duskin's. Joan said to Susie, "I'll take Rebe with me. Well, kid. I don't suppose there is anything that I can do here for you, is there?"

Susie replied, "No. Thanks, Joan. You and Ollie have done more than enough already, or at least I hope you have." Mrs. Secant, who had come in the door, said, "I'll say amen to that, Joan. Tom told me that Stewart is passed out at his house, thank God!"

Joan said, "Well, if it's OK, Rebe and I will take my car to the church." Joan drove to St. James and dropped Rebe off. Joan then drove back over to the Dulaires' gatehouse just to check on Stewart. To her horror she saw Stewart standing beside his big motorcycle. Joan froze.

When Stewart looked up and saw Joan, he shook his fist at her and called out angrily, "Goddamn you, Joan, all to hell! First, you and that fag Oliver tried to get me so drunk I couldn't get to Susie's wedding. Well, that just didn't work. Then you tried to lock me in my own house. Finally, you hide the key to my Tatra. You've also bashed up the ignition, haven't you?" Without waiting for her answer and with a malicious smile on his face, Stewart added as he stepped down on the crank pedal and the huge black motorcycle started with a roar, "Well, what you didn't know, Miss Smarty Pants, is that I can bypass the ignition switch by crossing the wires. I wasn't really sure until now that I was actually going to break up Little Miss Susie's fancy society wedding, but this, by the living Christ does it! If it's the last thing I do, I will say my piece when the preacherman asks if anyone knows any reason why Susie Secant and the Blinker can't get hitched. I am going to reveal certain facts so that you and everyone at St. James will never, never forget this particular wedding. Well, Little Miss Fix It, I will see you later, alligator!"

Joan turned around and drove swiftly back up the long hill to St. James. She had tears in her eyes. All of her plans seemed to have failed. As she was about to turn into the parking lot, she saw Ollie standing next to Corporal Roberts in the center of Bluner's Lane directing the traffic coming into St. James for the wedding. Ollie was just handing Corporal Roberts a piece of paper. Corporal Roberts, who was directing traffic, signaled her to come in and, having

Chapter 8 -- Let No Man Put Asunder

glanced at the paper, gave her and Oliver the high sign.

Joan had just time to say to Mr. and Mrs. Secant who were standing rather forlornly by the Baptismal font waiting for the service to get underway, "I have some really bad news. Stewart, in spite of everything, is back on his feet and is coming to St. James on his motorcycle. However, please don't give up just yet. There is another backup plan that Ollie and I have in place that may stop Stewart's fatal plans."

The Secants looked at one another in horror. They had no time to say anything because Mrs. Secant was led to the aisle by Mrs. Perry, the social secretary. Ollie took his aunt on his arm and walked her down the aisle to the first pew on the left.

Mrs. Perry formed the wedding procession and it got underway. First there were the six groomsmen followed by the six little children followed by the three bridesmaids. Then came Joan, the maid of honor. Finally, Mr. Secant came down the aisle with Susie on his arm to the traditional strains of "Here Comes the Bride." When Susie and her father reached the two little steps, they stopped in front of Reverend Piccard. He opened his *Book of Common Prayer* and was about to say "Dearly Beloved."

Chapter Nine

We Are Come Together

At 4:30 a single stroke on the big bell at St. James was the signal for the commencement of the wedding service. By then even the latest arrivals were seated as well as standing along the side aisles. The three bridesmaids with downcast faces and timid smiles came up the aisle following the six children and the six groomsmen striding two by two. The little boys were in blazers and white pants. The little girls were in long dresses made of white cotton decorated with flowers and had little coronets of ivy. Susie then came up the aisle on her father's arm to the familiar sounds of "Here Comes the Bride." Susie was smiling bravely. After they reached the two little steps before the chancel, Tom and Susie stopped. The church was totally quiet. The only sound was that of the four small fans below the chancel windows that were making a rhythmic purring sound. The atmosphere in the church was tense. Reverend Piccard opened the *Book of Common Prayer* and was about to say 'Dearly Beloved."

But Susie peeked around her father at her groom and whispered, "Father Piccard, before you begin ..." She motioned Phillip with her eyes to her bouquet. It was only then that Reverend Piccard saw that the bride's bouquet consisted entirely of dark green marijuana stems. Phil smiled and then pointed to a white cigar tube behind his handkerchief in his breast pocket. He pulled it out and handed it to Susie. Susie passed the bouquet and the cigar tube and a half finished pack of Winstons to Joan, who passed them to the first bridesmaid. The bridesmaids in turn passed the three items down the line. The last bridesmaid laid them all on the floor under the first pew. Phil and the bride exchanged smiles. Susie then again peered around her father and motioned Phil to step over to her. He did so and as he leaned down, she mounted the two little steps, stood on her tiptoes and put her two arms around him and whispered in his ear so that only Phil could hear, "Phil, my dear, you really must marry me. I am carrying our first child!"

Phil at first looked totally dumbfounded. Then he smiled broadly and put both of his arms around Susie and tenderly kissed her on the mouth. Father Piccard stood watching all of this. He beamed benignly, raised his hands in mock alarm and said to the bride and the groom but loudly enough so the whole congregation could hear, "Now, now, children. Please hold on. You seem to have forgotten that the first kiss comes at the end of the marriage ceremony, not at the beginning."

A ripple of good-natured laughter swept through the whole congregation. The tension was somewhat dispelled. Reverend Piccard, again addressing the whole congregation, said, "We, of course, are all here on the happy occasion of the marriage of Phillip and Susanne. But first, before we begin, the bride and groom came to me yesterday and asked if we could offer Holy Communion to the whole congregation. However, as we thought about it, they concluded, and I agreed, that Holy Communion for all those who have assembled for this wedding might well make this marriage service overly long. Instead, Phillip and Susanne decided to come together early this morning to this church. I administered both the Holy Rite of Confession as well as Holy Communion to the two of them. They especially asked, however, that the wedding service commence with an expression of their joint thanks to each and every one of you for attending and participating with them in their marriage."

Reverend Piccard paused, smiled again and said, "Also, you will notice children in the pews toward the front on both sides of the aisle. No, they are not children of the bride and groom." Again this evoked a little titter of laughter from the congregation. Reverend Piccard continued, "On the right side, as you face the altar, are Alice and Doris Simmons, the groom's little half sisters. On the left side are Timothy, Choa-Li, Rachael and Dabney. They are some of

Chapter 9 -- We Are Come Together

Susanne's pupils at the Tilton Center for Disabled Children. Susanne's students wanted to come and see their teacher get married in her beautiful white wedding dress instead of the blue jeans they have seen her in almost every day over the past year as their speech teacher. Also, if the truth be known, all these children have come to feast on the delicious wedding cake that they have been promised will be served at the reception after this service of marriage."

Reverend Piccard then looked over his glasses and said softly, "Susie and Phillip, ready?" When they nodded, he began.

"Dearly Beloved: We have come together in the presence of God to witness and bless the joining together of this man and this woman in Holy Matrimony. The bond and covenant of marriage was established by God in creation, and our Lord Jesus Christ adorned this manner of life by his presence and first miracle, at a wedding in Cana of Galilee. It signifies to us the mystery of the union between Christ and his Church, and the Holy Scripture commands it to be honored among all people.

"The union of husband and wife in heart, body, and mind is intended by God for their mutual joy, for the help and comfort given one another in prosperity and adversity: and when it is God's will, for the procreation of children and their nurture in the knowledge and love of the Lord. Therefore marriage is not to be entered into unadvisedly or lightly, but reverently, deliberately, and in accordance with the purposes for which it was instituted by God."

Reverend Piccard said, "The first reading will be by Miss Rebecca Haight, the bride's nurse and governess and a deaconess in the Episcopal Church of the Advent on the Island of Nevis."

Rebe had walked up the side aisle and now came to the lectern. Putting on her glasses, she said, "The first reading is Psalm 59:

> Rescue me from my enemies, O God;
> protect me from those who rise up against me.
>
> Rescue me from evildoers
> and save me from those who thirst for my blood.

See how they lie in wait for my life,
how the mighty gather together against me;
not for any offense or fault of mine, O Lord.

Not because of any guilt of mine
they run and prepare themselves for battle.

Rouse yourself, come to my side, and see;
for you, Lord God of hosts, are Israel's God.

Awake and punish all the ungodly;
show no mercy to those who are faithless and evil.

They go to and fro in the evening;
they snarl like dogs and run about the city.

Behold, they boast with their mouths,
and taunts are on their lips;
"For who," they say, "will hear us?"

But you, O Lord, you laugh at them;
you laugh all the ungodly to scorn.

My eyes are fixed on you, O my Strength;
for you, O God, are my stronghold.

My merciful God comes to meet me;
God will let me look in triumph on my enemies.

Slay them, O God, lest my people forget;
send them reeling by your might
and put them down, O Lord our shield.

For the sins of their mouths, for the words of their lips,
for the cursing and lies that they utter,
let them be caught in their pride.

Chapter 9 -- We Are Come Together

Make an end of them in your wrath;
make an end of them and they shall be no more.

The word of the Lord."

The congregation said: "Thanks be to You, oh Lord."

Rebe walked back down the side aisle and resumed her seat in the last pew. Reverend Piccard then said, "The bride and the groom will themselves read the second lesson responsively." Phil and Susie walked together to the lectern.

Phil began, "The lesson is from the First Letter of Paul to the Corinthians, Chapter 13: 'Though I speak with the tongues of men and of angels, and have not love, I am become as sounding brass, or a tinkling cymbal.'"

Susie then continued: "Love suffereth long, and is kind; love envieth not; love vaunteth not itself, is not puffed up."

Then Phil read: "Love never faileth; but whether there be prophecies, they shall fail; whether there be tongues, they shall cease; whether there be knowledge, it shall vanish away."

Then Susie read: "When I was a child, I spake as a child. I understood as a child. I thought as a child; but when I became a man, I put away childish things."

Then the two of them read in unison: "For now we see through a glass, darkly; but then face to face: now I know in part; but then shall I know even as also I am known. And now abideth faith, hope, love, these three; but the greatest of these is love. The word of the Lord."

Reverend Piccard went and brought the open Bible directly in front of Phil and Susie and read: "But from the beginning of the creation God made them male and female. For this cause shall a man leave his father and mother, and cleave to his wife; And they twain shall be one flesh: so then they are no more twain, but one flesh. What therefore God hath joined together let not man put asunder. The Holy Gospel of our Lord Jesus Christ."

The congregation said, "Glory to you, Lord Christ."

Reverend Piccard then addressed the congregation, saying, "Will all of you witnessing these promises do all in your power to uphold these two persons in their marriage?"

The congregation replied in unison, "We will."

Reverend Piccard said, "Who presents this woman to be married to this man?"

Tom said proudly, "Her mother and I do, as does Susie's nanny, Rebe."

As Reverend Piccard was about to go on, Susie made a little motion to him. Then she again went up the two steps, turned and put both her arms around her surprised father and kissed him. She stood on her tiptoes and whispered in his ear, "Dad, I thank you for your love and support all these years. Please forgive me for all that I have put both you and me through. Know that I have always loved you and I always will." She paused and added, "Say, Dad, let's both get back in shape and win the Club tennis championship again next June. Deal?"

Then with a final squeeze Susie went back down the two little steps. Though the congregation had not been able to hear what Susie had whispered in her father's ear, a murmur of approval ran through the congregation. As Tom turned to walk back to join Sarah in the first pew, there were tears streaming down his face.

Reverend Piccard then said, "I require and charge you both in the presence of God that if either of you know any reason why you may not be united in marriage lawfully and in accordance with God's will, now confess it."

Reverend Piccard waited a moment and said, addressing Susie, "Susanne, will you have Phillip to be your husband, to live together in the covenant of marriage. Will you love him and comfort him, honor and keep him in sickness and in health, forsaking all others, be faithful to him as long as you both shall live?"

Susie said, "I will."

Reverend Piccard turned to Phillip and said, "Phillip, will you have Susanne to be your wife, to live together in the covenant of marriage? Will you love her and comfort her, honor her and keep her in sickness and in heath, forsaking all others, be faithful to her as long you both shall live?"

Phillip said, "I will."

Chapter 9 -- We Are Come Together

Just then over the soft rhythmic sound of the four fans going back and forth could be heard the ever increasing sound of a motorcycle coming up the hill approaching St. James at a high rate of speed. Disregarding the sound, Reverend Piccard continued, saying "The Lord be with you."

The congregation replied in unison, "And also with you."

Reverend Piccard said, "Let us pray. Oh gracious and ever living God, You have created this male and female in Your image: have mercy upon this man and this woman who have come to You seeking Your blessing and assist them so that with Your grace, truth, and ability they may honor and keep the promise of the vows they made in Jesus Christ, our Savior, who lives and reigns with You and the Holy Spirit for ever and ever. Amen."

The roar of the approaching motorcycle increased. Reverend Piccard went right on. "Into this holy union Phillip and Susanne come now to be joined. If any of you have just cause why they may not be married, speak now or else forever hold your peace."

Reverend Piccard paused. The racket of the motorcycle as it came into the St. James parking lot and circled around the church became deafening. The members of the congregation looked at one another, their faces full of consternation. Because of the noise as the motorcycle thundered all the way around St. James, Reverend Piccard was forced to stop. He stood there waiting. Then the motorcycle came to an abrupt halt with the engine still running full blast right in front of the closed main doors of St. James.

The awful noise had changed the atmosphere of the church dramatically. The mood of pleasant anticipation had now given away to tension, dread and anxiety, which was reflected on the faces of all those in the church. The congregation had all turned around and now stood staring in horror at the main doors from which the terrorizing waves of sound were coming. Susie had turned deathly pale and clutched Phillip's arms. Susie said in an agonized whisper to Joan who was standing by her side, "Joan, I thought you had said Stewart wasn't coming."

The noise from outside increased when Rebe opened the main door just a crack and slid on out, pulling the door closed behind her. Joan said quietly with a reassuring smile to Susanne, "Hold on, kid. It ain't over 'til the fat lady sings." Phil put his arm around Susie and said quietly to her, "Steady, steady on, Susie. It will be OK. Just wait and see."

Sarah Secant had put both of her hands to her mouth with a look of unmitigated horror. She said in a terrified whisper to her husband, "Tom, oh my God! Tom, it's Charlie Jennings. After all these years, he's come back to make good on his curse on me by breaking up Susie's wedding."

Tom's face had turned bright red with rage. The large veins in his huge neck bulged out over his stiff white collar. He said in a whisper, "For God's sake, Sarah, get control of yourself! It's Stewart, not Charlie! But Stewart can't do anything, so hush up!"

Over the continued loud noise of the motorcycle engine, the sound of a woman's voice could be heard talking loudly right outside the church doors but the speaker's actual words could not be made out because of the din the motorcycle was making. Mrs. Oakley stood even more bolt upright and rigid, her eyes closed tight, and thought, "May God forgive me! Just what have I gone and done. I never, never should have tried to manipulate Stewart. I have now interfered with Susie's life just as she seemed to have come right again. By doing so I may have created a disaster for her and all of us by trying to manage things. May God forgive me!"

Mr. Oliver looked frightened. All at once, the motorcycle roared off at high speed, going out of the churchyard and back down Bluner's Lane. Its sound became fainter and fainter. Then all of a sudden the sound of the motorcycle could no longer be heard.

The main door of the church opened wide. Rebe was radiantly outlined by the afternoon sun. She was smiling serenely. She stood there for just a moment and then made the sign of the cross. Rebe walked back to the last pew and went down on her knees to pray silently. "Lord, thank You for hearing my prayer and turning back the powers of evil that sought to defile Your Holy Church and the Sacrament of Marriage between my precious Susie and her husband, Phillip."

Corporal Roberts came in the side door of St. James, taking off his hat as he came. He stood quietly at the back of the church

Chapter 9 -- We Are Come Together

folding some papers and putting them in the pocket of his uniform.

The only sound in the total quiet of the church was the rhythmic noise of the four fans going back and forth. The entire congregation turned back around and faced the bride and the groom and Reverend Piccard. There was a general sigh of relief from the congregation. The atmosphere was puzzled but serene.

Reverend Piccard said, "Let us pray together in the words our Savior taught us." The whole congregation joined in the Lord's Prayer: "Our Father who art in heaven, hallowed be Thy name, Thy kingdom come, Thy will be done on earth as it is in heaven. Give us this day our daily bread, forgive us our trespasses as we forgive those who trespass against us, and lead us not into temptation but deliver us from evil, for Thine is the Kingdom, the Power and the Glory forever and ever. Amen."

Reverend Piccard said, "Now, Phillip, take Susanne's right and repeat after me."

Phillip took Susanne's right hand. and repeating after Reverend Piccard, said, "In the name of God, I, Phillip, take thee Susanne to be my wife, to have and to hold from this day forward, for better, for worse, for richer, for poorer, in sickness and in health, to love and to cherish until we are parted by death. This is my solemn vow."

Reverend Piccard said, "Now, Susanne, take Phillip's right hand and repeat after me.

Susanne took Phillip's hand in turn and, repeating Reverend Piccard, said, "In the name of God, I, Susanne, take you, Phillip, to be my husband, to have and to hold from this day forward, for better, for worse, for richer, for poorer, in sickness and in health, to love and to cherish until we are parted by death. This is my solemn vow."

Reverend Piccard took the wedding ring from John Oliver and said, "Bless, oh Lord, this ring to be a sign of the vows which Phillip and Susanne have bound themselves to each other through Jesus Christ, our Lord. Amen."

Phillip turned and placed the ring on Susie's ring finger and said, "Susanne, I give you this ring as a symbol of my vow that all that I am and all that I have I honor you in the name of the Father, the Son and the Holy Spirit."

Then Reverend Piccard joined the right hands of Phillip and Susanne and said, "Now Phillip and Susanne have given themselves to each other by solemn vows and with the joining of hands and the giving and receiving of a ring. I pronounce that they are husband and wife in the name of the Father, the Son and the Holy Ghost. Those whom God have joined together, let no man put asunder."

The congregation replied, "Amen."

Reverend Piccard, raising his right hand, said, "The blessing of God the Father, God the Son and God the Holy Ghost, be with you and remain with you now and forever."

The congregation said joyfully and in unison, "Amen."

Phillip turned and took Susanne in both his arms, leaned down and embraced her and kissed her tenderly on the mouth. Then the two of them turned to the congregation. Phillip said, "At the commencement of his service, Susie and I expressed our thanks through Father Piccard to all of you for honoring us by coming and participating in this our wedding. We now want to conclude this wedding ceremony by repeating to you our thanks for participating in this, our matrimonial service."

Susie, now wearing a radiant smile, said, "And won't you all please join us in the celebration of our wedding at our wedding reception." She added, turning directly to the children in the front pews, "Timothy, Choa-Li, Rachel, Dabney, Alice and Doris, you have all been very, very good. Now comes the part of this wedding that you have all been waiting for. Please, all of you follow me and my new husband down the aisle and on out of the church. Then let's all go and eat tons of wedding cake, shall we?" As Phillip and Susie went by, the children on both sides of the aisle came out of the pews and followed the smiling bride and groom down to the front door of St. James. As Susie and Phil started down the aisle, Susie reached out and touched Tom's arm and did the same as she passed Mrs. Oakley.

The organist played the joyful anthem "The Prince of Denmark March." The bridesmaids, on the arms of the groomsmen, followed Phil and Susie and the children down the aisle.

Reverend Piccard closed his *Book of Common Prayer* and walked back through the sacristy to his office, thinking as he went, "Will

Chapter 9 -- We Are Come Together

miracles never end! Praise be to God, this wedding really did take place. But why in the world did Jennings suddenly leave. I and, I believe, the whole congregation thought he was going to come right on in!"

Joan smiled triumphantly at John Oliver as they walked gaily down the aisle together. She said, "Well, Ollie, in the end Stewart did not make good on his threat to break up Susie's wedding."

Rebe was standing in the shadows outside the front door, smiling as she watched Susie and Phillip, now man and wife, as they came out of the church and into the afternoon sunlight followed by the flock of children and the wedding party as well as the now beaming congregation. Susie, catching sight of Rebe, ran over and embraced her, saying, "Rebe, as always, you have come to my rescue. I don't know what you did but you saved our wedding from Stewart."

Rebe replied, "Susiekins, Phil, don't thank me. Thank the Lord!"

Phillip said, "Rebe, it may have been the Lord, but He surely worked through you this day."

As Phillip and Susie turned toward the limousine waiting to take them to the reception, Rebe took a moment to savor what had happened. When Rebe came out of the church, there was Stewart sitting on his roaring motorcycle looking at Corporal Roberts, who was walking toward him. Rebe came up to Stewart and tapped him on the shoulder, saying sternly, "Stewart Jennings!"

Stewart looked around, totally surprised. He said with disbelief and with a look of fright, "Rebe!"

Rebe said, "Stewart Jennings, years ago, I told you once and for all to leave Susie alone. Now you have come to God's church and are about to commit an act of sacrilege. Leave this holy place here and now!"

Corporal Roberts was standing on the other side of the motorcycle. Stewart suddenly put his motorcycle in gear and had gunned it away from her and Corporal Roberts. Stewart had then roared on out of the St. James parking lot, turned left and gone down Bluner's Lane.

Rebe crossed herself and said, "Oh God, thank you for your

help in driving that evil young man away from this church and the marriage of Susanne and Phillip."

Great cascades of joyous sound came from the pealing of the bells in the belfry of St. James and reverberated around the peaceful hills and valleys.

Chapter 9 -- We Are Come Together

A Social Note

Susanne Oakley Secant Marries Phillip MacPherson

September 18, Miss Susan Oakley Secant was married to Mr. Phillip MacPherson at St. James Episcopal Church by the Reverend William Piccard. Mrs. MacPherson is the daughter of Thomas and Sarah Secant and is the granddaughter of the late Robert Oakley and Mrs. Oakley. Mr. Oakley was a descendant of William Oakley, who came to Pennsylvania with William Penn. Ms. Secant graduated from Ethel Walker School and attended Bennett College. Recently she has been a full time volunteer at the Tilton Center for Disabled Children in Philadelphia. Mrs. MacPherson plans to pursue a career in speech and auditory therapy for impaired children.

Mr. MacPherson is the son of the late Robert MacPherson. His mother is Mrs. Charles Simmons of West Hartford, Connecticut. Mr. MacPherson graduated from Phillips Exeter Academy and the Woodrow Wilson School of Public and International Affairs at Princeton University. After a wedding trip in Alaska, Mr. MacPherson will go on active duty with the U.S. Navy in October. He has accepted a post as an intern with the U.S. Department of Defense and will assume that post when his naval service is complete.

Philadelphia Herald, September 18, 1973

Dearly Beloved

Out of Control

**Local Motorist Dies
As Foreign Motorcycle Goes Out of Control**

Stewart Bellack Jennings, age 21, was pronounced dead at the scene of an accident at 5:00 P.M. Saturday, September 18, when he lost control of his foreign made Tetra motorcycle at a corner on Bluner's Lane, according to Corporal Tim Roberts of the county police.

Roberts said Jennings was about to be stopped because he was riding a Czechoslovakian motorcycle that was not registered in Pennsylvania and did not have a valid Pennsylvania license plate. Before being stopped, Jennings sped away. Corporal Roberts said that Jennings was not being pursued at the time of the accident. he apparently lost control of the racing motorcycle as he came down the hill and tried to round the corner at the bottom of Bluner's Lane near Colonel Rider's estate. Jennings was not wearing a helmet and suffered head and internal injuries. Mr. Jennings was a student at Boston College and was a musician. Mr. Jennings is survived by his mother, Mrs. Charles Jennings, as well as cousins in Czechoslovakia and in Pennsylvania. Mr. Jennings had lived for a number of years in the gatehouse on the Dulaire estate. Mr. Jennings on his mother's side is descended from William Dulaire, an early governor of Pennsylvania. Mr. Jennings' grandmother was a noted Czech pianist.

As of this date funeral arrangements have not been completed.

Philadelphia Herald, September 20, 1973